John C. Hopkins

Life and Work of the Rt. Hon. Sir John Thompson, P.C., K.C.M.G., Q.C.

Prime Minister of Canada

John C. Hopkins

Life and Work of the Rt. Hon. Sir John Thompson, P.C., K.C.M.G., Q.C.
Prime Minister of Canada

ISBN/EAN: 9783337096830

Printed in Europe, USA, Canada, Australia, Japan

Cover: Foto ©Raphael Reischuk / pixelio.de

More available books at **www.hansebooks.com**

HER MAJESTY THE QUEEN.

THE RT. HON. SIR JOHN S. D. THOMPSON, P.C., K.C.M.G., Q.C.

Fourth Prime Minister of Canada.

LIFE AND WORK

OF THE

RT. HON. SIR JOHN THOMPSON

P.C., K.C.M.G., Q.C.

PRIME MINISTER OF CANADA

BY

J CASTELL HOPKINS

WITH A

PREFACE

BY

HIS EXCELLENCY THE EARL OF ABERDEEN

GOVERNOR GENERAL OF CANADA.

UNITED PUBLISHING HOUSES

TORONTO, LONDON AND BRANTFORD

1895

His Excellency The Earl of Aberdeen, P.C.
Governor General of Canada.

PREFACE.

THE "Life and Work" of a man.—The phrase is suggestive; and it is eminently applicable as the title of a biography of Sir John Thompson. His life was full of work, and of work to which emphatically might be applied the old maxim, "*Laborare est orare,*" for the labours of his busy life were pervaded and prompted by lofty aims and religious principles.

That a record, a description, of his career should be given to his country and to the world, is a matter not merely of appropriateness but of obligation; for the various grounds upon which a claim for a biography of any person may be made on behalf of the public, are in this case combined, whether regarded from the historical, the political, the legal, the exemplary, or the personal point of view.

To say this implies that the biographer will have no lack of material; but it does not follow that his task will be easy. Indeed it must be admitted that in no case can the authorship of a biography be free from difficulty; and of course, especially is this the case when the life to be presented is that of a statesman whose position and duties inevitably brought him not only into the midst of the stir and stress of a central place in public life, and the controversies and emulations with which it is surrounded, but also included the taking of an important part in international and other transactions requiring delicate handling and diplomatic skill.

The biographer of such a man will desire to exercise discretion, but he will also wish to avoid the criticism that in striving to exercise caution he has incurred the risk of dullness. He must enable his readers to understand the domestic and personal characteristics of his subject, but he must not too freely lift the veil that protects the sanctity of home and family life. Above all, while utilizing the opportunity for justifying any utterances or lines of conduct which he regards as having been misrepresented or misunderstood, he must not allow this proper sense of loyalty, this admiration for the character of his subject, to betray him into uncalled-for, perhaps unfair, disparagement of those whose attitude on the occasion in question was that of opposition. And the need of good judgment and discretion in this matter is of course increased, when the controversies referred to are of extremely recent occurrence.

But it is not necessary to say more about the functions of a biographer than will serve to draw attention to the manner in which the author of this memoir has performed his part. It may safely be predicted that the general opinion will be that he has done his work well. He has evidently aimed at maintaining the impartiality of a chronicler, together with the appreciation of an admirer. He has also shown that sense of proportion which is especially necessary in the picture of a life so many-sided and so full of interest as that of Sir John Thompson. It is indeed not too much to say that to describe fully the chief portion of his public career would be to write a history of Canada during the past decade; and it is thus that the author has evidently felt it requisite to give a descriptive sketch of several of the chief events and public questions which occupied or agitated the mind of the country during the period in view, in order that Sir John Thompson's actions and influence on these occasions may be properly presented to the reader.

It has already been remarked that the reasons for the appearance of this biography are numerous. A perusal of the volume will make this apparent, even to those not previously in any personal manner acquainted with the circumstances and the subject; while by those who were in any way brought in contact with Sir John Thompson, the book will be looked for with an eager, though melancholy interest.

But there is one feature in Sir John Thompson's character which adds especially to the value of any memoir of his life. He has often been described as a man of reserved and even cold demeanour. It follows therefore that he must frequently have been liable to be misunderstood, or at least that the beauty of his character and disposition cannot always have been fully revealed. Doubtless to those who were at all intimately acquainted with him the less apparent features of his character had become familiar. But if the more genial side of his nature was to some extent hidden, how desirable that this and every other distinguishing trait of the man should be as fully as possible described and portrayed! To the attainment of that object the publication of correspondence is doubtless a most important means, and it may be a cause of some regret that the present volume does not contain a larger number of letters. But it must be borne in mind that the publication of correspondence, especially of the correspondence of a person who has occupied an important position in public life, is a matter which requires time, for the purpose of deliberation. consultation, and classification; in addition to which, the lapse of a certain period is sometimes necessary before correspondence upon some questions can suitably be given to the world. The present volume, however, is published in order to meet the immediate demand of the public; and meanwhile it may be hoped that at some later date there may be an opportunity of becoming acquainted with at least a considerable portion of Sir John Thompson's correspondence.

Reverting to what has been said regarding the manner and appearance of Sir John Thompson, the writer of this preface, if asked to give a description of the personality of the late Premier, would say that the dominant impression left on his mind and recollection is that of combined strength and sweetness. When silent, his countenance no doubt often wore a composed, almost a stoical expression; but this, as a contrast, only made the bright and gentle smile more attractive.

His remarkable aptitude as a listener, combined with an extraordinary power of grasping and presenting in a clear and lucid manner the various aspects and bearings of a subject, must have struck all who had occasion to confer with him on matters of business; and his faculty in this respect is illustrated in a highly interesting manner by one of the personal reminiscences recorded in the text by Bishop Cameron.

Sir John Thompson had a ready and genial sense of humour. Many a quiet laugh have I shared with him, even during conversations on official matters, when anything drew from him a jocular remark, or recalled to either of us an amusing anecdote or reminiscence. With this sense of humour, as is often the case with those who possess it, there was the power of sarcasm, which (as members of the Dominion House of Commons could no doubt testify) was manifested on occasion.

As a public speaker Sir John Thompson has been described as somewhat cold, although possessing in a high degree the essentially important qualities of clear articulation, lucidity of expression, and an accurate sense of proportion in the division of a subject. I was debarred from having many opportunities of hearing him speak in public, but the occasions on which that advantage was enjoyed would lead me to demur to the designation of "coldness" as applied to his oratory. Doubtless his delivery was calm, and in a sense unimpassioned; but there was frequently a sympathetic ring -- almost a tremor — in his tones, which in a pathetic passage would readily have moved many to tears. And indeed it could not be that this note of sympathetic feeling, albeit as an undertone, should be absent from even the public utterances of one whose deep and true feeling was manifested so clearly in every relation of life.

In short, as has already been said, in him were united gentleness and strength—marks of true manliness and nobility of character.

Such were some of the characteristics of the subject of this memoir. And though the promptings of affection and appreciation would incite the writer to linger on the theme, this informal preface must be brought to a close.

Sir John Thompson was a great man. He has made his mark. His influence has been for good, and its impress is of an abiding nature. His country has reason to be proud of him; it has reason to be thankful for him; and it may be confidently recorded that his character and his abilities were such as would have fitted him to occupy with success and distinction the very highest positions that can be attained by any statesman in the British Empire.

Aberdeen

Ottawa, Feb. 25, 1895.

CONTENTS.

CHAPTER VI.

CHAPTER VII.

CHAPTER VIII.

CHAPTER IX.

CHAPTER X.

CHAPTER XI.

CHAPTER XII.

CHAPTER XIII.

CHAPTER XIV.

CHAPTER XV.

CHAPTER XX.

CHAPTER XXI.

CHAPTER XXII.

CHAPTER XXIII.

CHAPTER XXIV.

CHAPTER XXV.

CHAPTER XXVI.

CHAPTER XXVII.

CHAPTER XXVIII.

APPENDIX.

LIST OF ILLUSTRATIONS.

SIR JOHN THOMPSON,
Aged 21 Years.

CHAPTER I.

A Great Canadian.

The Right Honourable Sir John S. D. Thompson possessed one of those strong minds which, in different ages of the world's history, have occasionally swayed the destinies of nations and controlled the people, by pure force of intellect. He was undoubtedly a great man. Tried by ordinary standards, it is perhaps difficult to comprehend his marvellous success in public life. He had no adventitious surroundings of family or wealth. He did not possess a commanding personal appearance and had none of that magnetism of manner, that charm and fascination of speech and gesture, which enabled Sir John A. Macdonald, Lord Palmerston or James G. Blaine to lead men whither they would. Yet, by the power of ability, concentration of purpose, and force of character, he rose with unique rapidity to the highest place in his province, in his party and in his country.

The last nine years of his life were filled with triumphs which came not as the reward of popularity, nor upon waves of national passion, but as the results of a great mind working with patience and patriotic zeal; with clear insight and acute intelligence, upon the different problems which were presented. Triumphs over personal prejudice, born of that self-repression which made a strong man shrink from the arts of the ordinary politician and take refuge in a coldness of manner which concealed his really warm heart and many generous and sympathetic qualities. Triumphs over that deplorable sectarian sentiment which for a long time refused to admit the greatness of the statesman and the goodness of the man who, in early life, had obeyed his conscience and conviction by a change of religion. Triumphs of oratory at the Bar and in Parliament, upon the Bench and before the people. Triumphs of statesmanship, in the treatment of race and creed questions which, under the manipulation of demagogues, threatened the disintegration of the Dominion; and in the control of Parliamentary matters which more than once endangered the unity and strength of the party. Triumphs of diplomacy, which forced Mr. Blaine, with all his acuteness and ability, into the confession of a desire to obtain commercial control of Canada and a refusal to grant reciprocity on any other terms: and which compelled the settlement upon satisfactory lines of the long-standing Behring Sea troubles. Triumphs as an Imperial statesman which brought about the success of the Intercolonial Conference, created steam communication with Australia, paved the way to closer British unity, and led to the heaping of honours upon the head of Canada through its Premier and representative.

It was a combination of qualities which made Sir John Thompson so great in character, so successful in his career. He was undoubtedly self-confident as well as self sustained. He was conscious of his own strength and did not feel the necessity of intimidating others, or of asserting himself. And, as Archbishop O'Brien said shortly after the Premier's death, he had the quiet repose of strong minds, the dignified reticence of genius. In his profession: upon the Bench: in public life: in the Department of Justice: his mastery of details was marvellous, and contributed greatly to his success. No case for trial in his earlier career found him unprepared, and no argument came to him as a bewildering surprise. Lucidity of thought and language characterized him as a lawyer, marked his decisions as a Judge, and his State papers as a Minister. This faculty of clothing the most difficult and involved transactions or propositions in clear and concise language he possessed in an extraordinary degree. Judge Townshend, of Nova Scotia, once declared that, "in shaping, modifying and adapting resolutions and statutes to meet the views of public bodies of which he was a member, I think he was unequalled."

Like most really great men, Sir John possessed a wonderful capacity for work. He never seemed to be in a hurry, and yet succeeded in constantly déspatching an enormous amount of business, quickly and efficiently. For some time before the death of Sir John Macdonald, it is an open secret that the Chieftain leaned greatly upon his Minister of Justice, who, during that period, as well as later under the leadership of Sir John Abbott, bore the burden of work in the House of Commons, besides the many and heavy labours connected with his own Department. Since then, also, he has at times assumed diplomatic duties and taken a position and share in the settlement of questions, such as the Behring Sea and Copyright problems, which must have demanded much time and study. And in addition, there have been the continual and normal requirements of deputations, speeches and journeys. Perhaps it would be an elaborate state paper to-day upon the London election case, a speech in the House to-morrow upon the Tarte charges, an address the next day upon the unveiling of a monument to the Springhill N. S., miners. And Sir John Thompson never did anything by halves. Whatever he undertook was done as well as ability and close observation and application could make possible.

In reading Sir John Thompson's papers and speeches

upon questions like those of Riel's execution, the disallowance of the Jesuits' Estates Act, the Copyright Law, or the Manitoba Schools, one is struck by the completeness and thoroughness of his argument, the keenness and analytical quality of his mind, and the industry and skill displayed in obtaining and marshalling the facts of the case. In dealing with constitutional or international questions, he seemed to be entirely at home. Early training had no doubt made him familiar with the Fisheries question as it affected the Maritime Provinces, and his work in connection with the Halifax Commission gave him a still wider insight into both sides of the dispute. His later experience as a Nova Scotian Judge and Premier increased this knowledge, while his position as Minister of Justice finally brought him into touch with all the legal complications which followed the abrogation of the Fisheries' Clause of the Washington Treaty and the unjust seizure of Canadian vessels in the Behring Sea. The British North America Act was thoroughly familiar to him in all its intricacies, and every shade of public opinion in Canada recognized frankly his high judicial insight and knowledge when it was crowned by selection as one of England's arbitrators in that brilliant gathering of statesmen and jurists at Paris.

A marked feature of the late Premier's character was his entire unselfishness. Devotion to duty was his watchword, disregard of personal considerations and comfort his principle of action. Without any particular liking for politics as such, he left the Bench of Nova Scotia, with its life of comparative ease and affluence and the prospect of undoubted and high promotion, for the stormy career of statesmanship. No doubt he had that ambition for fame which all great men have and which the next few years so fully realized. Perhaps, also, he felt that it was possible for him to render greater service to the country which he loved so well. Judging indeed by his subsequent career, there can be little doubt that Sir John Thompson did deliberately surrender the ermine of ease, as he at a later period refused to take the Chief Justiceship of Canada, in order to devote himself to promoting the welfare of the Dominion.

This quality of unselfish loyalty was well exhibited in those dark days which followed the death of Sir John A. Macdonald. It was a time of political stir and stress; a moment when the Conservative party was bewildered by the greatness of its loss; a period when very little causes might have produced striking and startling results. A man actuated by ambition only would have thought and said in Sir John Thompson's position that he had earned the Premiership, and would have expected it as a right. But Sir John was a true statesman, and his appreciation of the situation made him see that the patriotic course was to step aside for the moment and to continue doing his duty in a high, though still subordinate, sphere. No doubt, too, he felt the consciousness of personal power, and realized that his time could not be far distant. But it must also be remembered that at the moment in question no one knew the full strength of the sectarian feeling in Ontario. It might have prevented Sir John Thompson from ever obtaining the Premiership, as the strength of a similar sentiment in Quebec in earlier days kept George Brown permanently out of power, and during many years in the recent history of Ontario, kept Mr. Meredith in Opposition.

In still another way was his self-sacrifice shown. No one doubts that Sir John could have made large sums of money at his profession, and maintained himself and his family in affluence. So also, had he remained a judge, or at any later period accepted a judgeship once more, there is every probability that his life would have been indefinitely prolonged, and his promotion rapid; while his eventual elevation to the lofty and remunerative post of a member of the Judicial Committee of the Imperial Privy Council would have been almost a certainty. But he preferred the path of public life and duty to the ease and dignity of the Bench, and his sudden death left a family unprovided for, which, but for unstinted devotion to his national work, would have had ample fortune and an assured future.

His was a peculiar style of oratory—typical of the man and his work. He was unable, and in any case would have been unwilling, to move the masses by appeals to prejudice and passion. But if eloquence finds its perfect expression in convincing minds and swaying intellects, then Sir John Thompson was emphatically a great orator. His memorable speech upon the Riel question placed the new Minister of Justice at one bound in the front rank of Parliamentary debaters, and there he remained until his death. Indeed the full supremacy of his master-mind could hardly be appreciated save by those who heard and felt its operation in the debates of Parliament. Sir John Macdonald held sway in that Chamber for many years by the force of matchless political skill and dexterity, and in the latter period of his life was aided by a ripe and respected experience; a deep personal affection on the part of members; a devoted and united following. But Sir John Thompson stepped up at once to the place held by Sir Charles Tupper and Mr. Blake, and upon their retirement from the scene his supremacy as a debater was practically unchallenged. In command of language he excelled Mr. Blake, who is known to have put much labor into the wording of his speeches; in beauty of expression he somewhat resembled Lord Rosebery; in clearness and incisiveness of style he might have been compared to Mr. Chamberlain. His rank amongst the trained debaters of the Imperial Parliament would have been high; his place in the Canadian House of Commons was the highest.

In the annals of the British Empire he will hold a permanent and lofty place. Under his leadership, though fostered and guided by the patriotic hand of the Hon. Mackenzie Bowell, the movement for closer British relationship found expression in the Ottawa Conference by means of which, tariffs, cables and steamship lines will be freely utilized in drawing the distant parts of our vast Imperial realm into commercial, political and personal union. As the *London Daily News* so well said, that step "established a precedent and suggested the possibility of an imperial federation. The calling of it belonged almost to the dreamland of statesmanship" But the result belongs also to the record of practical work and progress which Sir John perhaps appreciated more than sentimental considerations. The latter he by no means deprecated, however, and his mournful death, almost at the feet of the Sovereign he had served so well, illustrates, as did his life and policy, the famous utterance in a speech at Belleville: "He who serves Canada, serves the Empire, and he who serves the Empire serves Canada as well."

But while his statesmanship exceeded the bounds of the Dominion and stamped itself upon Imperial history; while his heart went out to the Mother-land and his policy strove to bind its children in close union and brotherly intercourse; yet the life work of Sir John Thompson was essentially Canadian. He was emphatically a son of the soil. Born and educated in Canada, his early political battles and later political successes were all fought and obtained within the Dominion. Imperial honours were showered upon him, and more of them might have come in the future, but they were bestowed for services which in benefiting Canada, benefitted the Empire as well. He was filled with a passionate patriotism which was neither understood nor properly appreciated by the people during his life-time, being as it was to a great extent concealed from view by his calm and cold exterior and by the even flow of his logical and unsympathetic oratory. But it was shown in his policy, and occasionally surprised the public in some unusually eloquent and striking phrase; while his death exhibits the man as he really was—unwilling to give up his post even under the physicians' warning of a fatal termination, because it might lead to party disorganization and the consequent defeat of the principles he held so dear, and of the policy he considered so necessary to the progress and welfare of the Dominion.

No one but a true Canadian, devoted to his country and his cause, could have led the Conservatives through the troubles following the fatal 6th of June, 1891. But Sir John inspired the rank and file of the party with thorough confidence in his ability, and impressed even his most bitter opponents with respect for his honesty and honour. The result was that his moderation, his intellectual strength, his justice, and sincere conscientiousness had become qualities to conjure with, and had lent a peculiar power to his leadership which it is safe to say would have remained unshaken by all the bubbles and foam of sectarian advocacy.

It is difficult to be critical concerning such a life and character as that of Sir John Thompson. Apart from the sympathy which the Angel of Death creates for all men and particularly when it comes amid such surroundings and with such dramatic and painful suddenness, it is not easy to find faults in either his public or private career.

THE RT. HON. SIR JOHN A. MACDONALD, P.C., G.C.B., Q.C., M.P.

First Prime Minister of the Dominion of Canada.

Men differed from him in politics, but all united in praise of his life, his motives his character, his attainments. When death came, the Opposition press was as eulogistic as were the Government organs. Men differed from him in religion, but his life was so pure, his change of faith has been proved to have been so conscientious and at the time so injurious to his material interests, that all criticism has been hushed, and the denunciations of Dr. Douglas, sincere as that eloquent divine no doubt was, are buried with him. His faults were undoubtedly few, his virtues many. He lived indeed as though he fully appreciated the fact that

"Our life of mortal breath
Is but a suburb of the life Elysian,
Whose portal we call death."

It is not fulsome flattery of a man, who was good as well as great, to say that his whole career and character constitute a noble example for young Canadians. There was never any doubt that Sir John Thompson would do right in any public emergency, in accordance with his convictions, and up to the extreme limit of his power. His inflexible purpose compelled respect from the leaders of his party, and combined with his high character and great ability, caused his Cabinet, as well as his followers in the House, and in the country, to give an extraordinary degree of consideration to his wishes. A well-regulated ambition coupled with concentration of aim and a wide degree of culture, brought him the highest place in a field which his patriotism had made as wide as the Empire. These qualities render the career of Sir John Thompson memorable, and important to all Canadians. They carried him from the reporter's table to the foot of the Throne; they made the young lawyer of other days Minister of Justice for this wide Dominion and a British representative upon more than one important occasion; they made the once youthful politician and debater a great Prime-Minister and powerful speaker. They will carry his name still further down the corridors of time, as

"Were a star quenched on high,
  For ages would its light,
Still travelling downwards from the sky,
  Shine on our mortal sight.
So, when a great man dies
  For years beyond our ken,
The light he leaves behind him lies
  Upon the paths of men."

CHAPTER II.

EARLY DAYS.

The Province of Nova Scotia has become famous for the men it produces. The broad Dominion of Canada from end to end has felt the impress of their virile force and unusual ability. The name of Sir Charles Tupper is stamped in vivid letters upon the pages of provincial, national and imperial history. The eloquence of Joseph Howe still thunders down through the years which have passed since his wonderful voice was hushed in death. The ability, energy and skill of Sir William Dawson have made McGill University one of the great educational centres of the world, and left his name a lofty one in the difficult realms of science. The great work of Principal Grant has built up Queen's University, Kingston, and his fame as an earnest and eloquent exponent of Imperial unity has not been confined to the shores of Canada. The financial ability of Hon. George E. Foster has been a tower of strength to three Canadian administrations; and the rapid rise of Sir Charles Hibbert Tupper in reputation and position, presage a place in history hardly second to that held by his distinguished father.

But history will probably say that the career of Sir John Thompson was more remarkable than that of any other native of Nova Scotia. His rapid rise, his lofty position, his great honours, his dramatic death, all combined to render the life of the fourth Premier of Canada the most eventful and remarkable in the national annals.

There was, however, nothing in his surroundings to indicate this future when John Sparrow David Thompson was born at Halifax on November 10th, 1844. His mother, a thoroughly good woman, was a native of the Orkney Islands, her maiden name being Charlotte Pottinger. His father, Mr. John Sparrow Thompson, was a man of culture and position, though not possessed of private means. He was a native of Waterford, Ireland, and had emigrated, when quite young, to the Province of Nova Scotia, then an isolated, out of the world sort of place, possessed of charms and resources which seemed to be buried in almost primeval obscurity. For some years, Mr. Thompson was Queen's Printer, and subsequently for a prolonged period, held the restricted but fairly comfortable post of Superintendent of the Nova Scotian Money Order system.

He seems, however, to have participated in other pursuits as well, and was assistant editor of the *Nova Scotian*, at a time when Joseph Howe as its proprietor was occupied in moulding public opinion with pen and voice and influence. Naturally, he fought with his chief during the struggle for responsible government in the Province, and naturally also, be taught his then youthful son an affectionate regard for the great tribune, which had its effect in later days. Mr. Thompson, who died in 1867, seems to have enjoyed in his day a high reputation as a graceful and well-informed writer, and an accomplished gentleman. The circumstances surrounding his son's boyhood therefore were not at all unfavorable to the youthful development of any remarkable qualities which he might possess. But, as in so many other cases, the child hardly seems to have been the father of the man. He attended the common schools of his native city, and afterwards took a course at the Free Church Academy in Halifax, besides receiving most careful home training and advice, in all his studies and pursuits.

At the early age of fifteen he commenced the study of law as an articled clerk in the office of Mr. Henry Pryor, afterwards stipendiary magistrate of Halifax, and was called to the Bar of the Province in 1865, when barely twenty-one. He is described in his student days as having been a slight and rather delicate youth, with a shy and timid manner, and as utterly devoid of anything like conceit or self-assertion. And the daily work of the junior articled student was not then made as pleasant or useful as it is at the present time. It was indeed of the dullest and apparently most useless character, including such labor as the copying of voluminous writs and pleadings, now long done away with, and the general performance of a class of work which is nowadays handed over to the office typewriter. Some one has said in this connection that it was a formidable undertaking even to peruse an ordinary set of the pleadings of thirty years ago; it was a still more difficult task to write out the complete copy of such a set; but the superlative was reached by the bewildered student in the attempt to comprehend the precise meanings of the super-subtle technicalities thus expanded upon so many pages of foolscap. Browning may indeed be termed the embodiment of lucidity in comparison with the intricate legal phraseology of some of the documents of a generation or two since.

But "Johnnie" Thompson, as he was called, not only found time to do his office work and to be an industrious student of the principles of law, but also to master the difficult art of stenography. Then as in the future, what he found to do, he did thoroughly. And when the early years of hard and constant struggle at the bar commenced, the young lawyer was only too glad to eke out his income by the use of an accomplishment not very common at the time. As a matter of fact also, there is as much difference between a first-class stenographer, such as he was, and one who can only take down words and then give a literal translation of them, as there is between the writer and the pen he drives over the paper. The one will summarize in a short time a ten-column speech so that it will not exceed a column in space and yet include every salient point, grammatically worded, and perhaps embellished in a way the speaker himself was incapable of doing. The other will take down his letters from dictation, and give an exact copy, as may perhaps be his duty, without the exercise of thought or of any special ability.

This was not the way with young Thompson. He practised law and, at the same time, reported the debates of the Legislative Assembly. In 1867, the Official Reporter of the House was Mr. John George Bourinot, now the learned and distinguished Clerk of the Dominion House of Commons. His volumes for that year make acknowledgment to John S. D. Thompson for assistance given, and in the succeeding year they bear the signature of Mr. Thompson as Reporter-in-chief. During the four following sessions he continued to report the debates with great advantage to himself in the gaining of a thorough and ready knowledge of the procedure of Parliament. It must also have given him a very complete acquaintance with the politics and political leaders of his province, and been of great assistance when he later on came to enter the House of Assembly. Meanwhile the reputation of the young lawyer was growing. When he had been at the Bar but little more than two years he had won the respect and confidence of the Bench and of his professional brethren. Simplicity, sincerity and fairness seem to have been the predominant qualities of the lawyer as they were afterwards of the judge and the statesman. His first partner was Mr. Joseph Coombes, for whom he did the office work and prepared briefs; his second, after a few years of indifferent progress, from a pecuniary standpoint, was Mr. Wallace Graham. The firm thus finally formed was a success, and Mr. Thompson soon rose in his profession until he attained the foremost place before the Provincial Bar.

During these years he worked exceedingly hard. Matters were complicated by his father's health failing, and for some years the son performed much of the work pertaining to his parent's Government position by sitting up and labouring far into the night. It is a melancholy fact stated by one of his friends in those seemingly distant days, that his ambition then was to make sufficient money to keep his own family from ever being in the difficulties he himself had experienced. As a lawyer during this period he contributed to the true dignity of a great profession, scorned pettifogging tricks, and was ever on the side of peace and settlement where such results were at all possible. His powers of concentration were very great, and of course aided him not a little in getting through multifarious duties and in winning legal successes.

In 1870, at the age of twenty-six, John Thompson was married to Miss Annie Affleck, daughter of Captain Affleck, of Halifax. To her, the partner of his early struggles and his later greatness, he was ever the most devoted of husbands, as he has been to his children a most thoughtful and tender parent. But the marriage was not accomplished without some difficulty. Miss Affleck was a Roman Catholic, he was a Protestant. His family were most devoted and pronounced Methodists: with perhaps a little of that undue religious prejudice which is apt to develop in small communities and in the hearts and minds of the very best of people. He was, however, drifting into closer communion with the Roman Catholic Church, and had about this time been deeply impressed by a series of sermons on the "Foundations and Doctrines of the Church," preached by Archbishop Connolly of Halifax, an ecclesiastic whom he greatly admired, and who soon came in turn to appreciate his young friend's ability and keenness of thought.

It seems clear that his future wife had little or nothing to do with his change of faith, which came later, and which so influenced the course of his whole life. It is indeed understood that they never discussed religious matters, either before or after marriage, until he announced his intention of becoming a Roman Catholic. During their engagement Mr. Thompson would frequently meet her at the church door and walk home, but he seldom or never attended the services with her. At the time the marriage was decided upon, Archbishop Connolly was unfortunately away and as mixed marriages were never celebrated in Halifax, arrangements were made with some little difficulty to have the ceremony performed in Portland, Maine. Canon Power ultimately gave Mrs. Affleck letters to Bishop Bacon of that place, who did everything possible to facilitate matters. She and her daughter reached there early in July, and on the 5th of the month the young couple were married in the Bishop's parlor.

A year afterwards Mr. Thompson joined the Roman Catholic Church. A change of religion is always a marked and striking action whichever direction it may take, and in his case was rendered especially noteworthy by the silent opposition of his relatives and friends, by the fact that as a boy he had been the pride of the Brunswick Street Methodist Sabbath School, and as a young man, one of its most efficient teachers. But there was no room for surprise in the matter. His friends knew that for years he had been

Hon. Alex. Mackenzie, M.P.,

Second Prime Minister of Canada.

debating the question, and that the final step was only taken after the deliberate weighing of arguments and conclusions which characterized him throughout life. He was never the creature of circumstances, and there cannot be the slightest doubt of his having made the change from the highest and purest of motives. As he remarked at the time to an intimate friend:—"I have everything to lose from a worldly standpoint by the step I am about to take." But so convinced were all his friends of his sincerity, and so much did they admire his high-minded indifference to any success which might be attained by refusing to run counter to public opinion or individual prejudice, that they clung to him all the more closely, and his popularity grew rather than diminished. A few months after the event he was elected an Alderman of Halifax in the fifth ward, and by acclamation. This position he continued to hold for six years, in 1874 being also elected a member of the City Board of School Commissioners. Of the latter body he was for a time chairman. In civic affairs the young Alderman soon took an active and prominent part, and his surviving colleagues, as well as the records of the Council itself, bear ample testimony to his ability and skill. And so with the School Board.

Education was then, as it always is in mixed religious communities, a difficult matter to deal with in Halifax. There were no Separate Schools, though of course many private institutions were maintained of a more or less religious character. The School Board was chosen without reference to creed and it had to manage the conflicting views of the different elements of the people. In this Mr. Thompson showed marked skill. It is said that he hardly ever offended any one. He did not believe in antagonizing people, and if his manner was too cold and distant to win popular affection, his qualities at least compelled public respect, while his quiet, dignified way of discussing matters prevented people from taking personal offence at his opposition to their views. He once warned a close personal friend, who now holds a high judicial place in the Dominion, that he was "too impulsive," and advised him to use every possible argument against the point in dispute, but never so as to personally offend the other disputant. And there is no doubt about his own success in these years of preliminary struggle. His influence in the Council was supreme, and no one could throw oil upon the troubled waters of the School Board better than he. Writing on Dec. 4th, 1877, the *Halifax Herald* says that "If any Alderman ever conducted himself in such a manner as to win popularity and confidence that man was Alderman Thompson."

During these years the young lawyer was for some time President of the Young Men's Literary Association of Halifax, and of the Charitable Irish Society, taking a deep interest in their affairs and general proceedings. Naturally also he was steadily developing his debating powers as well as increasing the stores of information and knowledge of precedents, which lie at the basis of a genuine and permanent Parliamentary reputation. The shyness of early youth soon wore away, so far as any outward manifestation was concerned, but the reserved manner remained and clung to him through life. But then, and always, he disliked public speaking, and for this reason, probably, was never a good campaign orator. Any audience, however, which desired to hear a clear-cut analysis of the questions at issue without oratorical frills or appeals to sentiment and passion, could appreciate an address from John Thompson, and would probably leave the building impressed by the honesty and honor of the man, as well as by the logical strength of his arguments.

At this time the storms which had swept over the

politics and parties of Nova-Scotia were somewhat abated, though much of bitterness still remained The great figure of Joseph Howe had passed from the scene and only the memory was left of a man whom the Canadian people of to-day can hardly appreciate at the full measure of his superb ability and disinterestedness. The historic battles which he waged for responsible government and against confederation had brought out a display of eloquence and power which in a less circumscribed sphere would have made Howe one of the great men of the age. The latter contest was a struggle of giants. The sledge-hammer blows of Dr. Tupper ringing against the shield of his eloquent antagonist made the prolonged battle a memorable one to all Nova-Scotians, and the literary part taken in it by Mr. Thompson, senior, as a devoted friend and follower of the Anti-Union leader, was by no means small.

During this period the Province was literally deluged with pamphlets and political literature of all kinds; the press was loaded with arguments and fiery denunciation; the air was filled with the sounds of oratory. Finally, on the 18th of September, 1867, the new Dominion was startled by intelligence of the terrific defeat which the supporters of Canadian federation had received in Nova-Scotia. Out of eighteen members of the Commons, but one Confederate, Dr. Tupper, was returned; and out of 38 members of the Provincial Assembly only two Confederates had survived the political hurricane. Howe literally held the Province in his hand and had he pleased, during the next year or two could have taken Nova-Scotia out of the Union and compelled the Dominion to conquer it or else wait for a turning tide. But the Imperial Government refused to grant constitutional repeal of the Union, and he was too loyal a man to dream of using force. Many of his followers however, began to assume a disloyal attitude and to even dally with American sympathizers.

Here was the opportunity for the Dominion party, which had been gradually regaining ground during the interval. And no one could seize an opportunity quicker than Sir John A Macdonald. He came to Halifax and saw Howe; played upon his love of British connection and closer Imperial unity; convinced him of the serious danger into which the Anti-Confederates were drifting and the utter impossibility of separation; offered him better financial terms for the Province, and finally won him over. Howe entered the Dominion Parliament and Government in order to more effectually guard the interests of Nova-Scotia, and though much of his marvellous popularity departed with that act, and the misrepresentation to which it was subjected, he nevertheless lived to occupy for a short time the Government House of his native Province, and when he died received the tribute of heart-felt and universal mourning from its people.

Mr. Thompson, who had in the meantime lost his father by death, was not sorry when circumstances compelled Howe to sever himself from his old-time associates. His admiration for the man was very great, his regard for his memory was afterwards deep and sincere, but he would never have followed him in any unconstitutional action or disloyal advocacy. This union of Tupper and Howe—the Conservative and Radical of earlier days—founded the Liberal-Conservative party in Nova-Scotia which, in Provincial matters, John S. D. Thompson was to lead in the course of a few years, and in later times was to represent in the Government of the Dominion. About 1874, he became known as a strong advocate of protection to native industries, and with a small coterie of active friends in Halifax, urged the issue which four years afterwards was to sweep the country like a whirlwind.

Meanwhile he was connected with various important

cases coming before the Supreme Court of Nova-Scotia, and was rapidly acquiring a foremost place at the bar, as well as in municipal politics, and in the appreciation of public men who were able to judge of ability in those rising around them. It was a curious friendship which existed at this time between the young lawyer, with his cold and reserved manner, his suppressed emotions and solid judgment, and the emotional and impetuous Archbishop Connolly, with his fervid temperament and characteristic Irish eloquence. Bishop Cameron of Antigonish describes his first meeting with Mr. Thompson as being at a dinner in the Archbishop's house some years after the religious change, which has been elsewhere referred to, and says : *— "Dinner over, His Grace invited us to his room and began to give us the detailed history of a case at law in which he was largely interested. As a listener, a perfect listener, he (Mr. Thompson) impressed me very much. And when he broke his dead silence, his rapid and searching examination was a study, soon followed by unbounded admiration at the easy skill with which he proved that he had already thoroughly mastered the whole complicated subject at issue and completely dissipated every difficulty that had the moment before seemed all but insurmountable."

Archbishop Hannan, who succeeded Dr. Connolly in 1876, was not upon very intimate or friendly terms with Mr. Thompson, and the latter's action in defence of a local religious sisterhood which appealed to him for legal aid, actually embittered their relationship. It seems that the sisterhood in question consulted the lawyer regarding certain regulations made by the Archbishop which they did not like, and he advised an appeal to Rome. After a prolonged controversy, in which Archbishop Lynch of Toronto was accidentally involved, the sisterhood finally triumphed.

*Letter to the Author, dated December 20th, 1894.

But this was sometime after the period now under consideration.

Meanwhile an important epoch in his career was at hand. During the thirty-three years of his past life he had proven the possession of certain qualities which almost ensure success to the man who has them. As a boy and a young man his affection for his parents had been something remarkable. His father naturally inspired respect, and the judicious and close intimacy to which he admitted the son, did much to mould the mind and character of the future statesman. He won and wedded his wife despite the difference of religion which his education and family influence made a considerable difficulty, and being the man he was, it is probable that he never even considered the fact that her lack of money made the future depend entirely upon his own exertions. He had clearly shown in the practice of law and in the practice of preliminary politics that the performance of duty and the maintenance of absolute integrity, were to him far more precious than the glamour of a fleeting popularity, or the glitter of success obtained by doubtful means. And in the public recognition of these qualities he had laid the foundation for a higher position and a permanent reputation.

CHAPTER III.

Law and Politics.

The time had now come for Mr. John S. D. Thompson to rise out of the Provincial sphere of legal practice and to take a place amongst the more or less leading lawyers of the Dominion. He had, it is true, already made himself felt before the Bench of Nova-Scotia, and had been connected with a number of important cases. He had thoroughly familiarized himself with the law and practice of his own Province, but as yet the sphere had been too limited for fame and not sufficiently remunerative for wealth. But in 1877 came the chance.

In the early part of that year the Halifax Fisheries' Commission met. It was the outcome of the Washington Treaty of 1871, by the terms of which the Americans had been given the right to fish for twelve years within the limits of Canadian waters in return for a similar right on the part of British subjects within the jurisdiction of the United States. As this latter privilege was almost valueless it was agreed that an International Commission should meet at some date to be thereafter arranged and settle the amount of the compensation which was to be paid Great Britain on behalf of Canada. From various causes nothing definite was done during the following half-dozen years. It was not the fault of the Canadian Government. On the 8th of February, 1877, Mr. Mackenzie's administration announced through the Speech from the Throne that in spite of every effort no advance had been made in obtaining a settlement from the United States as pledged under the terms of the Treaty. Sir John Macdonald in speaking to the Address admitted that the fault did not lie with Canada, and expressed the earnest hope that the incoming American Government would "remove the stigma that had been cast upon the good faith of the American people," by the previous and positive refusal to carry out this provision of the Treaty of Washington.

The expectations based upon the coming into office of President Hayes were promptly realized, and on June 15th the Commission met at Halifax. The central figure in the gathering was M. Maurice Delfosse, Belgian Minister at Washington, who was named by the Austrian Minister in London, and was expected to hold the scales with absolute justice between the British Commissioner, Sir Alex. T. Galt, K.C.M.G., and the American Commissioner, Hon. Ensign H. Kellogg. M. Delfosse was elected President, and performed his duties with dignity and fairness. Hardly less important personages were the two Agents, the British being Mr. (now Sir) Francis Clare Ford; the American, the Hon. Dwight Foster. There was a brilliant array of counsel, the British side being especially strong in this respect. It included such men as Joseph Doutre, Q.C., of Montreal; S. R. Thomson, Q.C., of St. John, N.B.; Hon. W. V. Whiteway, Q.C., of Newfoundland; Hon. L. H. Davies, of Charlottetown; and R. L. Wheatherbe, Q.C., of Halifax. Upon the American side were Richard H. Dana, Jr., and Francis H. Trescott. But, fortunately for the case he had to present, Mr. Dana recognized the necessity of calling in to his assistance some Nova-Scotian lawyer who was known to be thoroughly posted in Maritime Provincial matters and versed in the law of maritime nations. He selected Mr. J. S. D. Thompson and thus gave him the one opportunity he required. It was with him, as it is in such cases with all lawyers, a purely business transaction.

SIR JOHN CALDWELL ABBOTT, K.C.M.G., Q.C., D.C.L.

Third Premier of Canada.

Two sides in an important international case had to be presented before certain judges, and he undertook to aid in the preparation of the American brief. On the 30th of July and after the Commission had been sitting for three days, he was formally introduced in the following words, extracted from the official minutes:

"Mr. Dwight Foster then requested permission to introduce Mr. J. S. D. Thompson, of Halifax, and Mr. Alfred Foster, of Boston, who would attend the Commission to perform such duties on behalf of the United States as might be assigned to them."

Those duties, so far as Mr. Thompson was concerned, were sufficiently onerous. There was no publicity for him in connection with the case; his name only appears once upon the minutes of the meetings; he delivered no speeches and received no official thanks. Yet there can be no doubt that he prepared the greater part of the American case, and especially that which had a local application; that he had to make a profound study of the whole Fisheries question; and was required to analyze the evidence produced, for the benefit of the United States counsel. His reward was a large fee—estimated at $6,000—and a considerable increase in reputation. As the *Halifax Herald* said some months afterwards, "It is a point of pride with us that Mr. Thompson was deemed so eminent in his profession as to be sought after by the American Government"

The result of the Commission was not all that Canada desired or expected, but to the United States it was intensely unsatisfactory. The tribunal awarded Canada $5,500,000 by a majority vote, Messrs. Delfosse and Galt supporting, and Mr. Kellogg dissenting. For nearly a year the American Government delayed the payment to which they were in honour pledged, and while at least one-half of the fifteen millions paid by Great Britain in full for the

Alabama damages was lying in their vaults uncalled for and unclaimed. Finally, towards the close of 1878, the amount was handed over, but only after an ungracious protest from Mr. Welsh, the American Minister to England, in which he declared that "the Government of the United States cannot accept the result of the Halifax Commission as furnishing any just measure of value of participation by our citizens in the in-shore fisheries of the British Provinces." Mr. Thompson was afterwards, for political purposes, criticized for his share in the case, but the very general feeling was that he had acted perfectly within his rights as a lawyer, and that the very fact of a leading Halifax barrister being allowed without public objection to take such a part, showed the Canadian desire to give our rivals every fair right to assistance before the tribunal. It, no doubt, helped also in the moral compulsion afterwards required to obtain payment of the award.

In November, 1877, the opportunity came for one who had proved himself an able lawyer to show whether he also possessed the qualities of a politician and statesman. As a rule, and despite the number of lawyers who play at politics and the politicians who meddle with law, the qualifications are not often combined in any great degree. A training in law is apt to limit the intellectual horizon and restrict the broad-minded interpretation of precedents and that freedom of mental action, so essential to a man who aspires to true statesmanship. The great English party leaders have never been lawyers, and men like Brougham, Eldon or Campbell would perhaps have been greater in character and reputation had they adhered to law and not dabbled in politics. And it is probable that Mr. Thompson's first essay in political life was not in the end successful, from a party point of view, because he was inclined to look too much at legislation from the legal standpoint and think too little of popular sentiment in connection with it. Other and specific causes there were, but in a general sense this had much to do with the result.

However, all went well at the beginning. A vacancy had occurred in the representation of Antigonish county in the Local House of Assembly, and a movement at once commenced for the nomination of Mr. J. S. D. Thompson. At that time a little coterie of men were active in Halifax Conservative circles, all of whom afterwards attained more or less eminence. Robert Sedgewick is now a Judge of the Supreme Court of Canada; Martin J. Griffin, Editor of the *Halifax Herald*, is Parliamentary Librarian at Ottawa, and a well-known Canadian writer; Wallace Graham, Q.C., is a Judge of the Supreme Court of Nova-Scotia; C. J. Townshend became a member of several Nova-Scotian Governments, and is now a Judge of the Province; George Johnson is Dominion Statistician at Ottawa. There were others also, including Mr. J. J. Stewart, the present proprietor of the *Herald*. And the way in which they clung together was as remarkable as the manner in which the most of them rose to fame. Not less noteworthy, perhaps, was the regard in which Mr. Thompson was held by these rising men of his own home city.

On the 21st of November, the *Halifax Herald* came out with an editorial declaring that, "Should Mr. Thompson be nominated by the Opposition in Antigonish, should he accept a nomination, at least seven-eights of the city readers of the Government organs will be found hoping he may win. For the organs fight against him under the melancholy disadvantage of knowing that the majority of their party look upon Mr. Thompson as a man who ought to be in public life, who will be in public life, who will make his mark in public life, and who has the ability, character and standing to do credit to any public position in which he may be placed." Shortly after this high tribute, he was given the unanimous Conservative nomination, and during the brief campaign of a week which followed made ten speeches in the constituency.

But it was not all clear sailing. His opponent was a Roman Catholic Conservative named Joseph McDonald, who received the strong support of the Local Government, and who expected to obtain enough Conservative votes to defeat the Opposition candidate. The *Halifax Chronicle* commenced the campaign against Mr. Thompson by the charge that he was the nominee of Bishop Cameron, and that "his religion was expected to have more to do with his prospects in Antigonish than his politics." This was rather an absurd argument to address to a county which was overwhelmingly Catholic in population, but which had for years shown its moderation by electing one Protestant and one Roman Catholic. And in connection with this first appearance of a statement which has had considerable currency during many following years, a further extract from the letter of Bishop Cameron, which has been previously mentioned, will be of interest. He writes: "Towards the end of October, 1877, I was convalescing after a serious attack of illness, when one day I received a friendly visit from Senator Miller. A by-election was soon to take place in Antigonish. In that connection the Senator said: 'What do you think of the idea of inviting Mr. J. S. D. Thompson to become a candidate?' My reply was as follows: 'I should be delighted to see my native county represented by a man of Thompson's standing and ability.' Upon my being asked whether Miller would be allowed to make use of the above expression, I readily replied that my words were but the honest expression of my views, and that I was not ashamed of their being known to all whom they might concern." The Bishop then goes on to say that he resided at that time in Arichat and did not visit any part of Antigonish County during the campaign that ensued.

As a matter of course, the knowledge that Bishop Cameron favoured any particular candidate would help rather than hurt him under such conditions as prevailed in the contest, and there can be no doubt that the *Halifax Herald* hit the nail upon the head in saying that even if the *Chronicle* was true in its assertion, Mr. Thompson was to be congratulated on having secured the favourable regards of "one of the most able and scholarly, the most refined and powerful, ecclesiastics in the Lower Provinces." But in fact, he was the candidate of no one man. Halifax Conservative opinion almost pushed him into public life; his nomination papers were signed by the principal men in Antigonish County, which in any case had strong Opposition leanings; he did not seek the constituency, it sought him. After the nomination, his speech was described by a local paper, *The Casket*, as something unusual. "We have heard public speakers in Canada, in the States, and in our own Province, and we fear not to assert that Mr. Thompson is the most perfect public speaker we have ever listened to. In fluency and ease, and grace and vigour of expression, he is without a peer in this country." Other local references to his ability and gentlemanly bearing indicate the forces that were at work, and which finally resulted in the large majority of 517.

It was a very considerable victory for a young man who had hitherto only taken a quiet interest, and not a public part, in political matters. He had been compelled to fight the whole Government interest and an alleged Independent candidate, besides facing a constituency to which he was a stranger, and in which he had only a week to become acquainted. The Conservative Opposition in the Local House was jubilant, and the *Herald* congratulated the County of Antigonish on having secured the services of one of the ablest young men in the Province. It congratulated Nova-Scotia upon obtaining the public services of a man of high character and tried ability. It congratulated the Opposition upon such an accession of strength to its ranks.

The Government of Nova-Scotia was at this time in the hands of the Liberal party, under the leadership of the Hon. P. C. Hill. A large majority of the Legislature was at its back, but it had become somewhat weakened by a reckless management of the finances, by certain scandals in connection with details of administration, and by the growing unpopularity of the Liberal Ministry at Ottawa, coupled with that omniscient factor in political affairs—hard times. Mr. Thompson's victory in Antigonish marked the turning of the tide, and a year later, at the same time that the Mackenzie Government was swept from power by the rising waves of Protectionism, the Nova-Scotia Ministry was so badly beaten at the polls that only eight of its supporters were returned to the Legislature out of a membership of thirty-eight. All the ministers but one were defeated.

Mr. Thompson came back to the Assembly from Antigonish by acclamation, and on the 21st of October, 1878, a Conservative Government was formed by the Hon. Simon H. Holmes, who took the portfolio of Provincial Secretary, with J. S. D. Thompson as Attorney-General, and the Hon. Samuel Creelman, a veteran Radical of the days of Howe, as Commissioner of Works and Mines. Messrs. C. J. McDonald, W. B. Troop, J. S. McDonald, N. W. White, C. J. Townshend, and H. F. McDougall held office without portfolios. The new Attorney-General was warmly welcomed by a portion of the press, the *Herald* declaring him to be of high standing in every situation of public or private life, with a reputation as clear as noonday from all charges and even all suspicions.

Much was expected from the new Ministry, and in a very substantial way much was received. To extricate the Province from financial difficulties, to lift its railway system out of the hopeless muddle into which it had fallen, and to reform the loose method of municipal government, were the requirements of the moment. The Premier and his chief assistant set themselves to this task, and in three years of economy and retrenchment paid off $70,000 of the $400,000 debt incurred by their predecessors; reduced expenditures by $150,000; doubled the receipts from mines; and trebled the receipts from Crown Lands.

In another direction considerable success was achieved. The preceeding Government had subsidized Provincial railways to the extent of $1,400,000 during its term of office, but without securing the results aimed at. There now seemed to be difficulties in every direction. Grants had been expended without half the work being done, and in the case of the Eastern Extension Railway, the Company, contractors, and Government appeared to be in a perfect tangle of trouble. One or two minor roads were soon completed by the new Ministry, and its energies were then devoted to the production of a scheme which should effect the complete consolidation of the railways of the Province under the control of an English syndicate. Some local men of wealth were interested, but the principal members of the Company were Sir Henry Tyler, Lord Ashley, Lord Colin Campbell, and other Englishmen of similar standing. Under a voluminous contract prepared by the Attorney-General, the Company, after considerable discussion, both public and private, agreed to complete some of the existing roads, and to construct 140 miles of new railway. The Government in turn promised considerable grants of land, and consented to guarantee the interest on certain bonds.

There seemed to be no general opposition to the scheme. From one quarter, however, came steadfast and stinging criticism, and the ability with which Mr. W. S. Fielding, then editor of the *Halifax Morning Chronicle*, handled the question, not only effected the public mind injuriously to the Government, but helped to place him in the prominent position which he afterwards attained of Prime Minister of Nova-Scotia. But these attacks made no impression upon the Legislature. In opening the session of that body on January 19th, 1882, the Lieut.-Governor was very optimistic, and prophesied that the railway consolidation arrangements would "mark a new era in the development of the Province." On Feb. 1st, following, Mr. Thompson delivered a long and powerful speech upon the Railway Bill, which embodied the scheme in its entirety, and the measure was carried by a sweeping majority. It easily passed the Council, but the success of the Liberals at the polls a few months later prevented it from ever going into operation.

Another matter dealt with, and to the lasting benefit of the Province, was the reform of its municipal system. It was a most difficult task. The old method of municipal government was vastly inferior to that of Ontario, and even to the system which had been established in New Brunswick two years previously. Attorney-General Thompson, however, went into the matter with his usual thoroughness, and seemed to be utterly oblivious of local popular clamor or of political exigencies. His Municipal Corporation Act, which finally became law, effected a genuine revolution. Each county in the Province was incorporated and provided with municipal self-government,

Sir Mackenzie Bowell, K.C.M.G., Senator,

Fifth Premier of Canada.

largely upon the Ontario plan, in place of the antiquated method of rule by Sessions of the Peace and Grand Juries. The control of road and bridge moneys was vested in the municipal councils, and many abuses developed as the natural outgrowths of an old system were done away with. It was natural that a measure of wholesale reform such as this should create discontent in different quarters. The Liberal Opposition, as a matter of course, opposed and censured it. Magistrates all over the Province, whom it deprived of the share in governing the counties which they had hitherto held, were naturally indignant. And an army of officials who had been previously connected with the expenditures upon roads and bridges fought vigorously against the new proposals and against Mr. Thompson as the author of the reforms. But the measure was so good as a whole that the Legislature could hardly refuse to pass it, even though the majority knew that the conscientious labours of the Attorney-General would deprive the Government party in the coming elections of the support of what had practically become a political machine—the magistracy of the Province.

A prolonged effort was also made by the Holmes-Thompson Government, as it was called, to abolish the not very useful, and certainly expensive, Upper House. In 1879, the Ministry introduced a bill for that purpose, which was passed by the Assembly but thrown out by the Legislative Council. An address to the Queen was then carried through the popular chamber praying for such amendment to the British North America Act as would permit the Lieut.-Governor-in-Council to appoint enough members of the Upper House to carry the measure. The latter body presented a counter address to Her Majesty, and the Ministry followed that up with an able document prepared by Mr. Thompson, and endorsing the views of the Assembly.

The Imperial Government, however, refused to interfere, and the Legislative Council still stands as one of the institutions of Nova-Scotia. Other legislation was attempted or carried out and, taken altogether, the course of the Government won it a reputation which caused so well-informed a paper as the *St. John Sun* to declare that, "Nova-Scotia had never been so well governed" as it was during this period.

Meanwhile important changes were pending, and on the 25th of May, 1882, it was announced that a re-construction of the Cabinet had taken place. Mr. Holmes had resigned the Premiership on account of ill-health, and had accepted the office of Prothonotory of Halifax. The new Ministry was formed as follows:

Premier and Attorney-General............ .Hon. John S. D. Thompson.
Provincial Secretary. ....Hon. A. C. Bell.
Commissioner of Public Works ....Hon. S. Creelman.
Without Portfolio.........................Hon. W. B. Troop.
" " ....Hon. C. J. Townshend.

Mr. Thompson became Prime Minister as a matter of course. He was now, as a leading local paper declared, first in his profession and first in the Legislature, while, "as the son of one of the founders of Liberalism in Nova-Scotia, he still retains the spirit which actuated the men who won responsible government for us and made future reforms possible." But he was destined to hold the position for only a very brief period. Dissolution followed early in June, and in the elections which took place on June 20th the Thompson government was defeated by a majority of five.

The Premier himself was again returned for Antigonish, and amongst other notable selections at the polls was that of J. W. Longley for Annapolis, and W. S. Fielding for Halifax. Early in July the Government resigned, and on the 27th of the same month Mr. Thompson accepted a place on the Supreme Court of the Province.

There were many reasons for the defeat of the Ministry. The ability displayed by the *Chronicle* in its strong but unscrupulous attacks was one ; the enemies made by the municipal reforms was another ; and the following statement by Mr. Fielding in a speech at Halifax on June 1st was widely believed : "As Premier we have a gentleman who has many friends. It is well known that the Hon. gentleman who temporarily fills that office has no intention of remaining in politics, but will at the earliest opportunity take a seat upon the Bench which his recognized ability as a lawyer fits him to adorn."

There is no doubt that this was a popular impression, strengthened by the Attorney-General's disregard of the usual arts of the politician. And there seems also to have been a certain limited display of that sectarian spirit which had been shown in the first contest fought by Mr. Thompson in Antigonish. When a very few scattered votes could change the result in many constituencies, appeals to bigotry, whether secretly or openly made, would naturally have some effect in a general election. Of genuine religious narrowness, however, such as was developed at a later period in Ontario, there never had been very much in Nova-Scotia. But, whatever the measure of influence wielded by diverse causes may have been, the battle was now over ; Mr. Thompson had ceased to be Premier ; his star of political success appeared to have paled forever ; and he had assumed at the early age of thirty-eight the ermine of the Provincial judiciary.

There seemed to be no discord or disagreement in opinion regarding his appointment. The Liberals said : "We told you so." The Conservatives declared that the ablest lawyer in Nova-Scotia had taken the place which he perhaps most desired, and which he was splendidly fitted to fill. Long afterwards a few whispers were heard to the effect that he had deserted his party in its time of need, and that he should have stayed by the political ship in the shadow of failure as well as in the sunshine of success. But there was no public expression of this feeling at the time, and it was confined to a few who may have been offended by his political rectitude or judicial manner of dealing with party questions. The *Halifax Herald* gave the Tory view in a parting eulogium in which reference was made to his having brought order out of Legislative chaos; inaugurated many valuable reforms; secured the completion and publication of the Provincial Law Reports, and rendered the Province many other services which it would feel for all time to come. An interesting tribute, unexpected at the time, and destined to be of political service in years to come, was that tendered by the new Judge's most bitter critic and ablest journalistic adversary —the *Morning Chronicle.* Writing on July 27th, that paper spoke of him as probably the youngest Judge in the Dominion, and then went on to say:

"In politics we have differed from him, but our differences have never prevented a recognition of his fine abilities and high standing as a lawyer. It will be admitted on all sides that he is one of the foremost men in his profession, and possesses all the qualities necessary for a good Judge. . . . We predict for him a brilliant judicial career."

It was therefore under very favourable circumstances that Judge Thompson began what appeared to be his real life-work. Politics had been a sort of passing experiment in which he had not succeeded as a party leader, though proving himself more than successful as a masterful debater and legislator. And during the next three years he did good work for Nova-Scotia. The Judicature Act of 1884, by which the system of pleadings and practice in the Province was greatly simplified and brought up to the standard of Ontario and England, was chiefly his work. He took the greatest interest in the founding of the Law School at Halifax in connection with Dalhousie University; contributed liberally to its support at a time when his aid meant life or death to the institution; lectured for years in its halls without charge and while holding a seat on the Bench, and devoted much time in other ways to what is now a most successful and valuable legal establishment.

Personally he displayed many of the qualities of an ideal Judge. He was prompt in decision, fertile in precedent, invariably courteous to the members of the Bar, and was undoubtedly possessed of that indescribable qualification known as a judicial mind. He seemed to have a peculiar faculty for getting down through a huge mass of apparently relevant, or really irrelevant, questions to the crucial point in the most intricate of disputes. No student at college ever worked harder than did Judge Thompson. In pursuance of a resolution made when he ascended the Bench, it is understood that during the years he remained in his position he devoted at least five hours a day to the study of law. So deep was the impression this legal knowledge now began to make upon the public mind that when his lectures upon "Evidence," at Dalhousie University, were announced, a large number of the barristers of Halifax enrolled themselves as general students of the college for the purpose of hearing them. And these addresses upon a most difficult branch of legal study are considered to be of the highest value, as well as distinguished for lucidity and scholarly style. When therefore the call came to higher duties, and in his case to national responsibilities, Judge Thompson was prepared for advancement, as is every man who does thoroughly and well that which his hand finds to do.

CHAPTER IV.

ENTERS THE GOVERNMENT.

By the autumn of 1885 some important changes in the composition of the Dominion Cabinet had become necessary Sir John Macdonald was not all that he had once been in health and energy, though his cheerines; of disposition showed no signs of failing. Sir Leonard Tilley had found the Finance Department too great a strain for one of his years and strength, and the ministry was therefore about to lose the services of one of the best trusted of Canadian statesmen. Sir Charles Tupper intended also to shortly retire to the High Commissionership in London, and Sir Alex. Campbell was desirous of resigning his position. To find new men capable of in some measure taking the place of these distinguished veterans was the task which the Premier had to face. And it was all the more important that his selections should be men of vigour and ability because the Riel question was at this moment threatening the party with disintegration and the country with serious disaster.

It was, therefore, a happy stroke of wisdom and good fortune combined, when Sir John Macdonald called in Mr. Thomas White as Minister of the Interior, and Mr. George E. Foster as Minister of Marine and Fisheries. Both had been of considerable service to him in the preceding session when various causes had made debating talent rather scarce upon the Conservative side of the House, and both were well-known throughout the country as skillful speakers and clever politicians. But when it was announced a short time afterwards that the most important portfolio in the Cabinet at that moment—the Ministry of Justice—had been offered to a Nova-Scotian judge whom the Prime Minister had never even seen, and who, as a politician, had never filled the public mind of the country in any national sense, there were undoubted and natural expressions of surprise.

The Dominion Liberals did not attack the appointment of Judge Thompson on personal grounds, but made the mistake of trying to minimize it. Referring to the Ministerial changes generally, the *Toronto Globe* observed, on the 26th of September, the day after the new Minister of Justice was gazetted, that "these changes and shuffles are of very little consequence to the country. The men who remained in the Cabinet and the men who have lately been taken into the Cabinet, are small men who will exercise no influence on the country." Such a comment upon politicians of the calibre of White and Foster and Thompson is enough to make partisans on either side smile to-day, and it is quite safe to say would not be offered by the *Globe* under its present clever management, should any similar occurrence again take place.

The *Toronto Mail*, then under the able editorship of Martin J. Griffin, was on familiar ground in dealing with the Hon John S. D. Thompson, and naturally did him more justice. It was in a position to tell the Dominion something of his services as a lawyer; of his occasional successes as an orator; of his "high and unstained personal character"; of his eminence as a judge; and of his reputation since 1869 as "a most faithful, high-minded, unselfish, and respected advocate of the policy of the great chief of the Liberal Conservative party of Canada." Still it must be admitted that the country as a whole accepted the appointment largely on trust, and waited for time and experience to develop results before expressing any particular opinion.

The Conservative party, of course, had confidence in Sir John Macdonald's wonderful judgment of men, and those who followed politics closely knew also that there must be something remarkable in the new Minister or he would never have been selected to fill an exceedingly difficult post at the moment when a most complicated constitutional issue was darkening the whole national horizon with sectarian and sectional storm clouds.

The man most directly concerned did not want the position. His party had almost forced him into public life when he first consented to contest Antigonish for the Local House. During the following period, while Mr. Thompson held office in Nova-Scotia, he made as few public appearances as possible, seldom delivered platform speeches, and though he laboured earnestly and unremittingly, was known to have retired to the Bench with pleasure, when defeat ultimately came. And now his party had again demanded his aid. It was given with hesitation, and only from a final conviction of duty. The well-known statement of Sir John Macdonald's, that "the great discovery of my life was the discovery of Thompson," is, like most epigrams, somewhat inaccurate. It was absolutely necessary that a successor should be found to Sir Charles Tupper, and Nova-Scotia had, of course, the first claim to produce him. But it seemed very doubtful if the man was to be obtained in the Province.

Mr. (now Sir) Charles H. Tupper, and his distinguished father, Mr. Robert Sedgewick, Q.C., and the other local Conservative leaders urged upon Sir John the ability and services of Judge Thompson. The latter however told his friends he would not take the position, and there really seemed to be no one else upon whom the mantle of Howe

Hon. Wilfrid Laurier, Q.C., M.P.,

Leader of the Canadian Opposition.

and Tupper could for the time being fall. Meanwhile the claims of the Hon. George E. King, ex-Premier and then Judge of the Supreme Court of New Brunswick, were being pushed by friends in his Province, and the result seemed very doubtful. Finally, Mr. C. H. Tupper, Mr. Sedgewick, and others went once more and urged Judge Thompson to accept the post they thought him so well fitted to occupy. A letter from Sir John Macdonald was taken to him, formally offering the position, and stating that a County Judgeship had been accepted by Mr. McIsaac, the Liberal M.P. for Antigonish, and that his old constituency was once more open to receive him.

Sir Charles Tupper at the same time and with the consent of Sir John Macdonald, went down to Antigonish in order to obtain, if possible, the concurrence and aid of Bishop Cameron, who had now for some years been Judge Thompson's closest friend and confidant. He pointed out to the Bishop what a wide sphere of influence the change would open up for his friend, and how greatly in the interest of Nova-Scotia and of the country generally it would be to have such a strong man in control of the Department of Justice. Bishop Cameron eventually concurred, and under the varied pressure thus brought upon him the Hon. J. S. D. Thompson entered the Dominion Cabinet. The whole proceedure was a great compliment to the man and his ability, and it proves also that the astute Chieftain at Ottawa had been more than favorably impressed by what had been told him regarding the Nova-Scotian Judge. In this way he may be said to have "discovered" him.

But the fact that Mr. D'Alton McCarthy, Q.C., M.P., was first offered the Ministry of Justice before Judge Thompson was approached in the matter, rather tends to make the appointment one of those accidents of politics which bring about the most strange and striking results.

Mr. McCarthy's refusal of the portfolio really paved the way for the successful national career of his great rival.

It must have required considerable courage to face the large opposing majority in Antigonish. Several constituencies were offered the new Minister, in any one of which he would have been elected by acclamation, but he preferred going back to his old friends. Without hesitation, or taking time to "sound" the electorate, he faced a Liberal majority of 333; placed his faith and political future in the hands of the people of Antigonish; and despite renewed appeals in certain quarters to the old religious prejudice; and a natural local desire for a local representative such as Dr. McIntosh was, who opposed him as an Independent Conservative; the brief campaign resulted in a sweeping triumph for the new Nova-Scotian leader by the splendid majority of 228.

The comments of the Nova Scotian press had in the meantime been generally eulogistic and congratulatory. Unlike that of Ontario it could speak with knowledge of the past record and of the personal character and abilities of the lawyer and politician who was now to enter upon a career of broader statesmanship. The *Halifax Herald*, speaking on the 24th of September, when the appointment was first announced, represented very accurately the opinion of most of the intelligent Conservatives of the Province:

"As a gentleman the new minister has ever been a favorite among men of all parties, creeds and classes; as a lawyer he has no equal in the Lower Provinces, and few if any superiors, in Canada; while as a public man he displayed all the highest qualities of an ideal statesman. . . . Honest, industrious, broad-minded, clear-headed and courageous, with a thorough mastery of his profession and a patriotic ambition to be useful in his day and generation, Mr. Thompson is unquestionably of all the men in the Province the one best qualified to succeed Sir Charles Tupper as the representative of Nova-Scotia in the Government of Canada."

Fair minded Liberal opinion was voiced by the following from the Windsor, N.S. *Courier* :—

"We congratulate the people of Nova-Scotia upon having in the Dominion Cabinet a gentleman of Mr. Thompson's ability and untiring energy. He is an excellent speaker, a clear-headed lawyer, and will undoubtedly fill the office to the satisfaction of the country."

Well-informed opinion outside of the Province was represented by the *Toronto Mail*—already quoted—and the *Montreal Gazette*, which declared that in the new minister the Government would receive a valuable acquisition. It went on to describe him thus :—"A profound lawyer, universally admitted as being in the foremost rank of his profession, he combines the qualities of a sound jurist, with those of an eloquent and effective speaker, who will prove a valuable addition to the debating power of the Ministerial benches." How valuable, not even the *Gazette* had the faintest conception ! The rabid and extreme partisan view may be obtained from a despatch sent by the Ottawa correspondent of the St. John *Telegraph*, which declared that "the members of the Orange order are greatly enraged over the appointment. They say he supplants a Protestant and that Riel will not be hanged."

There was a very interesting discussion following upon the appointment, which was partisan in origin, constitutional in form, and not exactly personal in application. A good many years before this time Vice-Chancellor Mowat of the Ontario Judiciary had stepped down from the bench to assume the Attorney-Generalship of his Province, and to enter that political arena in which he has since had such conspicuous success. The Conservative press and speakers of that day had censured the Liberal party for thus degrading the Bench of Justice by making its occupants eligible for party favours and party rewards, and had especially denounced Mr. Blake, the retiring Premier of Ontario, who had nominated the distinguished Judge as his successor and had urged him to accept the post. Whatever force these arguments may have had in Provincial politics, and it is not probable that an occasional retirement from the Bench to enter political life will ever really injure the Judiciary, they had still less in connection with the Dominion post of Minister of Justice.

Who indeed could be better fftted to administer justice for the nation; to control the law-work of the Dominion; to look after and abolish, modify, change or amend its laws, than one who had previously possessed judicial experience? Then in a matter of precedents—those things which lawyers and politicians appreciate so much and which constitute such excellent reasons for action or inaction as the case may be—there is a considerable resemblance as to the duties performed, between the position of Canadian Minister of Justice and that of the Lord Chancellor in England. In the Mother-country many of the most distinguished holders of that great blue ribbon of the legal profession went from the Bench to the woolsack. Amongst them were Lord Hardwicke, Lord Bathurst, Lord Loughborough, Lord Truro, Lord Hatherley, Lord Camden, Lord Campbell, and, greatest of all, Lord Eldon. And certainly it has never been claimed that the English Bench was degraded thereby, though it is open to any one to urge that men like the late Lord Chief Justices Cockburn and Coleridge have left greater legal reputations than the vast majority of those who preferred the temporary glory of the woolsack to the lasting splendour of a distinguished judicial record.

But none the less the discussion was entertaining, and gave the party organs something to talk about. As there was nothing special about the new Minister to denounce, they fired a good deal of political ammunition over this little point, and it was one of the earliest matters referred to when Parliament opened its fourth session on the 25th of February, 1886. The new member for Antigonish was introduced for the first time to the House, of which in five years he was to be leader, by Sir John A. Macdonald and the Hon. A. W. McLellan, and at once took his seat as Minister of Justice. At the same time the Hon. Thomas White and Hon. George E. Foster went through the form of introduction and took their places, after having returned to their constituents for election upon appointment to office. Within eight years from that day four out of those five political leaders had passed through more or less eventful phases of political life, and had departed from the scene! How wonderfully true in this connection seem the beautiful lines by Lowell:

> "Life is a leaf of paper, white,
> Upon which each of us may write
> His word or two.
> Then comes the night."

On the following day the debate upon the Address in reply to the Speech from the Throne took place, and Mr. Blake, as leader of the Opposition, proceeded to pour the usual hot shot into the Ministerial ranks. He was particularly sarcastic concerning the two different opinions apparently held by the party in power regarding the appointment of judges to political office. It was with them, he declared, not a matter of principle, but simply one of expediency. And then speaking of the Mowat incident, he said: "I was told that I had degraded the Bench; that I had soiled the hitherto unspotted ermine; that I had created a feeling of want of confidence on the part of the people in the judges of the land; that I had rendered it impossible for the judges to conduct impartially the trials of election cases." And after this he paid his respects to the new Minister in a style which was meant to make prominent Conservatives feel secretly annoyed, and to make Mr. Thompson slightly uncomfortable had he really been, as Mr. Blake supposed, a small man in a large place.

"I congratulate the honorable incumbent of the office. He enters Federal politics, as the French would say, by the great gate. For him there is no apprenticeship in our Parliament. . . . No greater compliment could be paid a public man. The Government felt the office was important; they felt they had no one available in Parliament, and that they had to look outside. As a lawyer, the hon. gentleman has come to the front with a bound over many heads; as a legislator, he begins his Federal career at once as a Minister."

In his reply, Sir John Macdonald chaffed the Opposition leader in his usual effective style; spoke of him as "the dissolving view" of the Mackenzie Government, sometimes in and sometimes out; referred to the Hon. W. B. Vail having been brought into that Government from Nova-Scotia over the heads of many Liberal members in the House; criticized the retirement of Vice-Chancellor S. H. Blake from the Bench; and spoke of the elevation of the Hon. E. B. Wood to the Chief Justiceship of Manitoba by Mr. Blake as the employment of the Bench for the reward of political services. Finally, he had a few words, and only a few words, to say about the new Minister: "I looked out in Nova-Scotia when the (Ministerial) vacancy existed, for a lawyer who could fill that position creditably, and I found him in my hon. friend, and if he were not here at this moment I might enter more fully into the fact of his fitness, but I believe that even the hon. gentlemen opposite will admit before the Session closes the correctness of my selection and choice."

It is probable that a very few months of intimate association in Cabinet and private political discussion would be all that was necessary for a man of Sir John Macdonald's keen insight to have guaged the ability and knowledge of the new Minister of Justice. But in making that last prophetic remark, even he could hardly have foreseen the skill and value of Mr. Thompson as a Parliamentary debater, though, no doubt, he was able to make a shrewd guess at the truth. In the course of a few weeks, however, there would be no possible doubt concerning the matter.

CHAPTER V.

THE RIEL QUESTION.

The opening of this session of the Parliament of 1886, was perhaps the most critical period in the life of the new Minister of Justice. At a crisis in the history of the government which he had joined and of the party to which he belonged, he found himself called upon to bear the burden of defence against the fiercest and best organized attack in the annals of Canadian legislation. Fresh from the Bench of his Province and long unaccustomed to heated discussions and party strife, he was to endure the lash of sectarian bitterness and sectional prejudice, intensified as it was, by an external and seemingly successful campaign of unscrupulous misrepresentation. Unknown as a speaker to nearly the whole of his critical, or already prejudiced, audience in the House, he had to face the oratorical graces of Mr. Laurier, the powerful eloquence of Mr. Blake, and the fervid utterances of a score of others, who were borne by the excitement of the time to the crest of a storm-tossed political wave.

There can be little doubt that the position of the Ministry was very precarious. The old-time influence of the Conservative party in the Province of Quebec, seemed to have gone forever. The magnetic personality of Sir John A. Macdonald appeared to have lost its power. He was freely denounced in great French-Canadian meetings as "the enemy of our nationality," and was even burned in effigy at Montreal, whilst the Hon. J. A. Chapleau, the

THE EARL OF DERBY, G.C.B., P.C.,

Late Governor-General of Canada.

eloquent tribune of the people, was bracketed with Sir Hector Langevin and Sir Adolphe Caron, in public resolutions, as "traitors to their country." Riel was to be the hero of Quebec and one of the political martyrs of his nationality: Mr. Mercier was to be the leader of a new movement which in the sacred name of race and religion was to avenge his execution: the Parti-Nationale was to sweep out of existence the enemies of French Canada and of the Roman Catholic Church: Mr. Blake was to stir up the Province of Ontario against those who had committed what 30,000 people on the Champ-de-Mars in Montreal, declared "an act of inhumanity and cruelty unworthy of a civilized nation."

From the moment when the man who had caused so much of sorrow and bloodshed, suffering and death, was executed at Regina, on the 16th of November, 1885, this agitation had grown in force and sunk deeper and deeper into the hearts of the people. Popular passion is always easy to arouse when questions are raised touching even the fringe of creed or nationality, and Mr. Mercier, who was trying to ride into power upon a wave of sectarian prejudice, seemed utterly indifferent to the danger of his course. And in allowing the law to be carried out the Dominion Government had to face a double difficulty. Not only was the situation in Quebec critical: not only did *Le Monde*, a Conservative paper, represent the sentiments of its press as a whole in declaring, after the execution, that "Fanaticism wanted a victim: Riel has been offered as a holocaust: and Orangeism has hanged him for hate and to satisfy an old thirst for revenge": but the remarkable utterances of the *Toronto Mail* and *Orange Sentinel*, provided additional fuel for the flame of excitement. The former had declared on the 3rd of November, preceding the execution, that "as Britons we believe the conquest will have to be fought over again and Lower Canada may depend upon it, there will be no treaty of 1763." The *Sentinel* declared, in reply to fiery statements from Quebec, that the Government did not dare to hang the rebel; that "English-Canadians will not longer suffer this galling bondage: and the day may not be far distant when the call to arms will again resound throughout the Dominion."

Tremendous pressure had been brought to bear upon the French-Canadian Ministers to resign from the Dominion Cabinet. They were told, and truly, that Mr Mercier was about to sweep the Province of Quebec, defeat the Local administration, and then turn his attention to aiding Mr. Laurier at Ottawa. Many of their Conservative supporters pointed out that refusal to leave a doomed government meant political extinction, and that if they attempted to condone the execution of Riel, even a seat in Parliament would be an impossibility. Whole batches of French-Canadian Conservatives declared that they dare not support the Government in their proposal to let justice take its course, or in their subsequent definite performance of that duty. Meanwhile, Mr. Blake had not made the outlook more pleasant by vigorous speeches in Ontario, during which he denounced the whole North-West policy of the Government. If appearances could be trusted it seemed indeed as though a general break-up of the national Conservative forces was about to take place.

This then was the situation when the Hon. J. S. D. Thompson faced a storm-tossed House of Commons on the 11th of March, and listened with stocial composure to Mr. Landry's long-anticipated and now famous motion :—

"That this House feels it its duty to express its deep regret that the sentence of death passed upon Louis Riel, convicted of high treason, was allowed to be carried into execution."

Mr. Landry's speech was the key-note of much that followed during a week's debate. He described the Government's action in a strain of the fiercest invective. It was a provocation flung at the face of a whole nationality: it was a breach of the laws of justice: it was an evidence of weakness on the part of the Ministry: it was the gratification of a long-sought vengeance: it was the wanton sacrifice of the life of a French-Canadian Catholic upon the altar of sectarian hatred and bigotry. He spoke of the petitions that had been disregarded, and considered the actions of Riel to be those of an insane man or of a monomaniac. He quoted the pardoning of Jefferson Davis, the exile of Arabi Pashi, and the treatment of Abd-el-Kader by France, as affording ample precedents for the forgiveness of Riel. Lt. Colonel Amyot, another Conservative, followed, and declared with all the vigour of passionate declamation, that after an examination of the record in Riel's case, the Ministry had ordered the hanging in spite of the favourable nature of the record: in spite of the recommendation to mercy by the jury: in spite of the madness of Riel, which was admitted and proved: in spite of the petitions which they had received. "We go further" added the orator, "we say they did it after mature deliberation, in order to please a certain section of the country, not caring about offending the other."

Many others spoke. Mr. Clarke Wallace declared that out of 2000 Orange Lodges in the country not more than six had passed any resolutions whatever upon the subject. Mr. M. C. Cameron denounced the Government as having "trafficked in the destiny of a fellow mortal." Mr. Laurier made a speech which was remarkable for the purity of its diction, the beauty of its language and style. He stated his belief, and the belief of his Province, that the execution of Riel was "the sacrifice of a life, not to inexorable justice, but to bitter passion and revenge." He claimed that the American, English and French press, almost without exception, had taken the ground that the execution of Riel was unjustified, unwarranted and against the spirit of the age. He urged that Riel had been deprived at his trial of certain witnesses, and that papers and documents taken from him and his house had not been placed at the disposal of his counsel as requested. He compared Riel to Jefferson Davis, and quoted from the evidence of General Grant before a committee of the American Congress to show what were considered the rights of surrendered officers. If Riel had thought that he was going to be treated as a captured rebel he would have escaped instead of surrendering to Major-General Middleton. Mr. Laurier concluded an oration, which Mr. Blake afterwards characterized as the best he had ever heard upon the floors of Parliament, by appealing for that justice which, in his opinion, the unfortunate half-breeds had fought for and had never yet obtained.

Sir Hector Langevin, Minister of Public Works, and the nominal leader of the French-Canadian Conservatives, referred to the great difficulties which he and his colleagues had been compelled to contend with during the previous four months of wild excitement, of agitation in Quebec, and counter-agitation in Ontario. He spoke of the rebellion; its inception through the machinations of Louis Riel; its progress and final suppression by the gallantry of the Canadian volunteers. General Middleton had kept his promise to Riel, and had handed him over in safety to the civil authorities. He had been tried under a law which was put on the Statute book when the Liberal party had been in power. And so anxious was the Government to give the rebel leader every legal chance for his life that the case had been carried to the Supreme Court of Manitoba, and thence to the Judicial Committee of the Imperia Privy Council. He summed up strongly and eloquently in the following words:

"We are the Government of the country; we had no revenge against this man; he had done us nothing personally; but he had attacked the authority of the Queen; he had revolutionized that country; he had called the half-breeds to his aid and had deceived them in a most shameful way, as the missionaries of that country have all testified; he had destroyed their faith; he had destroyed their religion to establish one of his own, and my friends from the Province of Qnebec call that man a compatriot! No, Mr. Speaker, the sober second thought of the people will not be so."

Mr. Royal contended that the rebellion was a crime against God and humanity; Mr. Gigault thought it was a political scaffold and a political execution that took place at Regina, though he did not say how the matter could possibly have benefited the party in power. Mr. J. J. Curran (afterwards Solicitor-General) declared that the central figure in this war of races and religions which was being inaugurated, had been alternately exhibited as a hero, a martyr, a fool and a lunatic. He quoted from documents, speeches at the trial, interviews, etc., in order to prove that Riel was simply an ambitious and utterly unscrupulous schemer. Mr. Coursol denounced the attitude of the *Toronto Mail*, as did Mr. Langelier, who contributed the following remarks to the debate:

"Our ancestors, when only 60 000 in number, including men, women and children, stood their ground for five years against 50,000 of the best soldiers, not only of England, but of the world. Now that we are a million and a half we could offer a pretty stiff resistance to the Tory land grabbers who threaten us."

Sir Adolphe Caron, in an eloquent speech, declared that if circumstances should ever arise similar to those of last year, he would again do what he had then thought was his duty. He considered that Riel had deceived the half-breeds, and showed how he had offered to sell for a bribe both his followers and his "cause." He read letters from Bishop Grandin showing the trouble and misery the rebellion had caused, and from Riel to "Poundmaker," which proved that he had tried to raise the Indians in revolt. Mr. Chapleau, in a most able effort, defended the Government's position and his own share in supporting the law of the land. He referred to the brilliant offers made him by the Parti-Nationale; spoke of his refusal to take the leadership of that organization in Quebec, which for a time seemed, and was, all powerful; and urged strongly his conviction that Riel was entirely responsible for his own actions.

But the speeches around which centered the greatest interest, and upon which depended the ultimate verdict of Parliament, of the people and of posterity, were those of Mr. Blake and Mr. Thompson. The House was expectant when the leader of the Opposition rose to his feet. It looked for a powerful arraignment of the Government; for close reasoning; for a wide display of constitutional knowledge; for vigorous invective. But in the case of the Minister of Justice, it was simply curious. Conservatives anticipated a fair presentation of the case, but were hopeless of any real reply to the great speech which it was known Mr. Blake had prepared. And Liberals would have laughed exceedingly had any one hinted that Blake might meet his match in the short, stout, fresh-coloured, young-looking gentleman who had just come in from a Nova-

Scotian constituency, and who was to soon make his maiden speech in the House. Mr. Blake reviewed the whole matter. He went into the history of the rebellion; the discontents of the half-breeds; the action or inaction of the Government. He contended that the trial had not been a fair one; that the choice of the magistrate had been unfortunate, and that the evidence and facts of the case proved Riel to be insane. He spoke of the disregard of the jury's recommendation to mercy, and enlarged upon the question of executive interference by the Government, and as to when it was warranted. His case was a very wide and varied one; the reference to authorities was extensive, and many precedents were produced to show that as Riel, in his opinion, was not responsible for his actions, he should not have been executed. The speaker concluded by saying that though he knew that many of those of his own race and religion would differ from him, it was his conviction that the sentence should have been imprisonment for life; that by the execution a great blow had been inflicted upon the administration of justice, and that the Government was responsible for it.

In making what was really a great speech upon this occasion, there is no doubt that Mr. Blake fell into the fatal error of under-estimating his antagonist. Had he felt any comprehension of what was to follow, he would not have made his argument so general or so broad, and would have depended upon the strong points in the case without introducing weak ones, which seemed specious and plausible at first sight, but which could not stand the shock of logical and keen analysis. Unfortunately for him, too, it was past midnight when the speech was finished, and this gave the Minister of Justice an inestimable advantage—one which experienced debaters know how to appreciate and make use of. He promptly moved the adjournment of the debate, and, after a couple of days' interval, rose to reply during the afternoon of Monday, the 22nd of March.

It is very seldom indeed that a public man achieves a reputation of the highest order by a first speech in Parliament. If in England a future leader, or a man of admitted and commanding ability, makes a mere favourable impression upon the House, he is considered to have done exceedingly well for the first time. In Canada it had only been the case, and then in a very modified form, upon one previous occasion, when the Hon James McDonald, now Chief-Justice of Nova-Scotia, delivered a maiden speech in the Parliament of 1873. Of course, in the American Congress where only pluck and pyrotechnics are required, it is comparatively easy to make an oratorical success of a first effort. But in the case of the Hon. J. S. D. Thompson success meant the defeat of the greatest logician and debater in the House of Commons, and the defence of the Government's position in a matter involving most intricate constitutional issues. It meant that a new man was to pitt himself victoriously against a veteran in Parliamentary debate and knowledge of constitutional law. It meant that he was to become a power in the House and the nation, while failure involved results which would have made his subsequent rise impossible, or, at least, unlikely.

The Chamber was crowded to excess, and from the moment when the musical voice of the unpretentious, and not at all imposing, speaker was first heard, until he sat down at the end of two hours, he held the close and undivided attention of the House, and it may be almost literally said that a pin could have been heard to fall. Those who know the normal condition of the Commons, no matter who is speaking, in regard to attention and quietness, will appreciate the full force of the compliment thus conveyed. The speech was strong, clear and convinc-

Hon. Sir Oliver Mowat, K.C.M.G., Q.C., M.P.P.

ing. The Minister of Justice seemed to be master of himself, master of his subject, master of the law in its theory, practice and precedent, master of his audience. He pierced the armour of Mr. Blake's argument with the most direct and irresistible skill, and while not appealing in the least to his hearers' passions, prejudices or sympathies, he subdued a critical and censorious body of men by pure force of reasoning and logical argument. Before that speech was ended, it is absolutely accurate to say that he appeared to both friends and opponents as a

> "Tower of strength
> That stood four-square to all the winds that blow."

Mr. Thompson first deprecated the extreme feeling, if not actual animosity, which had been shown throughout the greater part of the prolonged debate. He made a statement of the part taken in the case by his own Department—that of Justice—and then proceeded to combat the claim that Parliament was a court of appeal in criminal cases, pointing out some of the evil results which might ensue in such an event. He defended the composition of the Regina Court, and met fully and squarely Mr. Blake's contention that the Judge was an inferior one and the choice unwise. He held that it would have been gross injustice, and a very dangerous precedent, to have enacted any special law to meet the case. After going over the evidence and proceedings at the Regina trial, Mr. Thompson took up the assertion that Riel was a political offender, and, therefore, should not have been hanged. He instanced the case of John Brown; dealt with that of Lord George Gordon; quoted Mr. Gladstone in connection with the Fenians and the murder of Constable Brett, and gave the opinion of the English Commission on Capital Punishment, which declared that "in cases of treason accompanied by overt acts of rebellion, assassination or other violence, the extreme penalty must be maintained." Lord Cranborne, now the Marquis of Salisbury, had said that "You must treat treason as the highest crime known to the law. If you impose capital punishment for murder you must for treason."

He pointed out that Lord Bramwell had declared that "Treason is worse than murder, because it involves the taking of many lives." The condition of a new country such as the North-West absolutely required strong enforcement of the law, and any laxity in the punishment of admitted crime would have been a criminal act on the part of the Government. He then dealt with the insanity question in a lucid and convincing manner, and asked in that connection how others who took part in the rebellion could have been dealt with if the head and front of the movement had been granted executive clemency. "I should like to ask how the Frog Lake murderers could have been punished if the man who incited them to rebellion was allowed to go free or to repose in a lunatic asylum until he got rid of his delusion?" And then, in a few ringing words, he concluded his speech amid loud and prolonged cheering:

"I think, Sir, it was absolutely necessary for us to show to those Indians, to every section of the country, to every class of the population, that the power of the Government in the North-West was strong, not only to protect, but to punish as well; and in the administration of justice, with regard to those territories in particular, it was absolutely necessary that the deterrent effect of capital punishment should be called into play. (Cheers.) I am not disposed, remote as that territory is, strong as the calls are for vigorous government there and for the enforcement of every branch of the law, to be inhuman or unmerciful in the execution of the penalties which the law pronounces; but in relation to men of this class, men who time and again are candidates for the extreme penalty, men who have despised mercy when it was given to them before, I would give the answer given to those who proposed to abolish capital punishment in France, "Very well, but let the assassins begin."

With the close of this speech there arose a new figure in Canadian politics and a chief amongst those who played the leading parts in the great game of public life. Three days afterwards the division was taken, and the Government found itself sustained by 146 to 42. Meantime, the echoes of the speech delivered by the new Minister of Justice had permeated every part of the Dominion, and the man from Nova-Scotia, the stranger who had entered the great arena of debate and overthrown the hitherto almost invincible Blake, found himself famous as a constitutional lawyer and powerful speaker.

Canada has every reason to be grateful for the firm disposition and straightforward character of its Minister of Justice during the crisis which prevailed in the autumn of 1885, as well as in that which has just been described. There is no doubt that Sir Hector Langevin had given his friends in Quebec secret assurances during the storm of protests which came in while the execution of Riel was pending, that a commutation of the sentence might be and would be granted. He spoke with the authority of a senior Privy Councillor and a right hand man of the Premier's for many a long year, and it is probable really believed that his influence over Sir John Macdonald, both as a personal friend and as the successor of Sir George Cartier in the French-Canadian leadership, would be sufficient to eventually obtain it. Hence his organ *Le Monde* was permitted to join the chorus of protesting papers and politicians; many Conservatives were deceived into joining the movement; and it was only when the agitation got beyond control and threatened the very existence of the Conservative party in the Province, that Sir Hector woke up at the same time to the dangerous situation he had allowed to develop in the ranks of his own followers, and to the probability that he would be unable to guide the issue in the Cabinet.

Stronger men than he were at the back of Sir John Macdonald, and had the chieftain entertained the least idea of interfering with the course of the law, the forceful personality of Mr. Thompson would have probably averted the evil. There is no indication or evidence that he ever did think of taking such an action, but Sir Hector appears to have been in a serious predicament, and the crisis was so acute that a weak-kneed Minister of Justice might have been cajoled or coerced into advising that the sentence be commuted. The excuse thus given for bending before the storm might have been accepted or it might not, the probabilities being that a large majority of the Cabinet would still have been in favour of the upright and honourable course which was in the end pursued. And this may be said without considering "the Old Man's" masterful disposition. But none the less was the fact of Mr. Thompson being a Roman Catholic and possessing a vigorous will and character of his own, very effective in keeping the Government united to all intents and purposes upon the question which was shortly to be the central one in a general election, extending from the shores of the Atlantic to the rock-bound coasts of the Pacific.

CHAPTER VI.

An Election and a Fisheries' Treaty.

The campaign which preceded the Dominion elections of 1887 brought the new Minister of Justice into personal contact with the people of Ontario. Hitherto he had been a sort of political myth, powerful in the Cabinet and in Parliament, but personally unknown to the public. He was now to be introduced to Ontario by the Chieftain himself, and to take a leading part in the battle upon which depended the fate of the party; for, as Ontario went, so it was felt would go the country. The Conservatives in Quebec were fighting a lost cause; Rielism, and all that it involved of racial agitation and revengeful cries, was uppermost, and the Province on Oct. 11th, 1886, returned the Liberals to power in the Local Legislature, and placed the sweets of office in the hands of Mr. Mercier. Nothing could, therefore, be hoped from what had once been the mainstay of Canadian Toryism, and everything turned upon the result in Ontario.

On the 11th of November, Sir John A. Macdonald, the Hon. J. S. D. Thompson, the Hon. Thomas White and Mr. W. R. Meredith, started in the afterwards famous private car "Jamaica" upon their political tour of the Province, commencing with a large meeting at Renfrew. Mr. Meredith, who was conducting his own campaign at the same time against Mr. Mowat, and who, in this election, came so near to winning the day, did not, of course, speak at all the meetings, and a little later the three first-named leaders were joined by Hon. George E. Foster. With them at occasional intervals were the Hon. J. A. Chapleau, the Hon. John Costigan and Mr. J. J. Curran, Q.C. Everywhere the reception given the Ministers was not only cordial but enthusiastic. All along the line vast crowds turned out to see the "Grand Old Man," and the hero of the Riel debate. The drill-hall, rink, or city hall, as the case might be, was invariably crowded to the doors, and it was not long before Sir John Macdonald found that far from supporting a lost cause in Ontario, he had the great mass of the people with him.

It was known to his intimate friends in that campaign that Sir John had expected defeat; that he thought Quebec was going solidly against him, while Ontario would do well if it left the party representation about equal; that he left Ottawa weak in health and dispirited to the last degree. But the greetings of the people were so cordial, the meetings so enthusiastic, and the reports began to get so favourable as the tour progressed, that he visibly improved in health and spirits and rapidly became himself again. Mr. Thompson was given a prominent place on the programme of almost daily speeches, generally opening the ball with a powerful arraignment of the Opposition's alleged policy of race and revenge in Quebec, secession in Nova-Scotia, annexation in New Brunswick, and detraction everywhere. He invariably handled the Riel question, urged the preservation of the Union, and spoke of the oneness of the Conservative policy as it was now presented in every part of the Dominion. Mr. White or Mr. Foster would follow, and then Sir John Macdonald would close with a few pithy, witty remarks. Very often there were two meetings—one in the afternoon, and one in the evening at the next town.

A preliminary mass-meeting and demonstration was held at London on Sept. 16th, 1886. Sir John Macdonald, Mr. Thompson, Mr. White, Mr. Chapleau, Mr. Meredith and Mr. Carling were the speakers, and the "Old Man" delivered a lengthy and elaborate address. The Minister of Justice received a splendid reception, and the eloquent speech of Mr. Chapleau, the great Quebec orator, was one which, it is safe to say, will never be forgotten by those who heard it. A little later, on Oct. 14th, Messrs. White, Foster and Thompson addressed an immense gathering at St. John, N.B., and the *Daily Sun* on the succeeding day observed that "Too much cannot be said in praise either of the style or matter of the address of the Minister of Justice. He is the more polished speaker of the three. Every sentence is clear, incisive and graceful."

At Owen Sound, on Nov. 15th, when the Ontario tour really commenced, the reception was particularly elaborate in arrangement and enthusiastic in spirit. Mr. Thompson was warmly received and brought ringing cheers from a great audience by the declaration that "one loyal man is as good as ten rebels." Then followed a large gathering at Dungannon in Huron County, and on Nov. 20th the party reached Hamilton. Here we find in Mr. Thompson's speech a rather amusing comment on the varied policies of the Liberals. "There, however, Mr. Blake did have a policy in his pocket. He had a right to christen his own baby, and, therefore, he called it the 'alternative policy.' A better name for it, however, would have been the 'all-turnative policy.'"

Galt, Listowel, Stratford, Guelph and Sarnia were then visited, with all the now familiar accompaniments of tremendous crowds, torch-light processions and loyal addresses. At Stratford the crowd was so great that the Ministers could hardly get through it to the platform. When they did get there, Mr. Thompson referred to "the warm-hearted hug" he had received as one which a man only wanted once in a lifetime. At Sarnia he said a rather good thing at the expense of one of the Liberal leaders:

"Sir Richard Cartwright has recently stated that the Prime Minister ought to pass into nothingness, but these demonstrations did not indicate such a result. Eight years ago he had himself passed into nothingness, and he was realizing to-day the bitterness of the old axiom that out of nothing, nothing comes."

In speaking of the recent Quebec elections, the success of the Nationalists, and Mr. Mercier's promised aid to Mr. Laurier in the coming Dominion contest, he referred—with more bitterness than usually characterized him—to "the blasphemer, Mr. Mercier, and the traitor, Mr. Laurier." It is not unlikely that he afterwards regretted the violence of this language, but the provocation was great, and the people of Ontario only partially realized then, and have forgotten now, the terrific storm of abuse and misrepresentation by which Quebec had just been carried for the Local House, and by the continued use of which it was hoped to capture the Dominion. The applause, however, upon this occasion was long and continued. The episode showed, as did a certain reply to Sir Richard Cartwright some years later, that the Minister of Justice could, when he desired, denounce his opponents as vigorously, as he could argue with them skilfully.

Immense meetings followed at Orangeville, Orillia, Sunderland, Port Hope, Peterboro', Cobourg, Deseronto, Welland, Essex Centre and Windsor. At Sunderland, on Dec. 1st, Mr. Thompson referred to the name applied by the *Globe* to the party of speakers, "the Chestnut Combination," as being in a certain sense correct. The successful receptions to different Ministers in New Brunswick, Nova-Scotia and Ontario were, no doubt, becoming unpleasant "chestnuts" to the Liberal organ. "And," said he, "there was another sense in which they might be called a 'chestnut combination,' and in respect of which they gloried in

HON. SIR CHARLES HIBBERT TUPPER, K.C.M.G.,

Minister of Justice.

the name. They were able to go from one Province to another, from one town to another, and tell the same story to the people." At Deseronto he joked with the same phrase in a rather effective way: "Why, Mr. Blake himself repeated but one speech in every part of Nova-Scotia. He dished up chestnuts roasted, chestnuts fried, chestnuts on the hard shell, chestnuts salted down, and reproduced long after they were stale and out of use."

Speaking at Peterboro of the good times which followed the depression of 1878, and as an illustration of the general progress under Conservative rule, he said that an old and wealthy Maritime Province man was once asked how he had acquired his money, and replied, "I bought property when the Liberals were in power: I sold it when the Tories came in." At Welland, Mr. Thompson declared that "Mr. Blake had better confine his attention to the laborious and malignant satire which suited his disposition so very much better than any allusion to facts or figures." At Windsor he once more struck at Mr. Laurier. as one who "justifies murder, pillage and rebellion under the sacred right of resistance. Do not the settlers, the Government officials, the mounted police and the volunteers possess some sacred rights as well as Riel and his associates?"

The closing meetings of the tour were at Lucan, Wingham and Chatham, with a final demonstration at Toronto. For some reason connected with the general campaign, Mr. Thompson was not present in the Queen City on Dec. 21st, but addresses were delivered by Sir John and by Messrs. White, Foster and Chapleau.

This prolonged tour made the new Minister deservedly popular, though, of course, never in the same sense as was Sir John Macdonald. His proper place was not upon the stump, though in this campaign many things combined to render his speeches exceedingly effective and useful to the party. He could be sarcastic, and at times humorous in narrative, though never magnetic with that personal merriment which has such influence upon a crowd. He was also much too self-contained and deliberate to arouse large gatherings. Meantime the campaign had been progressing all over the country. Mr. Chapleau had done much to even matters up in Quebec, assisted by the efforts of Sir Hector Langevin and Sir Adolphe Caron. Sir Hector had finally thrown in his lot with the Ministry, and his work in organization during that time of political uncertainty, and amid the loss of party followers and friends, and the smashing of party ties, was of great value. Sir A. P. Caron was always an effective and popular campaigner, and on this occasion he worked like a Trojan. Between them, they managed to hold the balance so that election day showed, instead of the expected Liberal sweep, a representation of about half and half.

On the 22nd of February, 1887, the ballot box settled the destinies of Canada for a few years longer. The Maritime Provinces returned a pretty solid Conservative contigent, Mr. Thompson being elected for Antigonish by a majority of forty over an old-time antagonist in local politics, Mr. Angus McGillivray. Manitoba, the North-West and British Columbia went straight Conservative, and Ontario gave a fair majority. Once more, Sir John Macdonald had appealed successfully to

"A weapon that comes down as still
As snowflakes fall upon the sod;
But executes a freeman's will
As lightning does the will of God."

The Riel question was thus disposed of so far as Dominion politics were concerned, but it was already producing, in the form of Mercierism, many serious evils, of which Sir John Thompson himself did not live to see the end.

The cessation of party struggles at home for the time being, now gave the Government an opportunity to deal with the trying and difficult Fisheries' Question. And in writing a number of years after the crucial point had been faced by Canada, Sir Charles Tupper declared that he only accepted the post of Plenipotentiary to Washington in 1887 upon the condition that he should be accompanied by the Hon. J. S. D. Thompson as legal adviser. There is no doubt that he very fully apprehended the situation, and after sitting for a time in the same Government with the Minister of Justice, understood how great the value his wide knowledge and clear grasp of international law would be in such a connection. It was the revival of the old, old question which had been settled in 1818, settled again in 1871, and re-adjusted by the Halifax Commission of 1877. Through the deliberate abrogation of the Fisheries' Clause of the Washington Treaty by the American Government in 1885, the Canadian Administration had found itself face to face with the alternative of giving the Americans a free hand in the immensly valuable in-shore fisheries of the Dominion, or else of falling back upon the treaty of 1818 which gave full power for the reguation and control of foreign fishermen in British waters.

The Government had naturally taken the latter course; made the necessary arrangements for the complete protection of Canadian interests and British subjects within the three mile limit; and prepared to endure with patience the outburst of American indignation which was of course inevitable. But unfortunately the United States refused altogether to recognize the Canadian construction of the Treaty of 1818; its Government denounced the protective regulations as unfriendly and illegal; its fishing interests clamoured for action, while their men and vessels proceeded boldly into Canadian waters and did as they liked without regard to either law or license. Armed coasting-steamers had been at once despatched to the disputed fishing grounds with orders to capture and carry into the nearest British port any vessel found poaching within British jurisdiction. These orders were freely obeyed, and during the next two years many American vessels were seized, the cases tried by the Canadian Maritime Courts, and not infrequently the cargoes and vessels confiscated. More than once there had been collisions between excited crews. More than once bloodshed was only averted by the merest chance, and not infrequently during this perilous period, the possibility of a war between the Empire and the Republic seemed to hang upon trifles light as air. Many were the menaces from the other side of the line. The abrogation of the bonding privilege, the refusal to permit Canadian vessels to enter American ports, the cessation of all commercial intercourse, were each in turn threatened either by the newspapers, by Congress or by the President. Canada, however, stood firmly by what the Government believed to be its rights, and the Minister of Justice was at one with the Minister of Marine and Fisheries in the determination to uphold the legal rights and Maritime interests of the Dominion and of its large fishing population.

The result was that on November 15th of this year, a Commission met at Washington to discuss the points at issue and make an attempt at settlement. The British Plenipotentiaries were the Rt. Hon. Joseph Chamberlain, M.P., the brilliant and keen-witted English Radical; the Hon. Lionel Sackville West, British Minister to the United States, and Sir Charles Tupper, G.C.M.G., Canadian Minister of Finance. The American Commissioners were the Hon. Thomas F. Bayard, United States Secretary of State, and Messrs. W. L Putnam and James B. Angell. With Sir Charles Tupper was associated Mr. Thompson as legal adviser.

No more fitting appointment could have been made. The Canadian Minister of Justice was closely in touch with the business and legal details of the whole question; he understood thoroughly the views and wishes of his colleagues; and the American side of the case was by no means new to him. It is very seldom indeed that a Plenipotentiary in negotiating a Treaty has the assistance of an acute legal mind which not very many years before had thoroughly mastered the other side of the questions at issue and prepared the brief for the representatives of the country which he was now to meet in discussion. And no doubt Mr. Thompson's acquaintance ten year's previously with American methods at Halifax, had given him an insight into the somewhat tortuous paths of American diplomacy which was useful to even the long experience of Sir Charles Tupper, or the trained intellect of Mr. Chamberlain. So far, however, as Mr. Bayard was concerned, he showed in this case how honourable, straightforward and honest an American statesman can be when he allows himself to rise above the narrow anti-British prejudices of his own environment.

A great deal of discussion and cross-firing of communications between the three Governments concerned, together with many and diverse comments by the newspapers of the United States, Canada, and Great Britain, followed. From November, 1887, until February, 1888, the negotiations were continued off and on. For a prolonged period meetings of the plenipotentiaries and their counsel were held almost daily. It is understood that many able papers were submitted to the British Commissioners upon different questions and phases of the general problem by Mr. Thompson, and that his knowledge and quick perception of technical and legal points were of invaluable service to Sir Charles Tupper. And Canadians of the future when they learn something of the wonderful ability and unique power of mental grasp shown by Mr. Chamberlain upon this occasion, and regarding a subject of which he had naturally known very little before coming to Washington, will indeed regret that Sir John A. Macdonald had not received the same keen appreciation and co-operation from the British Commissioners who helped or hindered him in negotiating the Washington Treaty of 1871.

On the 15th of March a Treaty was duly signed. By its terms an International Commission was to be appointed for the decision of the exact limits of Canadian waters, within which by the Treaty of 1818, the United States had renounced for ever all rights as to taking, drying or curing fish. A method of calculating the three marine miles of exclusion was decided upon. Privileges were mutually given as to vessels reporting, entering or clearing for shelter, for repairing damages, for the purchase of wood or the obtaining of water. Such vessels were relieved of compulsory pilotage and of harbour and other dues. Vessels under stress of weather or accident were to be allowed to unload, reload, tranship or sell all fish on board, subject to customs' regulations, when such action might be necessary as incidental to repairs. Full privilege was given for the replenishing of outfits, supplies, etc., when damaged or lost by disaster. Reciprocity was promised by Canada whenever the United States should remove the duty from fish, fish-oil and other produce of the fisheries of the Dominion. Upon this step being taken United States' fishing vessels were to be given annual licenses free of charge for the following purposes:

I. The purchase of provisions, bait, ice, seines, lines and all other supplies and outfits.

II. Transhipment of catch, for transport by any means of conveyance.

III. Shipping of crews.

Such was the Treaty finally made, in which, of course, Newfoundland was included. And in order to show international friendliness and prevent any possible friction before the ratification of the Treaty, Canada offered the United States a most favourable *modus vivendi* or temporary arrangement. This was accepted, and all seemed to be well at last in this most troublesome of disputes. In presenting it to Congress on February 20th, President Cleveland declared that "the Treaty meets my approval because I believe that it supplies a satisfactory, practical and final adjustment, upon a basis honourable and just to both parties, of the difficult and vexed question to which it relates." And in speaking of the *modus vivendi* which had been offered by the British plenipotentiaries, he said that it appeared to have been "dictated by a friendly and amicable spirit."

On the 2nd of March a banquet was given Mr. Chamberlain in New York by the Canadian Club and its President, Mr. Erastus Wiman. In his speech the distinguished English statesman pointed out the difficulties which the Commissioners had encountered, and declared that they had left the Treaty "to the calm and sober judgment, to the common sense and reason, and above all to the friendly feeling of the peoples of both countries." He gave a brief sketch of its terms and of the concessions made on either side; spoke strongly regarding the absolute justice and fairness of the Canadian policy in the whole affair; and concluded with an appeal to the United States Senate to accept the settlement. After a visit to Canada and a most eloquent address in Toronto, Mr. Chamberlain returned to England, and in a speech at Birmingham shortly after his arrival, declared that "the Canadian Government and its representatives were desirous of terminating a state of irritation, dangerous in its possible consequences, which had existed for a considerable time. They were quite willing to surrender the strict interpretation of their rights, and extreme contentions, and to deal with the matters submitted in a spirit of equity, and with the anxious hope of promoting neighbourly intercourse."

A little later Mr. Bayard wrote that "Conciliation and mutual neighbourly concession have together done their honourable and honest work in this treaty, and have paved the way for relations of amity and mutual advantage." In the beginning of April the measure came before the Canadian Parliament for ratification. Mr. L. H. Davies delivered a speech of general denunciation, and was followed by Mr. Thompson, who referred to the onslaught made upon the Treaty by the Liberal party and then to the equally strong claim of the Republicans on the other side of the line, that the interests of the United States were sacrificed in the arrangement:—"The enemies of the Administration, the enemies of this Treaty, the enemies of Canada, have been ringing the changes which he (Mr. Davies) has reversed here to-night." The Minister of Justice proceeded first to speak of the Fisheries as Canada's most valuable possession, and one that would as the years rolled by steadily increase in value; and then defended the Canadian interpretation of the Treaty of 1818—"It was always assumed, even in the courts of law, that the entering of an American fishing vessel in defiance of a treaty would result in the forfeiture of the vessel and her cargo, and we were only putting on the statute book in 1886 what had been the view of the law acted on from the earliest times, with the exception that the seizures in earlier times were by British vessels of war, and that lately they have been made by Canadian revenue cutters."

It had not been, he declared, an "anti-civilized policy,"

Hon. Edward Blake, Q.C., M.P. for Longford,

Late Leader of the Liberal Party in Canada.

as the Liberals had called it, but one of proper protection of Canadian interests, and one which the United States carried out to a far greater degree in its own ports and harbours. "I support this Treaty," he added, "because it contains fair concessions on the part of Canada and fair and liberal concessions on the part of the United States." He then pointed out that Nova-Scotian fishermen did not particularly want a treaty—so long, in fact, as their inshore fisheries were protected they did not care about it at all. "The only necessity that existed for one was the fact that our neighbors alongside of us were dissatisfied with the construction which we put on the Treaty of 1818." And then came an eloquent peroration: "If the Government had not protected the fisheries as they have, with vigilance and with strictness, instead of occupying the proud position we occupy to-day, we should have had no treaty on the Table; we should have had no concessions to make; we should have received no concessions in return; our fishermen would not have fared as well as they have during the past few years; our fisheries would not have been as valuable as they are to-day, and neither the United States nor any other country would have thought it worth their while to go through the solemnities of negotiating and making a treaty in regard to fisheries which the owners thought so little of that they did not take the trouble to administer the laws of their own country for their protection."

The Treaty finally passed the House of Commons without amendment and without a vote being taken. In the month of August following, however, the American Senate, actuated by considerations of demagoguery and unfriendliness, very far removed from the spirit of conciliation and good will to which Mr. Chamberlain had appealed, summarily threw out the whole arrangement. President Cleveland then issued his remarkable Message, dated the 23rd of August, in which he declared his belief that "the treaty just rejected was well suited to the exigency and its provisions were adequate for our security in the future and for the promotion of friendly intimacy without sacrificing our national pride and dignity." And then, in the teeth of all honour, friendliness and common sense, he recommends "a policy of national retaliation," one which "manifestly embraces the infliction of the greatest harm upon those who have injured us, with the least possible damage to ourselves"! "I recommend," he continued, "immediate legislative action conferring upon the Executive the power to suspend by proclamation the operation of all laws and regulations permitting the transit of goods, wares, and merchandize in bond, across or over the territory of the United States, to or from Canada."

Needless to say no overt action followed this extraordinary message. The President was given the authority desired but never used it: the ensuing election swept him from the power which he had hoped to strengthen by this very means; and the Canadian Government fell back once more upon its own regulations for the care of its fisheries. But it was not the fault of Canada or England that this measure of peace and conciliation had been refused. It was not the fault of the able negotiators who had spent time and labour in its preparation. It was the strength of that anti-British element in the United States to which even a President with the strong will, clear intellect, and vigorous convictions of Mr. Grover Cleveland, found it necessary to bow and to offer sacrifice, as did the men of old before Moloch.

On the 11th of September the work done by Mr. J. S. D. Thompson was rewarded by Her Majesty the Queen with a Knight Commandership of the distinguished order of St. Michael and St. George, bestowed "in recognition of his eminent services on the Commission." He accepted it with that loyal appreciation which is a natural accompaniment of true modesty and genuine ability. It is said that on the morning Mr. Thompson was apprised of the honour conferred upon him, Sir John Macdonald put his head into the room of the Minister of Justice and enquired: "How is Sir John this morning?" "You ought to be best able to answer that question," replied Sir John Thompson, forgetting for the moment his new designation. This mark of distinction was most fully approved by the Canadian press, and the *Montreal Gazette*, in the following comment, pretty well voiced public opinion:

"Though but a young man, in Dominion politics, Sir John Thompson has won a foremost place among the country's public men. As Minister of Justice it has been his duty to act in a number of cases calling for the greatest legal skill and the surest judgment, and in all he has acquitted himself with honour, even when in opposition to so powerful a legal authority as Mr. Blake." And a Parliamentary question was now about to darken the political horizon which would require all the skill and ability possessed by the Minister of Justice, and which was destined to leave its mark upon the remaining years of his public life.

CHAPTER VII.

THE JESUITS' ESTATES ACT.

The action of the Dominion Government in the case of Riel, had stirred to a white heat the prejudices of ultra Catholics in the Province of Quebec. Its refusal to disallow the Jesuits' Estates Act was now destined to have a similar effect upon the ultra Protestants of the Province of Ontario. The ablest defence of the refusal to pander to the sectarian elements of French-speaking Canada, had been made by Mr. John S. D. Thompson. And his great deliverance during the debate upon Colonel O'Brien's famous motion, defended up to the hilt the Government's policy of refusal to interfere with the Provincial legislation of Quebec, at the dictation of the sectarian elements in English-speaking Canada. By the first speech the Minister of Justice made his reputation. By the second he confirmed and enhanced it. And curiously enough, they were each made upon opposite sides of the semi-religious issue which has more than once threatened the Dominion with serious disaster.

In connection with this Jesuits' Estates question there seemed to be combined nearly every element which could embarrass a Government, provoke ill-will between the Provinces, raise sectarian issues, and make the action of the Dominion Ministry unpopular whichever line it might ultimately take. The Premier of Quebec, who had planned and passed the legislation, was intensely unpopular in Ontario and other Provinces, because of his speeches during the Riel agitation. The preamble to the Bill as carried through the Parliament of Quebec was exceedingly offensive in its terms to a great majority of Protestants. The measure itself seemed to be specially adapted to misrepresentation and to the uses of those who might and did believe in all honesty that Roman Catholicism was advancing its influence and power to a dangerous degree throughout the Dominion of Canada. And, although it is a delicate matter to refer to, there can be no doubt that the personal position of the Minister of Justice, as a converted member of that great church, was freely used to enhance this injurious sentiment.

The first stages in the history of the affair did not indicate any serious trouble. On the 3rd of July, 1888, a Bill for the settlement of the long-standing dispute between the Jesuits, the Clergy of the Roman Catholic Church, and the Province of Quebec, was passed without opposition or protest through the Lower House of the Quebec Legislature. It passed the Upper House also without opposition, and in due course was assented to by the Lieut.-Governor and became law, subject within a certain period to disallowance by the Dominion authorities should the legislation be considered unconstitutional or dangerous to the interests of the country as a whole. At first there was neither opposition nor serious criticism. With the exception of the Huntingdon *Gleaner*, not a paper in Quebec discussed the matter from a hostile standpoint, and the Protestant Committee of Public Instruction quietly accepted the promise of $60,000, included in the measure. Mr. Mercier was therefore justified in concluding while the Bill was before the Legislature that there could be no very strong feeling against the proposal in the Province interested. Indeed the Hon. Mr. Lynch, a Protestant representative, declared during the passage of the measure, that "there was nothing in it alarming in character."

The Hon. Mr. Starnes, in the Legislative Council, said

that "Protestants and Catholics ought to be satisfied with the manner in which the question is now settled." The Hon. David Ross, declared that "we had to deal with a question of justice and I gave it my support. The Protestants whom I represent in the Cabinet are well satisfied with the settlement." None the less however, Mr. Mercier was necessarily well aware of the ultimate result of such legislation, especially when the introductory portion of the Bill was worded in a way so peculiarly offensive to large elements of the national population. He supplied the provocation, and it is hardly unjust in view of his previous and subsequent record, to surmise that he did it deliberately, knowing the advantage which a sectarian agitation in Ontario would be to his own political position in Quebec.

The origin of the question was simple enough. Stripped of all technicalities and complex developments, it seems that in 1791 the King of Great Britain issued a proclamation suppressing the Order of the Jesuits in Canada, but leaving them the use of their estates so long as those who were then members should remain alive. In 1800 the last Jesuit died and the properties, it was claimed, were escheated to the Crown. But in cases of escheat a liberal proportion is generally appropriated to the carrying out of the intention of the donors, or to indemnifying those who morally may consider themselves entitled to it. And the re-instatement of the Jesuits at a later period, together with their incorporation, gave them this moral right—such as it was. Meanwhile through the suppression for a time of the Order by the Pope, it was also claimed that the estates instead of reverting to the Crown, passed to the dioceses in which they were placed. Hence the claims of the Quebec Bishops and a situation generally, which for a long period either precluded the sale of the lands by the Government or very seriously hampered its action in dealing with them.

At every step it was met by protests from the united hierarchy of Quebec demanding that the lands should not be diverted from the charitable and religious purposes to which they had been originally devoted, in some cases by private donors, in others by grants from the French King. Under these conditions, and it must be remembered in a Catholic Province, several Governments had attempted to adjust the question but without success, because they did not like to negotiate upon the fact that there was only one authority whom the Jesuits and the Bishops as branches of the same church, could each recognize as an arbiter, and as having the moral power to act for them in the settlement of the dispute.

By the calling in of the Pope, Mr. Mercier solved the problem, but by the way in which it was done, he created a storm in Ontario which it has taken years to calm. Summed up in a few words the head of the Roman Catholic Church consented to perform the part of an arbiter, and appointed the Archbishop of Quebec to act as his attorney in the matter. This latter arrangement was afterwards cancelled, and in a letter dated May 7th, 1887, which was freely used in the subsequent Ontario campaign, the Pope states that he has "reserved to himself" the right to settle the question. That is to say, he reserved to himself the authority previously given to the archbishop. Without, however, going into the matter further at this stage, it seems clear that the business arrangement was not in itself as bad as it has been depicted. The Quebec Premier claimed that some settlement was absolutely necessary; that the Pope was the only authority recognized in a church dispute by the two religious bodies in question; and that the $400,000 was made by his intervention a full, legal settlement of claims aggregating $2,000,000. Nevertheless the introduction of his preamble into the bill and some of the correspondence itself, was a gross illustration of political demagogism and a dangerous menace to the good-feeling in Ontario which had survived the ebullition of fanaticism of a couple of years before in Quebec itself.

There could be no doubt about the sentiment which the publication of the bill speedily aroused in many sections of the Upper Province. Aggressive Protestantism was stirred up; Orange Lodges passed denunciatory resolutions; the *Mail* renewed its vigorous and able but unjust and unwise attacks, upon Quebec and the great religious institutions of that Province; the Jesuits were painted in the blackest shades which tongue and pen could produce; and Equal Rights and Disallowance became the cries of the hour. Though this ebullition of strong and sincere sentiment was confined to a limited number of the people it had the usual effect elsewhere. Extremes in one direction are almost sure to produce the opposite extreme. The Protestants of Quebec therefore commenced to think themselves aggrieved and a section of them began to agitate and pass resolutions which served to fan the flame in Ontario. The unwise language which is always used in sectarian disputes stirred up both sides to the controversy and very soon the French-Canadian press was denouncing the fanaticism of the Upper Province in language very like that used by many Ontario papers during the Riel discussion.

This then was the position of affairs which Sir John Thompson had to face before the country, and in the great Parliamentary debate which soon became imminent. With the forgetfulness of his stand in the Riel matter, which always characterises a busy public, he was looked upon by ultra Protestants as the central figure in a great drama of surrender to the mandates of the Church which he was known to regard with such devotion. It did not seem to occur to many of them, although the great mass of enlight-

Hon. Geo. E. Foster, D.C.L., M.P.,

Canadian Minister of Finance.

ened Canadians believed otherwise, that a statesman could be a Roman Catholic and at the same time a patriotic citizen. If Sir John Thompson's career had served no other purpose than to dispel such bigoted and dangerous views he would not have lived in vain.

On February 13th, 1889, the first mutterings of the coming Parliamentary conflict were heard, as Mr. J. A. Barron, Q.C., rose from his place in the House of Commons to ask five questions regarding the consideration which the Jesuits' Estates Act had received from the Dominion Government. Sir John Thompson's reply was characteristically precise and complete:

"The answer to the first question of the hon. gentleman is that the Act referred to has been before the Government for their consideration; to the second question, that the Minister of Justice reported on the Act to His Excellency the Governor-General on the 16th January last; to the third question, that the Minister of Justice reported that the Act in question, together with the 112 other Acts passed at the same session of the Quebec Legislature, should be left to its operation; to the fourth question, that the report of the Minister of Justice was approved on the 19th January, 1889, and the result was at once communicated to the Government of Quebec; to the fifth question, that the Acts of the Legislature of Quebec for the session of 1888 were received by the Secretary of State on the 8th August."

This statement set at rest all speculation as to the course the Government intended to pursue, but it opened the flood-gates of sectarian agitation and made the Minister of Justice the theme of much fiery denunciation and eloquent invective. The Rev. Dr. Douglas, Bishop Carman, Canon DuMoulin, Principal Caven, Mr. James L. Hughes, and many others, denounced the action or inaction of the

Ministry in permitting the Act to go into operation. Great mass meetings were held in Toronto and elsewhere; and Mr. D'Alton McCarthy was urged to become the Protestant champion and to take the field against those who were willing—it was claimed—to sacrifice religion upon the altar of political expediency. Finally, after many rumours, and amid great political purturbation, Lieut. Colonel William E. O'Brien moved the following resolution in the House on March 26th:

"That an humble address be presented to His Excellency the Governor-General setting forth: I. That this House regards the power of disallowing the Acts of the Legislative Assemblies of the Provinces, vested in His Excellency in Council, as a prerogative essential to the national existence of the Dominion: II. That this great power, while it should never be wantonly exercised, should be fearlessly used for the protection of the rights of a minority, for the preservation of the fundamental principles of the Constitution, and for safe-guarding the general interests of the people: III. That in the opinion of this House, the passage by the Legislature of the Province of Quebec of the Act entitled 'An Act respecting the settlement of the Jesuits' Estates,' is beyond the power of that Legislature. Firstly, because it endows from public funds a religious organization, thereby violating the undoubted constitutional principle of the complete separation of Church and State, and of the absolute equality of all denominations before the law. Secondly, because it recognizes the usurpation of a right by a foreign authority, namely, His Holiness the Pope of Rome, to claim that his consent was necessary to empower the Provincial Legislature to dispose of a portion of the public domain, and also because the Act is made to depend upon the will, and the appropriation of the grant thereby made as subject to the control, of the same authority. And, thirdly, because the endowment of the Society of Jesus, an alien, secret and politico-religious body, the expulsion of which from every Christian community wherein it has had a footing has been rendered necessary by its intolerant and mischievous intermeddling with the functions of civil government, is fraught with danger to the civil and religious liberties of the people of Canada. And this House, therefore, prays that His Excellency will be graciously pleased to disallow the said Act."

Such was the famous motion which precipitated an able, but somewhat violent, debate in Parliament, and still further promoted the sectarian agitation in the country generally. It was skilfully worded, and was intended to obtain the support of all who believed in limited Provincial powers; of all who disliked or dreaded Roman Catholicism; of all who shared in the popular prejudice against the Papal spiritual and temporal power, and against the Jesuit body.

Colonel O'Brien delivered a speech which in ability and eloquence surprised the House. He gave the lead, however, in a direction which was very generally followed by his supporters in debate, and endeavoured to hold up the Jesuits to popular execration. He admitted the hardships, trials and sufferings they had endured in attempting to convert and civilize the Indians of early Canadian days, but would admit no good points in their work or history in any other country. Reference was made to the glaring difference between this grant of money by Quebec to a religious body, and the abolition of the Clergy Reserves in Ontario, in order that perfect religious equality might prevail. In dealing with the Pope's exercise of his moral authority over the parties to the dispute, he quoted from the instructions given to Governor Murray in 1762: "You are not to admit of any ecclesiastical jurisdiction of the See of Rome," and of those in which Governor Carleton is reminded in 1775, "That all appeals to, or correspondence with, any foreign ecclesiastical jurisdiction is absolutely forbidden under very severe penalties." The subsequent relaxation of restrictions was claimed to be simply toleration, and not the giving of any legal right. A Jesuit was described as "a being abnormal in his conditions; he has no family ties, no home nor country. He is subject absolutely to the will of his superior. Such a system, such an order, being subject to an irresponsible power, must be dangerous, as it always has been dangerous, to every community in which it has existed."

Mr. Rykert followed in a somewhat vigorous defence of the Jesuits, by quotations from Macaulay, Parkman, and others. Perhaps the most important part of his address was the following extract from a letter written by the Very Rev. Principal Grant, of Queen's University, Kingston: "If the matter was to be settled at all, let us remember that the great majority of the people of Quebec are Roman Catholics. I do not see what else Mr. Mercier could have done than require the sanction of the Pope to the bargain. It may seem astonishing to Protestants that Roman Catholics should acknowledge a man living in Rome as the head of their Church. But they do. Protestants must accept that fact in the same spirit in which all facts should be accepted." The delicate satire of the last sentence or two is simply inimitible. Mr. Rykert also referred to the Pope's interference in Irish matters, solicited, as it was upon more than one occasion, by the British Government, and notably, to his denunciation of the Plan of Campaign.

Mr. Barron went back to the days of Elizabeth, to statutes passed regarding foreign potentates and prelates at a time when England had been in serious danger from the attempted invasion of Philip of Spain. He claimed that the Act of Supremacy remained as much a living force in the Canada of 1888 as it had been in the England of 1554, and quoted Todd in support of his contention. He also instanced the Royal instructions to the Duke of Richmond when appointed Governor of the Canadas in 1818, and in reference to the people of Quebec: "It is a toleration of the free exercise of the religion of the Church of Rome only, to which they are entitled, but not to the powers and privileges of an established Church. . . . It is our will and pleasure that all appeals to a correspondence with any foreign ecclesiastical jurisdiction, of what nature or kind soever, be absolutely forbidden under very severe penalties." He claimed that the Jesuits' Estates Act was an usurpation of the right to make denominational grants, which had never yet been allowed a Province; and strongly denounced the Incorporation of the Jesuits in Quebec in 1887.

Mr. C. C. Colby, of Montreal, afterwards for a short time a member of the Government, made an eloquent and effective appeal for moderation and toleration. He referred to the many instances of it in Quebec, where for some time the Hon. H. G. Joly de Lotbiniere, a Protestant, had been Premier and the representative of a Catholic constituency; where the Hon. J. G. Robertson, "a good old orthodox Presbyterian," had for years been Provincial Treasurer under the Conservative *regimé*; where even at the time of speaking two Provincial Ministers out of seven were Protestants. Not long before, Cardinal Taschereau had presided over a mixed meeting, held for the advancement of temperance. And, in concluding, he expressed very strongly his opinions as a Protestant along lines which will be interesting to many in these times of unrest:

"The Roman Catholic Church—I will not speak of it

as a religious body—I look upon from a political standpoint as one of the strongest, if not the strongest, bulwark we have in our country against what I conceive to be the most dangerous element abroad in the earth to-day. The Roman Catholic Church recognizes the supremacy of authority; it teaches observance to law; it teaches respect for the good order and constituted authorities of society. It does that, and there is need of such teaching; for the most dangerous enemy abroad to-day in this land and on this continent is a spirit of infidelity; is a spirit of anarchy which has no respect for any institution, human or divine; which seeks to drag down all constituted authorities, emperors, kings, presidents, from their seats, the Almighty from the throne of the universe, and to lift up the Goddess of Reason to the place of highest authority."

The Hon. Peter Mitchell then spoke briefly, and was followed by Mr. D'Alton McCarthy. It is impossible to do justice here to the able effort of the Equal Rights leader. He was forcible, and sometimes, in view of the manifest unpopularity of his position so far as the House and its members were concerned, became almost bitter. And it would have been impossible to have denounced any body of men more strongly than he did the Jesuit organization. Mr. McCarthy, in commencing, claimed that he should have been allowed the privilege of a reply to some one of the Ministers, and evidently did not like the idea of being followed by Sir John Thompson without previously knowing the lines of Ministerial defence. He was, however, unwilling to let the occasion go by without explaining his reason for having to separate himself from "the political friends with whom it has been my pride and pleasure to act up to this time." He then went into the history of the Jesuit claims, and of the limits of religious toleration and privilege accorded by the British Government from the

Sir Adolphe Caron, K.C.M.G., M.P.,

Postmaster-General of Canada

days of the cession to the present time. Lengthy quotations from various sources were given to show that finally the estates in question were surrendered by the Crown to the Province for educational purposes and nothing else.

But there were other grounds. "I say," declared Mr. McCarthy, "that either this Act is unconstitutional, that it is *ultra vires* of the Province, that it ought to have been disallowed upon that ground, because it violates a fundamental principal of this country that all religions are free and equal before the law; or, if that be not so as a legal proposition, then, Sir, I claim that there should have been exercised that judgment, that discretion, that policy, which would at once stamp out, in whatever Province it reared its head, the attempt which has been made to establish a kind of State Church amongst us." Mr. McCarthy took his seat after a speech which those who heard it could not but admire, even while many of them disliked the speaker and had at every opportunity passionately denounced his views. It was a clear and cutting arraignment of the Government and the Opposition alike, and it made him immensely popular with the element in the country which had been recently stirred up to boiling point by various religious cries.

Sir John Thompson had a most difficult duty to perform in his reply, and that he was brilliantly successful from the logical and constitutional standpoint was afterwards almost generally admitted. In making his first great speech in the House he had been obliged to win his way to success over an audience to which his personality was unknown and against an antagonist whose place was thought too great and secure for successful attack. Upon this second occasion he had to face the bitter prejudice which only religious differences can arouse, and which is often none the less real because it is concealed beneath a nominal support and even a favourable speech or vote. He fully recognized also, the gulf which it would place for the time being between himself and many of the people, by saying in a few introductory remarks that he would have to speak "under a sense of the fact that with one large portion of the people of Canada nothing that I can say will be satisfactory, and that with another, and I hope the greater portion, no defence of the Government is necessary." But as in the Riel question, he did what he thought his duty and no man can do more.

The Minister of Justice began by pointing out in reference to Mr. McCarthy's charge of unfairness, that it was the place of the ministry, and especially of himself, as the minister most largely responsible, to hear the charges that were to be brought before making a reply. He complimented the member for Simcoe upon his "admirable address," and then pointed out that Mr. McCarthy, in a three hours' speech, had presented a very learned and complete case for the purpose of "proving that the Jesuits of Quebec had lost their title to the estates in question—a fact which is admitted in the preamble to the Act." He analyzed the Treaty of 1763, and summed up its provisions and their relation to the Act of Supremacy as follows:—"Obviously His Britannic Majesty (in granting the liberty of the Catholic religion to the inhabitants of Canada) meant that there should be perfect freedom of worship in the newly ceded country, subject only to the legislation which might be made upon this subject from time to time by the Parliament of Great Britain, certainly not that it was subject then to the laws as regards freedom of worship in Great Britain; for let me remind the House that instead of there being any such freedom at that time, the exercise of the Roman Catholic religion then amounted to the crime of high treason; and no dissenter under the risk of being imprisoned, could enter a conventicle or a meeting-house."

Sir John then proceeded to summarize the correspondence between Mr. Mercier and the Pope, and pointed out that the latter's intervention really only consisted of a mediator's part between two rival claimants who acknowledged his moral, spiritual and legal authority in any matter pertaining to the church, and that his "consent" to the Quebec Government retaining the proceeds of the sales of disputed property, was merely on behalf of the two other claimants and subject to a future settlement of the question. And then he hit at Mr. McCarthy's religious references and the abuse of the Jesuits which had been introduced into the debate, by a remark regarding "the theological questions which my honourable friend from Simcoe and I are to join issue on, with a view to the House passing judgment as to which is the better theologian forsooth, and as to whose advice on the subject of theology His Excellency the Governor-General, as the supreme theologian, is to take." He pointed out as a matter of business in this transaction, that the Premier of Quebec had stipulated that before the Province should be asked to pay over one dollar of the money, it should have a conveyance of all rights and titles, legal and moral, to the disputed lands; in the first place from the Society of Jesus, in the second place from the Pope himself, and in the third place from the Sacred College of the Propaganda and the Roman Catholic Church in general.

Sir John Thompson did not attempt, nor did he desire, to defend the manner in which the preamble was drawn up, or the loose way in which the correspondence had been carried on, and in which a power seemed to be recognized that did not really exist. But he did point out that all further claims in this connection were made impossible by the terms of the arrangement. And he also declared that in the history of the scores of Canadian Statutes disallowed in the Mother-Country, there was not one instance of a preamble to a bill being considered a reason for such action.

As to the supremacy of the Queen which Mr. McCarthy had just proclaimed "with gravity and force and eloquence" to be seriously undermined by the Act, Sir John observed: "It does not, I submit, place the public money of the Province at the disposal of a foreigner; it sets aside a sum of money for the extinguishment of a claim upon the public property of Quebec, and then calls upon those who are litigants in regard to it, to abide by the decision of their arbitrator in the matter. . . . In the ordinary course, it (the $400,000) would be paid to one of the claimants on the property; but as there happen to be two, it is paid in the hands, or held subject to the order of, the person who has to settle disputes between them."

Upon the subject of Provincial powers in legislation the Minister of Justice spoke with no uncertain sound. "I say that within the limits of its authority and subject only to the power of disallowance, a Provincial Legislature is as absolute as is the Imperial Parliament itself." He pointed out that thirty-seven years before—in 1852—the Parliament of Canada had actually incorporated St. Mary's College, Montreal, a body of the Jesuits, and that the division list on that occasion showed in favour of the action 29 Protestants and 27 Catholics. He referred to Stoneyhurst and other great Jesuit institutions in the England of to-day as showing what a dead letter the old religious laws of Elizabeth had become, and pointed out that not only had the Jesuits been incorporated by the Quebec Legislature in 1887, but that the whole body had been incorporated by the Dominion Parliament in 1871.

He claimed that a society of teachers and preachers is not a church, and that money paid to the Jesuits could not, therefore, be the endowment of a Church. And in conclusion he declared with emphasis and earnestness that "whenever we touch these delicate and difficult questions, which are in any way connected with the sentiments of religion, or of race, or of education, there are two principles which it is absolutely necessary to maintain, for the sake of the living together of the different members of this Confederation, for the sake of the preservation of the Federal power, for the sake of the good-will, and kindly charity of all our people towards each other, and for the sake of the prospects of making a nation, as we can only do by living in harmony and ignoring those differences which used to be considered fundamental; these two principles surely must prevail, that as regards theological questions the State must have nothing to do with them, and that as regards the control which the Federal power can exercise over Provincial Legislatures in matters touching the freedom of its people, the religion of its people, the appropriations of its people, or the sentiments of its people, no section of this country, whether it be the great Province of Quebec or the humblest and smallest Province of this country, can be governed according to the fashion of 300 years ago."

Mr. Alex. McNeill, the Hon. David Mills, Mr. Charlton, Mr. Mulock, Mr. Scriver, the Hon. Mr. Laurier, Sir John A. Macdonald, and Sir Richard Cartwright followed, and upon a division, the attitude of the Government as well as the view taken by the Minister of Justice, was endorsed by a non-partisan vote of 188 to 13. The speech of Sir John Thompson had been a magnificant success. At its close Mr. Edward Blake crossed the floor of the House, and amidst general applause congratulated him upon what had undoubtedly been his greatest effort in Parliament. As an argument of sustained power, delivered by a brilliant lawyer with all the "cold neutrality" of an impartial judge, it will remain a monument of oratorical and legal ability. From a party standpoint there was perhaps one blemish upon its success. A defence of the Jesuits was hardly required from the Minister of Justice, and no matter how strongly he might have felt, as was undoubtedly the case, that they were grossly misrepresented, it was unnecessary and under the stormy circumstances of the moment, worse than useless, for him to try and change the popular prejudice of Ontario and other Provinces.

But none the less was the action admirable, and it can only be properly appreciated by the supposition that at some critical moment in the future political development of Quebec, a Protestant member of the Government there should feel it his duty at whatever risk to his personal popularity, to defend some branch of his church from a long sustained and powerful attack made on historic grounds. The *Toronto Mail*, of course, denounced the Minister of Justice and his speech with great vigour; the *Globe* declared it to be "a combination of masterpieces. . . . In part a masterpiece of reasoning, in part a masterpiece of casuistry, and on the whole a masterpiece of audacity." Sir John Thompfon was in fact singled out for most of the attacks which marked the ensuing Equal Rights campaign.

Sir Frank Smith, K.C.M.G., Senator,

Minister without Portfolio.

CHAPTER VIII.

Equal Rights, the Fisheries and the French Language.

The phenomenal majority given by Parliament to the Government in connection with the Jesuits' Estates question, proved to have by no means silenced the agitation. Both political parties had hoped it would have that result, and both were sincerely anxious to get rid of the question before the general elections should loom upon the horizon. But religious sentiment had been aroused; racial prejudices had been stirred up; and just as it had been impossible to control the storm in Quebec over the execution of Louis Riel, so now it was found impossible to check the anti-Jesuit agitation in Ontario until it had run its course.

On the very day that Colonel O'Brien's resolution was proposed in the House of Commons, a mass meeting had been held in the Pavilion at Toronto, with Mr. W. H. Howland as Chairman. The Jesuits' Estates Act was condemned in no measured language, and the speeches of men like Rev. D. J. Macdonell, Mr. J. J. McLaren, Q.C., Principal Caven, and others, were fervent and denunciatory. The last motion was proposed by Mr. J. L. Hughes, and appointed a Committee to extend the movement throughout the Dominion against all who had supported or condoned the legislation in question. This was the beginning of the Equal Rights Association of a few months later. On April 22nd another large meeting was held in the Granite Rink in Toronto, and resolutions of approval and congratulation were tendered to the "noble thirteen," who had, as the phrase of the moment put it, stood up for civil and religious liberty, for the people against the politicians, for true British liberty, and against any union of Church and State. Mr. McCarthy delivered the principal address and accused the Minister of Justice of having adroitly mixed up the divisions of the question so as to create confusion in the minds of the people. "He had been perfectly amazed at the speech of the Minister of Justice. He had heard speeches in which the hairs were split very freely, but he had never heard any arguments more specious, misleading, and, at the same time, so captivating, as those used by the Minister of Justice."

In accordance with an address issued by the Citizen's Committee to the people of Ontario and an approving resolution passed at this meeting, a Provincial Convention was held in Toronto on June 11th and 12th. It was largely attended and very enthusiastic. The Equal Rights Association was duly organized, with influential officers, and with Mr. McCarthy as the Parliamentary leader and the real chief. Meanwhile action had been taken in Montreal by Mr. Hugh Graham, who petitioned the Governor-General to refer to the Supreme Court of Canada for hearing and consideration an inquiry as to the constitutionality of the Incorporation Act and the Jesuits' Estates Act. This was sent to the Minister of Justice for advice, and eventually the request was refused. A most able State paper was published in August, giving Sir John Thompson's reasons for recommending His Excellency not to grant the appeal. It was an exhaustive document, both in its wealth of legal learning and in the number of precedents produced.

His reasons were apparently very strong, and may be concisely summarized:

I. The petitioner was duly represented in the legislature by which these enactments were adopted, and his representatives there seem to have concurred in the adoption of both these statutes almost with unanimity.

II. He had the right of petition and remonstrance against the adoption of both these enactments, but does not appear to have used it.

III. Ample opportunity was afforded for such protests or petitions as are now being made, before the Lieut.-Governor of Quebec was informed that the Acts respectively would be left to their operation. There was an interval of several months which was not taken advantage of in any way, and Mr. Graham's petition was not presented until by lapse of time in the case of the Incorporation Act, as well as by the obligations of public faith and honour in regard to both of them, it had ceased to be in the Governor-General's power to interfere with their operation.

IV. The petitioner still possessed the opportunity of calling the attention of his Provincial Government to the desirability that the statutes referred to should not be acted upon by the transfer of the public money and property being completed.

V. The petitioner also possessed the right to call upon the Attorney-General of his Province to take legal proceedings, in accordance with the law of Quebec, to test the validity of the Act of Incorporation. "If that Act should be decided to be invalid and unconstitutional, there can be little doubt that the second Act will be nugatory, as the grant of money and land which the second Act authorizes is, by its terms, to be made to the corporation, established by the Incorporation Act."

Here was an opening for action pointed out with distinctness by the Minister of Justice himself. Had Mr. Graham and his friends taken the course indicated, it would have been a turning of the tables indeed upon Mr.

Mercier and his Mi istry, but the idea was not followed up. The object of too many of the Equal Rights advocates in both Provinces seemed from the beginning to be the embarassment of the Dominion Government, and not the genuine pursuit of equal laws and equal privileges as between race and race, religion and religion. Later on in Ontario, as Mr. McCarthy has so bitterly complained, this was indicated by the partisan conduct of Mr. Charlton and Principal Caven in the Local elections of 1890. Sir John Thompson summed up his advice to the Governor-General in the following words:

"The Acts referred to in the petition relate only to the Province of Quebec. They do not conflict in any degree with the powers of the Parliament of Canada, or with the rights and powers of Your Excellency. They do not concern in any way Your Excellency's officers, and they do not affect the revenue or property of Canada or any interest of the Dominion. They should, therefore, in the opinion of the undersigned, be left to the responsibility of those whom the Constitution has entrusted with the power to pass such enactments."

Previous to the publication of this Report, though some time after its submission to the Governor-General-in Council, His Excellency had received, on August 2nd, a deputation at Quebec, which presented an Ontario petition 160 yards long, and containing 156,000 signatures; another signed by the members of the recent Equal Rights Convention to the number of 860; and one from Montreal and the Province of Quebec bearing some 9,000 names. The petitioners asked for the disallowance of the Jesuits' Estates Act. Principal Caven was the chief speaker for the deputation, and the reply of Lord Stanley of Preston was listened to with deep interest and attention. As the Liberal journals throughout the country claimed in the discussion which ensued, that the Governor-General spoke practically from a brief handed him by the Minister of Justice, it is important to note how substantially his views really did harmonize with those of Sir John Thompson.

He declared that in his opinion the introduction of the Pope's name in this case had not in any way weakened or assailed the Queen's authority. He spoke from his personal experience as a one-time Secretary of the Treasury in England, regarding the frequency with which a moral claim is recognized when no legal one exists. He declared as a matter which had been carefully investigated, that in this nineteenth century, the Society of Jesus were not less law-abiding and loyal citizens than were the majority of people. He pointed out how utterly unconstitutional it would be for the Governor-General to disallow a bill in face of his Minister's advice, and in the teeth of a large Parliamentary majority. Such were the conclusions presented by the Governor-General, and endorsing the position assumed by his Minister of Justice. The delegates had nothing to say at the moment in reply to His Excellency's refusal to interfere, but later on they met and formally protested, urging at the same time that a more vigorous agitation and organization for the promotion of Equal Rights should now be pushed forward to a successful issue

Some time after this occurrence, in February, 1891, Mr. (now Sir) Mackenzie Bowell was addressing an audience at Madoc, Ontario, and stated that prior to arriving at a decision "Lord Stanley had telegraphed to the Imperial Government, and asked the law officers of the Crown whether the Act was within the power of the Province of Quebec to pass it, and three days later the answer came that it was strictly within the purview of the Legislature of Quebec, and further, that there was no necessity to refer it, as the petition which had been received suggested, to the Judicial Committee of the Privy Council." This particular step was therefore not advised by Sir John Thompson, but it is very probable that Lord Stanley was more or less influenced in his general conclusions by the clear and forceful reasoning of his Minister. There is absolutely no ground, however, for believing that the latter actually prepared the reply which was given to the Equal Rights deputation.

Shortly after this, the Protestant Committee of the Quebec Council of Public Instruction—25th September—passed a resolution accepting in the name of the Protestants of the Province the public trust imposed upon them to distribute the $60,000 given under the terms of the Jesuits' Estates Act. Certain conditions were made to which, however, Mr. Mercier, as Premier, agreed without hesitation, and on the 5th of November, the closing scene in a memorable drama took place in the City of Quebec. Here, amid a large gathering of the Provincial Ministers, the Roman Catholic clergy and sundry Protestant representatives, the $400,000 was paid over in the manner decided upon. A check for $160,000 was handed to the Jesuits; $40,000 went to Laval University; and the rest was distributed in sums of ten and twenty thousand amongst the different dioceses. In accepting the check on behalf of the Jesuit Order, the Rev. Father Turgeon, S. J., made a rather interesting remark: "I also thank Mr. Mercier as a Canadian. Thanks to God first, then to him and the Legislature, we are now recognized as citizens. In becoming a Jesuit I still remained a Canadian. Ancient Rome, I must say, conferred the title of citizenship for less than has been done by our fathers. Our Order has glorious pages in the history of this country. Our fathers have shed their blood for the country, and they surely deserve the name of Canadians."

THE EARL OF ROSEBERY, K. G.,

Prime Minister of Great Britain.

Meantime the Equal Rights party had not been idle in Ontario. On the 10th of October a mass-meeting had been held in Toronto, and the Report of the deputation to Lord Stanley of Preston, received. Principal Caven and Mr. McCarthy were the chief speakers. The spirit of the audience was pretty well shown in the hisses which upon one occasion greeted the name of Sir John Thompson. Mr. McCarthy declared himself against the teaching of French in the Ontario public schools; against the extension of the Separate School system through privileged legislation; against an official dual language system in Manitoba and the North-West. A few months later, on April 30th, 1890, the Jesuits' Estates matter came up once more before the House of Commons, upon a motion by Mr. Charlton, claiming that the question of the constitutionality of the Act should have been submitted to the Supreme Court of Canada. Sir John Thompson spoke in defence of the Government's course, and of the ground taken by the Governor-General.

Referring to an appeal made afterwards by certain representatives of the religious minority in Quebec, claiming the Act to have been an invasion of their rights, the Minister of Justice said:

"The petitioners presented their appeal and it having been referred to myself, I recommended that a day should be appointed on which the appeal should be heard; and it is quite possible that if the claimants had established anything like a case for the interference of the Governor-in-Council on the ground that the rights of the Protestant minority in Quebec had been infringed, a reference of the question as to whether it was an infringement or not might have been made to the Supreme Court of Canada. But before the day came the *appellants withdrew the appeal*, and they did it on account of the statement made by the

Premier of Quebec that the redress they desired would be given without any appeal being made."

It will thus be seen that on the broad question of the constitutionality of the Act neither the Government nor the Governor-General, nor Sir Richard Webster and Sir Edward Clarke, the Imperial law officers, would advise or permit an appeal; but upon any direct claim of injury done to a minority, they were at least willing to consider the question in all seriousness. In speaking of the charges of religious bias made against himself, Sir John Thompson took the opportunity to say: "I am very far from finding fault with those who, rightly or wrongly, were under the impression that I was swayed by my own private opinions in tendering the advice which His Excellency had acted upon. While I feel that that impression was unjust to me, I was only too glad when His Excellency was disposed to receive the deputation and to give them his answer upon the question."

The course of asking the Colonial Office to obtain the opinion of the Crown Law Officers was declared to have been His Excellency's own action "not by our advice and not by our request," though "we accept to the fullest extent the constitutional responsibility for such action." This debate terminated the question so far as Parliament was concerned. The Equal Rights Association flourished until the disputes connected with the Local elections of 1890 in Ontario practically destroyed its influence. Speaking in Toronto on June 2nd of that year, Mr. McCarthy vigorously denounced Mr. Charlton, M.P., for not supporting the Equal Rights candidates against the Mowat Government, and declared that he and others simply aided the movement for religious equality so far as it might injure the Dominion Government. And the absence of Principal Caven from the gathering spoke for itself. A little later, the Provincial Protestant Association rose from the wreck of the previous organization.

During the three years following the elections of 1887, many other important matters had been dealt with by the Minister of Justice, besides the much too prominent Jesuits' Estates question. One of these was the disallowance of the Montreal District Magistrates' Bill, passed by the Provincial Legislature under Mr. Mercier's auspices. This measure abolished the Circuit branch of the Quebec Supreme Court and vested its powers in two Judges clothed with a similar jurisdiction "for hearing and deciding civil matters as that exercised by the said Circuit Court of the District of Montreal." As the British North America Act gives the right of appointing Superior Court Judges to the Dominion Government, Sir John Thompson regarded this bill as a distinct attempt to take from the Dominion Parliament one of its constitutional prerogatives, by simply changing the name of the Court, and the designation of the Judge. Hence he recommended its disallowance.

Incidentally this action was the cause of his first speech in Montreal. It was in Sept., 1888, during the by-election in which Mr. Lepine and Mr. Poirier were the candidates for the vacancy caused by Mr. Coursol's death. The charge was freely made that the Minister of Justice in connection with this disallowance had been actuated by hostility to the French-Canadian people. And this at a time when he was suffering unmeasured abuse in certain other quarters for alleged subservience to their interests and religious sentiments!

Sir John Thompson went down to the commercial metropolis in order to support Mr. Lepine and defend the Government and himself. The old Bonsecours' market hall was filled to the doors by a mixed multitude of men. The Minister of Justice spoke in a low, measured voice and was listened to with marked attention. He explained the nature of the bill, and the reasons for disallowing it, concluding with a vigorous appeal for unity of race and creed. "We ask you," he said, "to stand by the old principles that Montreal has stood by so long—the National Policy. We ask you, above all, workingmen, English, Scotch, Irish and French-Canadian, to stand by your country which is threatened by the appeals made on behalf of sectarianism and race. When any man tells you that injustice can or will be attempted in this country against a French-speaking Roman Catholic Province, you can laugh in his face and tell him you are not a fool." The Conservative candidate was afterwards elected by a large majority.

On the 26th of February, 1889, the Fisheries' question again came up in Parliament. Mr. Laurier moved a resolution expressing regret at the present differences with the United States and urging that steps should be taken for their adjustment; and for the securing of unrestricted freedom in trade relations between the two countries; direct representation at Washington; and the renewal of the *modus vivendi*. The debate proceeded for some days and on March 1st Sir John Thompson rose to speak. As illustrating the fairness of the Government and its desire for the maintenance of friendly relations, he pointed out that on the abrogation of the Washington Treaty by the United States, the Canadian Government had offered to extend the operation of the Fisheries' clause until the close of the season. When the Opposition press urged that the United States would not accept this offer for fear of claims to future indemnity, the Government had asked Great Britain to inform the United States that it would give the use of the fisheries without stint or price. "Now the cry is that we folded our hands and did nothing."

The Minister of Justice then went on to say that "the

one supreme difficulty which the negotiators had to meet with in Washington last year, was the conviction which has gained ground in the United States, that we were perishing for reciprocity, and were raising the Fisheries' question in order to obtain reciprocity." He stated that the proposal made to the American Government was to consider the whole question of the fisheries, and in order to get a broad and liberal settlement of the question, "we throw open the fishing grounds as well as commercial privileges to the American fishermen for the remainder of 1885, on the assurance of the President of the United States, that he would recommend to Congess that a Commission be appointed to consider the fishery interests of the two countries." After six months enjoyment of the Canadian fisheries, together with the right of obtaining supplies, transhipment, etc., the President sent his Message to Congress, and the Senate replied by passing a resolution that such a Commission was not worthy of receiving a vote from Congress for its expenses! And only seventeen members voted against the motion.

When, owing to the vigour with which Canada protected its interests during the following period, a Treaty was eventually negotiated (as previously described), another *modus vivendi* was offered and accepted. The Senate received the courteous and generous offer of Canada by throwing the Treaty out, and thus once more disarranging the entire relations of the two countries. "Yet we are told that we have made no concessions to these people, and that every fault in the whole negotiations of the last twenty years has been with us." In referring to the President's Retaliation Message, which followed the Senate's rejection of the proposed arrangement, Sir John Thompson declared emphatically that "while no one would regret the enforcement of an Act of Retaliation by either of the two countries more strongly than I would, or apprehend more seriously the consequences than I would; if any such danger and difficulty should come, the Canadian Government would be able to leave its record to the judgment of any man of fairness, honesty and probity." And since then, owing to the wise, yet strong, administration of the Canadian fisheries, there has been no serious trouble with the American Government, and matters have adjusted themselves satisfactorily to the general terms of the Treaty of 1818. Such difficulties as have arisen were upon the Pacific Ocean and not on the coasts of the Atlantic.

In the following Session of 1890, a question which had been intermittently discussed for some months past was brought before Parliament. The dual language system in the North-West Provinces was one of those issues which must always have a rare charm for the agitator. It involved a stirring up of race sentiment and the revival of many of those old prejudices, and even animosities, which help so greatly in the agitation of any specific question amongst the people of a mixed community. And whatever else may be said regarding the debates in the House of Commons during the period in which Sir John Thompson's influence was felt within its walls, no charge can be made that they lacked interest. The Riel debate produced a score of eloquent speeches covering the whole ground of international law, and of experience in the punishment of rebels and the treatment and trial of political prisoners. The Jesuits' Estates agitation in the same way had been the cause of much oratory of a high rank and was conspicuous for research into the older history of Canada and into the constitutional powers once vested in the French King, then transferred to the monarchy of Britain, and now held in the main by the Government of Canada or the Executive of its Provinces.

Hon. W. E. Sanford,

Dominion Senator.

As studies in history, in constitutional law, and in the duties owed to one another by partners in a Federal compact, these debates may have been illustrative of the fact that good does sometimes come out of evil. Perhaps it would be more correct to say however that the evil which might have come out of the agitations in question, was to a considerable extent averted by judicious action on the part of men who were Canadians first, Provincialists second. And the discussion of the questions introduced into the Dual Language debate of 1890, was not less interesting and valuable in this educational sense than were the others which had been dealt with. The question in itself was an inevitable product of the race and religion cry which had been commenced by the admirers of Louis Riel, promoted by the assaults upon the Jesuits' Estates legislation, continued in the French language discussion and terminated, it may be hoped, in the Manitoba Schools' case.

As had been forshadowed by speeches during the Equal Rights agitation, it was Mr. McCarthy who moved in the matter. On the 22nd of January, 1890, amidst considerable excitement in political circles, he introduced his measure for an amendment of the North-West Territories Act, abolishing the official dual language system in that portion of the Dominion. His speech was afterwards the subject of very wide comment, and without at present going into the reasons for the denunciation of its terms, may very fairly be described as unwise, though clever and forcible in argument. The preamble to the bill made it in any case an impossibility : "It is expedient in the interest of the national unity of the Dominion that there should be community of language among the people of Canada, and that the enactment in the North-West Territories Act allowing the use of the French language should be expunged therefrom."

It had the effect of mixing up the question of an official French language in the Parliament of Canada and in the Province of Quebec with its use in the distant territories of the North-West, where comparatively few French Canadians were to be found, and where very little real importance could be attached to the question as a purely local matter. But, under existing circumstances, to urge its abolition there as a precedent for the future at Ottawa itself, was to arouse all the inflammable French sentiment in Parliament and to make the case absolutely hopeless from the first. Mr. McCarthy, in his address, gave a history of the Act which permitted the English or French language to be used in the debates of the Council or Legislative Assembly of the North-West Territories or in the Courts, and which rendered compulsory the printing of its records, journals and ordinances in both languages. He quoted many writers upon the necessity of one language in the building up of a common and united nationality; denounced the racial and religious difficulties of Canada as primarily due to the differences in language; pointed to Germany, Russia and France as countries whose greatness and unity depended upon their peoples speaking the same tongue in private and public life; and concluded by announcing that "My desire is to further and promote the welfare of this great Dominion, advance its national life and have a language common to all." Whatever his bare proposal might have done if submitted without a preamble or speech of this nature, it is hardly surprising that such remarks—made by a member whom the French Canadians were beginning to look at in a way not unlike that with which Ontario Orangemen regarded Mr. Mercier—should have aroused all their susceptible and sentimental regard for the language of their ancestors. The speeches at once became fierce in denunciation of the proposal and of its author.

Sir Hector Langevin denounced it as a development of the fanaticism shown in the Equal Rights movement. Speaking of the French settlers in the North-West, he declared that "Providence put them into this world, and they came here with French blood, and when they could speak they spoke the French language. They went there from the other Provinces knowing that the subjects of Her Most Gracious Majesty the Queen had the right under the laws of the empire to speak their language provided they did not speak treason." It could not be a matter of expense with Mr. McCarthy. During thirteen years the cost of public printing in the Territories by reason of this dual language system had only been increased by $4,000. "He wants to tyrannize over the French Canadians of this country. He does not like them. He hates them and has hated them from the time he came into Parliament." Sir Hector took the line which was followed by nearly all the speakers from all parts of the Dominion, and dealt with the proposal as an attack upon the language, and upon the French Canadians' freedom of speech. "Just now," he declared, "the French members of the House will stand as one man against Mr. McCarthy. It is not a matter of politics, but the question of the preservation of their race and nationality. The French are loyal to the British Crown, but at the same time they will not abandon their language and religion without a struggle."

The Hon. David Mills referred to the preamble to the bill, and the speech of the mover, as enunciating a principle far more important than the measure itself. Mr. McCarthy had in fact "laid down the principle that there could only be a Canadian nationality by having one language." He had spoken as though it were an offence for any of Her Majesty's subjects to speak the French language. But, said Mr. Mills, "I have never seen an oath of allegiance which required the subject to speak only English. The British subject may talk Italian in Malta, French in Quebec, Hindu at Calcutta, and Chinese at Hong-Kong, and so long as he does not speak treason will not sacrifice any of his rights as a British subject." He pointed out that the dual language system was in operation in Cape Colony, and Mauritius, as well as in other places within the Empire. He concluded by referring to a very similar attempt made early in the century by the King of the Netherlands, which resulted in the disruption of his kingdom and the establishment of the separate states of Holland and Belgium.

Mr. Laurier, who in 1877 had beocme leader of the Opposition in succession to Mr. Blake, illustrated in his speech the mistake which had been made in confusing the issue: "If it (the North-West Bill) were not to be followed by any other; if it were to remain, as it is here, simply the abolition of the French language in the North-West Territories; I would be tempted to say, let the measure pass." And then he quoted from a speech by Mr. McCarthy in which he declared that "we must buckle on our armour and make the French-Canadians British." He went on to speak of the high attributes and qualities of the people of Quebec in characteristically beautiful language: "There is not under the sun to-day a more honest, moral and intellectual race. If the honorable gentleman would come to Lower Canada it would be my pride to take him through one of those ancient parishes and show him a population to which, prejudiced as he is, he could not but apply the words of the poet:—

> 'Men whose lives glide on like rivers
> Watering the woodland,
> Darkened by shadows of earth,
> And reflecting the image of heaven.'

Let, therefore, the two races stand together, each with its own characteristics, and yet united in a common object."

Sir John Macdonald in his remarks voiced the principle of moderation—the true basis of union. "We have a constitution now under which every British subject is in a condition of absolute and perfect equality—having the same rights of language, of religion, of property and of person—the same right is extended to every race. There is no conquered race in this country; we are all British subjects, and those who are not English are none the less British on that account." He denounced Mr. Laurier, for having tried to make political capital out of the measure, and suggested that Mr. McCarthy had commenced at the wrong end. "If the butcher goes to kill an ox, he strikes him on the head; he does not cut a little piece off the tail." Mr. McCarthy should have commenced his agitation in Quebec. His measure was "like the sting of a gnat; merely a source of irritation." Sir John announced himself in favour of leaving the matter to the decision of the Territorial Assembly.

Mr. Chaplean delivered an eloquent and fervent speech. He referred to the fact that General Murray, the first English Governor of Quebec, had used the French language in all his dealings with the King's new subjects. "I take it for granted," declared the speaker, "that the quality of British citizenship is not incompatible with a foreign origin; that a British subject may be of French origin and a Roman Catholic." He spoke of the use of French in the Windward Islands, in Mauritius, and in the Seychelles. He referred to the teaching of Welsh in Wales; of Gaelic in Scotland; and of various native languages in the schools of India. So in the Austrian Empire, where a number of different languages were taught in the schools, and where the Fundamental Law, promulgated in 1867, declares that "all the races of the Empire are on a footing of equality, and each one of the nations severally has a right that the inviolability of its nationality and its language shall be secured." He quoted Montesquieu to the effect that men are governed less by terror than by love and confidence. "If absolute perfection in matter of Government is a myth, it is a fact that the best is the Government which adapts itself most closely to the climate, to the character, the usages, the habits, the prejudices even, of the country."

Late in the debate, Sir John Thompson rose to speak, and to put into shape the policy of the Government. Amendments to Mr. McCarthy's motion had been proposed by Mr. Bechard and Mr. Davin, but neither were considered satisfactory. What the Minister of Justice had to say was very little, but what he suggested in the form of an amendment was very effective. He pointed out how little real importance there was in the mere enactment covering an optional right to the use of either French or English. "I have seen that right conceded frequently in the Legislature of my own Province where there is no legislative guarantee on the subject, and the man who would object to the Acadian of Nova-Scotia speaking his own tongue in the Legislature of his own Province would be laughed to scorn, as unworthy to sit in that Assembly."

But he strongly urged the importance of the laws being published in both languages, where it might be desired in the interest of a minority; and the necessity of permissive legislation concerning the use of either language in the local Law Courts. He announced his intention to propose, therefore, that the regulations as to publishing the ordinances in both languages and permitting the use of English or French in the courts, should be left intact, but that the records, the journals and the debates of the Assembly should be referred to the control of the next duly elected Territorial Assembly. His amendment read as follows, and was carried by a vote of 117 to 63:—

Hon. William B. Ives, M.P.

President of Privy Council.

"That this House, having regard for the long-continued use of the French language in old Canada and to the covenants on that subject embodied in the British North America Act, cannot agree in the declarations contained in the said Bill as a basis thereof, namely, that it is expedient in the interest of the national unity of the Dominion that there should be unity of language amongst the people of Canada. That, on the contrary, this House declares its adhesion to the said covenant, and its determination to resist any attempt to impair the same. That at the same time this House deems it expedient and proper, and not inconsistent with the covenants, that the Legislative Assembly of the North-West Territories should receive from the Parliament of Canada power to regulate the proceedings of the Assembly and the manner of recording and publishing such proceedings."

This settled for a time a question which in itself was insignificant, but in its environment was exceedingly unpleasant and disastrous to the good feeling which ought to exist amongst all races and creeds within the Dominion of Canada.

CHAPTER IX.

THE ELECTIONS OF 1891.

The conflict at the polls which commenced by the dissolution of Parliament on the 4th of February, 1891, was in many respects the most momentous in the history of Canada. In 1874 a general election had overthrown a Government charged with corruption, and, whether right or wrong in this particular application of the principle, had clearly demonstrated that Canadians will not endure even a suspicion of dishonesty in their rulers. In 1878 protection to national industries had been proclaimed emphatically as the national policy of the country, and in 1882, amid the fair weather of good times and abounding prosperity that policy had been confirmed and strengthened. In 1887 a dangerous racial and religious agitation in Quebec had been rendered almost harmless by the patriotism of its people in rallying to the support of a Government which, whatever its faults, had acted in the best interests of the Dominion by allowing the law to take its course in the case of Louis Riel.

But four years later a new question had arisen and one which involved a clear and distinct issue to all who would honestly read the signs of the times. Leaving to one side all partisan cries and strictly partisan statements; accepting as a fact the loyalty of the great mass of the people in both parties; waiving present consideration of the utterances of men like Wiman and Farrer: it yet seems perfectly plain that the country had to consider during that campaign the principles of British unity, British commerce, and British sympathy, as against Continental unity, Continental trade, and Continental sympathy. There were side issues, of which the cry for Equal Rights was by no means the least, but this question of the British Empire versus "the Continent to which we belong," was the dominant and absorbing matter submitted to the consideration and decision of the people.

In stating this fact there is no intention of charging any one, whether leader or follower, with annexationist sentiments or with personal disloyalty. But in dealing with the principles which during this important contest, Sir John A. Macdonald defended with such vigour as to fatally undermine his health; which Sir Charles Tupper came from England to help in supporting; which Sir John Thompson aided by many a speech and with all the force of his clear and logical eloquence; which other Conservative leaders joined in urging with a passionate earnestness unusual in Canadian politics, it must be made clear that there really was some great underlying element of serious import.

Apart, therefore, from specific utterances and party charges, the great issue lay in the tendencies of the two policies. Everyone knows that a new country, like a young man, should have some high ideal, some great ambition, some future hope which constitutes in itself a living principle of conduct and a substantial basis for present action. During the dozen years in which it had held power, the Conservative party, with all its sins of omission and commission—and no public organization is devoid of them—had evolved and placed before the people some such principle and plan of national development. It was in this that Sir John Macdonald had shown his supreme statesmanship. Without the sentiment which surrounds the ideal of Canada for Canadians within the British Empire, the National Policy would have been a mere fiscal experiment, lasting as long as the good times continued, but blown away like chaff before the first storm of depression or financial difficulty.

But when the people clearly recognized that the whole tendency of this new policy was to build up the resources of Canada, by the development of trade, inter-communication, and investment within the Empire: when they heard and accepted the claim that it was none the less British for being Canadian: that it was safe from the charge of dependence on either Great Britain or the United States: and that it combined national sentiment and progress with a distinct tendency towards closer Imperial connection in the future; the natural effect was a strengthening of the protective system by the support of a large element of the people who considered loyalty of the first importance in conducting the affairs of our rising nationality.

On the other side of the political fence there had been, however, for several years, as Sir John Thompson pointed out in several of his more important speeches, a tendency to deprecate sentiment in the conduct of public affairs: to denounce loyalty as unimportant, or, at the best, of secondary importance: to place alleged material interests first, and national ideals and aspirations second. And as the campaign developed, this distinction between the parties came out even more plainly. The Commercial Union advocacy of the *Torontc Globe* and *Mail* in previous years; the unfortunate speeches of Mr. Laurier and Sir Richard Cartwright in Boston; the mixing up of the party papers and leaders with the annexationist ideas of Messrs. Wiman, Farrer, and Hitt; the scarcely disguised support given to the principle of discrimination against British goods, if necessary, in order to obtain American reciprocity; all combined to add strength and inspiration to Sir John Macdonald's famous Manifesto and to his equally vigorous denunciation of the alleged disloyalty of the Liberal leaders.

On February 4th, the Government gave to the press a despatch which had been sent by the Governor-General to the Colonial Secretary, on Dec. 13th, 1890, outlining the terms of certain negotiations into which his ministers desired to enter with the United States' Government. It was proposed that a Joint Commission should be formed similar to that of 1871, and with power to deal with the following questions:

I. Renewal of the Reciprocity Treaty of 1854, with necessary modifications.

II. Re-consideration of the Treaty of 1888, with respect to the Atlantic fisheries, with a view to reciprocity in fish, and in the privileges of buying bait, transhipment of fish, etc.

III. Protection of mackerel and other fisheries on the Atlantic coast and in the inland waters.

IV. Relaxation of the seaboard coasting laws of the two countries, and also of the coasting laws on the great lakes.

V. Mutual salvage and saving of wrecked vessels.

VI. Arrangements for settling boundary between Canada and Alaska.

It was stated that the presentation of these propositions arose through the negotiations which had for some time been going on between Newfoundland and the United States, and in which Canada insisted upon having something to say. The United States Government at first demanded separate negotiations, but eventually Mr. Blaine expressed a willingness to discuss matters, and a desire to know the basis upon which the Dominion Government desired to act. Lord Stanley's despatch was the result and its publication at this moment had the effect of making it a campaign document, and of taking the reciprocity wind to a certain extent out of the Opposition sails.

Naturally the Liberals were taken aback, and many were exceedingly angry at the clever political stroke. It was an instance of "the Old Man's strategy," which could be fully appreciated at the moment. And the terms of the preliminary announcement were strongly criticised. It was claimed that the American Government had never consented to negotiate; that the whole thing was a fraud intended to deceive the electorate; and that after the campaign was over nothing more would be heard of it. Strength was added to this view by the publication of a letter from Mr. Blaine denying that he had ever made any overtures in the matter, and asserting that only the very widest reciprocity would be considered by the American Government. Upon the other hand, Sir John Thompson declared emphatically at the great mass meeting in Toronto, on Feb. 6th, which practically opened the campaign, that "we had the proposition which was submitted to Mr. Blaine; the answer that Mr. Blaine made to us was that he was willing to enter upon a preliminary discussion to precede the more formal commission; he was willing to enter upon that discussion, and to consider all points embraced in it, but would not be prepared to do so until after the 4th of March, when the term of the present Congress expires." It is safe to say in this connection that where the personal statements of a Canadian and an American leader disagree, the Canadian people as a whole prefer to believe the former. And that was about all that could be said upon the subject at the time.

The Toronto meeting was a great success, besides being the occasion of Sir John Thompson's first appearance

Hon. A. R. Angers, Senator,

Minister of Agriculture.

before an audience in the Queen City. He had already been down in Nova-Scotia, accompanied by the Hon. C. H. Tupper, and had paid a hasty visit to Antigonish, where the Liberals had been raising a storm by attacking Bishop Cameron, and where the Minister of Justice had once more to meet the bitter feeling aroused through denunciation of clerical activity in elections. It seemed, indeed, as if it were his fate to encounter everywhere this religious prejudice, and to meet sectarian questions in every portion of his political career. The only thing which marred the success of the great gathering in the Toronto Auditorium was the rude interruption of some one in the gallery who shouted out the word "Jesuit" when the Minister of Justice was half-way through his speech. It appeared to have an unexpected effect upon the apparently cool and collected speaker, and to have considerably shortened his address. The fact is, that he was more easily moved upon these points than the public would have thought possible, and his calm exterior gave no indication of the passionate feelings and sensitive disposition of the man.

None the less was his speech a success and the impression made, a most favourable one. The other speakers were the Hon. Mackenzie Bowell, the Hon. G. E. Foster, the Hon. Frank Smith, and the Hon. John Carling. The Minister of Justice dealt largely with the Reciprocity question. At the first he spoke of himself in a characteristically plain and dignified manner: "Let me say at the outset that I am no orator, and that even if I had the gift of eloquence it would not be useful to me to-night in the task that is before me, because we are not here to carry away your feelings or to influence your passions by eloquent appeals, but to make a plain statement as behooves public men placing an issue of the greatest consequence before this country." He described the attitude of the

Opposition; reviewed the history of Canadian relations with the United States; and defended the Government in its dissolution of Parliament.

Upon this latter point he said: "If you and the people of Canada accept the policy that we put before you now, we will go to Washington with a Parliament behind us, and we will be able to treat with Mr. Blaine with the assurance that the Premier of this country has the renewed confidence of the people of Canada." He pointed out that the Liberals were everywhere criticising the Government's Reciprocity proposal as impossible of success. "Well, Sir, if it should fail, I will tell you why. It will fail because the followers of Sir Richard Cartwright have put on record whole volumes against Canada with regard to the necessities of this country, and with regard to her bankruptcy if she cannot get better trade relations with the United States. If it fails, it will be because of the cloud of witnesses he has produced against his country. The records of debates on Reciprocity in the House of Commons, the record of evidence given before Committee after Committee of Congress at Washington, have the names of these men appended as indicating that this country can be starved into submission."

Sir John Thompson concluded his speech with a very clear-cut definition of what the Government would do and would not do: "We appeal not to the sentiment of the United States. We do not, in the words of the gentleman who presided at the banquet in Boston, and which Sir Richard Cartwright addressed, look to them for the sign by which we conquer, but we appeal to our Canadian fellow-citizens, and if they sustain us in the policy I have stated to you to-night, the negotiations will proceed in March for a fair extension of the trade of this country—not for Unrestricted Reciprocity, not for any surrender of our tariff control, not for any discrimination against Great Britain—but for a fair line of interchange that will be beneficial to both countries."

The campaign was now in full swing, and it soon proved to be the most bitter contest ever fought in the Dominion. Sir Charles Tupper brought his forceful eloquence to bear upon the result, and at Toronto, Windsor, Hamilton, Kingston, London, Halifax and Quebec dealt sledge-hammer blows against the policy of the Opposition. The publication by Sir John Macdonald of the correspondence between Edward Farrer, Congressman Hitt and Erastus Wiman, followed by his eloquent and pathetic appeal to the British sentiment of the people, had a great effect. In his manifesto he characterized the policy of the Liberals as being veiled treason, and denounced it as involving discrimination against the Mother country; as necessitating direct taxation to the extent of $14,000,000 annually; and as inevitably resulting in annexation. Mr. Blake, after having resigned the Liberal leadership in 1887 into the hands of Mr. Laurier, now retired from Parliament altogether, and thus weakened his party by the defection of one whom all respected, whether they were in harmony with his views or the reverse.

The Conservatives however, did not have things all their own way. A manifesto was issued by the Equal Rights Association vigorously denouncing the Government for its action in connection with the Jesuits' Estates and French language questions. Mr. Laurier delivered a number of addresses in Ontario, and made the most of his power of persuasive eloquence and his personal charm of manner. On the 13th of February he published a manifesto dealing with Sir John Macdonald's charges and explaining his position regarding Unrestricted Reciprocity. He accepted the National Policy as the one issue put forward by the

Conservatives, and declared the platform of the Liberals to be "absolute reciprocal freedom of trade between Canada and the United States." He denounced the premature dissolution of Parliament, proclaimed the loyalty of himself and his party, and arraigned the protective tariff as a public curse. A strong point in the Liberal speeches was the effect which the McKinley bill might be expected to have upon the farmers, and the claims that these anticipated evils could be averted by giving the party a free hand for the negotiation of a wide reciprocity treaty with the American Republic.

Another source of aid was the influence of Mr. Mercier in Quebec. He had made every preparation to leave for Europe in order to float a loan of $10,000,000, but deferred his trip, because, as he declared at a mass meeting in Montreal on February 9th, "his place was beside his esteemed chief, Mr. Wilfred Laurier." It is not unlikely that he hoped to make a portion of the proposed loan unnecessary by thus helping into office a leader who was pledged to carry out the increased subsidies to the Provinces proposed by the Inter-Provincial Conference of a few years before. "Mr. Laurier accepted the resolutions," declared the speaker, "and promised to carry them into effect if he came into power. He (Mr. Mercier) had telegraphed asking him if he would ratify this declaration and Mr. Laurier had replied 'I accept the declaration as the expression of my policy.'" The Rykert scandal in the scarifying hands of Sir Richard Cartwright was also an element of substantial help to the Liberals, while the severe criticisms of the *Toronto Mail* and a speech or two made by the Hon. Oliver Mowat were of additional service.

As much can hardly be said of the assistance which Mr. Goldwin Smith tried to render. His letter to the *New York Times* of February 8th, stating that the Tories "seek to make Canada the engine of the Conservative aristocracy of Great Britain for averting the triumph of democracy in the New World," was merely regarded as a renewed effort to prejudice American public opinion against any Conservative attempt to obtain a fair and reasonable Reciprocity Treaty. And his subsequent letter to a Toronto paper denouncing the National Policy, only helped those who were trying to affix the disgraceful stigma of annexationism to the Liberal party. His aid was indeed an injury to the Opposition in this campaign as it might have been to the Conservative party had the distinguished English writer remained after 1878 a supporter of Protection and a follower of Sir John A. Macdonald.

Meanwhile Sir John Thompson had been making a speech or two in Nova-Scotia, and attending so far as was possible to his own interests in Antigonish, where his old opponent, the Hon. Angus McGillivray, was once more running against him. As his majority had only been 40 in the campaign of 1887, care was required at this juncture, especially in view of the somewhat unscrupulous nature of the contest on the part of the Opposition in the constituency. Mr. McGillivray was a man of considerable ability and standing. He had been first elected as a colleague of Mr. J. S. D. Thompson in Antigonish, to the Local Legislature, and had been re-elected in 1882. Three years' later he became Speaker of the Assembly and continued to hold that position until appointed a member of the Local Government in 1887. In this latter year he had for the first time opposed his old friend and fellow-Conservative in the elections for the Dominion House. In doing so he came into conflict with Bishop Cameron, which was not a very wise thing to do in that constituency, and had been beaten though not by a very large majority.

It had long been a matter of course in Antigonish

and a custom which the people regarded with respect, for the Bishop to intervene in the elections. Usually, several Catholics would be in the field, and he would express a preference for the one or the other. Then upon several occasions one Protestant would be returned to the Local House and one Catholic, showing clearly that there was no bigotry in the matter. When the close friendship, which has now become historical, grew up between the future Premier and the Bishop, it was not, therefore, surprising that the latter should help his friend, and it was not considered anything unusual in the constituency chiefly interested. In his earlier elections, Sir John Thompson had been greatly aided by this influence. In 1887, Mr. McGillivray, however, had allowed his supporters to spread abroad the impression that the Bishop's sympathy and support were no longer with the Minister of Justice, and that a letter to that effect was in existence. These statements brought out a characteristically vigorous manifesto from His Lordship, addressed to the electors, and urging them to support his friend. An extract from it will be of interest and importance, as showing the very substantial and effectual manner in which Bishop Cameron stood by Sir John:

"*To the Electors of Antigonish County:*

"GENTLEMEN,—I did not expect that designing politicians would disturb you by organizing a factious opposition to the return of the Hon. Mr. Thompson at the ensuing election, much less did I apprehend that either the factionists or their dupes would take such liberty with my own name as to oblige me in honor publicly to repudiate their misrepresentations of my views and sentiments regarding the present unseemly contest. In this and some of the neighbouring counties it is asserted, urged and confidently reiterated that my estimation of the Minister of Justice has undergone such a change that I have decided not to support him any more; that far from disapproving of his being ignominiously discharged by you, I have furnished Mr. A. McGillivray with an assurance of my entire unconcern; nay, that he had in his pocket a letter pledging me to strict neutrality. (It is scarcely necessary to remark that such a statement was never made either by Mr. McGillivray or any real friend of his.)

Hon. John F. Wood, M.P.,

Comptroller of Inland Revenue.

"Gentlemen, no such letter exists, no such assurances have been given; while my estimate of Mr. Thompson is even far greater now than when I last had the honor to ask your suffrages in favor of his election in 1885.

"About seventeen months ago, you chose him as your representative in the House of Commons, and you have since had abundant evidence of the wisdom of your choice. You have seen that he has proved himself to be one of the most gifted, most honoured, most influential and most irreproachable statesmen of the Dominion, and you have felt that his unequalled success is a source of legitimate pride to yourselves and to all Nova Scotians. You have seen, also, that while honouring you so highly by his eloquence in debate, and his wisdom in council and committee, he has never neglected your more immediate public interests—nay, that he has promoted them with a success altogether unprecedented.

"Seventeen months ago you needed postal communication and facilities in various localities, and already you have no fewer than five new post-offices opened, besides more frequent mails in several other places. You needed improvement in our railway tariff; through Mr. Thompson's strenuous efforts you have obtained it. You needed money to repair most useful public works, fallen into neglect and decay, to complete others and to originate more, and already no less than $34,346 has been placed at our disposal for that purpose; yet this magnificent sum is doubtless but an instalment of the amount which we may expect under the auspices of this most efficient benefactor, to be expended for our advantage. Lastly, he has been mainly instrumental in persuading the Cabinet to undertake to build a railway through Cape Breton, as a Government measure, and already forty-five miles of it are under contract and in course of construction. He has thus conferred an inestimable boon on Eastern Nova Scotia as well as on that fine Island in whose prosperity we all feel the liveliest interest.

"To give him his discharge, in existing circumstances, would be an act of senseless ingratitude, a public calamity and a lasting disgrace, for which I trust you will never be guilty of making yourselves answerable. In a word, to do yourselves full credit, you ought not only to return Mr. Thompson, but to return him by an overwhelming majority, since you have not been allowed the privilege of electing him as he deserved, by acclamation.

"The above is my reply to those who have unathoritatively dragged my name into the contest, and now, gentlemen, I confidently leave the issue in your hands, and remain,

"Your devoted well-wisher and servant in Christ,

"JOHN CAMERON,

"*Bishop of Antigonish.*

"Antigonish, Feb. 11, 1887."

During the canvass of the constituency which took place in the elections of 1891, Mr. McGillivray came out with a vigourous attack upon the Bishop, and in reply the Rev. Father Macdonald of Stellarton accused the former of having personally made the very statements which Bishop Cameron in the above circular charitably disbelieved. Archbishop O'Brien also came to the support of His Lordship, and indirectly of Sir John Thompson. In an address delivered at Halifax, he eloquently defended clerical intervention under certain conditions and in certain circumstances :

"The interest of the country and the fond, proud love of his country find a place in the heart and engage the attention of the true priest. Hence, should a candidate for Parliament advocate, say Unrestricted Reciprocity, and should a prelate conscientiously believe that to be the first step towards annexation—should he have good reason to believe that its promoters had that result in view, namely, to destroy our fair Canadian nationality and make of this country the battling ground of carpet-baggers and traitors—should he not advise, exhort, entreat, aye, and command, his people to vote against such a candidate?"

Needless to say, in a Catholic constituency like Antigonish it was not surprising that the influence of such appeals and the personal popularity of a prelate so respected and esteemed as Bishop Cameron, should have had great weight, and have prepared the way for the majority of 227 with which the Minister of Justice swept away his antagonist on March 5th. Before that final result of the campaign occurred, however, Sir John Thompson delivered two important addresses in the Province—one at Halifax in conjunction with Sir Charles Tupper and the Hon. C. H. Tupper, on February 14th, and the other at Kentville, four days later. The Halifax meeting was a great demonstration. Sir Charles Tupper in one of his old-time ringing speeches, stirred up the loyalty and enthusiasm of his audience to an unprecedented degree, and was followed by Sir John in a speech which seems to have been instinct with unusual earnestness and vim. He handled the Liberal party without gloves. Referring to the Reciprocity policies—restricted and unrestricted—he declared that "the Liberals made no offer to negotiate, but proclaimed in advance that they were prepared to give away everything The Liberals appealed to the manufacturers of Boston for 'a sign by which to conquer.' Sir John Macdonald appeals to the people of Canada, and says, 'To you I look for the sign by which to conquer. . . . When Nelson was once signalled to retire, he gave the command; 'Keep my signal for closer battle flying, and nail it to the mast.' Mr. Laurier had said at Halifax that he nailed his Unrestricted Reciprocity colours to the mast, but his mast has already been shot away, and his colours all tattered and torn are hanging in ribbons over the drifting hulk of his party."

The battle now progressed with intense vigour in all parts of the country to its termination. On the one side were "the Old Man, the Old Flag, and the Old Policy"; earnest appeals to British sentiment and allegiance; fierce denunciation of the alleged American sympathies, policy and environment of the Liberal leaders. Upon the other were vigorous protestations of loyalty; charges of wholesale corruption against the Government, departmental and national; advocacy of free trade with the States and wider markets for Canadian produce. Incidentally, there were Ontario protests and votes against those who had refused to support the disallowance of the Jesuits' Estates Act; while in Quebec Mr. Mercier directed all the smouldering fires of the prejudices aroused by the old Riel agitation, against the Dominion Government.

The result, however, was the sustaining of the Conservative party, policy and Ministry by a majority of between twenty and thirty. Two members of the Government, Mr. C. C. Colby, and Mr. John Carling, were defeated, while the Opposition lost Mr. A. G. Jones, Mr. Peter Mitchell and Mr. Weldon. And thus ended the most desperate fight in the history of the Dominion, and one which was destined to indirectly cause a greater loss to the Conservative party and to the country than any which had yet taken place. Sir John Macdonald, against the advice of his physicians, had taken a wonderfully active part in the campaign." The "Grand Old Man," with an energy perfectly phenomenal in one of his years and physical weakness, seemed to be everywhere urging on the battle; putting life and soul into his supporters; arousing the enthusiasm of vast audiences as only his magnetic personality could do; and giving to the struggle that swing of victory which was necessary to overcome the many adverse circumstances.

Without him, indeed, it is not unlikely, that the party would have been defeated, and of this he was quite well aware. Taking, therefore, his life in his hand, Sir John Macdonald had gone into the conflict determined to win one more success for what he believed to be the fundamental principles of Canadian nationality and progress—British connection and loyalty to the 'close and honourable union of the Dominion and the Empire. But his efforts in managing the campaign and addressing immense audiences almost daily for weeks—upon one day he spoke five times—were too much for his feeble frame, and after success had been achieved the inevitable reaction set in, and the laurels of victory instead of contributing to a new lease of power and influence, could only be used to crown the tomb of departed greatness.

CHAPTER X.

DEATH OF SIR JOHN MACDONALD.

On the 24th of May it became known to the public that the illness of Sir John A. Macdonald was somewhat serious. He himself did not appear to regard it in that light, however, and during the next day or two improved considerably. On the 29th, when the fatal stroke fell upon him, he had been dictating letters; holding a long conversation with Sir John Thompson upon questions of public policy and party tactics; and receiving a visit from the Governor-General. But shortly afterwards the paralytic seizure came and stilled the busy brain, numbed the marvellous faculties, and silenced forever the voice which had so long been the voice of Canada. During the week of anxious waiting which followed, a sorrowing people, a sympathetic Empire, and a Queen, who is as great a woman as she is a sovereign, watched beside the sick-bed at Earnscliffe, where the greatest of Colonial statesmen, the Father of Canadian confederation and the champion of Imperial unity, lay fighting his sad and hopeless battle.

As days and hours went by, and the great leader was passing slowly away, people began to realize what enormous consequences might follow. Sir John Macdonald to many minds seemed the actual embodiment of Canadian Conservatism. To them he was the party, and without him the party was nothing. Others, who understood more clearly the condition of affairs, knew that there were several men quite able to take the leadership, and that foremost amongst them stood the Minister of Justice. Outside of Canada, however, there is no doubt that the name of

Sir John Macdonald was at that time the only one which could be said to bear an international or imperial reputation. He had grown up with Canada. His policy had made itself felt abroad, and his name, in many places, was synonymous with that of the Dominion. His death, therefore, might involve political chaos, it might result in the disintegration of the party he had formed and led so long, it did undoubtedly imply serious political difficulties.

Parliament promptly adjourned upon the news of the Premier's fatal illness, and from that time till the end came, upon the memorable 6th of June, 1891, the pulse of the Canadian people was stirred as it had never been before. Publicly, of course, there could be no serious discussion as to the future leader, as to the future of the party or of the country. But privately there was a great deal. Ottawa was disturbed as it had not been since the days of 1873, when the fate of Sir John Macdonald's first ministry hung in the balance of a great parliamentary trial. Letters from all over the Dominion poured into the capital, rumours of a hundred kinds were current, considerations of all sorts were discussed. It was recognized then, and in the week which followed the Premier's death, that Sir John Thompson, by force of ability and political service, was the inevitable leader—if not at once, then in the near future.

Had there been an impression that Sir Charles Tupper would have cared to take up political life again, the opinion of the party would have probably united upon him, but the circumstances being otherwise there seemed a large majority of sentiment in favour of the Minister of Justice. Here, however, the sectarian element intervened. His religion it was claimed, in connection with the Jesuits' Estates and other questions, would fatally prejudice the chances of the party in certain portions of the country and it would be

Hon. Sir John Carling, K.C.M.G., M.P.,

Minister without Portfolio

better if, for a time at least, the Premiership of the Dominion were placed in the hands of someone who, in the existing crisis, would be able to unite all sections of the Conservative forces. The name of the Hon. J. J. C. Abbott was suggested, and his private correspondence at the time, as well as that of Sir John Thompson, illustrates the utter unselfishness which in this connection characterised the two men. In a letter written to an intimate friend on the 4th of June, and only two days before Sir John Macdonald's death, Mr. Abbott commented very frankly upon the proposal that the leadership should fall to him. He said:

"I have heard from many people lately very similar ideas of the situation to yours—but from none whose opinions I should place more confidence in. But I hate politics, and what are considered their appropriate methods. I hate notoriety, public meetings, public speeches, caucuses, and every thing that I know of that is apparently the necessary incident of politics—except doing public work to the best of my ability. Why should I go where doing honest work will only make me hated and my ministry unpopular; and where I can only gain reputation and credit by practising arts which I detest, to acquire popularity? Besides breaking up all my family arrangements in which I have settled down and hope to spend any time I may hope to have left, now that I have reached the allotted span. No doubt some such arrangement as you mention would be the best solution of the crisis—but there are lots of men better known than I, and better capable of working out the political problem; and who would be glad of the chance. My own impression is that Thompson is the man to be sent for, and I should think he could carry the work through, though of course I am not familiar with the feeling in Ontario.

"Yours sincerely, J. J. C. ABBOTT."

Such a letter, written by an old man who in shortly afterwards assuming the heavy duties of the Premiership, accepted a burden too great for his years and strength, has a pathetic ring in its every line. Little wonder that he hesitated to surrender his quiet home life, and in his declining days take up such a task. But none the less it was an honour which many would have liked to receive and a duty which few ambitious men would shrink from accepting, even in succession to such an unequalled leader as Sir John A. Macdonald. Writing to the same gentleman on the memorable 6th of June, Sir John Thompson breathed very similar sentiments :

"I am much obliged for your letter. At this crisis any member of the Government must feel grateful for the frank advice of sincere friends as I well know you to be. I fear, however, that you have conceived the idea that I aspire to lead the party, now or in the future. No greater mistake could be made. I am not willing to take that position now, or to enter on a period of probation with a view to that end. I hope that the party can be much better led, and I am willing to serve or to retire as may seem best to the man who shall take up the reins which have fallen from the hands of Sir John Macdonald.

"Yours sincerely,

"JNO. S. D. THOMPSON."

The death of the great Conservative leader on the very day this letter was written compelled action while for the moment interdicting discussion. Sir John Thompson had moved the adjournment of the House after brief speeches from Sir Hector Langevin and others. And the eloquent tribute paid upon that occasion to the memory of the dead statesman by the Hon. Wilfred Laurier is one of the bright spots in the record of Canadian political struggle.

Then followed the prolonged State funeral, amid such evidences of sincere national grief as are very rarely given to a public man, no matter how great he may have been in character or achievement. Sir John Macdonald was finally laid away in the distant cemetery at Cataraqui, amidst surroundings of almost unique sorrow :

> "Muffled peals and drooping banners,
> Bated breath and measured tread,
> Emblems of a nation's mourning
> For her great and noble dead."

With the passing of the Chieftain, came the imperative necessity for the selection of a new leader and a new Premier. Lord Stanley of Preston, had postponed action for six days and until the funeral was finished, but on the 12th of June, it was announced that His Excellency was in communication with Sir John Thompson and the Hon. Mr. Abbott. Meantime the intrigue and speculation customary in Cabinet crises had been going on. Sir Hector Langevin, as the member of the late ministry who had served the longest time in office, and who by virtue of his leadership of the French Canadian wing of the party, really had strong claims to consideration, was being strenuously urged for the Premiership by *Le Monde* and other journals of Quebec. Unfortunately, however, he was resting under the shadow of the Tarte charges, and was in a position which Sir John Thompson had declared in his speech at Halifax during the general elections, made an investigation absolutely necessary.

Mr. Chapleau was also vigorously opposed to him, and publicly urged the claims of the Minister of Justice to the position. "I regard Sir John Thompson," said he, on June 12th, "as the only man who can give the quality of stability in the re-organization of the Government. He may meet with Opposition from Ontario, but we believe that our Ontario friends will regard it as a duty and a necessity to join and co-operate for the best interests of the Conservative party. Sir John Thompson is essentially an Englishman and a Britisher, and as he himself has often pointed out in his speeches, is governed by political, not by religious principles." The *Ottawa Citizen* urged the distinguished services and abilities of Sir Charles Tupper, and in other quarters there was some talk of Mr. W. R. Meredith.

During a part of this period, Mr. D'Alton McCarthy was in Ottawa. And it was natural that the presence of the man who for years had been looked upon as Sir John Macdonald's successor; whose legal advice and political abilities had been so frequently utilized by the Chieftain prior to the coming of Sir John Thompson into office; whose place as an Ontario politician was now so peculiar and so antagonistic to the Province of Quebec; should have created much interest and discussion. The Equal Rights leader had one interview with Sir John Thompson during the crisis. Any political significance was denied at the time, but it is now understood that Mr. McCarthy took the opportunity to point out his claims to the Premiership, and to make suggestions, the details of which will probably never be known. Sir John was very non-committal in the matter, and a little later on, when the Governor-General discussed the formation of a Cabinet with him, and he felt obliged to decline the honour, it was Senator Abbott whom he recommended to His Excellency.

That Mr. McCarthy could not afterwards work with the Minister of Justice is therefore, not surprising, apart altogether from their differences upon the Jesuits' Estates, the French language, or the Manitoba Schools. That he was not consulted in the subsequent formation of the Thompson Government is still less surprising. And that

HON. J. J. CURRAN, Q.C., M.P.,

Solicitor-General.

he has since drifted entirely away from the Conservative party is a natural consequence of the rivalry of two able men of antagonistic ambitions, but of extremely diverse views and characteristics.

The Governor-General had not found it so very easy to obtain a Premier. When His Excellency summoned Sir John Thompson on the morning of the 12th of June, the latter hesitated, and advised that Mr. Abbott be sent for. After an hour's conversation, he left and spent some time in consultation with the latter. The two then returned to the Governor-General's office, and shortly afterwards it was announced that the Hon. J. J. C. Abbott had accepted the duty of forming a Cabinet. Four days later a communication was read to the House of Commons from the new Premier, stating that, "I have communicated with my colleagues, and requested their consent to remain in their present offices, and with their assent submitted to His Excellency my recommendation that they should be continued in their positions." This was, of course, approved, and Mr. Abbott himself assumed the post of President of the Council. For the time being, the Ministry of Railways and Canals, which Mr. Chapleau thought himself entitled to have, was administered by another member of the Government.

At a later date the promised re-construction of the Ministry took place, and the changes may as well be noted here. For months there had been rumours current concerning Mr. Meredith's entry into the Cabinet. There was undoubtedly a strong feeling in his favour throughout Ontario. Able, eloquent, popular and genial, the present Chief Justice of the Province had always held a warm place in the hearts of its people. Though unsuccessful in ousting the clever political strategist, who has so long held power at Toronto, he was almost equally respected by party friend and party foe. But the semi-religious cry of one or two campaigns and the anti-Separate School plank in his platform, had for good or ill antagonized the Roman Catholic vote and made it as difficult apparently for the Conservative Opposition leader in Ontario to enter the Dominion Government as it was for him to win success in the Local elections.

None the less a Cabinet position was offered him by Mr. Abbott during the re-construction. Why it was refused is not known, but that the offer was made, and with Sir John Thompson's full knowledge and approval, is beyond doubt. The Minister of Justice as leader of the Commons would have much to say in connection with such an important matter, and it is interesting to note how far removed from bigotry his views must have been. But this particular arrangement fell through, and by the end of January, 1892, all the other changes had been effected. Lieut.-Colonel J. A. Ouimet entered the Government in practical, though not immediate, succession to Sir Hector Langevin and took the portfolio of Public Works. Mr. John G. Haggart was promoted from the Postmaster-Generalship to the Ministry of Railways and Canals, and was succeeded by Sir Adolphe Caron, who handed over tne Department of Militia and Defence to the Hon. Mackenzie Bowell. Mr. Chapleau was given the Ministry of Customs—a decided promotion—and his old position of Secretary of State was filled by the elevation of Mr. James C. Patterson, a strong party organizer and popular politician, of clean and honourable record.

Such was Mr. Abbott's completed Cabinet. A word might be said in this connection about one of the most interesting personalities in Canadian politics—Mr. Nicholas Flood Davin. There is no doubt that the brilliant writer, orator and North-West representative had at this time strong claims to a Cabinet position. His friends had urged Sir. John A. Macdonald to make him Minister of the Interior in succession to Mr. Dewdney, and they continued to do so with Mr. Abbott, although the post had in the meantime been filled by Mr. Daly's appointment. Mr. Davin was finally offered the Lieut.-Governorship of the North-West Territories, but refused it, and the position went to Mr. C. H. Mackintosh. He would have made an ideal Governor.

The accession of Mr. Abbott had not been well received in all quarters. It was not that his self-denial and patriotism lacked appreciation, or that his ability as a manager of men and a wise tactician was not considered fully equal to the task before him. But there was a popular impression in French Canadian circles that Sir John Thompson was being put to one side on account of his religious views. *La Presse* of June 15th declared that "the Catholics are not going to be the victims of exclusionism because of their religious belief. Sir John Thompson is the most remarkable man in our Federal politics, and he has the right to be judged from a political standpoint." Mr. Chapleau was also dissatisfied: "I am still of opinion that Sir John Thompson is the best available man at this juncture. It seems apparent that the obstacle against him was his religion." The *Ottawa Citizen*, on finding that Sir Charles Tupper did not care to be put forward for the position, had already come out strongly for the Minister of Justice, and proclaimed on June 13th that "No more able, honourable, industrious, courteous and painstaking representative can be found in the ranks of the Conservatives. He is loved by all who know him, and the more responsible the position he is placed in the greater intellectual power will he display."

But these utterances were without result. Sir John

Thompson knew something of the difficulties which threatened the new Ministry, and he had no desire to add any sectarian complication to them if an act of personal self-sacrifice would avail to avert the evil. As it was, he at once assumed the leadership of the House of Commons in fact, if not in name. For a brief period courtesy gave Sir Hector Langevin a certain precedence, but it was not long before the aggressive and merciless Opposition placed the veteran Conservative leader in a position where self-defence was the only consideration. The *Toronto Globe,* and the Liberals generally, did not altogether like the new leadership. The organ declared that Sir John was too cold and grave; and pointed out that the blood and fire that leaps and flames in the men who seem born to lead their fellows, did not charge through the veins of this studious and deliberate politician.

This was hardly sufficient ground, however, for denouncing to the electorate the coming wearer of the mantle of Sir John Macdonald. The *Globe* could not charge personal or political corruption against him, so it alleged that he was returned for his county, not by the free votes of the people, but through "the strenuous intimidation of a Bishop." It could not criticise his administration of the Department of Justice, so it gravely alleged that he had been "a failure in the Local politics of Nova-Scotia." It was difficult to minimise the respect in which he was generally held outside of the ranks of extreme bigots and partisans, so the public were informed that "he came from a remote Province." However, these were not very severe or damaging charges. Far more injurious were the comments of the *Toronto Mail,* and it is not unlikely that the remarks of that paper on June 9th had influenced him considerably in his feelings as to the Premiership. After a reference to his admitted ability, unblemished character and high sense

Hon. J. A. Ouimet, M. P.

Minister of Public Works.

of honour, the Equal Rights organ went on to say that "the obvious objection to him is that he is a Roman Catholic and a convert, animated by a convert's zeal, as he showed when he came forward to lead in the defence of the Jesuits' Estates Act."

But whatever the future result might be, he had now done what seemed to be his duty to the party and the country, at a crisis which can only be appreciated by a recollection of the familiar phrase used for so many years by his opponents to depict the time when Sir John Macdonald would leave the scene of his struggles and his victories: "After me, the deluge." The long-looked for event had come, but other men had picked up the threads of power as they fell from the nerveless hands of the Chieftain, and his words uttered in Toronto on Dec. 18th, 1884, had assumed life and form: "I am satisfied that whoever may be chosen as my successor, he and those who act with him will move in the same line, will be governed by the same principles, and will be supported by the same party."

The first Session of the seventh Parliament of Canada resumed its work with a most satisfactory Budget Speech from Mr. Foster, following upon a motion of Mr. Laurier, which showed a Government majority of only twenty. The available surplus was placed at $2,100,000, and the removal of the sugar duties to the extent of $3,500,000 was met by an increased excise and a reduced expenditure. On May 20th, the interminable Franchise Act came up for discussion, on a Liberal motion for its repeal, as being inconvenient, cumbersome, and inefficient. Sir John Thompson showed how useless these continued debates were: "In 1885 we had a most elaborate discussion on every principle involved in the measure; in 1886, when I had occasion to introduce some amendments, we had a very long discussion, not only of the principles, but as to the expediency of repeal; in 1887, I think in 1888, and certainly last year, we had every argument exhausted and every argument reviewed." He then pointed out that the motion would make it necessary to fall back upon the franchises of the various Provinces, which change constantly and are never alike.

As it is, the Act "aids in securing uniformity. In some of the Provinces there are revisions by municipal authorities; in others by municipal officers; in others by sheriffs who are officers at pleasure of the Provincial Governments. . . . There is no pretence at uniformity; there is no attempt to secure any kind of legal qualification in the officers appointed to do the work of revision; whereas the Act now under consideration establishes a qualification for the office of revising barrister second to none required for any public office connected with the administration of any law; second only to that required for filling the highest judicial offices."

On May 29th, Mr. Laurier moved on behalf of the now aggressive and hopeful Opposition, a vote of censure upon Sir Charles Tupper for having taken part in the recent general elections whilst holding the post of High Commissioner in England; for having imputed treason against his opponents; and for having assailed the Grand Trunk Railway. Sir John Thompson in his reply made a vigorous defence of his old-time colleague and friend:— "Sir Charles Tupper in one place after another has shown that while certain persons had put themselves forward to promote the welfare and the designs of the Liberal party in this country, but really to subvert the institutions of this country—before the Liberal party could venture to go to the polls, they were compelled to dissavow all connection and all sympathy with any such designs or with individuals who were promoting those designs." Far, therefore, from imputing disloyalty to the Liberal party, he had simply shown that without this repudiation they would have been annihilated at the recent elections.

The Minister of Justice went on to point out that while the Opposition Leader made this general charge of imputing treason against Sir Charles Tupper, he had not laid on the Table of the House one single bit of evidence, or one solitary extract. Sir John then sketched the position and duties of the High Commissioner. "He is not a foreign ambassador. He is simply the Agent of this Government, living in London. His Excellency, the Governor-General, is the medium of communication between this and the Imperial Government. It is only when special views are to be passed or influence used that the High Commissioner comes into action. . . . It is necessary that he should be the confidential agent of the Government he serves; should be in sympathy with its policy; should strive to carry out that policy; should be the depository of its secrets. To be competent and efficient he cannot help having political sympathies."

After speaking of the Grand Trunk and Sir Charles Tupper's very moderate request that it should permit the employés to vote as they liked; Sir John referred to the general issue at the election in vigorous style:—"I think the Leader of the Opposition is somewhat mistaken in the choice of his expression when he declares that Sir C. Tupper 'stooped' to take part in those elections. Considering that the fate of this country was at stake, considering that the trade relations of this country were being discussed and fought over, and that the issues with regard to those trade relations were perhaps the most important ever submitted to the British North American Provinces, I do not think that anybody could fairly be said to have 'stooped' in order to take part in that contest." The motion was, of course, voted down, as had been the previous one in reference to the Franchise Act. But the majorities all through this difficult session were small—averaging about twenty—and requiring a most watchful care in debate and division on the part of the Leader of the House.

In September the adjournment came after a prolonged surfeit of scandals. It was the longest session but one in the history of the Dominion, and the worry and work which it entailed upon Sir John Thompson no doubt laid the foundation of the physical troubles which were to eventually carry him off. But he came through it all with flying colours as a Parliamentary leader, a debater and a minister. He proved himself capable of holding together a weakened, almost shattered party, in the face of a terrible personal loss; in the teeth of serious and injurious charges from a strong and united Opposition; in spite of a small and shifting majority. It was indeed a severe trial, but as on previous occasions, he had risen to the emergency.

Hon. T. Mayne Daly, M.P.

Minister of the Interior.

CHAPTER XI.

THE SCANDAL SESSION.

No country in the world can boast absolute purity in politics and administration. Few in this respect have stood as high in the scale as Canada. Elections in the Mother-land are known to cost millions; the constituencies are carefully "nursed" for years by would-be candidates at great personal expense; contracts upon occasion have notoriously been given to inefficient concerns upon very insufficient grounds. Yet no one will call England a really corrupt country. In the United States unfortunately there can be no doubt about the matter. There is corruption in the Presidential elections, in the Congressional elections, in the State contests, in the Civic governments, and in the city elections. It is a far cry from the Pension Bureau to the Lexow inquiry, but in all the varied departments of American politics between the one and the other, there is probably boodling to be found in a greater or lesser degree.

It is a matter of deep regret that the Dominion has not been able to keep its skirts altogether clean in this connection. But there are degrees of offence in this as in every other case. And, during the period now under consideration there were two parties to the charges of corruption. Quebec had covered itself with disgrace by allowing its Government to fall into the hands of a small clique of men who, under the brilliant but erratic and dangerous leadership of Count Mercier, had pillaged the Province without pity or remorse; had enjoyed for years a deficit of over a million dollars annually; had increased the debt by some $15,000,000; had rioted in luxury, in costly houses, in expensive horses, in journeys and fetes. The Baie de Chaleurs' case brought much of this home to the Provincial Premier and his Ministry; the Royal Commission did more in developing the investigation; the Lieut.-Governor finally gave the people their opportunity by dismissing his advisers and calling in new men and a new party. The elections which followed closed the drama and restored the Province to its former honorable position, while forever burying under the all-powerful ballot-box, the men who had disgraced its name and temporarily blackened its repute.

The Dominion case was different. The charges made against members of the Government were claimed by Sir John Thompson to be bitterly partisan; were proved, so far as personal corruption was concerned, to be without foundation; and dealt in the main with a system rather than with individual actions. Where charges were specified and proved against officials, punishment was swift and sure, though never merciless. Where they were vague, as in the case of Sir Adolphe Caron, every effort was made by Sir John to bring them to a point suited for investigation. Where they were, however, mere fishing expeditions, intended only for the purpose of throwing partisan mud in the hope that some would stick, he very properly refused to aid them or allow of their being carried beyond a certain limit.

But none the less the session which followed upon the death of Sir John Macdonald was a severe strain upon the heart and mind of a man such as the Minister of Justice. It may as well be frankly admitted that the great Premier whom Canada had just lost forever, was not afraid to use methods and means in building up the Dominion which would have been absolutely impossible to Sir John Thompson. They were necessary in the government of a new country, having crude and ill-defined institutions and strong internal opposition; permeated in many parts with lack of confidence in its own powers and resources and opportunities; and possessed of an immense area together with small available means for the management of great party conflicts.

In England party government is reduced to a science, and the vast sums of money required to manipulate elections are never seen or perhaps heard of, by the heads of the organizations, except in the most vague and general way. But in Canada the barest expenses can hardly be met, and money for the most legitimate and necessary purposes is difficult to obtain. Ministers here are more or less the party managers—though the fact is to be regretted—and it is therefore easy for some of the money contributed by strong supporters to come, without corrupt intent or consequences, from men who have received, or might receive in the future, an interest in government contracts or appointments.

During the general elections the most wholesale and unfounded charges had been made as to the "boodling" prevalent at Ottawa. It was alleged that the Departments were permeated with corruption; that vast sums had been obtained by members of the Government during many years past from contractors and others in order to purchase the constituencies; that the Conservative ministers, members and the government officials were all alike corrupt. Mr. J. Israel Tarte was elected for a Quebec seat in order to ventilate his charges against the McGreevy's and Sir Hector Langevin, and the Rykert scandal was used as an illustration of what was alleged to be the prevalent state of affairs. There was literally no end to the rumours current when the House met in April, and possibly the worry connected with this situation had a natural effect upon the already enfeebled frame of the Premier. Be that as it may however, his death postponed for a time the action which had been commenced regarding the Tarte enquiry.

There is no doubt that Sir John Thompson's treatment of the Rykert case during the previous session was approved by the country. Mr. J. C. Rykert had long been a popular and respected member of the Conservative party and it was hard indeed for the Minister of Justice to admit the unfortunate position in which the member for Lincoln had placed himself. But he did his duty in this as in subsequent cases. Sir Richard Cartwright had moved on March 11th, 1890, that Mr. Rykert's conduct had been "discreditable, corrupt and scandalous." It was claimed by him that the member for Lincoln had applied for and obtained certain North-West timber limits in the name of one John Adams. The latter in consideration of this service was alleged to have agreed to assign to Mrs. Rykert, one-half interest in the limits, and to pay one-half of all the proceeds from the sale of timber thereon. And it was further stated that on January 16th, 1883, the sum of $74,200 was paid over in accordance with this agreement. Receipts, letters and other documents were produced in proof of the charges. This in brief was Sir Richard's case, and he presented it in what the Minister of Justice termed a most "inflammatory speech."

Sir John Thompson defended the Government from the charge that this was a part of any general system and showed that so far as they were concerned there could have been no more corruption in granting Mr. Rykert a tract of 100 miles for a friend, than there had been upon one occasion under the Mackenzie administration when 200 miles had been similarly granted on the recommendation of Sir Richard Cartwright himself. A few days later when the

HON. JOHN G. HAGGART, M. P.

Minister of Railways and Canals.

debate was resumed, and after a brief but able speech by Mr. Blake, the Minister of Justice spoke out plainly and to the point; describing the affair as "a case in which the honour of Parliament is most deeply involved. I regard the authenticity of those letters as having been substantially established; I regard this correspondence as a most shocking correspondence, and one which appeals to the House as strongly as any case could appeal to its consideration for justice, as strongly as it can appeal to the mercy of this House. . . . I say that in the statements made by the member for Lincoln, he has failed to exonerate himself of the censure which, the resolution of the member for South Oxford makes him subject to."

He concluded by moving that the matter be referred to a committee, and so strongly had his preceding remarks convinced the House of his desire to do entire justice in the case, that Mr. Laurier supported the motion and added a somewhat unusual compliment: "I desire to say that after the strong declarations which have been made by the Minister of Justice, I am somewhat inclined to modify the conclusions at which I had arrived." Eventually the Committee reported, and so unfavourably to Mr. Rykert that he resigned in order to avoid the threatened expulsion. He was re-elected, but did not stand again in the ensuing general election.

This case is of interest only as showing that no matter how strong might be the personal and political reasons against a given line of action, Sir John Thompson was prepared to do his duty in the beginning of this regrettable series of scandals as well as in the end. Of course, it was impossible that he should please his party antagonists during the Session of 1891. Nothing but the expulsion of half the Conservative members of the House, and the retirement and prosecution of most of the Cabinet Ministers, would have satisfied enthusiastic Liberals such as Tarte, Lister, McMullen, Edgar, Cartwright and Charlton. But moderate men were pretty well satisfied that the abuses which had undoubtedly grown up during a dozen years of power would be rectified if the Minister of Justice could have his way. And after Sir John Macdonald's death there was no one in the Government who was prepared to dispute his practical, if not nominal, supremacy. So that the appeal made by Mr. Abbott in the Senate a couple of months after his accession to the Premiership was looked upon in the country as a fair indication of the new Government's policy: "I would ask the hon. gentlemen opposite to join with us in trying to find out what the facts are about this alleged rascality. We ask them to give us the benefit of their experience in this enquiry, to assist us in ascertaining the facts and placing them before the public, in order that they may be dealt with properly, and, if found guilty, that summary vengeance may be exercised upon those who are found guilty of appropriating public money—stealing—be they high or low."

The charges against Mr. Thomas McGreevy, M.P., were of a very serious nature. They were important because they affected the reputation of a prominent Conservative member of the House who had been the party's treasurer for many years in Quebec, and who was known to be a brother-in-law and intimate friend of the Minister of Public Works. They were important as indicating that Sir Hector Langevin had been either careless or criminal in a portion of his long administration of that Department, and as showing much looseness of principle to be prevalent amongst certain Quebec politicians. Sir John Thompson had already declared at Halifax that neither he nor the Government would defend Mr. McGreevy, or excuse him if guilty.

Mr. Tarte in this matter was a man with a mission. He had not always been so, and had at one time been under the ban of the Liberal party as an alleged "Tory corruptionist." The public interest, however, in his first speech and motion had been very great for some time, and the galleries of the House were crowded when on May 11th the slenderly-built, wiry little man, with glossy black hair, and wearing a fashionable costume, rose to his feet. Briefly summed up, the charges may be found in the following paragraph from his speech:

"Since 1882 or 1883, the secrets of the Department of Public Works have been penetrated and divulged for money considerations to public contractors by the hon. member for Quebec West, Mr. McGreevy, and according to the evidence I have got in my hands, money has been paid year after year on contract after contract, large sums of money; that during that period of time he has used his influence as a member of the Quebec Harbour Commission against the public interest on numerous and important occasions."

Various documents had been obtained through a quarrel between the brothers, Thomas and R. H. McGreevy, and were certainly very damaging in their nature. The claim was made that Sir Hector Langevin was implicated, and that large sums received from the interested contractors had gone into the campaign fund of the Conservative party. Mr. McGreevy, of course, denied the charges, and the Minister of Public Works demanded the fullest investigation. By permission of the Government, the whole matter was relegated to the Committee on Privileges and Elections, and the ensuing inquiry was most thorough—both sides showing every disposition to get at the truth. The Government retained Mr. B. B. Osler, Q.C., to help in the examination of witnesses. Finally, on the 25th of

August, the Committee met to consider their report, and its preparation was referred to a Sub-Committee composed of three Conservatives—Sir John Thompson, D. Girouard, and Michael Adams; and two Liberals—the Hon. David Mills and the Hon. L. H. Davies.

Naturally, they could not agree, the chief point of difference being the amount of responsibility which ought to be borne by Sir H. Langevin in the scandalous transactions proven to have taken place. Ultimately, a majority and minority report were presented to the House. The former, prepared largely by Sir John Thompson, concluded with the statement that "the evidence does not justify them in concluding that the Minister knew of the conspiracy before mentioned or that he willingly lent himself to its objects." The latter alleged that the fruits of the frauds went into the pockets of the contractors, towards the funds of the Conservative party, or to the support of *Le Monde*, Sir H. Langevin's paper. Both reports were considered by the House on Sept. 21st, and, after a prolonged debate, the majority one was carried on a party vote of 101 against 86. An amendment moved by Mr. McCarthy, acquitting Sir Hector of connivance but finding him guilty of inexcusable neglect, was voted down.

The expulsion of Mr. McGreevy followed upon the motion of the Minister of Justice, and a little later Sir Hector Langevin practically closed a prolonged political career of much useful service to his country, by resigning his place in the Ministry. Prosecutions were afterwards instituted by the Minister of Justice against those concerned in the frauds, and several convictions were obtained. Speaking at Perth on the 21st of November following, Sir John Thompson declared that the Minister of Public Works had no knowledge of the robbery which had been going on, but that he had fully accepted the doctrine of responsibility for what took place in his Department by resigning his position. And then he strongly denounced the Opposition, and at the same time explained the difficult position of the Government in attempting to do its duty under circumstances which would have been, from a party standpoint, greatly improved by a restriction of enquiry and a stifling of investigation.

"While our attitude was that of challenging investigation, inviting investigation even to the extent of paying the expenses of counsel who conducted the investigation on behalf of our opponents, what was the attitude of the Opposition? Why, during the discussion of these matters in the House of Commons, instead of feeling themselves impressed with the responsibility of judges, and the responsibility of being fair between man and man, every insult that could be heaped upon the accused member was rung out amidst the wildest cheering of the Opposition. When they were deliberating upon the question of whether a man should be found guilty of corruption or not, every incident of his political career, or the career of the men associated with him, was flung in his face; and the tribunal of the House was lowered as it never was before. As time went on and public feeling was aroused and excited by the reports of these scandals, finding that opportunity was given by the Government for wide investigation, they became bolder in their charges, and towards the close of the Session it came to this, and it has been in this state for some time past, that a public man has only to be accused in order to be adjudged guilty."

A lot of minor departmental scandals were unearthed, and considered by different committees. It soon became evident that a very loose idea of public morality had prevailed for a long time in various branches of the public service. But there was really nothing personally corrupt proved against the Ministers, though in one or two cases, carelessness in looking after their subordinates was very clearly indicated. The light that was shed upon the whole system of Departmental Government was so keen and searching, that the session, disgraceful as its results were in a certain sense, unpleasant as they were to the Government and the country, could not but do a great deal of good in purifying the service and lopping off the excresences of corruption which had developed during a long term of office. Sir John Thompson, as leader of the House, gave every possible aid to the investigations, and it is probable that had the desire of the Opposition to obtain political capital not been so keenly exhibited, even greater good would have resulted. As it was, many officials were dismissed or suspended, and others prosecuted and punished upon conviction. But the fierce party feeling which was aroused by the Liberal method of pushing charges in all kinds of directions, often with very little proof, and chiefly with a view to picking up something damaging to the Government, was so exasperating that the Minister of Justice often found it difficult to keep his followers in line.

As an illustration of this, the charges against the Hon. Mr. Haggart, then Postmaster-General, may be mentioned. Mr. Lister, of Lambton, whose fighting characteristics were fully exhibited during this stormy session, rose from his place in the House on the 23rd of September, and stated that to the best of his knowledge and belief, Mr. Haggart had been interested in the profits of a contract obtained by Alexander Manning, Alexander Shields, and others in the year 1879, for the construction of a branch of the Canadian Pacific Railway from Port Arthur to Rat Portage; that while a member of Parliament he had received large sums of money from these contractors which he had used for political purposes or had permitted the company to pay to

W. R. MEREDITH, Q.C., M.P.

Leader of the Opposition in the Legislature of Ontario,
—now Chief Justice of the Province.

other members of the Government for the same object. It may be readily imagined that such a wide and far reaching inquiry as was thus asked for in the dying days of a prolonged session was almost too much for the weary legislators to endure.

Mr. Haggart gave a prompt denial, and stated that the same charges had been made in 1880, when a Royal Commission was appointed to inquire into all matters connected with the C. P. R. In the evidence given before that body he had sworn positively that no such sums had ever been paid to him, or that he had any personal interest whatever in any contract with that railway. Mr. Peter McLaren, in whose name his stock was said to have been kept, had made at the time a similar declaration under oath, and they were both ready to repeat it. Sir John Thompson pointed out that Mr. Lister had so worded his charge in requesting a committee of investigation, that no responsibility would lie upon his shoulders in the event of his being unable to prove the statements made. He added that the Independence of Parliament Act could not be considered as infringed by a matter which had occurred during the lifetime of a Parliament long since superseded, and went on to claim that the whole thing was a mere scheme to fish up a little mud from the bottom of some old political stream: "Here is an accusation laid as the basis for an investigation as to things which occurred twelve years ago, against a Government, only one member of which sits in the House, and against that member there is not the slightest insinuation in this case. Under these circumstances, let us consider whether there must not in reason be some limit to the extent to which we are to go back."

The motion was rejected by the usual party vote, and two days later Mr. Haggart laid on the table a statutory declaration by Mr. Peter McLaren, in which he swore to the truthfulness of the Postmaster-General's statements, and explicitly denied the charge of corrupt payments to the Government. A little before this the Cochrane scandal, in which the member for East Northumberland was accused of having trafficed in Government offices in his constituency, had been investigated, and the majority report had admitted improper transactions, but cleared Mr. Cochrane personally. The inquiry into the Printing Bureau management resulted in the bitterest and most disgraceful wrangles of the whole session. It is almost impossible to discern the rights of this matter amid the partisan storms by which Mr. Chapleau's connection with it was surrounded, and in any case it would be useless to attempt it here. The brilliant French-Canadian orator has done his country splendid service in his day, despite any looseness of business management which can be charged against him in this connection, and he may do it still more.

But all these complicated questions, violent discussions, prolonged committee investigations, and the persistent abuse in Parliament, and in a portion of the press, made this session the most arduous since Confederation for the Leader of the House.

The air became somewhat purified after the adjournment, and much good was expected from a bill introduced by the Premier in the Senate, and carried through both Houses early in September, providing for the suppression of frauds against the Government. So also from the Royal Commission appointed to enquire into the working of the Civil Service. It must, however, have been an immense relief to Sir John Thompson when the murky cloud which had for so many hot and weary months rested like a pall over Parliament Hill was at last removed, and he was able to give to his department and to public business, time which had so long been given to debate upon most disagreeable subjects, and to party tactics which he never liked.

CHAPTER XII.

Redistribution and the Bye-Elections.

To the people of a young country the census is always an interesting consideration. To the politicians in Canada, where a redistribution of the seats takes place every decade, should the movements of population warrant a change, it is of special interest. Much was expected from the census of 1891, and the disappointment which followed was natural, though not altogether justifiable. A few pessimists expected it to show a steady drain of population from the country, a decrease in the total number of its inhabitants, a lack of progress in manufactures, and in all the elements of prosperity. But optimists, on the other hand, hoped it would show a population of six millions at least, and a tremendous industrial development.

An army of 4,300 enumerators and commissioners had been employed under the command of Mr. George Johnson, Dominion Statistician, and it was announced that the regulations respecting absentees, and the rules to prevent duplication, would be unusually strict. In England it may be said that 40,000 enumerators, and in British India nearly one million men, were employed in the same work. The difficulties encountered in taking a Canadian census are by no means small. The immense area of the Dominion had to be traversed by every conceivable method of locomotion. A steamer amid the islands and indents of the Pacific coast; pack-horses in the Rocky Mountain valleys; dog-trains on the plains of the Saskatchewan; canoes and portages in the great lake and river district to the north of

Lake Superior; buck-boards and boats on the prairies and in the rivers of Manitoba: a schooner in the Gulf of St. Lawrence; slow and toilsome pedestrianism in Algoma and other districts. Three months, however, sufficed to give to the public the full returns.

A summary of the results showed that the population of Canada had increased from 3,686,000 in 1871, to 4,324,000 in 1881, and thence to 4,829,000 in 1891. The increase, therefore, during the preceding decade had only amounted to 504,000, and there was naturally a good deal of disappointment and dissatisfaction expressed. A section of the press was, if such a phrase may be used, almost jubilant in its sorrow. The census seemed to reveal a complete failure in the vigorous efforts which had been made to promote immigration and to keep the people in the country, while by implication it was made to prove the absolute failure of the National Policy of protection. But second thoughts are proverbially best, and it was not long before people saw that there were two sides to the question.

Upon reflection, it seemed clear that population, following the universal trend of modern society, had during the past decade drifted into the cities. In protectionist Canada as in free trade Britain, people had flocked to the centres of population and industry. The larger cities of the United States had attracted many in spite of the inferiority which most Canadians believe to exist in American institutions, customs and modes of life. The introduction of agricultural machinery had further helped to deplete rural populations by doing away with much of the hired help formerly required, whilst the decrease in the price of cereals had in all countries enhanced the tendency to prefer city work to farm life. Just as in many portions of the United States population had decreased through the movement to other parts of the country, so in Canada many sections had been influenced by the proximity of the United States, and it must be added, by the praise of everything American, which has been, as Sir John Thompson more than once said, so often heard from the lips of certain Canadian politicians.

To Mr. Abbott's Government the local increases and decreases of population brought the unpleasant embarassment of a necessary redistribution of seats, and upon Sir John Thompson as leader of the House of Commons during the busy Session of 1892, fell the burden of the work in connection with this difficult and never popular matter. He was compelled to alter the representation in some places by cutting off a member altogether, in others by adding one, and again in others, by a re-organization of the electoral limits. Abuse in such a case was inevitable, and he had to bear the brunt of it.

The Redistribution Bill was presented to the House by the Minister of Justice, on April 24th. He commenced his speech in a jocular vein, which was rather unusual with him, and chaffed the Opposition upon their expectations of a pronounced gerrymander, a prolonged debate and a lengthened Session. "I am happy to know that the time of departure is very remote, indeed, and that there will be ample opportunity to consider all the merits of this Bill, and there are nothing but merits in it, I can assure my hon. friends opposite." Sir John then pointed out the necessity, under the terms of the British North American Act, for the redistribution of seats, and gave the figures of the census returns as follows:

	1881.	1891.
Ontario	1,926,922	2,120,989
Quebec	1,359,027	1,488,586
Nova Scotia	440,572	450,523
New Brunswick,	321,233	321,294
Prince Edward Island	108,891	109,088
Manitoba	62,260	154,442
British Columbia	49,459	92,767
North-West Territories	25,515	67,554

Under the provisions of the Act, therefore, the representation would have to be changed in several Provinces as regarded numbers, and in all of them, so far as the arrangement of constituencies was concerned. Ontario was entitled to retain its 92 members, and Quebec its 65 representatives. Nova-Scotia, with 21 members, was now only entitled to 20; New Brunswick, with 16 representatives, had to be cut down to 14; Prince Edward Island, which had six, could only retain five; Manitoba having five, was entitled to seven; the Territories would retain their four members, as would British Columbia, its old number of six representatives. But all over the Dominion population had fluctuated; many cities had increased enormously in size; and some rural districts had become entitled to increased representation, whilst others had decreased greatly in population.

Beginning with Prince Edward Island, Sir John Thompson described the various changes, in a detail which it would be wearisome to repeat. Following the township lines in the Island, five constituencies had been formed averaging 22,000 of a population each. The only change in New Brunswick was the taking away of one member from the combined City and County of St. John's, which had formerly possessed two; and the joining of the Counties of Sunbury and Queen's, which together, only boasted a population of 17,000 souls. In Nova-Scotia, the two Counties of Queen's and Shelburne—one with 10,610 people, the other with 14,954—were united, leaving the Provincial unit of population to a constituency, about 22,000. A number of changes were made necessary in Quebec, by the growth of Montreal. The Government's proposal was that Montreal and its suburb, Hochelaga, with a united population of 263,000, should have seven instead of four members; that a portion of the old constituencies of Montreal and

Hon. N. Clarke Wallace, M.P.

Comptroller of Customs.

Hochelaga should be added to the Counties of Jacques Cartier and Laval, so as not to increase the metropolitan representation unduly; and that the County of Ottawa should have the two members to which it was entitled. In order to make up the new constituencies, those of Three Rivers and St. Maurice were joined, and other changes were made in the thirteen counties lying north of the boundary of the Province of Quebec to the County of Nicolet. They were only entitled to nine members, but were allowed to retain ten. Napierville and Vercheres were absorbed in surrounding counties, and St. John's and Iberville were united.

Then the Minister turned to Ontario and remarked that very few changes were proposed. Dr. Landerkin here interposed one of those interruptions for which he is so well known in the House, by saying, "They are not needed." Sir John faced his opponent, and amid cheers and laughter rejoined: "I think there are some changes needed, at least in the representation of constituencies in this House. But we have decided to leave that in the hands of the electors who are doing it so admirably." As the Conservatives were just then sweeping the bye-elections, this little hit told. It was absolutely necessary to give Toronto another representative—in the city itself there was a strong demand for more than one—and to also give an additional member to the rapidly growing population of Algoma. This was done by giving West Toronto two members and creating the constituency of Nipissing. The two new seats thus given to portions of Ontario, were obtained by a re-construction of the constituencies in the Niagara Peninsula.

It so happened that there were in that district six seats contiguous to one another, and each smaller in population than the ordinary unit of representation—about 22,000. Monck had in round numbers 15,000 people;

Haldimand, 16,000; North Brant, 17,000; and South Norfolk, 17,000. The Government, therefore, proposed to wipe out North Wentworth, which returned a Liberal to Parliament, and Monck, which was represented by a Conservative. The four constituencies remaining were re-constructed so as to give an average of 23,000 people to each one of the four representatives, instead of the previous average of 16,000 to each of the six representatives. Other changes were made throughout the Province, but none of very great importance. Sir John Thompson claimed that those undertaken were all in the direction of equalization, and along lines which would make as little interference necessary with existing electoral divisions as was compatible with justice: "The re-construction which will take place is confined to Toronto, and in the group of districts about Lake Ontario, and every effort has been made to interfere as little as possible with the representation as it exists at present on geographical lines."

In Manitoba, Lisgar was changed by name into Selkirk, as being more historically appropriate; the City of Brandon was made a constituency; and Marquette was divided, one-half being made into an electoral division under the appropriate name of Macdonald, after "the statesman who devoted so much of his life to the development of the territories out of which the Province of Manitoba has been created." Some changes were made in British Columbia, by which the New Westminster district was enlarged geographically and given two representatives, while Yale and Cariboo were joined to Kootenay and allowed one member. Vancouver kept its one representative, and Victoria retained the two it had previously possessed. Such is a bare outline of the measure. To either defend or criticise it is useless. It seems indeed to be the fate of all redistribution measures in Canada to possess such an environment of partisanship as to make fair discussion almost an impossibility. Only combined action by the leaders of both parties would produce a generally acceptable arrangement, and that would involve an abrogation of ministerial responsibility which puts it out of the question.

Sir John Thompson's proposals resulted in a long and acrimonious conflict. The Conservative politicians and press lauded them as fair, moderate and equitable; the Liberals did the reverse. The *Montreal Herald*, for instance, denounced the bill as "a plan for deliberately stifling the voice of the people," while the *Toronto Mail* published perhaps the severest criticism of the Minister of Justice which had yet appeared in Canada. And according to the conclusions of the same paper, the Conservative party under the redistribution measure stood to gain eleven seats, and to lose only four at the next general election. In the House the discussion was prolonged in speech, and minute in debate. Every one had something to say, and usually from entirely different standpoints.

The address of Sir John Thompson upon the second reading of the bill, was a closely reasoned and fair defence of the Government's position and of his own measure. Rising from his place on June 2nd, after an energetic speech from Mr. L. H. Davies, he first pointed out that the bill had been introduced by the Government in the discharge of a compulsory, though unpleasant duty. "It was not introduced, nor was it proposed with any design to secure party advantage, and that I affirm in the most distinct manner. If the Government had designed to follow even the principle of re-adjustment by population, they would have made, with regard to each of the Provinces, a measure in which the application of the principle would have been far wider than it was in the present bill, and would have secured to them eminent party advantages."

He then spoke of Mr. Laurier's amendment proposing a reference of the whole matter to a conference or committee composed of both political parties, and denounced it as unprecedented and impracticable: "I have never heard in all the history of Parliamentary procedure, of a resolution being brought forward, the object of which was to subject legislation to the two political parties." The example which was alleged to have been set by the English Parliament a few years before was one of many cases in British history arising out of a deadlock between the Lords and the Commons. And the arrangement finally made in that case was not concerning the details of the bill, but upon the point whether it should form part of the general franchise measure or not. The Minister of Justice went on to say that the principle which it was claimed should guide such a conference, was that the equilibrium existing between the two political parties in the country at the present time must be maintained: "No more false principle could be allied with a measure of redistribution. What political party in this country has a vested right in the equilibrium of parties?"

He stated that not one of the papers criticising the measure had shown a careful study of the bill, and then placed his views upon the general question very clearly before the House: "He should say that whenever a redistribution bill was brought forward and discussed, the first object members should set before them should be to interfere as little as possible with existing lines, and not to interfere with them excepting some serious occasion called for it; but that when the serious occasion occurred the measure should be carried out without regard to the fate of either political party, or to the equilibrium of parties."

Later on in the Session, the Redistribution Bill with a few slight alterations, passed the House, and became the basis for the next ensuing general election. Meantime, on the sixth of April, Mr. J. D. Edgar had made voluminous and very serious charges against Sir Adolphe Caron, the Postmaster-General. They extended in their application over a period of at least ten years, and stated, in brief, that the Minister had aided in his capacity as a member of the Commons, and of the Government, in obtaining subsides of fully a million dollars for the Quebec and Lake St. John Railway. It was further alleged that Sir Adolphe during these years (1882-1891) had been a member of the Railway Company in question, and had received large sums of money from these subsidies, which he corruptly used in helping the election of himself, and certain supporters in different Quebec constituencies.

Mr. Edgar wished all these matters referred to the Committee on Privileges and Elections. Sir John Thompson in his reply pointed out what experience had proved during the preceding Session, and what he had himself consistently maintained even during that stormy period, that Parliament was not a suitable court to try cases of this nature. He concluded a speech of some length by refusing, on behalf of the Government, to consider the allegations in the way they were put forward by Mr. Edgar, stating very clearly the utter impossibility of the House consenting to a motion which involved the investigation of elections in some twenty-two Quebec constituencies during several general elections. Every opportunity would be given to a trial of the personal charges, but a Parliamentary consideration of the broad issues presented in a certain section of the charges, would be as unconstitutional, as it was impracticable from the standpoint of propriety and the limitations of time.

On the 4th of May, Mr. Mackenzie Bowell presented an elaborate motion which included every allegation made by Mr. Edgar, excepting the paragraphs involving an investigation into past elections, and asked for their reference to a Royal Commission of two Judges. This was, of course, granted, and, eventually, the Hon. A. B. Routhier and the Hon. M. M. Tait, of the Quebec Bench, were appointed with full powers to try the charges referred to them by Parliament. Then came the surprising refusal of Mr. Edgar to make his statements good, or to appear before the Commission on the ground that a portion of the original allegations had been eliminated. When the affair came before the House again, Sir John Thompson dealt at length with this question, and pointed out that the Tarte charges did not form a precedent, as they referred to matters connected with the improper expenditure of public moneys by the officers of a department. On the other hand, Clause 10 of Mr. Edgar's charges which had been eliminated was "an attempt to try some sixty or seventy elections," some of them already tried or closed in the Courts. "During all the practice of more than two hundred years, no such statement as that which has been eliminated from these charges has ever been preferred to the British House of Commons or any attempt made in that House to appoint a Commission on such a charge."

And then the speaker gave Mr. Mills a neat little bit of a lecture: "If you go back to the ages to which the member for Bothwell has gone, you can find precedents for anything." But they were "ages to which no man claiming the name of Liberal should be otherwise than ashamed to go back, either for Parliamentary precedents or for the maxims of a political creed." He concluded with a denunciation of Mr. Edgar's attitude, which will probably be long remembered for its vigour and strength: "Did anyone ever hear of a man occupying so contemptible a position in public life as to make nine or ten of the gravest accusations

HON. J. C. PATTERSON, M.P.

Minister of Militia and Defence.

which can be made against a public man, depriving him of honour, of character, of title, of a seat in this House and a seat in the Government, and when it is proposed that he should go before a judge and give his evidence, shrinking behind the privilege of a member of this House and saying we had no right to call him there. If there is an atom of manhood in his composition, body or soul, he will meet the man he has accused before any tribunal where British law will be administered and fair play will prevail."

Eventually, the Royal Commission reported such evidence as they had to the House without comment, and about four months afterwards—on March 22nd, 1893—Mr. Edgar returned to the charge with a motion declaring that the evidence taken had established facts which should have prevented Sir Adolphe Caron from again becoming an adviser of the Crown, and which rendered his incumbency of any office highly improper. Sir Adolphe defended himself vigourously, and after some debate the matter was disposed of by the resolution being defeated—69 to 119.

Another matter which claimed much attention during this Session, both in press and in Parliament, was the London election case. The charge in brief was that Judge Elliott, the revising barrister, had used his position to favour the Hon. Mr. Carling and to elect him in the teeth of an adverse majority. No one who knew the strict honour and honesty of Mr. (now Sir John) Carling would ever believe him guilty of benefiting by an act which he understood to have been fraudulent. But at the same time the whole question was so technical and so entirely a matter of law, that the Liberals were fully justified in pushing its investigation in the proper quarters and in the proper way. When the subject came up in the House, however, as it did on several occasions, Sir John Thompson found it necessary to protest against the aspersions which were cast upon Judge Elliott from a partisan standpoint, and to object—in reply to a speech made by Mr. Mulock when presenting some petitions from London—to the House of Commons entering into any enquiry of the kind in reference to County Court Judges.

He pointed out that assaults upon personal character; political attacks such as that of Mr Mulock; or the reading of anonymous newspaper articles, were not the way in which to try a judge or to claim the right to do so. "The progress of this debate illustrates the wisdom of the statute passed ten years ago, to provide another way of trying County Court Judges." The Minister of Justice deprecated the whole discussion, and especially in view of Mr. Lister's statement that there was no intention of impeachment or of making a formal request for the Judge's removal. Eventually, the matter was allowed to rest, and amidst strong protests from the Liberals Mr. Carling retained his seat.

While these matters had been interesting Parliament and a section of the public, the people at large had been stirred up by a series of bye-elections which constituted a complete sweep for the Conservatives. There were many reasons for this success. During the elections of 1891, Mr. Blake had announced his retirement from political life, and the day after the election a lengthy document addressed by him to the electors of West Durham, but really to the people of Canada, was published. In it he vigorously denounced the Government's policy of protection, as might have been expected, and also—as was not expected—repudiated the Opposition policy of Unrestricted Reciprocity. He described the latter as involving direct taxation; a uniform tariff with the United States; discrimination against Great Britain; and every probability of ultimate annexation. Such a manifesto, proving as it practically did, the assertions made by Sir John Macdonald and the Conservative party as to the meaning of the Opposition platform, was really a staggering blow to the popularity of the Liberals, although it did not immediately effect their position in the House or still the buoyant hopes which soon arose of benefiting by the scandals of the succeeding Session.

But even this latter solace was taken away by the revelations which came from Quebec. The corruption of the Mercier Ministry was the Conservative opportunity. It soon became a case of fighting dirt with dirt, and the very violence of the Liberal charges at Ottawa brought about a corresponding reaction in public opinion, when it was claimed that the very men who were posing as political purists at the national capital had received and used during the late elections large sums of money from the fund provided by Quebec boodlers. And it is safe to say that whether people believed or not the charges that Mr. Laurier had benefited in a political sense by these expenditures, they did very greatly dislike his refusal to repudiate Mr. Mercier in the Provincial elections which ensued, as well as the practical support which he gave to the culprits in urging the people to vote against the Conservative candidates, and "against Lieut.-Governor Angers," because of the latter's dismissal of his recreant ministry.

These two causes contributed greatly to the marvellous success of the Conservative party in the elections, which resulted from the unseating of numerous candidates in the Courts. And added to them was the wave of sentiment created by the death of Sir John A. Macdonald, and the accompanying manifestations of popular affection and sorrow. The first of the bye-elections had not, however, been very favourable. Richelieu went Liberal, and in a speech delivered at Halifax shortly afterwards, on the 16th of January, Sir John Thompson explained the result as due to the McGreevy influence, which in connection with the Richelieu and Ontario Navigation Company controlled some 300 votes in the constituency. "We found," said he, "as the result of that election, what we might have told you before, that you cannot prosecute a man in the Courts of Justice, and at the same time ask him to walk arm in arm to the polls with you. . . . My friends of the Opposition, we can afford to make you a present of Richelieu."

On February 2nd, however, the victories commenced with Soulanges—which came back into the Conservative column—and was followed rapidly by the gain of Prince Edward County, the capture of Lennox, the carrying of East Elgin by 494 of a majority, the winning of South Ontario and East Hastings, the really remarkable victory of the Hon. J. C. Patterson in West Huron, the gain of East Simcoe, the election of Mr. Carling in London, and the capture of Two Mountains in Quebec. Such was the partial record of a month, followed by the unexpected capture of South Perth, which for eighteen years had been Liberal without a break; the change in Monck from a minority of 260 to a majority of 323; the victory in West Northumberland after a keen and bitter contest; and the winning of East York after its vacation by the lamented death of the old-time and much respected Liberal leader, the Hon. Alexander Mackenzie. Many other seats were won in different parts of the country, and the Government of the Hon. Mr. Abbott found that instead of a fluctuating Parliamentary majority of about twenty, it possessed one of between sixty and seventy. And on the Queen's Birthday of this year, the Premier who had sacrificed so much of ease and comfort and health to the cause of his party and the country, was created a K. C. M. G., at the same time that Mr. Mowat, the distinguished Liberal Premier of Ontario, received a similar and deserved honour.

CHAPTER XIII.

SIR JOHN THOMPSON BECOMES PREMIER.

For some time previous to the retirement of Sir John Abbott it had become clear that he could not remain at the head of the Government very much longer. The Minister of Justice was during this period the practical chief of the Administration, as he had been the real leader of the Conservative party since the death of Sir John Macdonald. And this can be said without in any way reflecting upon the great services undoubtedly rendered by Sir J. J. C. Abbott in a time of trial and supreme party difficulty. But Sir John Thompson was leader of the House of Commons and his forceful character had so impressed itself upon the country while he held that position, and events had so clearly combined to make him the central figure in the politics of the hour, that it was not at all surprising to find him accepted by the public as the next Premier, long before the Governor-General had sent for him to form a ministry.

The logic of circumstances is sometimes irresistible, and the rise of a strong man in politics, as in most other matters, is occasionally aided by the absence of qualifications which to many people may have appeared absolutely essential. Though gifted with rare ability Sir John Thompson possessed one defect which seemed almost fatal to his success as a party leader. In ordinary cases a man who aspires to control a democratic electorate and a complex political machine, must possess the capacity of creating enthusiasm amongst his party followers and of stirring up a sentiment of warm personal allegiance. This the incoming Premier did not even pretend to or attempt. Yet it is probable that his dignified and reserved manner, combined with his reputation for honesty, kept at a distance the corrupt elements which instinctively seek the political centre here as in other countries, and helped his party through the critical scandal session and other unpleasant occasions, as no qualities of geniality, and mere personal graces of manner could have possibly done.

Up to his time it is also very questionable whether a Roman Catholic could have maintained himself in the Premiership of Canada. Before Confederation it had been possible, but under very different circumstances as regards population and balance of religious power. And the peculiar fortune which had compelled him to deal with such important issues in connection with race and creed, had apparently augmented this difficulty. But in reality it all tended to bring into prominence a question which the nation —if it were to be a nation—could only answer in one way. And that answer was greatly facilitated by the very strength of Sir John's convictions and the pronounced nature of his stand upon the subjects with which he had had to deal. For Parliament, the party, or the press, to refuse under such c'rcumstances to recognize him freely, fully, and honestly, as the heir to a position so well earned by ability and service, was to put out of court one-third of the Canadian people; shake the very basis of Canadian national life; and place the country finally under the fatal influence of bitter sectarian strife. It is therefore probable that the absence of the very qualifications which might have seemed most essential to Sir John Thompson's rise in power and position, contributed rather than otherwise to his success in public life. But, of course, only the certainty of his great ability could have enabled him to make these hostile circumstances subserv-

D'Alton McCarthy, Q.C., M.P.

ient to personal use. Otherwise, his cold manner would have involved Parliamentary unpopularity and loss of influence as a leader, while the religious difficulty would have hopelessly prejudiced any inferior man with a strong section of the people.

On November 25th, 1892, the retirement which had been imminent for some time was announced, coupled with the fact that Sir John S. D. Thompson had been summoned by His Excellency the Earl of Aberdeen to form a new Cabinet. A correspondent of one of the papers went forthwith to interview the new Premier and in the course of the evening found him at his house in Lisgar St., Ottawa. He describes a children's party which was being held, with the usual merry-making, home-made taffy and other delights of childhood, and expresses surprise at the fact that Sir John was spending the evening at home "in the most ordinary domestic manner imaginable."

During the next few days the usual rumours filled the air with every variation of political speculation and partisan criticism. The newspaper correspondents were kept busy telegraphing surmises as to the *personnel* of the new Cabinet. In one case it would be Mr. Meredith as Minister of Justice; in another, Mr. Christopher Robinson, Q.C., of Toronto; in another, some suggested arrangement with Mr. D'Alton McCarthy. One paper thought Mr. R. S. White, M.P., was going in; another alleged that Mr. W. B. Ives, M.P., was to take Sir John Abbott's place as the representative of the Eastern Townships and the Protestant minority of Quebec; another believed Mr. D. Girouard, M.P., was coming in, and the Hon. Mr. Chapleau was going out. Finally, the new Government was announced on the 6th of December as follows:

Premier and Minister of Justice....Sir John S. D. Thompson.
Minister of Trade and Commerce....Hon. Mackenzie Bowell.
Postmaster-General................Sir Adolphe Caron, K.C.M.G.
Secretary of State................Hon. John Costigan.
Minister of Finance...............Hon. George E. Foster.
" " Marine and Fisheries...Sir C. H. Tupper, K.C.M.G.
" " Railways and Canals....Hon. John G. Haggart.
" " Public Works.........Hon. J. Alderic Ouimet.
" " Militia and Defence.....Hon. J. C. Patterson.
" " the Interior...........Hon. T. Mayne Daly.
" " Agriculture............Hon. A. R. Angers.
Without Portfolio.................Sir Frank Smith, K.C.M.G.
" " ....Sir John Carling, K.C.M.G.
President of the Council..........Hon. W. B. Ives.

(In the Ministry but not in the Cabinet.)

Solicitor-General.................Hon. J. J. Curran, Q.C.
Comptroller of Customs............Hon. N. Clarke Wallace.
Comptroller of Inland Revenue.....Hon. J. F. Wood, Q.C.

There were a number of important changes in connection with the new Government. The proposed re-construction of the Department of Customs, the establishment of a Ministry of Trade and Commerce, and the appointment of a Solicitor-General to relieve the Minister of Justice of some of his too onerous duties, now came into effect. No better selection for head of a department dealing with the trade of the country could have been made than that of Mr. Mackenzie Bowell. His long control of the Customs and his interest in trade questions pointed him out as specially adapted for the post. The elevation of Mr. Curran and Mr. Wood was the reward of long party service which no one could dispute, and gave them positions which they were eminently fitted to fill. The appointment of Mr. Clarke Wallace was a stroke of political wisdom on the part of the new Premier. It not only brought to his side in the Government the recognized head of the Orange order in the Dominion, but it placed in control of the Customs a business man whose administration has since been both able and popular.

Mr. T. M. Daly, the genial member for Selkirk, Manitoba, had succeeded Mr. Dewdney as Minister of the Interior a month before Sir John Abbott's resignation, and he was confirmed in his place. Mr. W. B. Ives, M.P. for Sherbrooke, was a politician of long standing and bore the reputation of being a clear-headed and eminently successful business man. The retirement of the Hon. Mr. Angers from the Lieut.-Governorship of Quebec made room for the appointment of Mr. Chapleau to that position, and for the entry into national politics of one of the most interesting and honourable men whom Quebec has produced. Mr. Angers united culture and honour in public life with the fullest courage of his convictions, as he had shown in dealing with Mr. Mercier.

The brilliant qualities of the Hon. Charles H. Tupper and his honest, straightforward administration of the Department of Marine and Fisheries pointed to his remaining in that position, while the financial skill of Mr. Foster was retained in the Department whose dry details and principles of management he had enlivened with such genuine eloquence. Circumstances caused the retirement of Mr. Carling from a post to which he had devoted much time and patient labour, but if he was no longer Minister of Agriculture, he had shortly afterwards the honour of receiving Knighthood from Her Majesty the Queen. So, with Sir Frank Smith, whose business shrewdness and experience made his advice invaluable to any Cabinet. Sir Adolphe Caron had not long before left the Department of Militia and Defence, in which he had done such really strenuous service during the rebellion, and he once more accepted the Postmaster-Generalship.

Such was the composition of the Government which

Sir John Thompson was now to lead amid the shoals and rocks which are always strewn so plentifully before the ship of state. His accession to nominal, as well as real, power was well received throughout the country. The French-Canadian Conservative press was a unit in praise of the man and his record, his ability and his services. The *Ottawa Citizen* spoke of him as "a statesman of the weightiest calibre, deep in his knowledge of human nature and human affairs, of extensive reading and accurate and varied information, an orator and a tactician above all." It described him as one in whom the country had full faith. The *Toronto Empire* declared that "in every duty to which the necessity of the hour has summoned him, Sir John Thompson has been a conspicuous success. He has been a brilliant Minister. He is the absolute master of the House of Commons." The *Toronto Globe* announced that the man who by "pre-eminence of ability commands the Premiership," had at last got it, while the *Montreal Herald* with all its strong Liberal prejudices declared that "He has rendered the Conservative party more valuable service since Sir John Macdonald's death than perhaps any other living man could have done.'

The Maritime Provinces were enthusiastic in expressing pride at the success of the leader from Nova-Scotia, and the press was almost united in praise of his personal qualities and admitted abilities. But the unpleasant religious issue refused to be entirely suppressed, and the opinion of militant Protestantism was voiced by the *Toronto Mail* of a short time before his accession to power, and by the *Montreal Witness* of the day after. The former declared it "difficult to believe that the political managers of the Orange order will be able to induce the order for the sake of spoils to trail the effigy of William III. behind a political confederate of the order of Father Petre." The latter announced that "Sir John Thompson, nominee of the Archbishop of Halifax and disciple of the Jesuits, has become by the people's permission, absolute ruler of Canada." It seemed useless to argue with this sort of spirit. It was pointed out that a Catholic Premier would be apt to hold the scales of justice very rigidly in connection with those of his own religion so as to prove his entire freedom from bias or bigotry. It was urged that no man in a Canadian Cabinet, however strong might be his influence, could in these times of suspicion either counsel or practice an injustice towards any race or creed.

But it was, of course, little use placing such considerations—to say nothing of facts regarding a statesman's honourable character and career—before men who did not believe that a Roman Catholic could possess any qualities, good or bad, which were not subservient to the will of his Church. Perhaps in this connection the brightest and best indication of what was really the opinion of a vast majority of Canadians found expression in the *Globe's* further comment upon the new Premier: "With the fact that Sir John Thompson is a Roman Catholic, we have nothing to do. It would be a poor tribute to the liberality and intelligence of the Canadian people if it were laid down that a Roman Catholic may not equally with a Protestant aspire to the highest office within their gift, and any attempt to arouse sectarian prejudice over his appointment will not make for the dignity of Canadian politics or the welfare of the country."

In assuming the responsibilities of his position, however, the new leader was quite well aware of the difficulties before him. Canada will never be an easy country to govern, and whether its popular ruler be a Catholic or an Orangeman, an English-Canadian or a French-Canadian, he will have to encounter questions of the most conflicting interest, and the most embarassing import. And in speaking some time after this with reference to the arduous work which had been done by Sir John A. Macdonald, the new Premier gave a striking description of the labours required in the position which he was then himself filling. Day after day, he declared, was occupied by increasing toil, unwearying watchfulness and painful devotion to details. Night after night when men in all other occupations were enjoying rest in their homes. he would be at his work in the House of Commons, seldom leaving until early morning, and often beginning a long and arduous effort after midnight. This was the work which Sir John Thompson had now taken up in all its fulness, and that he never shrank from any portion of it, is writ large in the history of the next two years.

Meantime the four new Ministers had gone to their constituents, and been re-elected by acclamation; Mr. Wallace, in West York, Mr. Wood in Brockville, Mr. Ives in Sherbrooke, and Mr. Curran in Montreal Centre. The speech delivered by Mr. Clarke Wallace in the village of Weston upon the occasion of his re-election, on December 21st, contained an interesting explanation of his reasons for accepting office, and concerning certain Orange objections to the new Premier. "Sir John Thompson," said the speaker, "is the Premier of Canada to-day, and some people have objected to him, not on account of his lack of ability, for he is one of the ablest men in Canada; not because of his want of integrity, for no man's reputation is more unblemished; not because of his want of devotion to the interests of his country, but, and I will put it plainly, because he is a Roman Catholic. I do not view it in that light. I do not consider that an objection to a man's becoming Premier of Canada." He then went on to say that he was an Orangeman, and was proud of it; that he had been one for almost a quarter of a century; and

Hon. John Costigan M. P.

Secretary of State.

that he had been elevated to the highest position within the gift of the Orangemen, not only of Canada, but of the world.

But nowhere in the principles of the Order could be found word or line which would prevent a Roman Catholic from the free exercise of his national privileges: "Sir John Thompson is a loyal Canadian. He has the same right as any man in this Dominion to accept the office of Premier, and as an Orangeman, I am bound to support every man in the exercise of his constitutional rights. Therefore, I stand here to-day, on my obligations as an Orangeman, consistently, squarely, and I believe properly." This manly speech by Mr. Wallace did much to place the new Premier in a better and truer light before a portion of the community which had been inclined, perhaps naturally, to feel considerably prejudiced against him.

During the Session of 1892, immediately preceding Sir John Thompson's assumption of the Premiership, two events had occurred which are worth being recorded. Reference has already been made to the Redistribution measure, to the Elliott case, and to the Caron charges In his motion regarding the Crown Prosecutions, instituted as a result of the Tarte-McGreevy investigation, and in the speech which accompanied it, the Minister of Justice amply vindicated his own position and that of the Government. His resolution as presented to the House, on April 12th, was to the effect that all statements, admissions, and evidence produced before the Committees of the House, during the Session of 1891, should now be available for use in the Courts; that all clerks, stenographers, and other officials in the service of the House should be eligible as witnesses; and that all books, papers, and other documents which had been previously produced should be once more brought forward, and used in the trials now being instituted. The cases named were those against Connolly and McGreevy for conspiracy; against John R. Arnoldi for malfeasance in office; against Talbot and Larose for conspiracy; and against eleven other persons or firms for the recovery of money. Some opposition was made upon constitutional grounds, but the motion was, of course, carried, and enabled the Government to have everything that was possible done towards the conviction and punishment of those who had defrauded the country.

On the 28th of June an incident happened which delighted the Convervative members of the House beyond measure, astonished the country and the Opposition, and perhaps surprised the Minister of Justice himself. Some days previous to that date, Sir Richard Cartwright had announced that he was going to say something which he wished the Leader of the House to hear, and intimated that he intended to address him personally and particularly. When the time came he made a characteristically strong speech; denouncing the judiciary in connection with the recent election trials; the people for their action in returning so many "corruptionists" to the House in the bye-elections the Government for renewed evidences of boodling; the Minister of Justice for having, as he alleged, purchased a seat in Parliament, by obtaining in 1885 the appointment of Mr. McIsaac, to a County Court Judgeship in Nova-Scotia.

If the speaker had intended to "draw" Sir John Thompson, he was for once successful. To the amazement of its members, the House listened to a speech which was absolutely stormy in its character, bitter in its invective, and personal in its application. It was a perfect whirlwind of denunciation from a man upon whom the Commons was accustomed to look as the embodiment of dignity, of reserve, of suppression in language, and of moderation in tone. But the delight of the Conservatives was correspondingly great at the revelation of this new side to the character of their leader, and in its particular application to an opponent whom many disliked personally as well as politically.

The Minister of Justice commenced by endeavoring to find some reason for Sir Richard's effort in the dying days of the Session. "Perhaps," he said, "in ransacking his speeches of the past, he had found that there was some adjective which he had missed, and he wanted to get it before the House." Then he referred to the address just delivered, as "one of those war, famine, and pestilence speeches which have so often carried the country for the Government." He denounced the Liberal leader who had turned and pointed at him as having shown an intimate knowledge of criminal law, and as having, no doubt, been a successful defender of dangerous criminals. "Sir," said the Minister of Justice, "I decline the hon. gentleman's brief." Sir Richard Cartwright here interrupted with the remark, "You must have the fee first," and brought upon himself the following onslaught: "I have had some experience, both in defending criminals and in prosecuting them; I have never shrunk in my calling, as a member of the Bar, from taking any man's case, no matter how desperate it might be, for the purpose of saying for him what he might lawfully say for himself; but I have sometimes spurned the fee of a blatant scoundrel who denounced everybody else in the world, and was himself the most truculent savage of them all."

This last fierce sentence was long remembered by those who heard it, and is still cherished by the many who have suffered personally from Sir Richard's own powers of invective. Then Sir John Thompson went on to declare that the hon. gentleman would rather any day abuse his country and defame it than eat his breakfast. "I, as a member of the Liberal-Conservative party, owe him such a debt of gratitude that if it shall be necessary to retain his services in the party which he does not lead, and which would not have him for a leader, and which barely tolerates him as a supporter—if it be necessary in order to retain him in that capacity, I, for one, will propose a subsidy to Parliament to keep him there." He defended the Judges of the Dominion; referred to the pride which Sir John Macdonald had always taken in keeping the Judiciary free from the stain of partisan appointments; explained clearly but briefly the reasons for the transfer of Mr. McIsaac from Parliament to the Bench, and his own recommendation of the selection, aside altogether from his personal elevation to a position which he had twice refused before finally accepting it; and vigourously denied the fitness of Sir Richard Cartwright to sit in judgment upon the Judiciary —"He above all others made in the same mould, which, thank God, nature broke when she cast him."

Such, in a nutshell, was the famous speech which Mr. Laurier characterized in reply as a descent from "the language of Parliament to the invective of Billingsgate." No defence of Sir Richard Cartwright is required in this connection. He can always take care of himself. Nor is it necessary to criticise Sir John Thompson for the unique character of this utterance. That it was unusual is sufficient evidence of the tremendous provocation under which it was delivered, and that it was instinct with all the vigourous invective of a strong and generally suppressed nature, simply proves that the Minister of Justice was a man and not a saint, and that while his passions were as a rule thoroughly controlled, yet they could at times burst out and show his opponents that he was well able to answer fire with fire.

CHAPTER XIV.

Manitoba Schools' Legislation.

Manitoba has contributed several difficult problems for national solution. It produced Riel; it developed a hot agitation for Provincial rights; it has given the Dominion a separate school question. Struggles over religious education are, of course, by no means uncommon in Canada, and the one which Sir John Thompson had to deal with has been neither better nor worse than difficulties in the same connection which most other countries have at times had to face. Prior to 1863 Ontario was torn with dissensions concerning its educational system, and the Hon. George Brown led in an agitation against Roman Catholic separate schools, which was as earnest as it was finally ineffectual.

The result of this prolonged conflict was that it became tolerably clear, for good or ill, that it was impossible to harmonize Protestants and Roman Catholics upon the question of education, and that it only remained for the framers of Confederation to effect some compromise by which a Protestant minority in Quebec and a Roman Catholic minority in Ontario should be provided with a secure system of separate schools. This was achieved by giving them in each case a constitutional guarantee of all rights and privileges existing at the time of the Union. They were, necessarily, subject to the jurisdiction, in other respects, of the Provincial Legislatures; and, curiously enough, the concessions made to the supporters of minority schools in each of these two Provinces have been the cause of complaints from the religious majority. The separate schools, therefore, have had nothing to complain of in either Ontario or Quebec.

But in Manitoba it has been very different. The system was not the same as elsewhere; the Province did not enter the Dominion under similar conditions; and the fate of the schools has since become involved in the general and complex question of Provincial rights. Manitoba entered the Union in 1870. The population was about equally divided, between Catholics and Protestants, and as a large influx of French Canadians was expected in the future, it was at that time very generally believed that the balance would be more evenly preserved than has been the case. Under these circumstances the Dominion Parliament had to consider the power which it might be desirable to invest the future majority with, and, following the precedent of the Confederation Act, authority was given to the Legislature over education, subject to the preservation of rights existing at the time of the Union. And it was afterwards claimed that the privilege of an appeal to the Governor-General-in-Council was also allowed in the event of any of those rights being infringed.

It has been since admitted that no law, ordinance or regulation existed at the time of union with respect to education. The point of the future dispute turned, therefore, upon how far the "practice" then prevalent was a privilege and right under the laws. Archbishop Tache, whose evidence in the subsequent Barrett case was accepted as accurate and complete, states that there were a number of effective schools for children, some of them being regulated and controlled by the Roman Catholic Church, and others by various Protestant denominations. The means required for the support of the Catholic schools were supplied partly by fees and partly out of funds contributed to the Church by its members. During this period neither Catholics nor

Wm. Paterson, M.P.

Brantford.

Protestants had interest in or control over any schools but those pertaining to their respective beliefs.

In 1871, shortly after joining the Dominion, a law was passed by the Manitoban Legislature which established a system of denominational education in what were then called the common schools. By this act twelve electoral divisions, comprising in the main a Protestant population, were to be considered as constituting twelve Protestant school districts, under the management of the Protestant section of the Board of Education. Similarly, twelve districts, made up chiefly of a Roman Catholic population, were constituted an equal number of Catholic school districts, and were placed under the control of the Catholic section of the Provincial Education Board. Each school division raised the contribution required in addition to the amount given from the public funds, as might be decided at its annual meeting. And without the special sanction of its section of the Board of Education, only one school could be established in each district.

Changes suited to the differing proportions of the population were made in 1875; but the general principle was still maintained. And the system cannot be said to have worked badly, or to have caused any very serious trouble between the religious divisions of the Province. In 1890, however, a portion of the sectarian wave which had failed to engulf Ontario, overcame the Protestants of the Prairie Province—now in a large majority—and the Premier, Mr. Thomas Greenway, with his able lieutenant, Attorney-General Martin, seized the favourable and popular moment to establish a common school system. By the Act then passed, all school taxes, whether derived from Protestants or Catholics, were appropriated to the support of the new public schools, and the old arrangements constituting two Boards of Education, were of course repealed. Needless to say the

Roman Catholics all over the Dominion were seriously aroused by this action. It seemed to threaten their rights everywhere as well as those they claimed in Manitoba.

Strenuous pressure was brought to bear upon the Dominion Government to disallow the Act as infringing the rights of the minority. A petition dated 6th March, 1891, and signed by the Roman Catholic Archbishops and Bishops of the Dominion, was presented, stating that both the Schools' Act and the one abolishing the dual language system in Manitoba were "contrary to the dearests interests" of a large portion of the loyal subjects of Her Majesty; contrary to "the assurances given during the negotiations" which determined the entry of the Provinces into Confederation; contrary to the terms of the British North America Act, and of the Manitoba Act; contrary to the principles of public good faith. A little later, on April 4th, the French press of Quebeç, published a pastoral letter, issued by Cardinal Taschereau and the hierarchy of the Province, which was read in all the Catholic Churches, and claimed that the legislation in question would "destroy the faith of the Catholic children" of Manitoba, and would "despoil the Church of its sacred rights." It urged once more "the control of the Church over the education of Catholic children in the schools," and called upon all Catholics "to pray and to work for justice."

Following, however, the precedent set in the Jesuits' Estates Case, the Public Schools' bill was allowed by the Government to go into operation, as well as the one abolishing the official use of the French language in the Provincial Legislature. But in the case of the Schools' Act the Government intimated its willingness to pay the expenses involved in testing the constitutionality of the measure. Meantime, appeal had been entered by Mr. J. K. Barrett, of Winnipeg, in the interest of the local Catholic ratepayers and against two city by-laws which imposed a rate of taxation upon Catholics and Protestants alike, for the support of the public schools. He claimed that the old law was still in force, and based his case upon the 22nd section of the Manitoba Act, under which the Province entered the Union, and which states that "Nothing in any such law (Provincial) shall prejudicially affect any right or privilege, with respect to denominational schools, which any class of persons have by law or practice in the Province at the Union."

The Manitoba Government maintained, as against this plea, that a Separate School system was not really in existence prior to the Province entering the Confederation and that consequently the Roman Catholic minority possessed no guarantee whatever. On the 2nd of February, 1891, the Court of Queen's Bench in Manitoba had sustained the validity of the Act, three Judges being favourable and one opposed. Chief Justice Taylor gave an able review of the case, holding in substance that the general educational interests of the people had been dealt with under the disputed legislation and that no rights or privileges possessed before confederation had been affected. Mr. Justice Dubuc—a French-Canadian—dissented and upheld the Catholic contention. The case was at once appealed to the Supreme Court of Canada.

Towards the end of October judgment was given by the latter body declaring the Act *ultra vires,* allowing the appeals, and quashing the city by-laws. Chief Justice Ritchie in presenting the unanimous decision of the Court held that the Act of Union prohibited the abolition of Separate Schools by Local Legislatures. There was, of course, great excitement in Winnipeg over the result, and the Local Government announced its intention of at once appealing the case to the Imperial Privy Council. At the same time a similar test case on behalf of the Church of England in Manitoba, and claiming the right of that body to have separate schools, on the ground that the Episcopalians had possessed parochial schools prior to the Union, was also sent forward on appeal. Late in July, 1892, the decision of the highest British Court of Appeal upheld the Manitoba Courts, declared the legality of the Act of 1890, and reversed the judgment of the Supreme Court of the Dominion. Meantime, in advising the Governor-General-in-Council to allow the Act in due course, Sir John Thompson as Minister of Justice, submitted a Report on March 21st, 1891, which has since been the cause of considerable controversy. He reviewed the admitted legal powers of the Provincial Legislature with regard to education, and the questions of fact, of practice, or of privilege which he declared it would be wiser to leave to the decision of the Courts, than for any Government to attempt to deal with. "If the appeal should be successful these Acts will be annulled by judicial decision and the Roman Catholic minority in Manitoba will receive protection and redress." He then pointed out that if on the other hand the legal controversy should result in the Manitoba Courts being sustained the time would come for consideration by the Government of the various petitions which had been presented on behalf of the ministry, under the terms of a portion of Section 22 of the Manitoba Act which reads: "An appeal shall lie to the Governor-General-in-Council from any act or decision of the Legislature of the Province, or of any provincial authority affecting any right or privilege of the Protestant or Roman Catholic minority of the Queen's subjects, in relation to education." . . . Parliament may make remedial laws for the due execution of the provisions of this section, and of any decision of the Governor-General-in-Council."

It has often been said since, that Sir John Thompson

expected the Schools' Act to be declared *ultra vires*, and did not anticipate that this right of appeal to the Government would ever be asked for or utilized. But his language in concluding this Report does not seem to admit of two meanings: "Those sub-sections contain in effect the provisions which have been made as to all the Provinces, and are obviously those under which the constitution intended that the Government of the Dominion should proceed if it should at any time become necessary that the Federal powers should be resorted to for the protection of a Protestant or Roman Catholic minority against any Act or decision of the Legislature of the Province or of any provincial authority, affecting 'any right or privilege' of any such minority 'in relation to education.'"

Upon the decision of the Judicial Committee of the Privy Council being announced, the agitation for an appeal to the Government and for remedial legislature was renewed, and, of course, drew increased strength from the Report just quoted, although Sir John afterwards claimed, and especially in the House during a debate on April 26th, 1894, that he only referred to the petitions received at that time and took this method of indicating that they could not then be considered while the matter was still pending in the Courts. Strong language was used upon both sides in connection with the possibility of executive interference. The *Toronto Mail* declared on August 2nd that "the tribunal of last resort has pronounced Manitoba free; and free that Province shall be if the English population has any voice in the government of this country." Mr. Mercier, speaking in Montreal on February 23rd following, urged with equal emphasis upon the people of Quebec that "we must put aside all the divisions and hatreds of the past, and join in a fraternal union to place two millions of French Canadians against the oppression of the other Provinces."

Meantime the Dominion Government had appointed a Sub-Committee of Council composed of Sir John Thompson, the Hon. Mr. Bowell and the Hon. Mr. Chapleau, to hear the appeals which had been previously presented, and to listen to Mr. John S. Ewart, Q.C., of Winnipeg, on behalf of the petitioners. On November 27th, Mr. Ewart introduced his case and made a strong deliverance, and on January 6th following, the Sub-Committee reported to the Governor-General-in-Council a synopsis of the whole matter, prepared, in all probability, by Sir John Thompson, and recommending that another hearing should be given in which the Government of Manitoba might be represented. The Provincial Ministry refused, however, to consider the question as in any way open or to send a representative. The Report also indicated certain bases for consideration as to whether the Governor-General-in-Council really had the power to grant remedial legislation under existing circumstances.

These suggestions were subsequently brought before the Supreme Court in the form of six questions, and were dealt with on February 26th, 1894, by a judgment of interpretation, which held that the Roman Catholics had no ground upon which to ask for such legislation. The Court stood three to two upon the question, Mr. Justice Sedgewick not taking part in the case as he had assisted in its preparation while acting as Deputy-Minister of Justice. Curiously enough, Mr. Justice King, who, as Premier, had many years before assisted in abolishing the New Brunswick Separate Schools, supported the Catholic contention, while Mr. Justice Taschereau, a French Canadian, opposed the claims of his own co-religionists. Incidentally, this illustrates the high character of the Canadian Judiciary. From this decision the minority once more appealed to the Judicial Committee of the Privy Council, and it was not until after the death of Sir John Thompson that a decision was finally reached by that distinguished body, declaring that the Dominion Government under the British North America and Manitoba Acts did possess the right to grant the remedial legislation which had been so clearly foreshadowed as constitutionally possible by the Minister of Justice's famous Report in 1891.

Following upon the Government's assumption of judicial functions in connection with the hearing of the petitions, and prior to the submission of the new phase of the question to the Imperial Privy Council, an interesting debate took place in the House of Commons on March 6th, 1893, which was engineered by that master of political fireworks, Mr. J. Israel Tarte. The member for L'Islet had just returned from a campaign in his constituency during which he had vigourously abused the Judiciary of Quebec, and threatened innumerable revelations of Tory and national corruption. He was, therefore, in splendid trim to fight on behalf of the Manitoba minority, or in fact, upon any other question which might injure the Government of the day. His motion expressed "disapproval of the action of the Government in dealing with the Manitoba school question, and in assuming to be possessed of judicial functions conflicting with their duties as constitutional advisers of the Crown."

His speech was, as usual, rather interesting, and introduced, as was also generally the case, a new charge. He declared that in December, 1890, when the general elections were coming on, Mr. Chapleau had been sent as a delegate from the Government to see Archbishop Taché, who was then in Montreal, and that during the interview which took place he made distinct and formal promises as to Conservative policy in the Manitoba Schools' question. The impulsive Frenchman then pointed triumphantly to the report of the Minister of Justice in the month of March following, as being the public pledge resulting from the private promises. Of course, this statement aroused considerable discussion, although Mr. Tarte's tendency to make rash and irresponsible charges at a moment's notice, hardly made it a matter of importance. In a subsequent criticism of the member for L'Islet, Mr. Lariviere, a Conservative member from Manitoba, was decidedly witty. He declared that Mr. Tarte "had belonged to all parties, past and present (and he was going to say, future) in Canada. He had said that he came to the House as a Conservative to make the party pure, and what was the result? Mr. Tarte was the first man to be out of the party."

Sir John Thompson in his reply made a lengthy and elaborate defence of the Government. It cannot be said that he had a sympathetic audience. However wise might be the action of the Ministry in exercising care; in giving every side a fair and full hearing; in having every legal security for its policy in the premises; the delay could hardly be popular with the great body of ministerial supporters from the West or from Ontario. They wanted the question out of the way, as did the Opposition members from the latter province, and disallowance was so against the current of thought and sentiment in Ontario that the principle of full justice to a minority hardly obtained fair play, so far as individual feeling was concerned, though receiving it in practice through the votes and passive support of the members. Upon questions of this nature Mr. McCarthy would have been naturally the leader of his Province, had he not in so many ways estranged Conservative sympathy. And perhaps, in the interest of Canadian unity, it is as well that such was the case.

The Premier claimed that Mr. Tarte and Mr. McCarthy,

Rev. Dr. Carman.

Superintendent of the Methodist Church in Canada.

though as opposite as the poles in their opinions, were in this motion working together against the Government. He referred to the New Brunswick school case and to that of Prince Edward Island, and pointed out that in both cases the Roman Catholic minority had appealed on the ground of its rights being prejudicially affected. Parliament had then laid down the principle that such questions ought not to be settled by disallowance, and this position had been further sustained by the action taken in the Jesuits' Estates question, although the latter dealt with a Protestant minority. In dealing with Mr. Tarte's charge regarding the alleged promise to Archbishop Taché, he "denied that any such promise had been made, or that any Minister, or any other gentleman, or any living person was sent or delegated or authorized by the Government of Canada to go upon any such mission." Archbishop Taché "knew, as the Government knew, the folly of exercising disallowance in such a case."

Replying to the question whether the decision in the New Brunswick case was not sufficient in its general application, without new appeals, Sir John pointed out the obvious fact that the rights of the respective minorities rested on different statutes. Then he continued: "In consequence of the phraseology of the Supreme Court Act, the Government had no other alternative than to submit the case the way it did, but they were far from being influenced by any desire to assail the province. The litigation which went to the Judicial Committee of the Privy Council was from first to last on the subject of the validity of the statutes complained of. The question as to what rights the minority might have in an application by way of appeal to the Governor-General for redress, had nothing to do with the question decided there in the first appeal, and the litigation had nothing to do with it."

He spoke of the ground taken by Mr. Blake in 1890, when calling the attention of the House to these very matters, and claimed that his arguments at that time "applied with powerful force to this particular question; that Sir John Macdonald accepted the resolution submitted by Mr. Blake in the sense in which it was put forward; and that in the following year it was assented to by the whole of Parliament in being embodied in the Supreme Court Act. The exact machinery which the Government had followed in the Manitoba schools' case was that which Mr. Blake had suggested and Parliament had adopted."

A vigourous defence of the right of the Government under the constitution to receive petitions in a judicial, and not a political sense, was made, and the Premier instanced as a case in point the duties assigned by Act of Parliament to the Railway Committee of the Canadian Privy Council. He concluded a strong speech with the expression of a belief that Manitoba as a constitutional province would "obey the dictates of the highest Court of the Empire as to what its constitution was."

Mr. McCarthy on the succeeding day replied to this defence, and soundly denounced the Government for its delay in settling this much vexed question. The decision, one way or the other, was vital. "It was whether the Province of Manitoba, with a population of 150,000, of whom not more than 20,000 were Roman Catholics, was to have imposed upon it against its will, a Separate School system." He declared that three-quarters of the people in Ontario were altogether opposed to that method of education, and thought "nothing more dangerous, nothing more subversive of the principles of our constitution, could be tolerated than that the Cabinet of the Dominion should assume to act in this or any other question, as a judicial body.

Mr. Laurier made an interesting assertion in connection with a new claim from the Manitoban minority to the effect that the limited religious teaching allowed in the public schools of that Province made them, in fact and reality, Protestant, and not national, schools. "If," said he, "this be indeed true; if, under the guise of public schools, the Protestant schools are being continued and Roman Catholic children are being forced to attend these Protestant schools, I say, and let my words be heard by friends and foes over the length and breadth of the land, the strongest case has been made out for interference, and though my life as a public man depended upon it, I would undertake to say on every platform in Ontario and in Manitoba that the Roman Catholics of Manitoba had been put to the most infamous treatment." But the force of this utterance is somewhat modified by the fact that the genial Liberal leader afterwards visited the Prairie Province but refused to make any definite pronouncement upon the question of whether the schools were in any degree Protestant or were not. After three days' debate, the division was taken and Mr. Tarte's resolution was defeated by 120 to 71.

There can be little doubt in an unbiassed mind as to what were Sir John Thompson's private views upon this question. It would naturally be one of sympathy with his co-religionists in the hardships they claimed to have suffered and in the injustice alleged to have been meted out to them, and which had been so vigourously pourtrayed by the hierarchy of his own Church. To the sincere Roman Catholic, religious schools appear to be as vital and important as is free speech to the agitator, liberty of worship to the Protestant, or British connection to the loyalist. Publicly, his policy in this matter indicated the fullest intention to do his duty by the State whichever way the verdict of the Courts might eventually go, but it also pointed very distinctly to the expectation, if not hope, that some measure of remedial legislation would be ultimately found necessary, and thus harmonize duty and inclination. And who can blame an honest Canadian, be he Protestant or Roman Catholic, for desiring such an end to any vexed question? So long as a public man and a statesman puts duty first and personal wishes second, he cannot be fairly criticised for hoping that the two may be eventually combined. Nor can Sir John Thompson be blamed by any honourable man for giving a Canadian religious minority every possible opportunity for obtaining consideration of alleged wrongs and the use of every available judicial privilege.

Looking at the question, therefore, from his standpoint as a public man, it was essentially a legal and constitutional issue; one which ought to be kept from the heated arena of party politics; and one which might well be decided upon a non-partisan basis of toleration and liberality.

CHAPTER XV.

CANADA AND THE UNITED STATES.

Upon no question was the stand taken by Sir John Thompson more clear and distinct, more honourable and popular, than his position regarding Canadian relations with the United States. He was known to hold strong opinions as to American treatment of the Dominion, and concerning the policy for Canada to adopt in return. He despised any attitude of weakness or timidity; he disliked all bluster or attempts at intimidation; he was honestly anxious to be upon the friendliest terms with the great Republic which might be compatible with the protection and development of Canadian interests. But he was firm as a rock in the refusal to discuss any reciprocity which might endanger national industries or give the slightest hostile treatment to British interests.

For many years past the American government has been apparently willing to come to some commercial arrangement with Canada which might give the manufacturers of the United States control of the markets of the Dominion, and at the same time weaken British connection by the congenial process of cutting away the ground from under British trade and diminishing the Imperial sentiment in both Canada and England through a commercial system of discrimination against the products of the Mother-Country. To this end the Commercial Union movement was aided by American influence and, according to party statements, by American money. For this thinly disguised purpose, the fulminations of Mr. Goldwin Smith against Canadian protection were joyfully welcomed by the enthusiastic supporters of American protection. With this in view, resolutions favourable to commercial relations of the closest kind were passed by Congress, while limited reciprocity was absolutely refused by the Government. Now and then, when the success of other methods was recognised for the moment as impossible, threats were freely used against the Canadian Pacific Railway, attacks were made upon the Bonding system, or fiscal coercion was tried such as that embodied in the agricultural schedule of the McKinley bill.

Yet it can be safely said that Canada has more than done its duty towards the United States. It has never abrogated a treaty, never broken an arrangement, never obtained American territory by playing upon the natural weakness of friendly negotiators. It has given much and received little. Many unavailing attempts have been made to obtain a fair measure of reciprocity. Friendly manifestations have been constant from the days when 40,000 Canadians served in the armies of the North, to the time when all Canada joined the Republic in mourning for the murdered Garfield. The partial abrogation of the Washington Treaty, the Behring Sea seizures, the Atlantic Fisheries' dispute, and the Washington negotiations of 1892, occupy the other side of the shield.

And not the least of the services which Sir John Thompson rendered the Dominion was his share in the attempt made in 1892 to obtain a reciprocal trade arrangement with the United States. That last prolonged effort indicated in its results as clearly as language could express, the impossibility of obtaining a treaty such as Canadians could honourably accept. It proved to a demonstration that the American Government would consider no arrangement which did not discriminate against British goods, place a uniform tariff around the continent, and establish some system of international receipts and excise, controlled by a Joint Commission. This statement, of course, applies only to a Republican policy. The Democratic party will make no reciprocity treaties with any country, believing that they do more harm than good, though no doubt it would negotiate upon the basis of annexation.

On the 31st of March, 1891, and some three weeks after the general elections, Sir Charles Tupper proceeded to Washington in order to confer with the British ambassador, Sir Julian Pauncefote, concerning the proposed reciprocity negotiations. On April 2nd he visited Mr. Blaine, the Secretary of State, and explained the desire of the Canadian Government to obtain some immediate basis for discussion. Mr. Blaine apparently received the proposition with favour, and Sir Charles, returning to Ottawa, obtained the cooperation of the Hon. Mr. Foster, Minister of Finance, and Sir John Thompson, Minister of Justice, who were appointed to act with him at the informal interview which had been arranged, and during the further negotiations which were expected.

The three delegates arrived in Washington on the morning of the 6th inst. only to find that they had missed a telegram from Mr. Blaine, asking for the postponement of the meeting on the ground that the President desired to be present during the discussion—which his engagements just then did not permit. However, accompanied by the British Ambassador, they waited upon the Secretary of State and were cordially received. The conference was, of course, very brief and the visitors left for home the same day. The *New York Herald* very pleasantly announced that their return was "neither desired nor expected," and that "apart from his own reasons for not letting down the McKinley barriers raised against the introduction of Canadian live stock, and farm and dairy produce, the President had excellent grounds for believing that the Senate would not ratify any reciprocity made with Canada." On April 9th following it was stated that the negotiations would be renewed on October 12th. At that date another postponement took place on account of Mr. Blaine's ill-health, but finally the conference was held early in 1892, commencing on the 10th of February.

The discussion which then took place between Sir John Thompson, the Hon. Mackenzie Bowell and the Hon. G. E. Foster, representing Canada; Sir Julian Pauncefote representing Great Britain; and the Hon. James G. Blaine and General J. W. Foster representing the United States, was exceedingly important. An understanding was come to regarding the Alaskan boundary, the adoption of joint regulations for the protection of the fisheries, for reciprocity in wrecking, salvage, and towing in conterminous waters, and for the marking of the boundary-line on Passamaquaddy Bay. But it was upon the question of trade relations that the hitch occurred and it was in the same connection that the results were so vital. The official minutes of the meetings, from which a few extracts must be given, are signed by the three Canadian Ministers, and then in addition there is each day appended the statement "I concur in the above minute of proceedings," signed by Sir Julian Pauncefote. Strong partisans might possibly dispute a statement supported only by the signatures of members of the Canadian Government, but no one with any knowledge of the honourable traditions and practices of British diplomacy, and of the high rank and reputation held in it by the British Ambassador at Washington, can for a moment doubt the accuracy of minutes endorsed by him as correct.

During the conference which took place on the first day, Mr. Blaine pointed out that no treaty or arrangement

Hon. John Christian Schultz.

Lieut.-Governor of Manitoba

could be made which did not involve the admission of American manufactures into Canada. Mr. Foster asked in return "whether the United States would insist on differential treatment." Mr. Blaine replied "that the treaty would be of no benefit to the United States if the like treatment were given to other countries, especially as Great Britain was in active competition with the United States in almost every line of manufacture." On the following day "Mr. Foster frankly and fully explained the difficulties which prevented Canada from giving any discrimination to America over British goods or of arranging for the admission of all products free from one country to the other. Revenue considerations, national sentiment, and trade reasons all intervened. Mr. Blaine was equally frank in his reply and declared that "he could easily understand why Canada was reluctant to enter into a treaty of unlimited reciprocity, but that it was clear to his mind that no other arrangement would suit the United States, and that it must be accompanied by discrimination in favor of the United States, especially against Great Britain, who was their great competitor, and that it must likewise be accompanied by the adoption of a uniform tariff for the United States and Canada equal to that of the United States."

Such was the announcement which might have been expected to set at rest all question concerning reciprocal trade relations between Canada and the United States. But it was very far from doing so. The Budget debate in Parliament during the succeeding Session bore ample evidence of the fact that the Opposition proposed to adopt in this connection, and in its fullest meaning, the words "No surrender." After a number of speeches, protesting, urging, explaining and denying, Sir John Thompson took the floor on March 29th, and gave a very complete history of the origin, procedure, and results of the negotiations. Their commencement had been very simple. In connection with Newfoundland's attempt to make a separate treaty in 1890: "We requested Her Majesty's Government to ask that we should be included in any negotiation that took place between the United States and Her Majesty's Government in regard to the relations of Newfoundland with the United States, and the answer of Mr. Blaine was that, while he was not willing that Canada should be included in negotiations in regard to the Treaty with Newfoundland, he expressed a strong desire to conclude a wide reciprocity treaty with Canada."

Then followed the basis for negotiations cabled to London, which also furnished the reason for the dissolution of Parliament in February, 1891. Meantime Lord Knutsford, Colonial Secretary, had wired the Governor-General to the following effect on January 2nd of that year:

"Mr. Blaine replied that to endeavour to obtain the appointment of the formal commission to arrive at the reciprocity treaty would be useless, but that the United States Government was willing to discuss the question in private with Sir Julian Pauncefote, and one or more delegates from Canada, and to consider every subject as to which there was hope of agreement, on the ground of mutual interests; *if not, and to run so grave a step until* by private discussion he has satisfied himself that good ground existed for expecting an agreement by means of a commission. He added that he would be prepared to enter into private negotiations at any time after 4th March."

In this despatch, Sir John Thompson pointed out, there was no request, as there had been none in any of the previous or following correspondence, for secrecy as to the fact of the negotiations taking place. The discussions were to be private, as a matter of course in all diplomatic negotiations, but there was apparently nothing to prevent the Government from making a public announcement in the matter. Hence his great surprise when Mr. Blaine, on April 1st, and after the elections were over, complained to Sir Julian Pauncefote that a breach of faith had been committed. It now transpired, said Sir John, that a serious blunder had occurred in the sending of the above despatch from London to Ottawa, and that in the place where it will be noticed a hitch in the composition occurs, a sentence was originally included asking that "all public reference to the subject should be avoided." This explanation was received with satisfaction, and if proof were required that the American authorities had long since understood the mistake it had been offered in the sitting of the Conference itself.

During this year the Canal Tolls' question came up for international consideration. It was another illustration of the unreasonable demands made by the United States in circumstances where Canada was, in a very moderate way, following the example of the Republic and guarding its own interests. By the Washington Treaty of 1871, the American Government had engaged in return for the use of the Canadian canals on terms of equality with the citizens of the Dominion, "to urge upon the State Governments to secure to the subjects of Her Britannic Majesty the use of the several canals connected with the navigation of the lakes or rivers traversed by, or contiguous to, the boundary line." This was never done, although in all the years that followed, the Americans freely used the canals upon which Canada and its people had spent over $50,-000,000 in improvement and enlargement.

In every way the Americans and Canadians were placed in Dominion waters upon an equal footing. But of late, the Canadian Government had passed regulations which granted a rebate of 18 cents per ton to any vessel of either country which, coming through the Welland Canal and without going to an American port for transhipment, should send her cargo *via* Canadian ports or canals to Montreal. Yet this little measure of legitimate protection to Canadian interests raised such a stir as to finally result in a Retaliation Message from the President, and in all kinds of threatened complications. And this from a country which by some miserable quibble had got out of the privileges granted in American canals under the sacred form of treaty obligations! President Harrison's proclamation of August 21st, compelled Canadian vessels to pay 20 cents a ton in passing through the Sault Ste. Marie Canal, and the same toll was to be levied on American vessels bound for Canadian ports.

Naturally this measure interfered considerably with the Canadian vessels, which in 1891 used the Sault Canal, and carried freight to the extent of 314,000 tons, and passengers to the number of 10,000. The Government did not at first feel like yielding a point in which they had both right and justice upon their side. Speaking at Petrolia on September 7th, Sir John Thompson declared that Canada had never adopted a hostile attitude towards the States, or that the Government in this matter had acted unfairly or contrary to treaty obligations. He pointed out that the enormous sums which had been expended by Canada upon her canals had "resulted as much for the benefit of the people of the Western States as for the people of Canada. Every foot which Canada had deepened her canals or widened them, and every additional lock or canal which Canada had built, helped the western farmer of the United States to reach his market, and enhanced the value of his products."

He announced, however, that the Dominion would not

meet the irritating enactments of the United States in a beligerent mood, although the Americans had so long used these canals "upon the same terms as our own people, bearing not one dollar of the burden which it had cost to build them." What the Government had done in this connection was entirely within its rights, and consisted in the grant of "a bonus to our lake marine and shipping to cause them to seek our own ports." They had been urged to retaliate, as they well could do, but they were anxious to avoid quarrels even though, as he believed in this case, the spirit of the Canadian people would fully sustain them throughout. Hence the Government had said that "while the rebate system was not a violation of any treaty, they were willing to discontinue it after the present year, not because of any wrong involved, but simply for the sake of peace and good neighborhood." There was, of course, some criticism regarding this apparent surrender, but it is tolerably obvious in view of the rapid work then being done on the Canadian canal at the Sault—which would soon render the country entirely independent in the matter—that the issue was hardly worth a prolonged dispute with unreasonable neighbors.

Another subject of serious controversy in which the relations of Canada and the United States were more or less involved at this time, was the Bond-Blaine treaty. Mr. Robert Bond was a member of the Whiteway Government in Newfoundland, and like so many of the politicians in that unhappy island seemed to possess a narrowness of view, and an inability to appreciate imperial considerations which it is difficult to understand, when united with the possession of admitted ability. He was exceedingly anxious to negotiate a reciprocity treaty with the United States, and does not appear to have cared very much as to the methods he might adopt in attaining the result, or as to the way in which the desired end might affect other countries with which Newfoundland was connected by the mutual tie of allegiance.

Early in October, 1890, Mr. Bond arrived in Washington with permission from the Imperial Government to enter upon negotiations, subject to the assistance of the British Ambassador, and, of course, to the final approval of the arrangements when completed. Hitherto, in 1854, in 1871, and in 1888, any negotiations concerning the fisheries, in which the Maritime Provinces of Canada were almost as much interested as the people of the Island, had proceeded concurrently. Necessarily, therefore, the Dominion Government was aroused to action, and Sir John A. Macdonald at once cabled to the High Commissioner in London: "Can scarcely believe Newfoundland has received authority from Imperial Government to make separate arrangement regarding fisheries. The relations of all the North American provinces to the United States and the Empire would be affected. Please represent strongly how the fishing and commercial interests of Canada will be injured by such an arrangement as Bond is currently reported to be making. . . . Our difficulties under the new American tariff are sufficiently great now."

An elaborate report was also submitted to the Governor-General-in-Council, signed by Sir John Thompson, Minister of Justice, and by the Hon. C. H. Tupper, Minister of Marine and Fisheries. It dealt with the history of previous negotiations and with the general condition of the fishing interests which would be affected by the Bond-Blaine proposals. Then, in reference to the McKinley bill; the infringement of the Treaty of 1818; and the obvious fact that an arrangement such as that exhibited in the draft which had just been published; would permit Newfoundland to discriminate against Canada in favour of a foreign country, Sir John and his colleague entered the following vigourous, effective, and now historic, protest:

"The protection afforded by the Treaty of 1818 for upwards of seventy years would thus be taken away from Canadian fishermen and Newfoundland fishermen alike, but there would be special compensation to the fishermen of Newfoundland in the shape of removal of duties, while the Canadian fishermen would be made to pay enhanced duties under the new American tariff. While this would, perhaps, be the most effectual method of impressing on the minds of the Canadian people the lesson that they cannot be British subjects and enjoy American markets, Her Majesty's Government can hardly, on reflection, feel surprised that Your Excellency's Government have not for a moment believed that Her Majesty's ministers would co-operate with the authorities of the United States in inculcating such a lesson at the present time."

The report was accepted by the Cabinet and sent to England. Although previously favourable to some arrangement, no British Government of the present day would act in the teeth of such a protest from Canada, and the treaty was promptly "hung up." Then followed the effort by the Dominion to obtain a joint treaty of reciprocity, and its failure after prolonged negotiations. Meantime the indignation of the Islanders was very great, and the correspondence between their Government and those of Canada and England became peppery in the extreme. Newfoundland tried to retaliate by refusing to sell bait to Canadian fishermen, while giving Americans all they desired, and the Dominion returned the compliment by putting a moderate duty on fish coming from the Island. Eventually a Conference was agreed upon and in November, 1892, Sir John Thompson, the Hon. Mackenzie Bowell and the Hon. J. A. Chapleau, representing Canada; Sir William Whiteway, the Hon. Robert Bond, and Mr. A. W. Harvey, representing Newfoundland; met at Halifax to discuss a mutual arrangement, and incidentally, on the part of the Canadian Ministers, to see if the troubles could be settled upon a basis of confederation.

The Canadian Minister of Justice in opening the discussion, reviewed the history of previous negotiations; pointed out that the Bond-Blaine Treaty would have resulted in a distinct discrimination against Canada; and would have greatly restricted the rights and privileges of her fishermen. He suggested that the following principles should be assented to:

I. That Canada as well as Newfoundland should have the right to take part in such treaties or any negotiations which would affect the interests of both countries.

II. That at the very least, no convention should be concluded which both countries should not have the right to avail themselves of.

He went on to say that "the efforts to obtain a fair arrangement with the United States were only relaxed (by Canada) when it was found that the conditions imposed would sow the seeds of Imperial disintegration," and he thought that "any separate arrangement such as the Bond-Blaine Convention would divide the hitherto united interests of the British American dependencies." Mr. Bond claimed that his Treaty did not involve any discrimination against Canada, but Mr. Bowell promptly pointed out that in flour and other articles it provided for admission into the States under lower duties than were granted similar Canadian products. Then followed a discussion of an informal kind upon Confederation. Mr. Bowell in an earnest speech urged it as the best and, in fact, the inevitable, settlement of all their material difficulties, and as a means of strengthening British power upon this continent.

Very Rev. G. M. Grant, D. D.

Principal of Queen's University, Kingston.

Sir William Whiteway expressed himself as favourable to the principle, but thought the time had not yet come.

Sir John Thompson thought it ought to be carefully considered by the Conference, and might constitute "a solution of all pending difficulties." Mr. Harvey opposed its being dealt with at this time, while Mr. Chapleau discussed the French Shore question. Eventually, an understanding was arrived at with regard to many of the minor causes of friction, and a little later the Dominion and the Island substantially resumed their old relations. But the Canadian Government positively refused, speaking through Sir John Thompson, to withdraw its protest against the Bond-Blaine Treaty. Thus ended, for the time, another incident in the external relations of Canada.

CHAPTER XVI.

Connection with the Roman Catholic Church.

Sir John Thompson was not a man who wore his religion upon his coat-sleeve. In that respect, as in all other matters of daily life, daily routine, and daily action, he was unobtrusive and undemonstrative. But none the less was he firm and earnest in his belief, and strong in a life which practically embodied his deep sincerity. To him, as it is to many others, religion was a matter of the most vital personal importance, but it was one with which the public, or even his own friends, so far as he was concerned, had nothing to do. It was in his estimation and as far as can be judged, the guide to conduct in his private life; an aid to right living and to right dying.

But no man's religion ought to be a subject of political discussion or consideration. There can be little doubt that he even thought the topic one too sacred for ordinary conversation, and that the denunciations which rang from more than one Protestant pulpit and permeated the utterances of sundry fervent and hot-headed divines during recent years, were exceedingly painful to him. The miserable insinuations which were current in certain circles ever since the line of action which he considered it a duty and necessity to take in French-Canadian and Separate School matters were shafts which pierced far deeper than could have been thought possible by those who viewed the statesman only by his generally impassive demeanour, and his stoical composure under attack.

This particular mode of hostile action was indeed one

which he found it impossible to deal with. Religion would in his opinion have been deeply degraded by a transfer from the pulpit to the political platform. No defence was possible or necessary for an honest man's change of creed, and if he were dishonest in such a case there could be no sincerity or honour about him. Reply therefore was out of the question, and Sir John was obliged to endure in silence the unfortunate attacks of sincere but misguided bigotry. His life meanwhile was so clear, his reputation so high and untarnished, that it is difficult to understand how honest men could have persisted in the circulation of slanders respecting his change of faith.

Though Sir John Thompson believed in religion as a personal factor in daily life, there is everything to show that he never intruded it upon the sphere of politics. Upon this latter ground Christianity was a word wide enough in application and meaning to cover all sects and creeds, and the relations of a statesman to all national organizations. He might have strong convictions upon certain points and a strong sympathy with a certain church in private life and private thought, but he was not in office because of those beliefs or on account of that sympathy, and therefore in administering the affairs of a complex nationality they had no public place. This was apparently the way in which Sir John looked at these sectarian issues and this standpoint made the unprovoked attacks of the Rev. Dr. Douglas, of the Protestant Protective Association and of other men and organizations, all the more difficult to bear.

And he was absolutely right in this view of a subject, the great importance of which in his peculiar environment is the only excuse for its consideration. But in all countries, religious conflict and struggle has been more or less a curse. In some few cases it has made "the bounds of freedom broader yet," and has indirectly done much good through the promotion of liberty in discussion and government. On the other hand, however, nearly all the historic battle-fields of Christendom show the principles of bigotry to have filled a far larger place than did ever the true spirit of Christianity. Liberty would have come to the nations in time had the feuds of sects and creeds never disgraced the name of religion. When therefore the old-time sentiment of intolerance was revived in a new country of mixed races and creeds, it was as much to be condemned as was ever the Inquisition of Spain or the execution of Roman Catholics at the dictation of Titus Oates.

And when this feeling was promoted in order to further personal prejudice, pander to individual ignorance, or aid political ends, it became still more deplorable and dangerous. Looking back over the period now passed away forever, it is hard indeed to understand why such fierce personal attacks were made upon Sir John Thompson, or how some of the men who led in the campaign could have been so blind. It was perfectly legitimate to criticise the policy of the Minister and of his party, as well as that of the Opposition, in connection with the Jesuits' Estates Act. It was within the right of every public man, and of every individual, to denounce that policy from a political or national standpoint. But why should the Minister of Justice have been picked out to be the victim of so many charges of undue religious influence? Mr. Laurier never encountered them, though a sincere Roman Catholic in faith and practice. The real reason seems to have been his leaving one Church to join another. Yet under the circumstances of the time the change involved serious danger to his prospects in life. His friends were in the main Protestants, and strict Methodists; he had then never seen Bishop Cameron and could have had no idea of the services he was afterwards to render; he had no desire for public life and certainly knew very little about Antigonish, which happens to be one of the very few Catholic constituencies in the Maritime Provinces; his future success in law depended chiefly upon Protestant support; his wife had no means of her own and therefore could not have proffered him any lure of wealth, even had he been so despicable in character as to have considered such a matter. Yet all these things were alleged against him, by men of undoubted sincerity.

No one now questions his honour and the earnest honesty of his convictions. Archbishop O'Brien, of Halifax, has stated in a communication written shortly after the Premier's death, that* "It has always been well known that conscientious convictions were the sole cause of his submission to the Catholic Church. Such conversions are not at all uncommon here. There was no earthly hope of gain by the change; rather the prospect of temporal loss. Yet, so convinced were all Protestants of his sincerity, that not one of his former friends deserted him." Bishop Cameron writes in a similar strain, and uses language which shows how great was the friendship existing between the two men: "Neither then (the first election in Antigonish), nor before, nor since, till the hour of his death, was the subject of his religion discussed in anyway between us. With an habitual realization of the Divine presence, he was in every relation of life an exceptionally good man in the best meaning of the word. I never expect to see in the public life of Canada, another such man, take him all in all."

What the exact process of reasoning was by which he gradually, but surely, changed from Methodism to Roman Catholicism, is shrouded in uncertainty. Possibly the friendship in early days of a brilliant young Catholic *litterateur* and controversialist, long since deceased—James

*Letter to the author, Dec. 19th, 1894.

Foley—may have first turned his thoughts in that direction; undoubtedly the eloquent sermons, some years later, of Archbishop Connolly, had something to do with the final consummation. Probably also his own lack of imagination, his dislike of the merely emotional in religion and life, his preference for precedence and power, over appeals to passion or prejudice, had an influence upon the result. And there is much in temperament. John Wesley, warm and impulsive by nature; liking publicity and excitement, could not endure the cold religion of the Church of England, and the dull formalism, which in his time, obscured its worth and hampered its work. He sought some brighter and more popular form of religion and found it in Methodism. Sir John Thompson, on the other hand, with his cold disposition, his dislike of familiarity in the individual or on the part of the public, his fondness for retirement, and reverence for authority, must have naturally found the Methodist Church uncongenial. One can hardly conceive such a man as he in the post of class-leader, or mixing in the pleasures of a congregational tea-meeting.

Hence there is no great difficulty in perceiving the tendency of the man. And in his search after something upon which to rest his mind, and in which to obtain comfort and release from perplexity, he seems to have been deeply impressed by the spectacle of the Church of Rome, based upon centuries of tradition, and building itself up in power and prestige from the mists of antiquity. It had already impressed and won over the great minds of Newman and Manning, and no strong reason exists why the same influences should not have modified, and finally controlled, the faith of Sir John Thompson. The sense of spiritual exaltation as experienced by many Protestants does not appear to have had great force with him, and strong as was his belief in a Divine Being, and in the pracical support derivable from prayer, he was probably greatly helped in the earlier stages of his religious experience by the external aid of authority as voiced by the Church, with all its impressive forms and its many ceremonies.

It took Cardinal Newman six years of mental difficulty and gradual development to become a Roman Catholic. Yet during the four years which preceded the period of doubt, he tells us that he "honestly wished to benefit the Church of England at the expense of the Church of Rome." To Newman eventually, all the world outside of his Church appeared drifting into atheism; Catholic inquiry had in the course of centuries been transmuted through the power of great minds into a sort of science; revealed dogma as originally committed to the Church, and as declared by the Church to the world, had assumed all the charm and certainty of infallibility. It was this that eased his mind of doubt, and enabled him without the spiritual sense required from a sincere Protestant, to throw himself into the arms of Rome, and to say some time after his change of faith: "I have had no anxiety of heart whatever. I have been in perfect peace and contentment." So it may have been with Sir John in his gradual change from Methodism. And it is interesting to note in this connection upon the authority of an intimate friend, who also served under him in a high position, that the Minister of Justice before finally deciding any important case—especially if it affected the life or the property of an individual—would spend a few moments in silent prayer.

Observers of sectarian agitation and its baneful results may well ask how many of Sir John Thompson's critics along these lines could be said to have thus brought their religion into their daily life. There is much also to reflect upon in Archbishop Walsh's statement regarding the

Premier who had then just died: "In his search after truth, he but followed the Protestant principle of private judgment, and yet for daring to do that which Manning and Newman, and other brilliant, learned, and good men had done before him, he was abused, vilified, and denounced." There is equally a sad degree of truth in the assertion of the Hon. G. W. Ross upon an important political occasion at a later date, in the City of Toronto that the late Premier of Canada, the greatest and ablest man in the Conservative party of the last few years, could not have personally carried in an election some of the wards in that Conservative centre. It is at least sufficiently near the truth to point a serious moral in support of civil and religious liberty.

Sir John Thompson could not for a long time understand the motives or reasons behind the attacks of the Rev. Dr. Douglas. They were so fierce and unreasonable and grossly untrue, and yet emanated from a man so highly respected, so eloquent and admittedly sincere, that it is little wonder he was puzzled. The Methodist orator declared the Premier to be "a clerical creation"; pictured him as "enthroned in order to manipulate with Jesuit art the affairs of this country"; described him as "a lay Jesuit in the Government"; spoke of "the contrast between the great Chieftain of the past and the man who now sits in his seat and wears the brand of pervert on his brow"; gravely accused him of having "transformed Mercier into a political brigand," and seemingly endeavoured to make his hearers and readers and followers believe that Sir John Thompson accepted Roman Catholicism in order to promote his political chances, and used his political power in order to advance the interests of his Church. Such allegations concerning a man who notoriously lacked political ambition in the ordinary sense, and who possessed a sincerity and strength of personal honour all too rare amongst public men, should have borne their own answer with them.

But it appeared probable that Dr. Douglas must have received inspiration from some special direction in making these attacks. Sir John Thompson believed they were instigated by outside influence at a time when the brilliant intellect, or judgment, of the old man was somewhat weakening. Though a Liberal in his politics, it was never thought that the denunciation was dictated by personal partisanship. It is understood, however, that Sir John had ultimately every reason to believe that the information, or mis-information, supplied to the eminent divine came from a Methodist minister in Nova-Scotia who united with his sacred profession a very violent dislike of the Conservative party and its leaders. As illustrating the nature of other religious attacks, it may be said that after a certain series of bitter letters and miserable insinuations had appeared in the *Montreal Witness*, Bishop Cameron wrote from Antigonish saying that if one of the anonymous detractors would come out from his concealment, he (the Bishop) would prove his statements to be a mass of untruths. His Lordship's challenge was, of course, never accepted.

Yet this was the treatment accorded in certain circles to the man who took his political life in his hand, and on behalf of the law, the whole law and nothing but the law, defied in 1886 the prejudices of his co-religionists in Quebec, and saved the Government by a speech which embodied the truest doctrines of equal rights for all, under the constitution of the country. As he well said at London, Ont., on Sept. 16th of that eventful year: "An attempt has been made, as you know, to deceive the people of the Catholic faith in the Province of Quebec and in the Lower Provinces by the assertion that the law was carried out in Louis Riel's execution at the demand of the Orange Association of Ontario. That statement we do not hear so much of in the Province of Ontario, but the slander that I was deserting my principles and evading my faith was made because I denied then, and solemnly deny now, that there was a particle of truth in that statement. The people of this country, whether they are Orange or Catholic, French or English, have the right to entertain or to express any opinions they feel regarding the administration of public affairs."

And the man who could thus defend true liberty of speech and the right of Orangemen as well as of Catholics to be heard upon important questions; the man who, as a result of his stand upon the Riel issue, almost lost that alleged pocket borough of clericalism—Antigonish—in the elections of 1887; was the object of these unjust denunciations by Dr. Douglas and Dr. Carman, and of private insinuations which afterwards formed the basis of many a P.P.A. organization. This Association sprang into sudden prominence during Sir John Thompson's Premiership. It was the product of religious prejudice united with ignorant sincerity. It was formed out of the more violent and uncontrollable spirits of the Equal Rights movement, and had been easily moulded into shape by American agitators upon the lines of the American Protestant Association. The organization obtained a marked success in the municipal elections of 1894, and carried two or three seats in the subsequent Ontario election.

Its chief, the Rev. J. C Madill, won a brief period of prominence by sacrificing the true principles of Christianity upon the altar of ambition or bigotry. Speaking at Stratford on August 16th following the Provincial contest, he declared that Sir John Thompson "was not Premier by the voice of the people. It was Sir John A. Macdonald who carried the country, and Sir John Thompson was merely filling in his time. He could not be elected as a Papist or a Jesuit, and no Papist or Jesuit would be allowed to rule at Ottawa. Before they would submit to that they would fight Derry over again and give them a taste of the Boyne."

Such talk was to all sensible people simply demagogic and disgusting. Even the *Huntingdon Gleaner*, the staunch Protestant and Liberal organ of the Eastern Townships of Quebec, denounced it as inclining all fair-minded men to support the Premier in order to prevent him being "hounded down" in such a cowardly fashion.

Organizations of this nature, however, do not last long. The P. P. A. served its apparent purpose, in causing difficulty to an honourable man in the pursuit of duty, and now that he has passed to the bourne whence no man returneth, it may rest in peace. In this connection it is interesting to note how often the word "Jesuit," was hurled at Sir John Thompson. Though intended to be offensive, it is questionable whether the epithet really was so to him, aside from the obvious motive. As a devout Catholic, he would naturally disbelieve most of the allegations made against the Society of Jesus. Indeed his admiration for controversial history was never very profound. Speaking in the House upon one occasion, and in reply to some inquiry (25th April, 1890), he said, with a simplicity which is worthy of comment: "I do not know. There are many facts in the history of this country, of which I am not aware, and a great many statements of facts in regard to history, I find controverted so often, that I am not able to state a positive opinion in regard to them."

It was a couple of years after this that Cardinal Moran, of Sydney, Australia, in dealing at length with the question of the Jesuits' Estates Act, defended the Canadian order with an earnestness far in advance of that shown by Sir John Thompson, during the famous debate in Parliament. And they both agreed in expressing admiration for the services of the Jesuits in the early history of Canada. The Cardinal, in the course of his address, also made a most interesting defence of his Church as a friend of liberty, of science and of true progress.

If, therefore, the political and judicial career of Sir John Thompson has been a great service to the State, as everyone believes, his change of faith in early days, before the future of power or success was dreamed of, has turned out an equal benefit. It has proved that despite limited but always noisy sectarianism, an honourable man can win his way to position and popularity in Canada. It has proved to the ignorant or indifferent or prejudiced that a Roman Catholic can do his duty in governing this mixed community as well as a Protestant. It has, through one man bearing successfully the brunt of vigorous and sustained attacks, done much to bring both divisions of the people together in the bonds of true brotherhood and real Christianity. And if a message of warning is still required for the future, it can be found in the absolutely accurate statement made by the Minister of Justice, as he stood at the threshold of the Premiership, on Sept. 7th, 1892: "The one calamity above all others which stands before this country is that political divisions should follow the division of race or the division of religion. The one danger which menaces the future of this country and the union of this country, now so happily being accomplished, is that men should stand arrayed against each other on the question of government, because they differ with regard to religion, because they differ with regard to race."

CHAPTER XVII.

Fiscal Matters and Political Parties.

The administration of Sir John Thompson assumed office with the intention of carrying on the historic policy of the Conservative party. The principles of that party under Sir John Macdonald, under Sir John Abbott, and now under the leadership of another statesman were announced as being one and the same. They involved a continuation of protection as applied to Canadian interests and industries. The "National Policy" was to be preserved and strengthened, and free trade opposed as impracticable in arrangement, and injurious in operation.

But none the less was the air full of rumours. There was an undercurrent of serious agitation going on, caused in part by the success of the Democrats in the United States and in part by the first touch of the wave of depression. It was assumed by the Liberal party in all sections of the country that a free trade tide was sweeping over the Continent and that the success of Mr. Cleveland indicated pronounced American legislation along those lines, together with some sort of an opportunity for Canadian reciprocity. And it was argued that as hard times had so greatly helped the Democracy in the States, the same cause must also help the Liberals in Canada.

The indications indeed seemed rather unfavourable to protectionists generally, and Liberal speakers and papers everywhere compared the National Policy to the McKinley Tariff, and prophesied a free trade revolution in Canada similar to that which had just stirred the Republic. Meanwhile the farmers began to organize in somewhat more serious fashion than had hitherto been the case. The Farmers' Institutes which had for a long time been under the friendly patronage of the Ontario Government, were formed into Patrons of Industry lodges and an order was established which its friends and members expected to see sweep the Province at the first ensuing Dominion elections. And its success in the Provincial elections of 1894 greatly encouraged this hope.

Mr. McCarthy constituted another disturbing element in the political outlook of the new Ministry. To his other differences with them he had now added a tariff issue, and had come out squarely for lower duties upon English goods, and reciprocal terms with the United States as soon as that country might be willing to consider an arrangement which would include manufactures as well as agricultural products and raw materials. But upon the question of discrimination against the Mother-Country he was as firmly opposed to the Liberal policy as he was upon other issues to the Conservative platform. At Stayner on January 25th, 1893, he emphasized two points of opposition to the existing tariff. The first was the alleged existence of numerous combinations which enhanced the prices of necessaries to the public, and the second was the suggestion that as the Americans were about to adjust and lower their duties, Canada should do the same. Accompanying this reduction however, was a proposal for the establishment of a maximum and minimum tariff by which the Dominion should discriminate to the extent of ten per cent. in favor of Great Britain.

Tariff reform of some kind was therefore in the air, and when it was announced that Sir John Thompson would deliver an address at the important annual banquet of the Toronto Board of Trade on the 5th of January, much curiosity and interest was felt in the coming deliverance of the new Premier. It was a great occasion Always successful in these efforts, the Board of Trade seemed to have this time excelled itself in the providing of distinguished speakers and guests. The Governor-General, Lord Stanley of Preston; Sir John S. D. Thompson, the Premier of Canada; the Lieut.-Governor of Ontario; Sir Oliver Mowat, the veteran Premier of the same Province; the Hon. George E. Foster, Minister of Finance; and Mr. W. C. Van-Horne, President of the Canadian Pacific Railway, were amongst those who graced the occasion, where were found

> "Again the feast, the speech, the glee,
> The shade of passing thought, the wealth
> Of words and wit, the double health,
> The crowning cup, the three-times three."

It is needless to refer at length to the speeches. All were good, but that of the new Prime Minister was the most important and certainly the one which had been most looked forward to. Sir John Thompson commenced his speech by a jest which created much amusement. He referred to the fact that his Government consisted of sixteen gentlemen, thirteen of whom averaged 47 years of age. "Their youth and their robustness excited the imagination of a Toronto poet, who indited some verses to me and put into my mouth words which were put into Cæsar's when he said: 'Let me have fat men about me, sleek-headed men who sleep at nights'—and I could, ladies and gentlemen, make you to-night a little boast about the girth and weight of my colleagues, if it were not that my friend Cassius here—the Finance Minister—breaks the record and utterly destroys the average."

The Premier then handled in a more serious vein the national problems of the moment, and the first of these in his opinion was the Manitoba schools' question. He pointed out that moral and religious problems which come home to the convictions of the people are dangerous to the welfare of the State if approached in any partisan or political spirit The only safe guide to any safe result which he could see in such a connection, was the exercise of tolera tion and of concession, so far as it did not infringe upon principle. The Government proposed to be guided by the constitutional law of the country, and to obey its dictates. As to his personal position, he said in words which have the ring of true and manly sincerity :

"I have no plea for toleration to make for myself. I want no sympathy through toleration in that regard. I am not occupying the responsible position which it is my honour to hold to-night through any effort of my own or any struggle of mine for political distinction. I occupy that position simply because those who were qualified to decide, and who were bound to decide, thought that I could serve the state occupying that position. I am nothing more than a public servant, and if I should succeed in serving the state well I shall have achieved the only ambition which I have in public life."

Amid the loud and constant cheering which interrupted and closed these sentences, Sir John Thompson turned to consider the trade question, and first referred to the desire of Canada to be on the most amicable terms with the United States. In order to aid this object, the Dominion had practically given way upon the Canal Tolls' question, and had arranged the sugar duties, which had been a cause of uneasiness and complaint to the Republic: "We think that we have shown to them what the policy of this country is, and shall be for the future, in so far as I have the right to speak for it—a policy that will make us to the United States the best of neighbors, although, please God, we shall never be anything but neighbors."

THE RIGHT REV. JOHN CAMERON, D.D, P.H.D.

Bishop of Antigonish, N.S.

But he spoke with doubt regarding the attitude of the President, and indicated the possibility of his attempting some further evidence of hostility before making way for Mr. Cleveland. One month later President Harrison sent his message to Congress, asking for the abrogation of the bonding system, which, however, he was fated not to get

The Premier went on to express grave doubts regarding the extent of the free trade legislation which the Democrats were likely to introduce, but announced the intention of his Government to take advantage of the experience of the United States; to watch its tariff changes; and to "adopt the policy for this country which will be found best for Canada first, and best for the Empire next." Replying to some one who had asked him if he considered the National Policy perfect, and assuming for the moment that only the fiscal part of that policy was meant, he replied in words which were afterwards widely discussed:

"I do not know of any tariff which has been perfection, and I know of defects both in the framing and administration of the present tariff which require a remedy. And therefore, sir, we do propose to take your good advice which this motto gives us, and 'lop the mouldering branches away.'"

The speech was a decided success, but the occasion had its limitations, and the one which followed on January 14th, in the Toronto Auditorium, was of a kind more calculated to attract popular attention. The former was important as affording hints concerning the policy of the new Government; the latter was of intense political interest, as being the first address delivered by the new Premier to his party and the country at large. And the affect of the demonstration was increased by the presence of ten other ministers. A feature of the meeting was the spontaneous and enthusiastic reception accorded to the Hon. Mr. Angers, as a tribute to his manly administration in Quebec. And the aggressive oratory of the Hon. C. H. Tupper was of a nature calculated to stir up any Canadian audience.

Sir John Thómpson's speech must be read to be appreciated. Most of the great audience had never seen or heard the Premier and seemed to be somewhat surprised when the full, deep, satisfying voice which seems to come only from down by the sea, as it breaks upon the shores of the Maritime Provinces, sounded through the building. As he went on in grave, serious, but sincere, style, the interest deepened and there were few present when the speaker concluded, who did not realise that he was a man who would do what seemed his duty in any emergency and in face of any difficulties. And there was no doubt about the Conservatism of that speech. It meant to the assembled throng and to the myriad readers of the succeeding day, that the third Sir John was worthy to carry the flag planted by Sir John Macdonald, and supported by Sir John Abbott. It meant that he was going to stand by the principle of Canada for the Canadians, and the British Empire for all.

Some portions were especially vigourous, as for instance, when he declared that a little while ago "we were taunted with waving the old flag; and a lot of traitors, a lot of cowards who have not the courage to be traitors, although they have the will, would sneer at the old flag: sneer at the loyalty we inherited from our fathers: sneer at the institutions which our fathers were so proud to leave us." This was sufficiently energetic language, and it certainly pleased the audience immensely. But the memorable demonstration had its pathetic side, as did so many other events in the last crowded years of the Premier's life. When President Armstrong of the Young Men's Conservative Association introduced Sir John to the audience as one who would provide "a great future for the Conservative party, and would not only legislate for the demands of the hour, but for the demands of the future," it seemed as if the new leader presented the very picture of health, vigour and manliness. What a commentary upon assertions and appearances that future was destined to be!

Parliament met on the 26th of January. The chief topic of political conversation was the tariff and the proposed changes. Several Conservative members had declared in favour of some amendment. Mr. Cockburn of Centre Toronto, Mr. Davin, Mr. Boyd, Mr. Calvin and Mr. McInerney of New Brunswick, all desired some alterations, though their proposals were not very radical. Mr. McCarthy, however, and his faithful colleague, Colonel O'Brien, were pronounced in their advocacy of lower duties. The Session commenced with an eloquent speech from the new Maritime orator, Mr. McInerney, who moved the Address and wound up his peroration by quoting lines eminently appropriate, not only in a general sense, but in a particular application to the statesman who was then at the head of the Government:

> "Build that these walls to coming generations,
> Your skill, your strength, your faithfulness shall tell;
> That all may say as storms and centuries test them,
> The men of old built well."

And, so far as Sir John Thompson was given the time, he did build well. Incidentally, Mr. Laurier in addressing the House four days later, referred in generous terms to the successful career of the new Premier. "There has been no public man in Canada at any time," he declared, "whose advancement has been so rapid. He came into this House at a comparatively recent date, preceded by a high reputation for ability, which he had earned in his own Province, which led everybody, friends and opponents alike, to expect a great deal from him, and that expectation has been realized since he entered this House." On the 14th of February following, Mr. Foster delivered his Budget Speech and announced the proposed alterations in the tariff. They were not numerous, and consisted merely in a reduction of the duty on binder twine from 25 to 12½ per cent., and the abolition of certain restrictions on coal oil. But it was stated that at the close of the Session a thorough inquiry into the tariff would be carried out by himself, the Minister of Trade and Commerce and the Comptrollers of Customs and Inland Revenue. Personal interviews would be had with the merchants, manufacturers and farmers, and a measure of Tariff Reform was promised for 1894 as the result of this investigation.

As Sir John Thompson was required in Paris within a couple of months to fill the distinguished position of a British arbitrator on the Behring Sea Commission, an effort was made to have a brief session. Mr. McCarthy, however, came forward in March with a long tariff amendment and a long speech, each of which embodied very fully his views on the ever burning fiscal issue. He contended that the protective tariff had answered its purpose, and was now merely useful for the development of trusts and combines; that it was becoming burdensome to the consuming classes and the farmers; that it ought to be amended by the substantial reduction of cutoms duties in favour of the United Kingdom; and that a light reduction might well be made in favour of the United States and of different portions of the Empire, where they were willing to reciprocate. Upon one point he spoke with no uncertain sound. He was "absolutely and unequivocally opposed to any kind of so-called free trade, no matter whether it gave us a continental market or not, which discriminated against the Mother-Land." Dr. Montague replied with characteristic eloquence and ability, and the discussion eventually closed with a Government majority of 54.

Another incident in which Provincial rights were involved took place during this Session. Early in the year certain important coal mines in Nova-Scotia had been handed over by the Local Government to an American syndicate under terms which were declared to be extremely advantageous to the Province. But many Conservatives opposed the arrangement, and a deputation of members of Parliament waited upon the Governor General, and asked him to disallow the measure on the ground chiefly that foreigners in control of the mines might fire or flood them in time of war, thus cutting off the coal supply of the navy, and proving of Imperial as well as Provincial injury. Constitutional questions of some interest were raised as to the propriety of individual members trying to usurp the power of the House as a Legislative body, and of the Government as an advisory and executive body. Mr. Mills brought the matter up on February 17th, and after some slight discussion Sir John Thompson stated that the whole affair was a mere conversation and entirely informal; that the Governor General had asked to have the matter put into such a shape that he could lay it before his constitutional advisers; and that no opinion could be expressed as yet because the statute in question had not reached the Department of Justice. Eventually, Sir John took the ground that the mines belonged to the Province and that the Federal authorities were not entitled to interfere with them. The bargain might be bad, but it was for the people of Nova-Scotia to deal with the matter, and not the Dominion Government.

Towards the close of the session, which, as expected, was a very short one, the Premier left for Paris and Mr. Foster acted as leader of the House. A couple of months after the adjournment on April 1st, a new departmental scandal developed itself and one which was promptly dealt with. Summarized, it showed an expenditure of $450,000 upon the reconstruction of the bridges over the Lachine Canal at Montreal, in place of the estimated cost of $175,000. A Royal Commission was at once appointed and Mr. Haggart as head of the Department of Railways and Canals had the enquiry pushed in every possible direction. It was soon found that the contracts had been fraudulently handled and that large sums had been wasted without the knowledge of the Minister. Of course the question immediately became a party one, the Opposition contending that the head of the Department should have known something of what was going on and prevented it: the Minister and his friends declaring that the usual care was exercised in making the payments, but that the frauds had occurred through forged pay lists and gross misrepresentation on the part of the contractors. The Engineer in charge of the works was suspended and later on the Minister of Justice had a suit instituted against the contractor for $143,000.

There is no doubt that Sir John Thompson felt keenly such occurrences as this. They showed a tendency to carelessness or dishonesty in the connection of officials with the public business to a degree which would not be endured for a moment in the conduct of any large private concern. Of course, a Minister cannot as a rule, go behind the properly certified pay sheets and documents of his department, but a very clearly defined impression existed in the minds of the public at this time and had been growing since the scandals of 1891, that members of the Government should individually exercise more control over the choice and qualities of their subordinates, as well as over the antecedents and characters of the men who were given contracts, and permitted to aid in the great and necessary work of carrying on, or completing, the country's public undertakings. And it is safe to say that Sir John Thompson sympathized strongly with this view.

Meantime tariff questions and politics had been coming more and more to the front throughout the country. The Ministers recently selected for the purpose started their inquiries; the Patrons of Industry formulated their platform; Mr. McCarthy announced his policy through the medium of a League and the employment of an organizer; the Liberal party met in convention and passed resolutions both varied and voluminous. The Patrons declared themselves in favor of British connection; the abolition of the Senate; the election of county officials, with the exception of County Judges; a tariff for revenue adjusted so as to tax luxuries; reciprocal trade with any countries which were willing to negotiate; prohibition of railway grants; and the preparation of the Dominion and Provincial voter's lists by municipal officers. The McCarthy policy has already been pretty well outlined, but the new organization had some very distinct planks regarding the absolute right of the provinces to control education, the necessity of having no interference with the Manitoba Schools' law, and the desirability of any future redistribution of seats being based upon an equality of population and upon county and city boundary lines.

The Liberal Convention at Ottawa early in July was a great success, and the delegates certainly could not complain of the warmth of their reception. But though the weather was tropical, the work done in platform making and speaking was very considerable. The policy finally evolved by a gathering which boasted the presence of nearly every prominent Liberal in the Canadian community, and which was representative in ability as well as in numbers, may be summed up as follows:

1. Denunciation of the protective tariff.
2. The necessity of low revenue duties.
3. Reciprocity with the United States in natural products and in a selected list of manufactured articles.
4. Arraignment of the Government as corrupt.
5. The necessity for great economy.
6. The repeal of the Franchise Act.
7. A Dominion plebiscite on Prohibition.
8. Reform of the Senate.

About this time also the Protestant Protective Association rose out of the ruins of the Equal Rights organization, and prepared to forward a mission of error and misunderstanding. So far as can be authoritatively gathered, its platform declared bitter opposition to Roman Catholicism as an element of political power; denounced all religio-political organizations (except itself) as enemies to civil and religious liberty; favoured one general unsectarian school organization and the taxing of all church property; repudiated the use of public funds for any sectarian purpose; and proclaimed it "unwise and unsafe to elect to civil, political or military office in this Dominion men who owe supreme allegiance to any foreign potentate or ecclesiastical power."

Such, in brief, were the various political divisions and party policies which the Conservative Premier had to face upon his return from Paris late in August. A tour of the Province of Ontario followed with very favourable results to Sir John Thompson personally through an increased acquaintance with the people, and with useful results to the party through the promotion of public familiarity with its policy and with the new leaders who were so rapidly replacing those of a previous period.

CHAPTER XVIII.

The Behring Sea Question.

In 1886, the year following Sir John Thompson's entry into Dominion politics, news of a somewhat serious character had come from the far north of the American continent. While engaged in seal-hunting, out of sight of land, and in what is generally understood to be the open sea, three Canadian schooners were seized by the United States revenue cutter *Corwin* and taken to an Alaskan port. There the officers were tried in the American Court for the District of Alaska, and condemned to fines and imprisonment, while their vessels were confiscated—on the general charge of contravention of the United States laws.

This high-handed proceeding attracted immediate and wide-spread attention. Throughout Canada the feeling was one of indignation, though not altogether of surprise, as the people had some knowledge of the American tendency to claim everything in sight where international relationships were concerned. But aside from any injury done to Canadian citizens and British subjects, these seizures—which were continued from time to time during ensuing years—opened up wide and important questions of Maritime jurisdiction. It has been generally assumed that the law of nations gives complete territorial rights to the extent of one marine league (three miles) from the shore. In specific cases, by custom or treaty, the right of a nation to control a greater distance may have been admitted, but these were the exceptions which are usually taken to prove the rule. On the Atlantic coast of Canada, the United

States for years, both before and after setting up this claim on the Pacific, had tried to break down the Canadian right to control even three miles from the shore. But whatever the local circumstances might be, this claim to jurisdiction, sixty miles from the coast, was practically an arbitrary assertion of a complete right to the ownership of part of Behring Sea, and if sustained or allowed would have placed that great body of water, eleven hundred miles long by eight hundred miles broad, largely under the control of Russia and the United States.

The charge laid against these vessels, their officers and owners, was that of being found "engaged in killing fur-seal within the limits of Alaska territory and in the waters thereof, in violation of section 1956 of the Revised Statutes of the United States." Obviously, therefore, to make these and subsequent seizures legal, a great part of Behring Sea, or what was really a portion of the North Pacific Ocean, had to be included within the limits of American jurisdiction. And as the claim to this authority was as extensive as might be the wandering instincts or fancies of the Alaskan seal in the vast waters of the Pacific, it will be appreciated as a pretty large one. Several reasons were given by the United States for its action. One was nominal and reasonable in appearance. It was evidenced in an invitation extended to Great Britain, France, Germany, Sweden and Norway, Russia, and Japan, in 1887, asking them to "enter into such an arrangement with the Government of the United States as will prevent the citizens of either country from killing seal in Behring Sea at such times and places, and by such methods, as are at present pursued, and which threaten the speedy extermination of these animals and consequent serious loss to mankind."

This philanthropic cloak was exceedingly pretty in appearance, but, as so often happens in diplomatic matters, it covered a very sordid reality. For many years the Alaska Commercial Company had enjoyed a practical monopoly of sealing in the Aleutian Islands and on the Alaskan coast, the value of which to them and to the American Government may be estimated by the report of a Congressional Committee in 1889, which declared that the Company had under the terms of their contract paid the Government $5,597,000 up to June 30th, 1888. And the total amount received from customs duties on Alaska dressed seal skins imported from England was, during the same period, $3,426,000. As the total amount paid by the United States to Russia for the purchase of Alaska in 1867 was only $7,200,000, and the expenses of Government from then to June, 1888, had not exceeded $400,000, the advantage of a continuance and extension of this monopoly is apparent.

It was further claimed that the Russian Government had exercised exclusive control over these fisheries and over the seals in the disputed waters, until the cession of Alaska, when its rights passed naturally to the United States. The British Government, on the other hand, expressed every desire to regulate sealing so as to preserve the species, but altogether denied the American claims of wide Maritime jurisdiction, and pointed out that the United States had more than once protested against the Russian attempts at exercising similar powers. Lord Salisbury, in voluminous despatches, apparently proved by extracts from the diplomatic correspondence of many years before, that England had always refused to admit any Russian claims in this matter of jurisdiction; that a Convention between the countries in 1825 had been regarded on both sides as a renunciation on the part of Russia; and that Behring Sea had always been considered a portion of the Pacific Ocean, and not in any sense a closed sea, as was at first claimed by Mr. Blaine on behalf of the United States.

Despite the most conciliatory correspondence on the part of Great Britain, and every effort on the side of Canada, to bring matters to some satisfactory conclusion, the element in the United States which is always delighted when some trouble arises between the Republic and the Empire, continued to urge active aggressive measures, and to praise the seizures of Canadian vessels which were still taking place. Canadian fishermen pursuing an honourable and legal occupation were stigmatised as "poachers," and every effort was made to hamper and injure them in their work. Finally, when it was announced in the American press early in 1890 that the same system would be continued during the ensuing season, Lord Salisbury apparently concluded that the time had passed for conciliation, and that bluster should be met by a firm announcement of the inevitable result of maintaining such a policy. Accordingly, on June 13th, Sir Julian Pauncefote, British minister at Washington, was finally instructed to make the following declaration:

"Her Britannic Majesty's Government are unable to pass over without noticing, the public announcement of intention on the part of the Government of the United States to renew the acts of interference with British vessels navigating outside the territorial waters of the United States, of which they have previously had to complain. The undersigned is in consequence instructed formally to protest against such interference and to declare that Her Britannic Majesty's Government must hold the Government of the United States responsible for the consequences that may ensue from acts which were contrary to the established principle of international law."

This last sentence is practically the diplomatic way of stating that if a certain course is pursued, force will be employed, or in other words that war will follow. It not only supplied ample food for thought to those who asserted that the Mother-Country would never fight for Canadian interests against the United States, but, as is always the case when honest boldness encounters unmeaning bluster and brag, it brought the whole question down from the clouds of controversy to a reasonable basis for settlement. And no more seizures were made. Early in 1891, negotiations for arbitration were commenced, and each country appointed Commissioners to investigate the real habits and environment of the seal. Sir George Baden-Powell, M.P., a strong friend of Imperial unity, and Professor George M. Dawson, of Canada, were the British Commissioners; and Professors Mendenhall and Merriam those appointed by the United States. A year later an arrangement was consummated pending the submission of the questions to Arbitration, and the Treaty to that end was finally ratified on May 7th.

The Tribunal as appointed in June following, was composed of some very eminent men. Under the terms of the treaty, Great Britain selected two arbitrators, the United States two, France, Italy, and Norway and Sweden, one each. The British arbitrators were the Rt. Hon. Lord Hannen, and the Prime Minister of Canada. The former had been for many years a distinguished English judge, and was a man of much intellectual force, and of strong character. Sir John Thompson afterwards said of him that from first to last he "exhibited the strongest determination that Canada should attain justice, both as to legal questions and as to the regulations, and was not in the slightest degree moved by the persistent effort which was made from beginning to end to divide the British from Canadian interests in the matter."

The American arbitrators were men of ability and standing, though thoroughly imbued with the idea that the Republic was always right, and that in no case could the ends of justice be served unless the American contention was maintained up to the hilt. Mr. Justice Harlan had been a Republican in politics, and Senator Morgan was a Southerner, and a somewhat fiery Democrat. Baron de Courcel, who represented France, was a distinguished jurist and diplomatist, and was ultimately selected to preside over the Tribunal, which he did with a grace and dignity worthy of the highest commendation. Italy sent the Marquis Venosta, a jurist, an ex-Minister of State, and a Senator. Sir John at a later period described his written opinions at the private meetings of the arbitrators as having shown great learning in legal precedents; skill in the analysis of evidence; and wide comprehension of English law. Mr. Gregors Gram, the arbitrator appointed by Sweden and Norway, was Minister of Foreign Affairs in his own country and had obtained much varied experience from twelve years' spent on the Mixed Tribunal of Egypt.

Meantime, Canada had been further honoured by the selection of the Hon. Charles H. Tupper, to act as British Agent, in the preparation of the case. Sir Richard Webster, Q. C., Sir Charles Russell, Q. C., Christopher Robinson, Q.C., of Toronto, and the Hon. W. H. Cross, M.P., were the British Counsel. The American Agent was General J. W. Foster, and the Counsel were the Hon. E. J. Phelps, formerly Minister to Great Britain, Judge Blodgett, and Mr. J. S. Carter. The points submitted for decision were as follows:

I. What exclusive jurisdiction in the sea known as the Behring Sea, and what exclusive rights in the seal fisheries therein did Russia assert and exercise prior and up to the time of the cession of Alaska to the United States?

II. How far were these claims of jurisdiction as to the seal fisheries recognized and conceded by Great Britain?

III. Was the body of water now known as the Behring Sea included in the phrase, "Pacific Ocean," as used in the treaty of 1825 between Great Britain and Russia, and what rights, if any, in the Behring Sea were held and exclusively exercised by Russia after said treaty ?

IV. Did not all the rights of Russia as to jurisdiction and as to the seal fisheries in Behring Sea east of the water boundary, in the treaty between the United States and Russia of the 30th March, 1867, pass unimpaired to the United States under that treaty ?

V. Has the United States any right, and, if so, what right, of protection or property in the fur seals frequenting the islands of the United States in Behring Sea when such seals are found outside the ordinary three-mile limit.

Besides these questions it was stipulated that in the event of the United States being declared to have no exclusive rights outside of the three mile limit, a decision should be made as to the necessary concurrent regulations for the preservation of the fur seal, and that the arbitrators should say whether damages were to be awarded Canada in the event of the decision upon questions of right going against the United States.

Sir John Thompson's appointment as an Arbitrator was hailed with general satisfaction. Even his strongest opponents conceded the fact that in judicial qualifications and breadth of intellect no better selection could be made. It was felt that his known firmness of character, his knowledge of maritime law, and previous experience in minor diplomatic missions, peculiarly fitted him for the maintenance of Canadian rights at this important juncture. Confidence was also entertained in his justness of view and ability to discriminate between blustering claims and those founded upon at least a measure of right. The Speech from the Throne in proroguing Parliament on April 1st, 1893, practically embodied this sentiment of fairness in words no doubt approved, if not prepared, by Sir John Thompson himself; "the nomination of the Prime Minister of Canada as one of the Arbitrators affords a guarantee that the interests of our sealers will be properly, though not unduly, safeguarded." Only those who have been able to closely follow American diplomacy as displayed in the various Washington Treaty negotiations, and in the Alabama and other questions, can fully appreciate the distinction between the calm dignity of that simple sentence and the assertive and aggressive nature of American claims in general international differences.

Every possible environment of luxury and hospitality awaited the Arbitrators when they met in Paris on April 4th. Spacious rooms in the Foreign Office were placed at their disposal, and entertainments without number and without price were given them by the kindly leaders, social and political, of the French Republic. But it was a period of very hard work as well as one of enjoyment in the form of banquets and receptions. There were specialists present in every branch covered by the arguments of the counsel —the British staff included more than fifteen—and besides the necessity of mastering all the voluminous special reports thus presented numberless drafts of each argument had to be studied, and modified or elaborated by the arbitrators to suit the circumstances and their convictions in the premises. The position of Sir John Thompson was peculiarly difficult. As the Canadian Premier he was responsible to the Canadian Parliament for whatever decision he accepted. As a British arbitrator he was responsible to the Imperial Government in this attempt to settle a question which could now only be disposed of by arbitration or war.

He had to find or accept some plan by which the ultimately admitted right of Canadians to seal in Behring Sea

Hon. Thomas Greenway.

Prime Minister of Manitoba.

might be reconciled with the equally proper desire, as expressed by the Americans, for the preservation of the species from final destruction. He had to face the contention of the United States that Canada was the cause of the whole trouble; that it was aggressive and hostile to the Republic; that its influence was so great in the Imperial Government as to make it a constant source of annoyance to the United States and the cause of unfriendly relations between that country and the Empire. Fortunately for a satisfactory solution, Lord Hannen became greatly impressed with the knowledge and forcefulness of character displayed by Sir John, and supported him strongly in the various discussions which took place. And it was natural that such should have been the case. A weak Canadian representative would have involved a lack of backbone in the British arbitrator, no matter how well intentioned the latter might have been. A strong Canadian meant two British Commissioners working for the interests of both Canada and Britain, instead of one who might have aimed chiefly at the making of a Treaty which would relieve England of a serious diplomatic trouble, even if it sacrificed some unappreciated Canadian interest.

The arguments of counsel on both sides were long and able; although the Americans, as usual, were away ahead in the amount of talking done and in the length of speeches. One unfortunate occurrence, was the use by the American counsel of certain documents which appeared to prove the Russian claim to exclusive jurisdiction in Behring Sea, but which, after submission to the Tribunal, were found to the astonishment of all concerned, to have been very clever forgeries, perpetrated by an employé of the United States Department of State. They were promptly withdrawn, but with them went a part of the American claims. Finally, judgment was given on August 15th, and on every claim advanced by the United States regarding maritime jurisdiction and exclusive rights, decision was given against the Republic, and in favour of the contentions so long and skilfully maintained by Canada and Britain. But the Tribunal decided to prescribe regulations, and by a majority vote—Judge Harlan and Senator Morgan dissenting because they were not sufficiently vigourous, and Sir John Thompson for the opposite reason—it was settled that no seals were to be taken within a zone of sixty miles of the Pribyloff Islands; that the close season was to be from May 1st. to July 31st; that only sealing vessels with a special license, and a distinguishing flag should be allowed to seal; and that the use of nets and firearms should be forbidden. It was also decided that an indemnity—the amount to be afterwards settled—must be paid Canadian sealers by the United States Government, for the vessels and cargoes which had been unlawfully captured.

The result was really a great victory for British interests in both the Imperial and the purely Canadian sense. In the former connection it secured an invaluable principle regarding maritime jurisdiction which it would have been madness for the Empire to have allowed any infringment of; it settled a difficult and dangerous question; it restored friendly relations with the United States. In the latter it proved Canada to have had justice and right upon its side; it vindicated the policy of Canadian statesmen; it showed that the Mother Country was standing behind the Dominion, and guarding local as well as Imperial interests; it freed Canadian sealers from the charge of poaching; it promised to restore to them the property so unjustly taken away. The only objection was the fear which Sir John felt as to the effects of the regulations upon the Canadian sealing industry, which, however, were so happily dissipated by experience, and by the unequalled catch which followed during the season of 1894.

Rewards and honours were freely bestowed upon those taking part in the British case. Sir Richard Webster and Sir Charles Russell were each given the insignia of a G.C.M.G. The latter also became, not long afterwards, Lord Russell of Killowen and Chief Justice of England. Mr. Christopher Robinson, Q.C., of Toronto, was offered Knighthood, but for personal reasons declined the honour. The able young Minister of Marine and Fisheries, who had devoted so much time and labour to the preparation of the case, was made a K.C.M.G., and last, but not least, the Premier of Canada was called to the Imperial Privy Council—and became entitled to the greatly valued prefix of "Right Honourable." Membership in Her Majesty's Privy Council is a rare distinction outside the United Kingdom, and within its bounds is considered by many public men to be ample reward for a lifetime of loyal service. For many years Sir John A. Macdonald was the only Colonial statesman who had attained the distinction; then William Bede Dalley, the eloquent Australian politician, who was instrumental in sending the famous contingent to the Soudan, joined the ranks; and a few years later Sir Alfred Stephen, the greatest of Australian jurists, and a man of the highest character and most distinguished political reputation, was appointed. All are now dead, including Sir John Thompson himself:

"Like clouds that rake the mountain summits,
Or waves that own no curbing hand!
How fast has brother followed brother
From sunshine to the sunless land."

Apart from the distinguished honour bestowed by his Sovereign, the Premier's services upon this great Imperial occasion were recognized in Canada with no grudging praise or half-hearted approval. Politics for the moment were dropped, and although there was some slight attempt afterwards to make capital out of the apparent danger of the sealers from the new regulations, all agreed as to the commanding ability shown by Sir John Thompson at Paris. Speaking at Belleville on September 28th following their return, Sir Charles Hibbert Tupper referred enthusiastically to the work done by his chief:

"I desire to say, and history will tell you that what I say is true, that our own leader, a true Canadian, a Canadian born, took first rank at that Tribunal. While I don't say that your interests would have been unsafe in the hands and under the management of English statesmen, I know that the Britith Foreign Secretary will agree with me when I tell you, in reference to this question and the regulations in reference to the settling of the immediate interests of the people on our Pacific coast, that we would have come out very small indeed had we not had Sir John Thompson forming one of the court which heard that case."

Senator Miller, speaking to an interviewer after his return from a prolonged visit to Europe during the months in which the Arbitration had been progressing, declared with equal emphasis that two things had been conclusively proved in this connection: first, the ample justice of the British case, and second, the transcendant ability of Sir John Thompson: "Although the deliberations of the tribunal were private, it is an open secret that the Canadian Premier was the master mind of the Arbitration, and I am told that his concise and able replies to the theories advanced by Senator Morgan and Judge Harlan, in their lengthy addresses, created the most profound impression on the minds of the neutral arbitrators." And somewhat similar tributes have since been paid by Sir R. Webster and Sir C. Russell.

Upon his reaching Quebec on August 25th, accompanied by Sir Charles Tupper and by the Minister of Marine and Fisheries, Sir John was received by a number of prominent men and welcomed back to Canada. In an interview with a *Toronto Empire* correspondent, the Premier dealt at length with the issues which had been involved. He pointed out that the British Government had already compensated Canadian sealers to the extent of $100,000 for abstaining from seal hunting in Behring Sea during the operation of the *modus vivendi*, and that under the terms of the Award the United States would be compelled to pay damages for the vessels illegally seized during many years' past. The claims for compensation had all been filed in London, and carefully adjusted. It may be said here that the amount ultimately agreed upon—$425,000—has not yet been paid by the American Government.* He went on to indicate the importance of the decision. The contentions of the United States involved nothing short of "absolute dominion over the Behring Sea for all purposes," and the American claims were so aggressively urged that "there could have been but one solution of the difficult situation if arbitration had not been resorted to, and that was war."

The next day Sir John Thompson arrived at Alexandria on his way to Ottawa, and was welcomed by a crowd of people, a band and a royal salute from some guns which had been mounted for the purpose. An address was presented, and in his reply the Premier dwelt upon the national import of the mission from which he had just returned; its removal of a cause of serious dispute; and its proof of the advantages accruing from British connection. A little later in the day he reached Ottawa, and was met by assembled citizens and presented with an address from

*February 12th, 1895.

the Civic Council. But the compliment he most keenly appreciated in this connection was the banquet tendered by the St. James' Club, Montreal, on November 21st. The commercial metropolis had already on September 12th, done something in the form of public addresses and a public reception to welcome the Prime Minister home, but it remained for the St. James' Club dinner to complete the pleasant tribute.

A large number of prominent political opponents shared in the demonstration, and it was this which so greatly enhanced the pleasure with which Sir John is known to have regarded this particular incident. Always disliking partisanship, it was to him like a green and beautiful oasis in a desert of political expediency and party considerations. An interesting feature of the occasion was a letter from Judge Davidson, of Montreal, regretting his inability to attend, and stating of the Premier that, "In a sense which is far away from and far above the strife of parties, he deserves this tribute to his life and character as a public man, for to all of us Canadians he stands out as an example of the lesson taught by Demosthenes that 'man is not born to his parents only, but to his country.'"

Sir John Thompson appreciated these kind words so greatly that he wrote privately on November 27th to Mr. Justice Davidson in a style which indicates how much he really felt political abuse and misrepresentation:

"My Dear Judge—

"Our friend, Judge Wurtele, showed me your very kind letter to him on the occasion of the dinner of last week at St. James' Club. I thank you most sincerely for this and all the other indications of your kindness which I have had. The banquet was a splendid affair, and the cordiality of everybody was very charming. I owe more thanks than I can ever give for such a splendid compliment. We, who are in political life, have to endure many insults and suspicions which we do not deserve, and must, therefore, be permitted to take with equanimity kindnesses like these which far exceed our merits. Friends like Wurtele and yourself, and a few others, work out this law of compensation in such a way as to relieve public life of its cares and odium.

"I remain, dear Judge, yours sincerely,

"JNO. S. D. THOMPSON."

At the banquet itself, which was presided over by Sir Donald Smith, M.P., the Premier spoke strongly concerning the valuable results of the arbitration:

"Canada received everything she would be glad to have accepted after a triumphant war, and she got them without any of the losses which war would have entailed. The lesson which bears on our future was to be derived from the attitude of Great Britain. Her forbearance and sagacity avoided war, and the treatment accorded Canada was an achievement of which we might well be proud. When we appear with Her Majesty's commission in our hands, no foreign diplomat dares to question our credentials."

A few months later, on March 16th, 1894, and during the debate on the Address, Mr. Laurier attacked the Treaty on account of the regulations, and accused Sir John Thompson of having returned home and spoken of the proceedings in a spirit of brag and bluster. Nothing could be more incongruous with the known character of the Premier than such a charge, and his speech in reply brushed away the attack like cobwebs from a ceiling. He showed his complete knowledge of the intricacies of the whole question, and in a very short time demolished his opponent's fine-spun theories, concluding with the statement that:

"I have professed great satisfaction at the upholding, in the most solemn way and before all the nations, of the doctrine for which we in this House have contended, for which we have contended in our correspondence with the Imperial Government, and for which no people in this country have so zealously contended as my hon. friend and those who sit beside him, namely, for the right of Canada to have a ruling voice in negotiations which affect her interests."

CHAPTER XIX.

Sir John Thompson and Mr. McCarthy.

During the comparatively brief, but important, period of what may be termed his national career, Sir John Thompson had no mean opponents to encounter and to overcome. Mr. Blake was a foeman worthy of any steel. From a purely intellectual standpoint he was probably the equal of any man in the House of Commons and the superior of most. Oratorically, he was not unlike the Minister of Justice in the days when they were pitted against each other. They both had the same faculty for amassing information and conveying it to the listener in logical and well-sustained periods. But Mr. Blake does not appear to have been as ready in his command of language, and the toil which he used to bestow upon the preparation of an important speech and the committing of it to memory, is a familiar matter to those who knew him. As politicians all that can be said in a few words is that one succeeded while the other failed.

Mr. Laurier was a delightful opponent, and no one appreciated his courtesy, tact, and natural graces of manner and oratory more than did Sir John Thompson. In many respects they were as opposite as the poles. The Liberal leader was apparently open in speech and style, excitable at times as is characteristic of his race, impetuous, and somewhat changeable. Sir John was always a reserved man, and this tendency increased rather than diminished with additional responsibilities. He never appeared to be excited, or so rarely as to make it almost remarkable; was never rash or hasty; and when once his mind was made up it was seldom changed. With Sir Richard Cartwright there was, of course, many a tilt, but on the whole Sir John Thompson appears to have rather admired the uncompromising political hostility of the Kingston knight. And this may be said in spite of the scathing Parliamentary attack of a certain memorable occasion. He is known also to have appreciated the ability displayed in the Budget criticisms, which during so many years, have helped to fill up the bill-of-fare in the House of Commons with a never failing raciness of invective and retort. In this respect Sir Richard is probably the most powerful speaker Canada has ever possessed. Without the ruggedness of George Brown he has a sarcastic style which seems to permeate not only his speech but himself, and which certainly makes his invective the bitterest of that of any man in Canadian public life.

The Hon. David Mills was another opponent whose knowledge of constitutional precedents and deep reading in general history made him worthy of every respect and attention. Mr. L. H. Davies, of Prince Edward Island, has for a long time been one of the Liberal leaders whose place is secure in the event of party success at the polls, and his characteristic Maritime eloquence had been known to Sir John Thompson since the period of the Halifax Fisheries' Award, when they found themselves for the first time prominently opposed to each other. And so with many more —the eloquent Paterson of Brant; Fraser, the forcible free-trader from down by the sea; Lister, the fighting Liberal; the fiery Tarte; the irrepressible Devlin. But the one man who stands distinctly out as the head and front of the opposition to Sir John Thompson during recent years is Mr. D'Alton McCarthy. Circumstances seemed to combine in order that the two men should appear in sharp antagonism to one another. Mr. McCarthy had refused to join the Liberal Opposition. He had declined to any longer support the Conservative party. And his hostility to the Conservative leader, whether personal or political, was voiced in nearly every important issue which has come before the House or the country since 1887.

The unquestioned ability and force which the member for North Simcoe displayed in his speeches, furnishes, of course, all the greater tribute to the success with which Sir John Thompson surmounted the difficulties so greatly augmented by Mr. McCarthy's attitude and advocacy. And in the same way the high rank which so many of the Liberal leaders took in debate, oratory, and upon the stump illustrated the qualities of courage, concentration and conviction which were needed to place a comparatively new man firmly in the saddle of political supremacy and to maintain him in power.

It is safe to say in this connection that the public life of Canada has never seen two men so diametrically opposed in convictions and characteristics as were Sir John and Mr. McCarthy, able to remain so long within the ranks of the same party; working together in the interests of the same political leader. The one entered the national arena in 1885 under the local auspices, and with the warm co-operation of the hierarchy of his native Province. Though his appointment in itself was a tribute to personal ability and to judicial services, it is none the less a fact that his environment was such as would have imperceptibly influenced any man not possessed of strong principles and a still stronger sense of duty. He reached Ottawa entirely new to his surroundings, to the leaders with whom he had to serve, and to the politicians whom he would be expected to lead. He came also heralded as a lawyer of high ability and a jurist of considerable reputation.

There he found Mr. D'Alton McCarthy established as a politician of long standing, of experience, and of cabinet rank. A close friend and intimate advisor of Sir John Macdonald, he was in addition the leader of the Ontario bar, and it was currently and very correctly supposed that he had been offered the particular portfolio which Mr. Thompson had just assumed. Naturally too he had been consulted for some years past upon constitutional issues as being an eminent lawyer, and upon political questions as being President of the Conservative Union of Ontario and the recognized party leader in that important Province. But when the new Minister of Justice forged to the front as an authority upon legal matters, and as one upon whom the Prime Minister in his growing physical weakness could confidently throw much of the burden of what may be called working government; it was inevitable that the position of an outside supporter and friend should become, not necessarily less confidential, but certainly less influential. And this might occur without reflecting in any way upon the ability and services of Mr. McCarthy.

It was simply the inevitable result of a strong man taking the place which the former might himself have filled with eminent success. For a time the two men worked together in apparent harmony, but it was not long before the divergence began to commence and develop. The Riel platform should have served as a mutual standing ground, but even here the contrast came out sharply. Mr. Thompson (as he was then) made a tour of the Province with the Premier during the elections of 1887. Everywhere he preached moderation; justice and fairplay to all races and creeds; toleration and a united Dominion. Meantime, Mr. McCarthy—Barrie February 4th—was paving the way for a very different policy: "Do you suppose," he declared, "that the men of Ontario are willing to submit for a prolonged period to a condition of subjection to one race—and I speak not of Ontario alone but of every man outside of the French nationality? . . . Do they mix with us; assimilate with us; intermarry with us; do they read our literture or learn our laws? No: everything with them is conducted on a French model, and while we may admire members of that race as individuals, yet as members of the body politic, I say they are the great danger to our confederacy."

Then came the Jesuits' Estates Question, and the differences along these lines became still more evident and distinct. Sir John Thompson did what he conceived to be his duty in a time of sectarian danger and sectional strife. He even went slightly out of his way to defend a religious body against which so many Protestants have been, and are, hopelessly and sincerely prejudiced, and which Mr. McCarthy attacked with much power. He endeavoured to throw a wet blanket upon the agitation which Mr. McCarthy was stirring up and fanning into a flame. While the one was counselling moderation and talking of the rights of Provinces, the dangers of strife, and the necessity of governing a mixed community upon principles of toleration and kindliness to all, the other was telling the people of Stayner, and incidentally of Canada—July 12th, 1889—that "now is the time when the ballot box will decide this great question before the people, and if that does not supply the remedy in this generation, bayonets will supply it in the next." And with the coming of the French language and Manitoba schools' questions, the divergence between the two leaders became so marked that in looking back it is difficult to see how they remained in even nominal alliance as long as they did.

Necessarily, therefore, as Sir John Thompson grew into leadership, and as his views continued to have more and more weight with the Conservative party, in opposition, at least, to those ennunciated by Mr. McCarthy, a public political separation of some kind became inevitable. And at the last moment the thread became so attenuated that the friends of both leaders were simply awaiting the movement which should make it snap. As it happened, the initiative was taken by the Government party through the medium of the *Toronto Empire.* On December 30th, 1892, that paper in a brief, and not particularly impressive editorial, announced that "for some time past the political course of the member for North Simcoe has been a prolonged and entertaining series of 'wobbles'." It declared that Mr. McCarthy had been holding quiet meetings in his constituency and warning his friends confidentially that he was about to leave the Conservative party. The article was sarcastic in tone, and was eminently calculated to be offensive to the politician who was the object of the attack.

A wide political discussion was the immediate result. Mr. McCarthy seized the occasion to say that he had been "read out of the party," and really did not seem to mind the operation very much. The importance of the newspaper deliverance turned, however, upon whether it was inspired by, or known to, the leaders at Ottawa. Amongst those who understood the close relations existing between the *Empire* and the Government, there could only be one opinion, though it might not have been a wise one to announce at the moment. And now that this particular page of journalistic history is closed forever, it can do no harm to say that the political policy of the paper was guided very largely by the opinions and wishes of Sir John A. Macdonald, and of Sir John Thompson after the Chieftain's death. Not that either of the leaders would offer suggestions masked, but Mr. Creighton, as the Managing Director, was very frequently in Ottawa, and was always there before any move of importance was made, either in politics or in the policy of the *Empire*. Financially, it was not aided by advertising and Government patronage to even a fair proportionate extent, and certainly not by the individual help of Ministers; although outside opinion seemed to think that a Government organ naturally lived upon the Government.

However that may be, the denunciation of Mr. McCarthy, while not inspired in its exact wording by Sir John Thompson, was without a shadow of doubt, approved by him as a matter of party policy and party tactics. The severance was coming anyway, and at the critical moment the friends of the Premier might as well be allowed to take the initiative. And aside from any other authority, a comprehension of the close relations existing between *The Empire* management and the Conservative leader would show how impossible it was that such an important step should have been taken without the latter's knowledge. No doubt also this fact was fully appreciated and understood by Mr. McCarthy himself. Whether it was a wise step to take, or not, is a debateable question, but that the drifting apart of the two men would come to some such result had long been absolutely inevitable.

After this occurrence their public relations were naturally not very friendly. That there was any personal hostility felt by Sir John Thompson towards his opponent and critic is altogether improbable. Neither by word or deed, in speech or document, with perhaps one exception, did he exhibit any anger or bitterness in this connection. At Belleville, during the demonstration in honour of Mr. Corby, the Premier made one significant reference, but it stood alone in the many speeches of that autumn tour: "The men who would divide the Conservative party, the men who would divide the country—for their ambition goes far enough to divide Canada as well as the party—thank God, have passed out of our ranks, and must pursue their nefarious work outside of them." When Sir John did allow himself scope he usually spoke strongly. Mr. McCarthy's position in his own defence, and in reply to *The Empire* was at first strong and dignified. In a letter published on January 2nd, following the famous editorial, he claimed as much right to belong to the party "if services and devotion count for anything, as any man now in public life." He then outlined the points upon which he differed from the Conservative leader:

"1. With reference to the Act respecting the Jesuits' Estates, which I thought, and still think, ought to have been disallowed under the veto power by His Excellency the Governor General, and I spoke and voted accordingly.

"2. With reference to the provisions regarding the North-West Territories, whereby the French language had been made official and put on the same basis as the English tongue, which, I endeavored, with a measure of success, to expunge from the statute book.

"3. The enactments as to the separate schools in the North-West, which I have sought, and at times aided by some of those who are now Ministers of the Crown, to repeal.

"4. I did most strenuously object and protest against the scheme of redistribution of seats which the Government introduced last Session and which, shorn it is true of some of its most objectionable features, passed into law."

But here came the statement which has made this matter historical, and which lends the personal element to what should have been merely a political incident. Mr. McCarthy goes on to speak of the National Policy, and points out that "Not having had any part, and not having been consulted in either the formation of the Government

Most Rev. Alex A. Taché,
Archbishop of St Boniface, Man.

or the framing of its policy," he is unable to reach a satisfactory conclusion as to its tariff intentions. This sentence seemed to indicate a certain amount of personal feeling which under the circumstances, is not altogether surprising. And at the same time it proved that he regretted the causes which had so perceptibly and steadily driven him along a road which seemed to most people capable of only one termination. When, upon Sir John Macdonald's death, he had approached the Minister of Justice, in connection with the formation of a new Cabinet, it is obvious that he then believed himself as fully a member and leader of the party as was Sir John Thompson himself.

The statement thus made was widely commented upon, and was practically repeated on the 25th of January following at Stayner: "It is not so much a question of policy that has driven me out of the ranks. It is the first time since I have been in public life that I have been ignored in the formation of a new Government. If I cannot be taken into the confidence of the councils of my party it is time to assert my independence." This assertion was followed up by the claim that the Government were responsible for the action of *The Empire*, and that the latter incident was a principal reason for his now formally withdrawing from the Conservative party for which in days gone by he had fought so brilliantly and well.

There are two points which ought to be considered in coming to a conclusion upon this historical matter. One is that an injustice has been done to Sir John Thompson in supposing that Mr. McCarthy's opposition to a certain line of Government policy was the secret reason for a break between the leaders. It must appear from what has been said that such a result was inevitable, apart altogether from the one being a strict Roman Catholic and the other having an environment of stern Protestantism. The fact is, that only Sir John Macdonald's leadership could have held such divergent sympathies in any kind of union. When Sir John Thompson became the practical leader in 1891, there existed no earthly reason for his consulting and working with Mr. D'Alton McCarthy. It might have been better had he tried to do so, but only along the lines of party expediency, and even the wisdom of that was doubtful. The truth is, that Mr. McCarthy had so antagonized his own party friends, that it would have been almost impossible for a Prime Minister or leader to have asked his co-operation in those days of sectarian and sectional suspicion.

But justice must be done Mr. McCarthy, in a statement which is made with all deference to his distinguished abilities and public services, he was hardly to be blamed for expecting consideration and attention from the leaders who had succeeded his old chief. And there can be no doubt of his consistency and independence of thought and action in regard to French Canadian and Roman Catholic questions. For years he had felt earnestly and strongly that something must be done to check what he considered dangerous aggression, and a man who had really sacrificed the Premiership, or a very great chance of obtaining it, for principle, deserved as much praise as he very often received blame. As a matter of fact also the particular questions which he brought to the front—the Jesuits' Estates Bill, the French language, and the Manitoba schools—were never made really party issues, and he was therefore justified to a certain extent in believing himself still a Conservative. And this despite the fact that the whole tendency of these agitations was against the national unity and good feeling for which both the political parties were nominally struggling.

He probably thought the issue a personal one between himself and Sir John Thompson. For a long time indeed they agreed upon the fiscal question, and while that was the case, it is difficult to see how Mr. McCarthy could have been "read out" of the party unless he wanted to go. But finally that link went also, and the only thing which continued to evidence a bond of fellowship was loyalty to a common sentiment regarding British union, and objection to any touch of Continentalism in trade or principle. The personal element, however, showed itself more and more strongly as time went on, and this must be pointed out in order to illustrate the justice of Sir John's conclusion that they could not longer work together within the same party. During a speech at Toronto in April following *The Empire* episode, Mr. McCarthy referred to what he called "the maintenance of the dual language iniquity and the separate school anomaly in the North-West," and asked if they constituted Tory doctrine. If so, then, "I am not a Tory. If it is a Conservative plank, I want to know when it was put in the platform. Was it when Sir John Thompson took charge of affairs? I think it was."

Speaking on May 1st at Orangeville, he was still more explicit. He pointed out that he was "an older man than Sir John, older in political experience, and older, too, than most of the statesmen he had summoned." But the Premier had formed his Cabinet. "They had all seen it and perhaps they liked it. It was a wonderful organization, so nicely balanced between the orange and the green. The equipoise was so excellent that it could not move forward—it had no volition." This is rather bitter, and shows the tendency of the speaker. At Listowel, on October 12th, he observed: "I am perfectly indifferent, politically speaking, as to what the future may have in store for me. I am not going to allow any man to silence me; I am not going to bend the knee to Sir John Thompson or Mr. Laurier, or anyone else." Again, on Dec. 19th, at Millbrook, this feeling came out even more distinctly. Referring to the then recent Liberal victory in Winnipeg, he declared that his friends there had done much towards Mr. Martin's success, and concluded by denouncing Sir John Thompson for his somewhat famous phrase used about this time in describing the two Liberal champions of Roman Catholicism and Protestantism respectively, as "the Black Tarte and the Yellow Martin": "Mr. Martin is the man who framed the law which repealed Separate Schools in Manitoba. Is he entitled to such an epithet for that act? Martin will be remembered long after the Premier is forgotten."

It is, therefore, evidently impossible, after a perusal of Mr. McCarthy's speeches before and since the event, to blame Sir John Thompson for his action in December, 1892, or to suppose that, so far as he was concerned, personal or religious feelings had anything to do with the matter. Nor is it incompatible with sincere respect for the late Premier's memory, and regard for his great life-work, to feel that the Equal Rights champion was sincere and consistent both in wishing to remain within the party and in finally leaving it.

And aside from the later developments in connection with trade and tariff matters, upon which opinions will differ, both Sir John Thompson and Mr. McCarthy seem to have been honestly consistent, and honestly antagonistic. The one thought that in a country of mixed nationalities and creeds, the only possible and permanent union was a system of working by mutual sympathy, forbearance and toleration. The other considered it absolutely necessary to build a nation as you would a house, upon a foundation of stone unmixed with any other article—a basis of similarity in sentiment, uniformity in language and approximation in creed. The one was a man of iron will, with intellect and passions under stern subjection to his sense of duty. The other also possessed a strong will, but with a somewhat impetuous and enthusiastic temperament. The one was willing to work and mould existing material with the aid of time and patience; the other was ready to overturn existing institutions or policies on the chance of replacing them with something better. Both had great ability. One is gone from the land he tried so well to serve, the other has still the opportunity for great and useful service to his country and empire.

CHAPTER XX.

THE NEW GOVERNOR GENERAL AND A POLITICAL TOUR.

Immediately following Sir John Thompson's return from Paris he had the privilege of joining in the welcome extended to the Earl and Countess of Aberdeen, who had come to take up the reins of vice-regal authority, and incidentally, to cement the warm friendship which had already grown up between themselves and the Prime Minister. Lady Aberdeen, in an article contributed to an English journal shortly after his death, vividly pourtrays the occasion of their first meeting Sir John. It was on the *Parisian* during a trip to Canada in 1891. "'I want to introduce to you the Minister of Justice,' said another Canadian friend, himself a former Minister; and but few words were necessary to impress one with a sense of confidence and trust in this quiet, strong, earnest-looking man, in whose eye, however, there played a twinkle, and whose smile lighted up a countenance full of sympathy and kindliness. It was not difficult to accept his friend's description of him as 'the ablest man in Canada.'"

Her Excellency then speaks of the rare nature with which he was endowed; of his power for deep, true friendship; of his constant and beautiful thought for others; of the strong friendship which had gone on deepening between them from that day until his sudden and mournful death. And there was much in this case to create that bond of sympathy and mutual respect without which real friendship is impossible. Sir John Thompson's ideal in life was the performance of duty, his chief motive the rendering of service to his country and empire. The ideal of Lord and Lady Aberdeen, as exhibited in their innumerable public, political and philanthropical enterprises, was the improvement of the condition of the poor and the elevation of surrounding humanity in comfort, in education, in thought, and in that spirit of personal aspiration which contributes so greatly to the uplifting and ennobling of those engaged in the drudgery and routine of ordinary life. The Canadian Premier had sacrificed much of his time for domestic happiness, his chances of financial prosperity, and positions of ease and dignity, upon the altar of national duty. The Governor General and the Countess of Aberdeen, on the other hand, had for many years surrendered the time which might have been devoted to the enjoyment of boundless luxury, and the pleasures of high position, in giving themselves to energetic and unceasing efforts for the promotion of the people's welfare in the different countries with which they had become connected.

It is not, therefore, a matter for surprise that this warm feeling of friendship should have grown up and strengthened, until the cord was snapped by death. Lord Aberdeen's first public appearance as Governor General of Canada was most successful from every point of view. Upon arriving at Quebec on September 17th, Their Excellencies were welcomed by a large gathering of Cabinet Ministers and others, and on the following day Lord Aberdeen was duly sworn in. His address upon this occasion deserved and received the careful consideration and sincere respect of the Canadian people. Especially noteworthy was the definition of a Governor General's duties: "Aloof though he be from actual executive responsibilities, his attitude must be that of ceaseless and watchful readiness to take part by whatever opportunity may be afforded to him in the fostering of every influence that will sweeten and elevate public life; to observe, study and join in making known the resources and development of the country; to vindicate, if required, the rights of the people and the ordinances of the constitution; and lastly, to promote by all means in his power, without reference to class or creed, every movement and every institution calculated to forward the social, moral and religious welfare of the Dominion."

There is a whole volume contained in this eloquent sentence, and despite the difficulties surrounding the position, and the occasional criticisms which are inevitable in any free community, the vast majority of the Canadian people feel with Sir John Thompson in some of his private correspondence, that Lord Aberdeen has earnestly and successfully lived up to the aspirations contained in that opening speech, and that he has been nobly aided by Her Excellency. And it is interesting to note in this connection that wherever the late Premier formed a personal friendship, the respect and admiration of those with whom he was thus intimate, became almost unbounded. Close acquaintance with his character seems indeed to have inspired feelings which show how true he was to principle, how unassuming he appeared to be, and yet how impressive he really was, in private as well as in public life. Familiarity, instead of breeding contempt or indifference or modified respect, in his case enhanced every sentiment of trust and esteem.

During the six crowded years following 1887, Sir John Thompson could hardly be said to have kept in personal touch with the important Province of Ontario. At that time he had campaigned with Sir John A. Macdonald, but it was as a new man, and in company with one whom many people almost worshipped. It is true that he then made a most favourable impression, and that his treatment of the Riel case had ensured him popularity and respect, but still the public memory is fickle, and the passing of a few years practically wiped that important tour off the slate. In the meantime, however, he had grown into the central figure of Canadian public life; had developed an Imperial reputation; and had pursued in regard to Provincial legislation, a certain line of policy which had not conduced to popularity in portions of Ontario. Yet he was unknown personally to the bulk of the Canadian people. In a Democratic community he had in fact climbed to the top without the aid of so-called popular qualities, and without being in personal touch with the all powerful electorate.

But it was now felt that a series of speeches was desirable, and that the Premier should be made acquainted, so far as was possible, with the local leaders and the people of Ontario. Especially was this the case in view of the trade and tariff conditions prevalent in the United States, and voiced in Canada by the various organizations and proposed policies which made 1893 a period of such widespread fiscal discussion. He had, of course, outlined the party policy during the first weeks of the year in Toronto, but six or eight months is a long time in politics, and much had happened since then, notably the financial crash in the States. Hence the interest taken in a tour which was immediately preceded by a great demonstration and reception in Montreal on the 12th of September. It was an occasion of considerable importance, and the address presented by the united Conservative clubs of the commercial metropolis was so full and complimentary, and embodied so clearly the policy of the Premier and his party, that it deserves to be given here, just as it was presented to Sir John Thompson in the crowded City drill hall with its dense mass of cheering people:

Honourable Sir,—

On this, your first public visit to Montreal since the representative of our Most Gracious Sovereign entrusted you with the formation of the Government, we desire, on behalf of the several Conservative organizations of Montreal, to extend to you a most cordial and hearty welcome.

We are proud to have the privilege of greeting you as a leader of the Conservative party, and in that capacity as the exponent of the principles to which we are cordially attached, through whose application in the administration of public affairs Canada has now, for many years, enjoyed a progressive prosperity in material concerns, contributing to the promotion of her status among the nations of the world, while strengthening and still more firmly cementing her attachment to the great Empire to which we are proud to owe allegiance.

We are especially gratified at the opportunity of congratulating you upon the successful completion of the important duty which you have just discharged as a member of the Court of Arbitration for the settlement of the dispute arising out of the control of the Behring Sea fisheries. We recognize in your appointment as one of the British arbitrators on the joint high tribunal not only the selection of one of the most able, astute and learned subjects of our Queen, but what is equally gratifying, an admission by the Government of the Mother Country of the right of Canada to a full and equal voice in the decision of all matters that nearly concern our peculiar interest, and we may be permitted to add from the result of the deliberations of the court, of which you were so distinguished a member, that in common with Canadians we deeply appreciate the splendid services rendered by you to Canada in that capacity.

In the conviction that the best interests of every class in our beloved country are wrapped up in the perpetuation of the cardinal principles of the policy upon which the administration of public affairs for the past fifteen years has been based, we beg to tender you the assurance of our continued devotion to the cause of the Conservative party whose honoured leader you are. Its policy, we are well aware, has been assailed by foes within and foes without; but we believe that the practical results flowing from the application of that policy have afforded so striking an object lesson to the electorate of this country, that when the time of trial comes, the principles we espouse will be once more triumphant. And that object lesson has been peculiarly emphasized during recent months by the happy condition of trade in Canada compared with other countries.

We are persuaded, moreover, that the Government of which you are an honoured and trusted leader will continue as in the past to vindicate its claim to the confidence of the people of Canada by shaping its policy to meet the varying conditions of trade, and by harmonizing every interest, whether labouring, manufacturing, agricultural, mining, fishing or otherwise, and shaping all in unison to a common end—the advancement of the welfare of a'l classes in our beloved Dominion.

In conclusion, permit us to renew the assurance of pleasure it affords us to welcome you to Montreal, and to wish yourself and Lady Thompson the richest blessings of health, long life and every prosperity.

Signed on behalf of the clubs,

FRED. C. HENSHAW,
President Junior Conservative Club.

P. B. MIGNAULT,
President Club Cartier.

C. A. MCDONNELL,
President Sir John A. Macdonald Club.

J. ADELARD OUIMET,
President Club Conservateur.

JOSEPH H. JACOBS; BEAUMONT JOUBERT,
Hon. Secs. United Conservative Clubs.

The Premier received this tribute, accompanied by Sir Adolphe Caron, the Hon. Mr. Angers, the Hon. Mr. Foster, the Hon. Mr. Ouimet and Mayor Desjardins. He spoke in reply first in French and then in English, the latter being of course the speech of the evening. In this connection it is worthy of note that when Sir John first came to Ottawa in 1886 he could hardly speak a word of French. But recognizing the desirability of being acquainted with the language of nearly two millions of the Canadian people he had devoted himself with characteristic energy, and amid all the innumerable demands upon his time, to its acquisition. The address was delivered in his usual calm, deliberate and judicial style; every word being well weighed and every sentence well rounded. It was not, however, a stump speech, and from current comments it is questionable whether the effect was as great as the ability and honesty of the effort deserved.

But it was the utterance of a statesman; the matured thought and expression of an earnest and sincere mind. In his opening remarks Sir John Thompson spoke of what his predecessors had accomplished, and added: "I venture to express the hope, as the highest ambition I can have, that I should be worthy, at least in effort, at least in disinterestedness, and at least in earnestness and zeal and purpose, of those great men." He then referred to the late Liberal Convention in a somewhat sarcastic way, and pointed out that the Conservative party did not require one because its policy and principles were known to all men, and had been over and over again approved by the people of Canada. But it was different with the Opposition: "They had great need of a convention because they were a party about to change their platform. They had done it very often before. We had seen them going to the country with even greater confidence than they expressed in Ottawa in convention, on other platforms altogether. They had declared for continental free trade. They then had a platform of commercial union, and only nine or ten months ago their leader declared that on Unrestricted Reciprocity they would live or die."

He went on to say that the protective policy was not a fixture in application, though regarding its general principles it was always the same. It was a fiscal method which permitted modifications and in fact made changes absolutely essential, in accordance with the constantly changing circumstances of the time. Hence the recent appointment of Ministers to investigate the condition of different industries and interests; hence also the promise of moderate tariff reform during the next session of Parliament. And then the Premier, amid great applause, eulogised the National Policy as a whole: "We think, while we admit that our policy in the past has not done all we hoped for, that it has achieved very great results for Canada. We think it has increased immensely the volume of Canadian trade both as regards our exports and imports.

We think it has succeeded in a marvellous degree in developing the interests of every class of the working community. We think it has been marvellously successful in establishing public works all over this country, of which any country in the world might be proud, and which have made Canada envied by other nations. We think, and we know, that it has been the means of increasing inter-provincial trade—of giving the home market to our people, to the industrial classes of different sections of the country, and thereby creating a greater sentiment in favour of union between the different provinces of this great Confederation."

Sir John then spoke of the idle and breadless working-men who were being fed in the streets and public parks of the great American cities; of the failures of innumerable banks in the United States; of the great commercial, industrial and financial crash which had taken place in that paradise of the advocates of unrestricted reciprocity; and pointed out that the Canadian artisan and Canadian interests were going along comparatively undisturbed by neighbouring disasters: "Every one knows that the social and commercial life of the people, the comfort of their homes, their abstention from crime and outrage, their obedience to order and to law, their respect for religion and authority, are a hundred-fold better—in this beloved country of ours—than in that boasted land from which these gentlemen sought to take their policy."

He referred to the effect of free trade and the absence of protection upon the unfortunate farmers of England; to the American depression in the prices of products and lands; to the condition of the English artisan and labourer. He declared the policy of the Government to be the maintenance of a home market for the Canadian people and announced it to be their intention to write upon the tariff in broad distinct terms, that the industries of the Dominion should "never be at the dictation of a foreign country." He claimed that under Mr. Mackenzie's Liberal administration the national debt had increased $8,000,000 per annum with little to show for it, while under Conservative rule it had grown only $6,250,000 a year, with the C. P. R. and many great public works as a result. He stated that Canadian commerce had fallen off $20,000,000 annually under a revenue tariff, but had increased $28,000,000 a year under protection.

The Premier then turned to the Manitoba Schools' question and discussed it freely, fully, and honestly. He referred to the charges made by Mr. Tarte, regarding a promise of remedial legislation said to have been given to Archbishop Taché, and mentioned "the solemn denial in writing by the venerable Archbishop himself." He added his belief that the people of Canada would accept the word of that "venerable and saintly man in preference to that of ten thousand Tartes." In reference to his own position he pointed out that "time and again I have been accused, with respect to this question, of pandering to Catholic interests. Time and again in another province I have been accused of entering into a league with the Roman Catholic hierarchy for the purpose of subverting the constitutional rights of a province of this Dominion."

He went on to deal with the problem historically and constitutionally; handled Mr. Laurier without gloves for his charges of cowardice; and then made a somewhat significant declaration regarding the Liberal leader's claim that if the public schools of Manitoba were *de facto* Protestant schools, then Federal interference might be necessary:

"Once for all we have to decide, if the public function is imposed upon us by the Courts, not what the schools are, but what the citizens of the Province make them; and, therefore, if the statutes of Manitoba do not make the schools of the Province Protestant schools and do not justify the public schools of that Province being made Protestant schools, the Federal Government would have no power to interfere if any contravention of the law there, was made to the oppression of the minority."

The Dominion, therefore, if given the power to intervene by the Courts, could only do so upon the legislation itself and not in connection with any system which might have developed in spite of, or through lax enforcement of, the law upon the statute book. The speech concluded with a vigourous denunciation of the Canadian independence idea and a rousing expression of loyalty to British connection.

This address gave the keynote for the ensuing tour of Ontario. At Belleville, a couple of weeks' later, perhaps the most important of these series of meetings was held-- the occasion being a demonstration in honour of the popular local member, Mr. Harry Corby. It was an out-of-doors meeting and over eight thousand people gathered from neighboring counties to welcome the Premier and his visiting colleagues. Mr. Baldwin Falkiner, President of the West Hastings Conservative Association, acted as chairman and an address was presented from the Associations of six ridings in the vicinity. Sir John Thompson was given a great reception and stated that though many of his colleagues as well as himself, were new men and unknown to the audience personally, they none the less stood for old principles. Amid great cheering he declared that "the ship of state has not been a ship lying to in the storm, but it is a ship which has made many prosperous voyages, a ship which carries the British flag still aloft, and now carries forward the hope of the young Canadian people, fuller of ambition to-day than it ever has been since the Union was formed."

Attention was drawn to the wonderful stability of Canada during a time of international distress: "We have seen the Australian Colonies swept by a whirlwind of disaster. We have seen the markets of Great Britain paralyzed by financial depression,--and later still we have seen the Western States swept by a cyclone of disaster, which the President of that country officially declared was stopping every wheel of industry and turning thousands of men into the streets." He spoke of the McKinley bill having checked exports to the Republic by $5,000,000, during a year which had seen trade increase with the Mother Country to the extent of $17,000,000. He stated that although reciprocity in any fair and practicable degree had been declared impossible by Mr. Blaine as representing the Republican party, yet his Government had informed the new Democratic administration—opposed as that party was on principle to reciprocity with any country—that if it "was disposed to make fair tariff concessions based upon legislation, such tariff concessions would be met by the Canadian Government in a proper spirit." More could not be done and even that much turned out to be useless. He denounced the Liberal party for its general pessimism and its constant changes. In this respect his words might well have brought to the minds of the audience those expressive lines:

> "Drifting, drifting, ever drifting,
> And never a harbour in sight.
> A pathless sea, a moonless night,
> And the clouds are never rifting."

Other addresses were delivered by Sir Adolphe Caron, Sir Charles Hibbert Tupper, Mr. Haggart and Mr. Angers. In the evening a banquet was held at which the Premier again spoke, together with Mr. Costigan, Mr. Daly, Mr. Clarke Wallace, Mr. Curran and Mr. Wood. On the morning of September 25th, Sir John reached Berlin, accom-

Louis Henry Davis, Q.C.

Formerly Premier of P. E. Island.

panied by other ministers, and visited many of its flourishing industries. In the afternoon they arrived at Elmira, and were enthusiastically welcomed at both the open meeting, and the great gathering in the evening. The next day Clinton was reached and a large audience of farmers from all over the county, was addressed in the afternoon. Sir John concluded a brief speech by expressing the hope that "the spirit of Canadian fellowship and enterprise, and of attachment to the British Empire may continue to grow. We are a determined, self-reliant people, determined to make a name for our country—the best half of this Continent."

Extensive preparations had been made at Stratford to welcome the Premier and his colleagues. The skating rink in the evening was filled to the doors with probably nine or ten thousand people, and the numerous addresses presented to Sir John were—it is to be hoped—as satisfactory to him as were the speeches delivered in reply, to the people. At Palmerston, a warm welcome was given on the afternoon of the 27th inst., and in the evening the largest political demonstration which is said to have ever been seen in Bruce County, was held at Walkerton. The town was literally packed with people, and after the public meeting a banquet was tendered the Premier. On the following day, flying visits were paid to Tara and Port Elgin, and a banquet was received at Southampton in the evening. The mass meeting in the Tara rink was especially interesting, as evoking a declaration from Sir John in favour of woman suffrage: "We look forward to it as one of the aims which are to be accomplished in the public life of Canada. because the Conservative party believe that the influence of women in the politics of the country is always for good. I think, therefore, that there is a probability of the franchise being extended to the women on the same property qualifications as men."

Lucan was next visited, and then Durham. At the latter place Sir John asked, amid loud cheers and in reference to the situation in the States: "Where would Canada have been to-day if the people of this country had accepted the Liberal proposition for Unrestricted Reciprocity?"

At Mount Forest, Kenilworth and Arthur, Sir John Thompson and his colleagues were greeted with veritable ovations. At the latter place, and on behalf of the North Wellington Conservative Association, Mr. Wm. Kingston presented an Address, part of which was unusually interesting:

"We watched your course during the lifetime of our late lamented leader with ever-increasing interest and respect. We learned to value the loyal support and energetic help you gave him while a member of his Ministry. We feel that you, better than any man living, understood his views and policy, and are fitted to become the depositary of his traditions. New circumstances require to be met and dealt with, and we believe that you will meet and deal with them in an independent and masterful way as in the past. We belong to a party whose motto it is to live in the present—abreast of the times—not forgetting our past, but connecting our policy smoothly with it."

North and South Perth seemed to meet at Mitchell on October 3rd to do honour to the Premier. Owen Sound contributed a demonstration on the following day as great as that which had welcomed the new Minister of Justice and the old Chieftain in 1887. Markdale, Dunnville and Glencoe followed suit, and on the evening of Saturday, Oct. 7th, the tour closed at the last-named place. Sir John took the train for Montreal, where he was to meet Lady Thompson on her return from Europe, and the other Ministers returned to the Capital. The two weeks thus spent must have been most gratifying to the Premier. The innumerable addresses which were presented indicated the high respect and esteem in which he was held; the constant references to the Behring Sea Commission showed how the results of the arbitration, and his connection with it, were appreciated; the receptions and banquets, the waiting crowds at the stations, together with the great processions in many places and the enthusiasm and interest everywhere exhibited, conveyed a popular tribute which could not fail to be satisfactory, even to a public man who cared so little for mere partisan applause as did Sir John Thompson.

CHAPTER XXI.

AS MINISTER OF JUSTICE.

Sir John Thompson possessed in an eminent degree the mind, the training, and the aptitude of a jurist. And he was therefore especially well qualified to administer successfully the Department which he controlled for some eight years. However disparagingly opponents might speak of him as a politician, a diplomatist, a leader, or a Prime Minister of his country, they were compelled to respect the admirable judicial attainments, natural and acquired, which he was able at all times and under all circumstances to bring to the consideration of great legal and judicial problems.

His career, in this sense, was curiously compact. Each important success seemed to fit into some future development and aid in furthering his interests, perhaps years afterwards. His first important case at the Bar was the defence of a negro accused of some petty crime, whose acquittal he secured. His first appearance in the Supreme Court of Nova-Scotia was in 1874, nearly nine years after being called to the Bar, when he acted as junior counsel with Mr. R. L. Weatherbe, now a Judge of that Court. He may be said to have made his reputation in pleading in the celebrated case of Woodworth vs. Troop *et al.*, during the same year. It was a case of Provincial and constitutional importance. The plaintiff was a member of the House of Assembly, and in a speech made during the Session had charged the Provincial Secretary with having altered and falsified certain public records and documents of the Crown Lands Department, after the signature of the Lieut.-Governor had been appended. A committee was appointed to investigate the charge and reported that there was no foundation whatever for it. The House then passed a resolution demanding an apology in the most abject terms from Woodworth—the plaintiff—which he declined to make. Another resolution followed, ordering his expulsion from the House, and the Speaker instructed the sergeant-at arms to eject him, which was done. Mr. Woodworth then brought action against the Speaker and the members of the Committee.

The whole question turned upon whether the Courts of the Province had power to review the action of the Legislature. Mr. Thompson, and Mr. Macdonald, Q.C., acted for the plaintiff and carried the matter through the various Courts until it was finally argued before the Supreme Court of Nova-Scotia, in 1876. In the meantime, party feeling had been aroused and the whole Province had taken sides for or against. Then it was that the future Minister of Justice first displayed that remarkable knowledge of the rights, duties, and prerogatives of Parliament, which afterwards so greatly distinguished him. His argument won the case and settled the question of the power of the Provincial Legislature to punish for contempt. The force and ability thus shown is said to have surprised his friends, while the natural result was an immediate accession of public favour, and his subsequent appearance in many important cases before the Supreme Court of the Province.

In 1879 Mr. Thompson became Attorney-General of his Province and in the following year was gazetted a Queen's Counsel. In 1882 he was appointed a judge of the Supreme Court. He sat as a justice of the Supreme Court of Nova Scotia untill 1886, when he resigned from the Bench and re-entered political life, being called upon to preside as Minister of Justice over the administration of

Canadian law and constitutional practice. His career in this high office appears to divide itself naturally into four distinct phases. The political control of great constitutional issues such as the Jesuits' Estates act, the Riel case, and the Manitoba schools forms one; his attitude upon moral and legal reforms and upon minor and technical questions in the House is another; his policy regarding general Provincial legislation is a third; and his efforts concerning important Parliamentary proposals and the initiation of legislation, such as the Criminal Code or the Copyright Law is a fourth. The first phase has been considered with more or less fulness.

It is interesting to note in a general way how thorough the Minister was in everything connected with his work and the administration of his department. Not satisfied with the reports of subordinates, he himself visited most of the prisons and penitentiaries under his jurisdiction. In 1887 he travelled through Manitoba, the North-West, and British Columbia for this purpose alone; making no speeches, and devoting himself entirely to business.

In the House of Commons, the influence of the Minister of Justice was all for good. It was a reforming, purifying, yet judicious power. He was incapable of legislating in a hurry, or of putting upon the statute book to-day reforms which would have to be modified or altered to-morrow. And he could be very sarcastic in dealing with those who made proposals which did not commend themselves to his judgment. Upon one occasion—June 6th, 1888—Dr. Sproule, a well-known member of the House, moved that in view of the Jubilee celebration it was expedient to pass an Address to the Governor General, asking that clemency in different degrees be granted to all convicts whose conduct had been meritorious during their term of imprisonment. In his speech Sir John dealt both shortly and sharply with the idea:

"The sentiments which actuate the hon. member who has brought the motion forward are, I find from the experience which I have had in office, those which actuate three-fourths of the members of this House; who are under the impression apparently that the unfortunate persons who are confined in the penitentiaries are confined there either through mistake or from some unforeseen misadventure which it was impossible for them to provide against. . . . I think if I may express the sentiment without offence to the gentlemen who are supporting this motion, that the most unsuitable way we could devise of celebrating Her Majesty's Jubilee or attempting to confer any benefit upon the public, would be to let loose upon the community a class of people who have shown themselves able by long experience to inflict the greatest injury upon the community."

This was not a very conciliatory way of discussing the suggestion of a prominent supporter, but it illustrates the principle of justice which permeated the speaker's character. To him, divorce legislation was a peculiarly difficult subject. As a Roman Catholic, all divorce was objectionable; as Minister of Justice he had to guide the House in its decisions upon the divorce bills which came down from the Senate. In one case—June 15th, 1887—he made an able speech in favour of the divorce asked for, and one which Mr. Davies, who followed, described as "a clear and lucid opinion." It certainly showed a very complete knowledge of the law as voiced by decisions in the English High Court of Justice and the House of Lords; in the different American States; and in legislation during centuries past and gone. He concluded with the significant remark: "I only refrain from voting for this Bill for the reasons that I should give for voting against any Bill for the dissolution of the marriage tie." Upon another occasion—April 21st, 1890—he vigourously opposed a certain petition on grounds which were expressed as follows:

"The proposition, then, is that we shall dissolve the marriage simply because she found that she was married to a person not able to support her as well as she hoped he would be. I cannot imagine a ground of divorce which would be more stigmatised in those countries where laxity of principles as regards divorce is prevalent; I cannot imagine an application for divorce, the granting of which would do more dishonour to this Parliament than the passage of this Bill. I shall, therefore, apart from my objection to divorce on general principles, oppose this Bill from every point of view." Needless to say the "relief" asked for was not granted.

Early in 1888, it was announced that the Government intended to take some steps to check gambling in stocks and merchandize and to control or abolish the "bucket shops," which were leading so many young men along the slippery path of speculation to ultimate ruin. Speaking upon the measure which was finally carried through the House, the Minister of Justice declared that,

"There is a limit beyond which speculation becomes merely a vice and profligacy and a temptation to everybody to get riches quickly, even if they do not get them honestly. . . . I know from experience that numbers of persons belonging to respectable classes in the community are in our different penitentiaries now, in consequence of bucket shop transactions which led them on to embezzlement and fraud of different kinds."

About the same time, the Minister moved an amendment to the law relating to the fraudulent marks on merchandize, which, as he said, was "an adaptation of the English Act to Canadian conditions." By this measure protection was given through criminal process to registered trade marks; the burden of proving the absence of fraud was thrown largely upon the defendant; all offenders became subject to summary conviction; the law was enlarged so as to deal with false trade descriptions; provision was made regarding search warrants, and for the seizure by the Customs authorities of goods which might infringe the law. And it is not likely that these and other enactments lacked severity in view of Sir John Thompson's well known hatred of dishonesty in all its forms.

The records of Parliament contain a number of debates turning upon more or less legal issues, in which the Minister of Justice was, of course, the controlling figure. The Baird election case was one of these. On April 28th, 1887, the matter was brought up in the House, and it was stated that G. G. King as the Liberal candidate in a Prince Edward Island constituency had received 1191 votes, whilst his opponent G. F. Baird, had received 1130. The returning officer, however, declared Mr. Baird elected on the ground that his opponent's nomination papers were invalid because of his deposit not having been made by a duly qualified agent. In his reply to Mr. Skinner, of New Brunswick, who had urged the House to take action, the Minister of Justice stated that it was not a matter for Parliamentary interference, but for the Courts to deal with. The precedents quoted had occurred previous to election cases having been transferred from Parliament to the Courts, both in Great Britain and Canada. All details, he pointed out, were now relegated to the Judiciary, the House only retaining the right to pass upon the qualification of the person returned as elected. In this connection he instanced the case of O'Donovan Rossa, whose election had been voided in 1870, by the British House of Commons, because of his being a convicted felon. But this particular question was one for the Courts to pass upon, as it involved purely technical and legal considerations.

Later on, the matter came up again, though in a very different form. Mr. Baird had voluntarily resigned his seat and been re-elected. Prior to this the case had been taken into the Courts and had resulted in Mr. J. W. Ellis, M.P., proprietor of the *St. John Globe*, being imprisoned for abusive language contained in his paper, and directed against one of the Judges. Meantime the returning-officer was brought before Parliament, but was eventually discharged. On June 6th, 1894, Mr Davies introduced a motion of serious censure upon the returning-officer, who had been dealt with by the House seven years before, and upon the Judge who had tried the more recent case. Incidentally, he made a somewhat violent speech. Sir John declared in the course of his reply that "Judges have been censured for having left their business of judgment and having gone into politics. We are being asked to leave our business of politics and to go into the business of judgment."

As usual, he urged the House to look after its own affairs, which were sufficiently onerous:

"Our business is confined to the politics of the country —I use the word 'politics' in its larger sense, as embracing legislation—and when we step out of our sphere and undertake to deliver judgment between subject and subject, much more when we undertake to reverse or to sit in review on the judgment of one of the highest Courts of the country, we lay ourselves open to the very condemnation that this resolution would pronounce against the Court whose opinions it criticises." The Premier concluded by declaring that all "the abominations of the Star Chamber" were included in this one resolution. Needless to say it did not pass.

Another case which came up—May 9th, 1888—and was widely discussed as involving the rights of the press was the imprisonment of J. T. Hawke, Editor of the

Moncton Transcript, for contempt of Court in commenting most violently and personally upon a judgment of the Supreme Court of New Brunswick in the Westmoreland election trial. Without going into details, it is sufficient to say that Mr. Davies urged the commutation of the Editor's sentence, and that the Minister of Justice stood firmly by the dignity and impartiality of the Bench. Referring to the attacks of the *Moncton Transcript* upon Judge Fraser in particular, he declared that: "I have nothing to say now in regard to the propriety of such language being used to public men, but it is in the interests of the free administration of justice that the men who sit on the Bench, apart from the hurly-burly in which we live and struggle day after day, should be free from such attacks."

A little later he moved an amendment to the Criminal Procedure Act by which a newspaper proprietor, publisher or editor charged with defamatory libel could be indicted, tried and punished in his own Province, and not run the risk of being taken, against his will, to another Province under varying local laws and conditions.

A brilliant illustration of Sir John's knowledge of legal precedents and constitutional principles occurred on March 18th, 1890, when Lieut.-Colonel Amyot moved a sudden amendment to the Committee of Supply resolution in which he urged the exclusive right of the Provincial Executives to appoint Queen's Counsel for all Provincial Courts and to establish rules and rights of procedure therein. The matter came as a surprise to the Minister of Justice, but he was fully equal to the emergency. After analyzing the case of Lenoir vs. Ritchie, which had been largely depended upon for the Provincial argument, and proving it to actually support the opposite contention, he referred to many other cases and to various reports, and went on to say: "I venture to differ from the hon. gentleman that he has established that the Crown is an integral part of the Legislatures of the Provinces. . . . . In reference to all the Provinces of Canada, I think I am speaking within the lines of the decisions—which have all run one way—proceeding from the Judicial Committee of the Privy Council, when I say that all the Legislative powers and constitutional functions which existed down to that time (1867) in the various Provinces of British America were for the instant taken back by the Imperial Government and re-distributed under the terms of the British North America Act."

An elaborate argument followed upon the degree in which Her Majesty could be bound by Provincial legislation enacted in her name. The speaker claimed finally that the Queen did not really form a part of the Provincial Legislatures, and that as a consequence of certain decisions the Provincial Government did not appear to have the power to create a Q.C. or to bestow titles of honour.

During this Session Sir John had to deal with two very technical and difficult subjects in the amendment of the law relating to bills of exchange and promissory notes, and in the discussions, negotiations, and arrangement of the "Bill respecting Banks and Banking." Several deputations, composed of Mr. B. E. Walker, Mr. D. R. Wilkie, and other leading bankers of the Dominion, waited upon the Minister of Finance and the Minister of Justice at Ottawa, and the details of the present very satisfactory law were gradually evolved. It is understood that Sir John Thompson strongly impressed his visitors upon this occasion by his broad views and intimate acquaintance with those common sense principles, which after all, form the only true solution of such intricate questions as those relating to finance and banking.

A very onerous portion of the duties which Sir John

Thompson had to perform was connected with the reviewing of Provincial legislation. The Acts passed by each Province are referred after the prorogation of the Assembly to the Minister of Justice, who in turn has to advise the Governor General regarding their constitutionality and the desirability of allowing them to become law or the reverse. He has a great many things to consider in connection with these varied and numerous enactments. One Province may pass legislation conflicting with another or with the Dominion, and the rights of the Federal Government in taxation, in property, in legal matters, in its general jurisdiction or in its control of the thousand and one things which come under the authority of the Dominion rather than of the Provinces, may be infringed. Sir John generally took the ground in all matters involving national and political issues that the provinces were themselves the best judges of their legislation, and he, therefore, refused to advise the veto of any such measures. Where there was a constitutional doubt involved, he considered the Courts the proper medium for deciding the result.

There were exceptions to this rule. According to the contract made between the Dominion Government and the Canadian Pacific Railway, dated Oct. 21st, 1880, it was agreed that for twenty years following, no independent line of railway should be constructed south from the C. P. R. in Manitoba, so as to unite with the American lines and thus introduce American competition. Subsequent Provincial and Dominion legislation recognized and strengthened this enactment. On July 4th, 1887, however, an Act for the construction of the Red River Valley Railway came before the Minister of Justice, and he promptly advised its disallowance on the ground that it infringed the general authority of the Dominion regarding railway legislation, and that the provision for connecting the proposed line with others outside the Province was in excess of powers held by the Legislature. The measure was accordingly disallowed and the action resulted in raising a perfect storm in the Province interested.

Vigourous protests, fresh legislation, an appeal to Her Majesty the Queen, threats, and even personal encounters between the officials representing the two Governments at the scene of construction, followed. A sub-committee of Council, composed of the Ministers of Justice and the Interior, was appointed and in a most elaborate report submitted on January 4th, 1888, went into the whole question, and declared that "the manifest international character of the enterprise, and the absence of all pretence of reason for it as 'a local work or undertaking,' fully justifies its being dealt with by the Government of Canada, and in the interest of the whole Dominion." The sub-committee referred to the great sacrifices which Canada had made in order to construct the C. P. R. and was "unable to recommend that there should be an abandonment of the policy of preventing the trade of Manitoba and the North-West from being diverted for the benefit of foreign railway corporations."

In this particular case Sir John Thompson seems to have considered the interests of Canada as a whole to be the important consideration; illegality being a secondary matter. In a special report some two months later he declared that "it cannot be asserted that in pronouncing the veto upon Acts which were deemed to have an injurious tendency as regards the country at large, Your Excellency has deprived the people of Manitoba of any of their rights." Eventually the matter was settled by a compromise between the two Governments, and the measure was allowed to go into operation. But it is interesting as being an exception to Sir John Thompson's general policy regarding disallowance. With Provincial legislation he never stood upon technical or constitutional objections where no apparent harm could result from allowance. Occasionally, however, Acts were vetoed by the Minister's advise, which glaringly infringed Dominion rights, or perhaps injuriously affected special interests, but such occurrences were rare. One of these was a Manitoba bill for authorizing external companies to do business within the Province. Another was "the District Magistrate's Bill," passed by the Quebec Legislature on the 2nd of October, 1888. The Report of the Minister of Justice upon this occasion was a most elaborate historical disquisition, and it constitutes a valuable State paper.

A very different case, with a different result, was the allowance of the Ordinance passed by the North-West Territorial Assembly in 1892. It amended the law respecting education and placed that subject under the control of a Council of Public Instruction. As in Manitoba, the Roman Catholic minority appealed to the Dominion authorities, and were strongly supported by Archbishop Taché. But acting on Sir John Thompson's advice, the veto was refused and the law went into operation. In a lengthy speech upon the subject on April 26th, 1894, the Premier pointed out that disallowance would not have redressed any of the grievances complained of; that the petitioners had not asked for an appeal to the Supreme Court; that they were mistaken as to the nature of the regulations which had existed prior to 1892. "I think," said he "that the House will be disposed to agree that after all we came to the safer and wiser conclusion, although it has created, I admit, considerable irritation on the part of those who had formed expectations of a more speedy, decisive, and heroic remedy being given to the petitioners."

With Sir Oliver Mowat the Minister of Justice was upon the most friendly personal terms, and their political or legal differences were conducted upon an unusually high plane. The former, in fact, has not hesitated to express his high appreciation of Sir John Thompson's business aptitude, facility for settling up matters long in dispute, and general legal attainments. Sir John was determined to get all the old questions at issue between the Provinces and the Dominion out of the way, and had initiated several suits against Ontario in connection with Indian claims and titles to land.

An important case along these lines was that arising from the treaties made with the Indians at Sault Ste. Marie on 3rd September, 1850, under which the Ojibeways surrendered to the Crown all the land north of Lakes Huron and Superior to the Height of Land, in consideration of certain fixed annuities. The treaty contained a provision that if the surrendered territory produced sufficient revenue to enable the Crown to do so, without incurring loss, the annuities in favor of the Indians would be augmented. This had since proved to be the case, and their claim had been pressed for consideration.

Under Section 111 of the British North America Act the Dominion engaged to assume all the liabilities of the late Provinces of Canada, so that primarily the Dominion was admitted to be liable to the Indians in this connection. Sir John Thompson, however, on behalf of the Government, claimed that Ontario having obtained the benefit of the land and the revenues received from it, should restore to the Dominion the moneys already expended and pay the whole of the annuities, past and future. Three arbitrators were chosen to deal with the question: Hon. J. A. Boyd, Chancellor of Ontario on behalf of the Province of Ontario; Sir Napoleon Casault, Chief Justice of Quebec, on behalf

Hon. G. W. Ross, LL.D., M.P.P.
Minister of Education in Ontario.

of the Province of Quebec; and the Hon. Mr. Justice Burbidge on behalf of the Dominion. As a large sum of money was involved the result was awaited with much interest. And as ultimately decided it was very largly in favour of the Dominion; partly in favor of the Provinces.

Under the terms of another treaty made with the Indians before Confederation and dealing with certain territories west of Lake Superior covering thousands of square miles in extent, sundry disputes regarding jurisdiction had occurred. Over two-thirds of the land in question was eventually decided by the Imperial Privy Council in the St. Catharines Milling case, to belong to Ontario. Meantime, however, the Dominion Government at great expense to itself had extinguished the Indian title to these lands by incurring heavy liabilities for large perpetual annuities and by other payments during many years past, which alone had reached $800,000. Sir John Thompson finally brought the matter before the Courts and it is still pending, but with every possibility that Ontario may eventually find itself interested to the tune of some millions of dollars, and Quebec in a smaller sum.

It seems to have been in connection with these cases that Sir Oliver Mowat was able to speak so highly of the late Premier at the time of his death:

"He was an earnest Canadian, a man of great ability and industry, and possessed of a judicial mind and sound judgment. From my official intercourse with him after his appointment as Minister of Justice I formed a high opinion of his great forwardness and business aptitude. I think the Conservatives of Canada have never had a better Minister, if they have had one as good."

Another legal matter in which Sir John Thompson took great interest, but which he was fated to leave still unsettled, was the question of an Insolvency Law. For a long time it had been felt that the existing system was inefficient and required reform. Finally the feeling amongst Canadian merchants grew so strong that a conference was held at Ottawa on January 16th, 1893, between delegates from the Montreal, Toronto and London Boards of Trade, and the Premier, the Hon. Mr. Foster and the Hon. Mr. Angers; with a view to the introduction of a measure at an early session of Parliament which, while extending reasonable means for relief to the debtor, would at the same time protect the creditor in realizing upon the assets of bankrupts. In accordance with the decision afterwards arrived at, Mr. Bowell brought a Bill before the Senate on April 4th, 1894, dealing with the whole subject in great elaboration. Unfortunately, many causes combined to prevent it getting through the Commons beyond the first reading. Promises were made however, by Sir John that it would come up and be pushed at the ensuing session.

It is interesting to note in connection with this particular portion of his career, how strongly he felt regarding the powers of the Local Legislatures. As already pointed out he seldom used the right of disallowance. But he went even further than a tacit admission of the wisdom of letting the Provinces govern themselves as a rule, and during the debate upon the Jesuits' Estates bill, declared that "a Provincial Legislature, legislating upon subjects which are given to it by the British North America Act has the power to repeal an Imperial Statute passed prior to the B.N.A. Act affecting those subjects." And upon this point he quoted several important precedents. In subsequent discussions upon the Copyright Law the power of the Dominion to repeal certain Imperial acts, so far as they affected Canada, was urged with equal distinctness and with far greater earnestness.

CHAPTER XXII.

THE CRIMINAL CODE AND THE COPYRIGHT LAW.

Multifarious as were the duties of the Minister of Justice during the years in which he filled that onerous office, he still managed to find time for great reforms as well as for the ordinary work of his department and for the innumerable matters which require the attention of a party leader. The review of Provincial enactments; the supervision of the national laws and of general legislation; the control of his department; the preparation of an immense number of reports; the presentation of the Government's views or defence upon nearly all important Parliamentary subjects; the preparation or supervision of leading appeal cases before the Supreme Court or the Privy Council; the inspection and charge of the prisons and penitentiaries of the Dominion; the making of campaign speeches; the participation in diplomatic negotiations regarding Behring Sea, the Fisheries, Reciprocity, or Newfoundland; composed but a portion of the vast amount of work which he had assumed.

In the midst of it all he managed to put into shape and pass through the House of Commons a Codification of the Criminal Laws of Canada, which in itself would constitute a lasting monument to the ability, industry and knowledge of any average statesman. During the Session of 1891, the measure was first brought forward by the Minister, chiefly in order to obtain suggestions from all who were competent to deal with the subject. In 1892, it was again introduced and was found to be greatly modified and improved by the advice of Judges and of other leading authorities in the legal world. The measure was probably the most voluminous ever presented to the House of Commons, and contained more than a thousand clauses, covering fully 350 pages. It was referred early in the Session to a Joint Committee, composed of the very ablest men in both parties, who went over it clause by clause and dealt with it in an honest, thorough manner.

Here it was that Sir John Thompson showed his power. In Committee he was always at his best, and in dealing with a non-partisan, legal question of this kind he naturally held the very highest place and most strongly impressed himself upon the legislation under discussion. So skilfully, ably and persistently did he stamp his views upon its every page that, in point of fact, the Canadian Code of 1892 deserves to be called after its maker far more than did ever the famous Code Napoleon. Under its terms Canadians were enabled to boast that they had led the way amongst English-speaking peoples in the enactment of a comprehensive code of criminal law. In briefly introducing his measure to the House on April 12th, the Minister of Justice announced that "It will deal with offences against public order, internal and external; offences affecting the administration of the law and of justice; offences against religion, morals and public convenience; offences against the person and reputation; offences against the rights of property and rights arising out of contracts, and offences connected with trade; it will deal with procedure and proceedings after conviction and actions against persons administering the criminal law."

The final report of the Joint Committee to which it had been referred did not appear till nearly the end of the Session, but it was accepted without serious objection, and the new Code became the law of the land. Its important features were numerous, and in fact may be said to have almost effected a legal revolution. Up to 1869, when a first effort was made at consolidation, English regulations and proceedure had prevailed in all the provinces, and even after that date the English law, when not inconsistent with that of Canada, or when dealing with offences not provided against in the Canadian law, still obtained. The new Code covered all the ground hitherto untouched by Dominion regulation, and declared the English criminal law to be no longer applicable in Canada. No person, therefore, could in the future be proceeded against for an infraction of any Act of the Imperial Parliament, unless by express terms such an Act was made effective within the Dominion.

Important legislation was settled concerning insanity. No person could be convicted because of an offence committed, or an act omitted, by him, when labouring under natural imbecility or disease of mind. The condition specified was one in which incapacity existed for appreciating the nature of the act, or omission, with which he was charged, or of distinguishing between right and wrong. All persons, however, who might be slightly affected, were not excused, and if labouring under specific delusions, though in other respects sane, could not be acquitted on the ground of insanity. Various crimes were defined, including murder, treason, sedition, corruption, libel and theft. The following provision is especially interesting: "Culpable homicide, which would otherwise be murder, may be reduced to manslaughter, if the person who causes death does so in the heat of passion caused by sudden provocation. Any wrongful act or insult of such a nature as to be sufficient to deprive an ordinary person of the power of self-control may be provocation if the offender acts upon it on the sudden, and before there has been time for his passion to cool."

Treason was defined as an attempt to kill Her Majesty or the Heir Apparent, or exhibiting a desire to do so; as an effort to depose the Sovereign or levying war in order to compel a change in legislation; as an endeavour to overawe the Parliament of Canada. Sedition was described as involving an attempt to bring the Sovereign into hatred or contempt; exciting disaffection against the Queen, the Dominion Parliament or any Provincial Legislature; endeavouring to procure an alteration of any State enactment or regulation, by unlawful means. And then came an interesting provision: "Everyone is guilty of an indictable offence and liable to one year's imprisonment who cites or publishes false news or tales whereby discord or slander may grow between the Queen and her people, or which may produce other public and private injury."

The libel law was modified and improved while strenuous regulations were made regarding corruption. Following the lines of Mr. Abbott's measure in the preceding year, any judge or justice accepting a bribe was made liable to fourteen years' imprisonment; the sale of contracts and offices was made punishable with other indictable offences, and the offender was to be disqualified for five years; the contribution of money to election funds by public contractors was declared illegal; and public officers were prohibited from accepting commissions.

Another important provision was that by which either husband or wife were allowed to give evidence in a case where the other was concerned, only excepting any evidence which might be based upon private conversation between the two. Then there was the not less vital change in the law, by which the accused could testify on his own behalf. A distinguished Judge is authority for the private statement that during the last two years, since this enactment has been in force, he has found it most useful. Guilty parties seemed very often disposed to perjure themselves and to finally reveal their own guilt by attempts to flounder out of difficulties On the other hand it was found to be a great help to really innocent persons.

Of course the measure had its critics. Mr. Justice Taschereau, of the Supreme Court, a jurist of distinguished reputation, published an elaborate denunciation of the whole code. His position in the matter was, however, much weakened by failure to make a single suggestion during the prolonged period in which the bill was being considered, and by omission to, in anyway, respond to the requests for advice which were frequently made to him. No one but a lawyer of wide research could deal with the technical objections raised by His Lordship, but it must seem to any impartial layman who looks at this completed code, that its defects are like spots upon the sun—merely incidental to a vast and varied surface of light. As the poet has so well said:

> "In every work regard the writer's end,
> Since none can compass more than they intend,
> And if the means be just, the conduct true,
> Applause in spite of trivial faults, is due."

Sir John Thompson's work in this connection is indeed a lasting memorial to his wonderfully luminous legal intellect, and to his rank as a really great Minister. And there is much to think of and remember in the eloquent tribute paid to this particular achievement by Mr. J. T. Bulmer, of Halifax:

"The completion and passage of the criminal code marks a new era in criminal legislation and penal reform, not only for Canada, but for the world as well. It is as true as a proposition in Euclid, that the criminal law of Canada is above that of any nation or State on the face of the earth. It embodies most of the suggestions of Bentham,

Becarri, Livingston, Mackintosh and Romily, and hundreds of others which never occurred to them, and is the first attempt on a national scale to make criminal law synonymous with justice, and substitute civilization and Christianity for barbarism."

It may safely be said also that the rank and place thus taken by Sir John paved the way for the offer which would inevitably have come in subsequent years, of membership in the Judicial Committee of the Imperial Privy Council. Whether it would have been accepted by a man who declined to take the vacant Chief Justiceship of Canada, with all its environments of ease and dignity, because he thought his duty lay in assuming the Premiership; or whether it would have had any effect upon the leader, who practically let life slip away from him in the attempt to do his duty, and his whole duty, by the State; depends upon circumstances which can now be only guessed at. But when an authority like the late Sir James Fitzjames Stephen, declares the English legal system to be merely "a mass of ill-arranged Acts of Parliament. . . . finally consolidated into a small number of acts, faithfully preserving the confusion and intricacy of the material from which they were put together," it is not difficult to understand the eventual appreciation which must have followed the achievement of the Canadian Minister of Justice.

Upon another subject in which Sir John Thompson was enthusiastically interested, and in the mastery of whose technical and difficult details he had expended much research and labour, success did not come during his lifetime. On the very verge of an arrangement regarding the Canadian Copyright Law, which no one else understood so thoroughly and could have handled with so many probabilities of a satisfactory result, he was stricken down. The points in this prolonged dispute are not, perhaps, appreciated at their true importance. The question involves the discussion and, perhaps, re-arrangement, of various international treaties; it affects the general question of Colonial self-government; it includes the complaints of Canadian publishers and the fears of British authors; it dates back through fifty years of contention; and requires on the part of anyone who would deal with it in statesmanlike form, a mastery of the official communications and voluminous arguments produced by half a century of vigourous disputation.

The origin of the trouble was the Imperial Copyright Act of 1842, which gave copyright throughout the British dominions to any book published in the United Kingdom, whether printed there or not. Though intended to give a free circulation to British literature within British territories, it was soon found that English editions were too expensive for Colonial requirements, and in order to meet this difficulty an amendment was introduced in 1847 which allowed the Canadian Government to impose a nominal author's royalty of 12½ per cent., to be collected at the Custom Houses, and to be handed over to the Imperial Government. Under this new regulation, cheap American reprints soon flooded the market to the advantage of Canadian readers, but to the very evident injury of the local book and publishing trade.

Then followed complications in connection with the Berne Convention of 1886, and the ensuing International Copyright Act, passed by the British Parliament, which practically threw the Canadian market open to British and American publications, without any control by the Dominion Government on behalf of the Canadian publisher. In 1875 a local enactment had been passed, limited, however, to the rights of Canadian publishers, in connection with local works. But on the 20th of April, 1889, Sir John Thompson introduced a measure by which he proposed to end this sort of thing; to test the power of the Dominion Government to protect the Canadian publisher; and to take firm ground upon the rights derivable from the Confederation Act of 1867. The constitutional position he described very clearly:

"I think we have the right to legislate in respect to this subject irrespective of any Statute of the Imperial Parliament passed before the British North America Act was passed. The Imperial Copyright Act was passed in 1842. The Act which declared that Colonial Statutes were invalid if they were repugnant to Imperial Statutes was passed in 1865. Two years after that, we received the ample gift of powers which the British North America Act contains. In the exercise of those powers, we have repealed, sometimes by implication, and sometimes directly, scores of Imperial enactments, in addition to volumes of the Common Law of the United Kingdom; and, if the objection were sustained in regard to the exercise of our powers on the question of copyright, it would strike off at least one-half of the Revised Statutes."

In dealing with the difficulties under which Canadian publishers laboured, the Minister of Justice pointed out that by the local laws an author can obtain copyright in Canada only on condition of his printing and publishing, or reprinting and republishing, in the Dominion. No such condition, however, is attached to the copyright of English works in Canada, and practically there is no restriction upon the sale of American reprints. "While a Canadian publishing house is not at liberty to republish an English copyrighted work, a publishing house in the United States, having obtained a transfer of the rights to Canada possessed by an English author, can republish in the United States and have complete command of the Canadian market, while, on the other hand, it is impossible for a citizen of Canada, under any circumstances, to obtain copyright privileges in the United States."

Residence in a British country which was at first required, had become entirely nominal and a perfect farce, so that, to sum up, the American author by obtaining copyright simultaneously in both the United Kingdom and the United States was able to capture, without any consideration in return, the absolute control of the Canadian market.

The Minister proposed in this measure that unless the author who had obtained British copyright should at the same time obtain a copyright in Canada, and republish his book there within a week after, the Minister of Agriculture should be at liberty to give a license to any Canadian to publish the work. He added that this might be thought "a strong step in the interests of all those connected with the publishing industry in Canada, and it may be supposed to be a strong step against the British author." But, on the other hand, it was intended to enact that there should be an excise duty on all the books published under that license; and, said the speaker, "Those who have made a study of the subject assure me that the proceeds to be derived from that excise duty, will give the British author far more compensation for the sale of his works in Canada than he could possibly derive by other means." He concluded a vigourous and most effective speech by a declaration of his belief that "we have these powers; if not, the sooner we get them the better."

Passing Parliament unanimously, the Act was sent to the Imperial Government for approval, which had not been given up to the day of its author's death. Protests regarding the delay, and urgent State papers drawn up by Sir John Thompson have been forwarded, while various other efforts have been made to get the law into operation. But the opposing influences have been too great. It is claimed by the Imperial Government that such an enactment involves the abandonment of the policy of international and Imperial copyright which was after difficulty, asserted in 1888 to the considerable benefit of the British author in various markets; that it is inconsistent with the policy of making copyright independent of the place of printing—in other words, that it does not harmonize with the English free trade idea—that it would probably modify, if not destroy, advantages gained in the United States by the arrangement of 1891; and that it would be injurious to the British authors by whom the Canadian market (via United States publishers) is chiefly supplied.

In an elaborate memorandum addressed by the Minister of Justice to Lord Knutsford, as Colonial Secretary, on July 14th, 1890, these and other contentions are thoroughly handled, and the position of the Canadian publisher is most vividly depicted. The results of the present system were declared to be exceedingly disastrous:

"The American publisher, unrestrained by any international copyright law or treaty, is free to reprint any British work and to supply it, not only to the reading public of the United States, but to the reading public of Canada, while the Canadian publisher is not free to reprint any such work on any terms, unless he can obtain the permission of the holder of the copyright in Great Britain. In some noted instances, this has actually led to the transfer of printing establishments from Canada to the United States. In other cases English publishing houses have set up branches in New York or other American cities with the view of reprinting for the United States and Canada the copyright works which they have issued in London."

He points out how impossible it is for a Canadian publisher to compete in making arrangements for the right to reprint any given English work, with American firms which not only command and hold their own market of 60,000,000, but in addition have a practical monopoly of the Canadian market :

"Inasmuch as the Imperial Copyright Acts forbid the reprinting of copyrighted works, but permit the importation of the American reprints. In many modern instances, the British copyright holder has preferred to sell his right to an American publisher rather than to a Canadian, and has even bound himself by the terms of sale to prosecute any Canadian who may reprint his work for sale in Canada —the operation which the American sets himself about at once."

Sir John then gave at length, though as concisely as was possible, the history of the whole question, together with correspondence which had taken place from time to time. The report constitutes in fact a most complete and logical presentation of the case, and it is not difficult in view of the compact, yet varied knowledge, displayed in this and other documents,to realize the confidence which was felt in his eventual settlement of the controversy. And it is none the less interesting to note the strong expressions of praise which in this connection have been since awarded to the late Premier by political opponents of the most pronounced kind. If Sir John Thompson could have received these expressions of non-partisan approval during his lifetime, there is no doubt that it would have been the greatest pleasure which he could possibly have been given.

But as so often happens, the public forget during a leader's fighting career to express their appreciation in a tangible manner or in one which a sensitive and sometimes greatly abused statesman can enjoy ; while political opponents let slip many an opportunity to sweeten and render pleasant, the surroundings of party stress and struggle.

CHAPTER XXIII.

AN IMPERIAL STATESMAN.

Sir John Thompson never appeared before the public as an enthusiast. The unwillingness to express his own strong feelings to others and intense dislike of those who used patriotic phrases as a cloak for unpatriotic policies were dominant forces in his character. No Canadian was ever more earnest in believing that the maintenance of British connection and the development of Imperial unity were the greatest and wisest objects for Dominion policy. But it was only by slow degrees that the people of Canada generally, came to appreciate the strength of this sentiment and then more by the practical results of his policy than by any special public belief in his loyalty or Imperialism.

Where Sir John A. Macdonald, by phrase or precept, would embody the national regard for Britain, in a way calculated to arouse all the enthusiasm of the people, and thus aid him in the carrying out of an Imperial policy, Sir John Thompson would proceed first to plan, and then to quietly put his schemes in practice before inviting that public approval of which he was always reasonably assured. Yet his utterances upon these lines were by no means few, and as time went on the strength of his views would have become more evident and more widely known. Speaking, for instance, at the Ministerial Banquet in the Mansion House, London, on Aug. 6th, 1890, and in response to the toast of the "Army and Navy and Reserve Forces," the Minister of Justice for Canada—as he then was—referred to his pride as a colonist that "the day had come when friends and foes alike, in considering the strength of the Empire, had to take into account the strength of the Colonies across the sea."

Upon all the questions which came up from time to time in regard to Canada's duty to the Empire, he spoke with no uncertain sound. The very idea of discrimination against British products in favour of American goods was abhorrent to him; the advocacy of Independence he considered dangerous to the Dominion, both in the present and in the future; and the best policy to pursue was, in his opinion, one which would make the interests of Canada and the Empire identical, and gradually bring the wealth and power of the Mother Country into operation as substantial factors in the development of Canadian territory. In resisting successfully the efforts of Newfoundland to introduce the wretched precedent of discrimination into the Colonial relationship, he did a great and perhaps not sufficiently appreciated service to the Empire. His action served as an ample protection against any discrimination in favour of American goods in the treaty afterwards made between the British West Indies and the United States. It will also prove an efficient precedent, and a reason for the use of the veto by the Imperial Government in the event of any future Canadian administration being so lost to a sense of national honour as to introduce the principle into a reciprocity arrangement with the American Republic.

At the same time Sir John Thompson was too thorough a Canadian to permit of his ever considering British interests first and those of the Dominion second. The way in which he stood out for Canadian rights in regard to the Atlantic fisheries, and the Pacific Coast sealing interests; the Copyright question, and the British treaties which limit the freedom of Canadian fiscal action; are proofs which sufficiently illustrate the fact. He believed in Canada having the very fullest power compatible with its position as a State of the Empire, and had its interests come in conflict with those of England, he would have stood for Canada first. But he considered the whole matter in a very different spirit from that wh'ch must have actuated those who were always looking forward to such a divergence of destiny, and speaking of it as something inevitable, when in reality it was barely possible.

National existence he considered compatible with British connection, one, in fact, being dependent upon the other. Speaking in Toronto on January 6th, 1893, the new Premier declared that "every man who is a Canadian at heart feels that this country ought to be a nation, will be a nation, and, please God, we shall help to make it a nation; but, sir, we do not desire that it shall be a separate nation, but that it will be a nation in itself, forming a bulwark to the British Empire, whose traditions we admire, whose protection we enjoy, and who has given to this country in the fullest degree the right and the power of self-government, and agreed to extend to the people of this country every facility which a self-governed and independent people could desire to have."

At the great meeting which followed a week later in the Auditorium, he proclaimed amid ringing cheers that "the very corner-stone of the policy which we have endeavoured to carry forward. which we will build our future upon, is British connection." He went on to say that it was the bounden duty of both Liberals and Conservatives to take care that the question of that future was not trifled with; to see that Canada was developed as "a firm, strong British nationality"; to base political action upon confidence and not pessimism; to spurn the annexationist emissary from the door of every true Canadian: to cease trifling with the idea of annexation "by paltering

Sir John Thompson,

Speaking in the Canadian House of Commons.

with independence." It was not, he thought, an unworthy ambition to look forward to a distant possibility of independence when Canada might contain a great and populous nation, but "to talk of it as being practicable or reasonable within the present generation, is to talk absurdity, if it is not to talk treason."

At the present time, Canada was independent in the truest sense of the word, with the greatest possible liberty of self-government, and the protection of so powerful a parent that no one could menace that independence or hamper its free operation and development But in view of the immense power and intense aggressiveness of the United States "it required the fullest care and help of the Empire in order to keep the independence of Canada and to safeguard the rights of Canada." The man, therefore, who advocated independence while the Dominion was in this stage of national existence, advocated not only separation from Great Britain, but practically the absorption of this country into the United States: "If the sentiments which animated the people of the Dominion were destroyed by British connection being severed, and the moral help and the prestige of Great Britain were withdrawn from it, the United States would have us at her disposal whenever she pleased."

In an elaborate interview given the papers upon his return from the Arbitration Tribunal at Paris,—August 26th—Sir John Thompson was even more plain and forcible: "The propagandism for Canadian independence is a direct and plain agitation in favor of annexation. Nobody in the country ought to be deceived about that. If anyone wants to know what fate Canada would meet in dealing with any international question standing outside of the British Empire, he had better read the record in the Behring Sea discussion. Great Britain stood by us nobly from first to last, and she guarded every interest, that she was necessarily asked to guard, and she dealt with Canada in all matters of arbitration as fairly and as zealously as if Canada had been a part of the United Kingdom. Standing alone by herself Canada would not have received one moment's consideration, and any discussion of rights would have been disposed of in short order."

A few weeks later at the demonstration in Montreal, on September 12th, he denounced "the wretched, feeble voices of the miserable creatures," who raised the cry of annexation, and declared that after closing their little office in Toronto, some of them had gone to the other half of the Continent "for which they have such a profound affection, but in which they will find the people have a profound contempt for renegade Canadians." It will not be surprising in this connection to those who appreciated the strong though suppressed feelings which characterized Sir John, to know that he entertained of late years sentiments of intense dislike to Mr. Goldwin Smith, as the champion of views for which he felt the keenest aversion. He found it difficult, indeed, to understand how a cultured Englishman and brilliant writer could hold such dishonouring and ignoble opinions.

Turning to the Behring Sea matter, he pointed out that it had been a struggle of five millions of people against sixty millions, and that "it was not by chattering annexation and independence that Canada had her rights assured and maintained in the face of the nations." It was because Great Britain had thrown the majesty of her flag around the humblest craft which ploughed the waters of the North Pacific; it was because the Mother Country gave Canada an equal voice in the deliberations of the Tribunal; it was because the Queen of England declared that at the bar of international justice the voice of able and eloquent Canadian counsel should be heard upon an equal footing with that of the great legal lights of Britain. And once more he pronounced the moral: "The people who are attempting to deceive you with the story of independence are just as renegade to every interest in this country as is the annexationist himself."

Referring again to those who spoke of it merely as a possibility in the distant future, the Premier continued: "That is a worthy aspiration for those who may come after us, many long years hence, to contemplate; but those who speak of independence in the present state of Canada, or in any condition in which she is likely to be within the time of you or your children, are not talking independence from the heart, but they are talking it with the lips, and with black treason in their hearts to every true Canadian interest to which we should stand firm."

Yet, with all his strong feelings of loyalty and intense aversion to anything savouring of annexation or continentalism, Sir John Thompson was extremely moderate and fair in his views of the every-day policy which should actuate Canada in its relations towards the United States. As an instance of this, and apart from his well known attitude regarding reciprocity, the Alien Labour Bill presented to the House in 1890, and urged very frequently afterwards, may be mentioned. For years the United States had dealt in a harsh, almost brutal, manner with Canadian workingmen who had crossed the border to seek employment, who had perhaps obtained it, or who were found to be Canadians after having held a position for possibly many years. Under the terms of the U.S. Alien Labour Law, and with the aid of inspectors, or of the lynx-eyed representatives of some labour organization, these men would be discovered and promptly put out of the country, with little consideration and less respect.

Naturally, strong feeling was aroused by these indications of international friendship and courtesy, and on January 27th, Mr. George Taylor, a strong Conservative and prominent supporter of the Government, introduced what was really a retaliatory measure—a Canadian Alien Labour Law. Sir John, in his speech during the debate, urged moderation. He pointed out that the contract labour regulations of the United States applied as much to Italy as to Canada in principle, although naturally their operation was more immediately felt in the Dominion. Canadians could not be exempted from the terms of the American law, even by special arrangement, without the exemption of all British subjects. For the United States to exempt the Dominion would be to make Canada the back door by which English immigrants of an undesirable class might gain admittance. For the Republic to exempt British citizens generally would be to practically give up its control over the incoming of the product of European slums, to be added to the already ample population of American slums.

It was, he thought, a matter of internal policy, entirely under the control of the United States, one which they could not affect and in which they should not endeavour to intervene, even though American officials enforced the law with harshness and individual ignominy. As to retaliation: "I do submit that it would be an insane policy to adopt, simply because harsh and irritating legislation has been used against Canada." Another point to consider was the fact that it would interfere with immigration, and unlike the United States, we needed more people rather than less: "It would be unwise, situated as this country is, to impose restrictions of this kind on any immigration we can possibly get." The proposal was not passed, but the incident shows, as did the *modus vivendi* given during the Atlantic and Behring Sea fishery disputes;

the Canal Tolls, and other questions; how anxious Sir John always was to be upon the best possible terms with the United States.

Reference has been frequently made in these pages to Sir John Thompson's dislike of any proposal to discriminate in favour of the United States against any part of the British Empire. Speaking in the House of Commons on April 25th, 1892, he declared that "we must recognize the sovereignity of the Monarchy of which we are subjects, and our relations to the Empire are utterly inconsistent with the idea of giving a preference to foreign countries in the markets of this country, over our fellow subjects in other parts of the Empire, and in Great Britain itself." For this reason indeed he had protested so energetically and successfully against the Bond-Blaine treaty; for this reason he had watched so closely the American and West Indian treaty; for this reason he had denounced so vigourously the Opposition appeals to pessimism, and representation of the country as wrapped in misery and permeated with poverty for want of the great American market—which could only be obtained by discrimination against the Mother Country.

In this particular speech he expressed strong disapprobation of the previous utterances of Mr. Davies, on account of this dismal and sombre hue:

> "Outside of my darkening window
> Is the great world's crash and din,
> And slowly the autumn shadows
> Come drifting, drifting in."

It was nearly all shadow and no sunshine; national despair with but few gleams of hope or brightness. He then went on, as if speaking to the Mother Country, to define the Canadian position: "You, with our choice and by our wish, have laid certain burdens upon us as part of this Empire we have to a certain extent to maintain our own defence, we have to keep up the British institutions which we got from you, and in bearing our own financial burdens, it is absolutely necessary that we should be masters of our own tariff, saving one thing only, and that is, that we shall not forget the duties we owe to the Empire by agreeing that any foreign country shall have a preference over you in the tariffs which we make."

This is the declaration of a man and a statesman. It defends Canadian rights without infringing British interests; it seeks to make the two identical rather than to discover some material or sentimental flaw in the bond of union by which separation may be aided; it proclaims that each section of the Empire owes a duty to the other portions, but should at the same time cultivate a spirit of mutual independence in all matters of local import. And it does not particularly appeal to sentiment. In all of Sir John Thompson's speeches, as in his general policy, duty seems to have been the first consideration. He sought to express and explain the obligations Canada was under to the Mother Country; the obligations which Great Britain bore to the Dominion. Each had a duty to perform—in one case the bearing of true allegiance, in the other the giving of true protection. And the mutual performance of duty would result in benefit to all concerned.

From the standpoint of sentiment he said little in his earlier natlonal speeches, although his fierce denunciations of annexation and the advocates of that idea, indicated clearly enough that he felt deeply upon the subject. The future was not a thing which his strong, practical mind, cared to deal with very much, except in the way of warning. Imperial Federation he did not publicly discuss, although his whole policy was permeated with the principle upon which it must ultimately be developed. Closer union with the Empire in a sentimental sense, he did not specially urge. Yet, no man expressed more strongly and sincerely the necessity of conserving British unity in all practical political directions.

Upon the question of trade with Great Britain and with the Colonies there could be no doubt whatever concerning his views. Canada was to him the pivot upon which the commercial and maritime destinies of the Empire must eventually turn. Hence the importance of the C.P.R; the steamship connection with Australia and England; the problems of cable communication and preferential trade. The latter he hoped for rather than expected. With the other Colonies the policy was, of course practicable; with England the difficulties were very great. Speaking in the House on February 29th, 1892, he declared in this connection that "with or without a preferential market, the market of Great Britain is at present the grandest field for the products of this country." There could, in his opinion, be no comparison between the demand for Canadian productions in the Mother Country and that furnished by the United States.

Imperial Federation, or the future of the Empire in a constitutional sense, Sir John Thompson never discussed in public. It was too purely speculative, and while such closer unity was desirable, and eventually necessary in some form or other, was probably in his opinion best served and hastened by building carefully the foundations of mutual affection and respect, of trade interchange and personal intercourse, of cable communication and general defence. Appreciation of the greatness and power of the British Empire, of the desirability of its remaining undivided, of the weakness of Canada standing alone beside the United States, of the good-will and substantial aid given in recent years by the Mother Country to the Dominion; all these were apparently more potent forces to the mind of the late

Premier in the bringing about of complete Imperial union, than were any number of proposed constitutions, theoretical propositions, or appeals to abstract sentiment. Unlike Lord Rosebery and Sir John Macdonald, he, therefore, never identified himself directly with the Imperial Federation movement, although his British policy and principles were, of course, in complete accordance with the work of its promoters.

There can certainly be no doubt concerning Sir John Thompson's rank and place as an Imperial statesman. Apart from the Inter-Colonial Conference, which may be thought to constitute the central event of his administration, he had shown himself in diplomacy and in arbitration a man worthy to hold his own amongst the best and highest of the Mother Land. In complications of iong standing with the United States he proved himself a careful Minister and ashrewd opponent; a protector of Canadian interests, but averse to anything which might unduly endanger British interests. In the Newfoundland matter he indicated his ability of looking ahead in a practical way, and his desire to stand up for future Imperial unity even against present Imperial Ministers. But he was none the less keen in his recognition of any sympathetic statesmanship in the Mother Country. Upon one occasion, he asked Lord Aberdeen as Governor General, to convey to Lord Ripon the warm appreciation of his colleagues and himself, concerning the Colonial Secretary's general administration of affairs with which Canada had been connected. In the Behring Sea arbitration, he showed the inheritance of those judicial qualities of mind and intellect which make British diplomacy and legal administration the admiration of the world. His broad views thus gave him an Imperial reputation and standing; his conduct of Imperial matters made him a British statesman in the fullest sense of the word.

CHAPTER XXIV.

The Inter-Colonial Conference.

The most striking event of Sir John Thompson's brief Premiership was undoubtedly the gathering of representative men from various portions of the Empire, which met at Ottawa with a view to the promotion of Imperial interests and unity. In the future it may loom larger than even at present, and in history the Inter-Colonial Conference of 1894 will be recorded as a memorable incident in the chain of circumstances which helped to produce a united British Empire. It has been the great mission of Canada to forge many of those links of union.

By the Confederation of its Provinces in 1867 an impetus was given to the federal principle which now permeates the local politics and fills the aspirations of the people of Australia and South Africa. By the construction of the Canadian Pacific Railway it opened up vast territories to British settlement and cultivation; created cities and towns which are now reaching out for trade with the distant east; provided an Imperial highway for the transport of troops and munitions of war; and completed commercially that unity of Canada which in a national sense had been commenced at Confederation. By the creation of a steamship line from Vancouver to Sydney, and the voting of the large subsidy which indicates the ultimate completion of a fast line of steamers between Canada and England, the Dominion has formed a substantial basis for the closer commercial relations which should in the future exist between the different sections of the Empire.

What the statesmanship of Sir John Macdonald initiated, the brief ministry of Sir John Thompson continued. The mantle of the great Imperialist had fallen upon one who was well able to appreciate the importance of the inheritance and to aid in developing the practical side of the far-reaching problem which is the noble birth-right of every British citizen. Early in September, 1893, Mr. Mackenzie Bowell, Minister of Trade and Commerce, had been sent on an official mission to the Australian Colonies for the purpose of seeing what could be done in the direction of extending interchange and promoting a mutual knowledge of requirements and resources. His intimate acquaintance with Canadian affairs made him in this connection an ideal diplomatist, an advantage which was further enhanced by a personal enthusiasm in the mission. But—fortunately as it turned out—he found it was impossible to negotiate satisfactorily with so many distinct Colonies in the short time at his disposal, and arrangements were therefore made for the Conference which met at Ottawa on the 28th of June, and to which South Africa and the Imperial Government joined in sending representatives.

During his Belleville speech on the 21st of September, Sir John Thompson had referred to this Imperial policy in words which seemed to arouse the strongest sympathies of his audience: "We have sent different lines of steamships to every part of the world. We have subsidised them on the Pacific to the Eastern countries. We have subsidised them to Australia, and we are holding out inducements to get upon the Atlantic the finest line of steamships, or as fine a line, as crosses the ocean in any part of the world. To-day one of those steamships on the Pacific is carrying the Hon. Mackenzie Bowell to seek to extend the hand of fellowship and friendship and intercourse of trade with the Australian Colonies, in the most distant part of the Empire."

Referring to the matter in the House early in the Session of 1894, the Premier pointed out in reply to some criticisms from Mr. Laurier—March 16th—that the Governments far away on the Pacific had received Mr. Bowell "with the cordial hand of fellowship, as warm and generous as one colonist could extend to another," and had intimated their intention of discussing the proposals in a conference to be held in Canada. "I venture to say," continued the speaker, "that a proposition which is thus warmly received, and is being acted on by four or five Governments in Australia and New Zealand is not one to be derided as unworthy of the ambition of a Government representing this country, for we can see not only that commercial interests may be developed and extended by the promotion of trade between those countries and Canada, but that we shall be doing honest yeoman service to the interests of the Empire if we draw together in closer bonds our fellow-colonists and ourselves."

The result, as shown by the meeting at the capital of the Dominion in the following summer, was a gathering of most notable men from various parts of the British realm. From Great Britain came the Earl of Jersey, G.C.M.G., who had been for some years a most popular Governor of New South Wales. From South Australia came the Hon. Thomas Playford, formerly Premier, and now Agent-General in London. New South Wales sent the Hon. F. B. Suttor, M.L.A., Minister of Public Instruction; Tasmania had the Hon. N. Fitzgerald as its representative; New Zealand sent a prominent business man in the person of Mr. Alfred Lee-Smith; Victoria sent Sir Henry J. Wrixon, K.C.M.G., Q.C., and the Hon. Simon Fraser, a Canadian of days gone by. Queensland was represented by the Hon. A. J. Thynne, M.L.C., a member of the Local Government, and by the Hon. William Forrest. Cape Colony—now the centre of a new policy of Imperial expansion under the inspiring influence of Mr. Cecil Rhodes—sent Chief Justice Sir Henry de Villiers, Sir Charles Mills, Agent-General in London; and that most striking personality, the Hon. Jan Hendrick Hofmeyr, the loyal leader of the Dutch element at the Cape. Canada was represented by the Hon. Mackenzie Bowell, who was deservedly elected President of the Conference; Sir Adolphe Caron; the Hon. G. E. Foster; and by Mr. Sandford Fleming, C.M.G., whose enthusiastic interest in the question of cable communication had made his name so familiar in what may be called the politics of the Empire.

The opening of the Conference in the Dominion Senate Chamber was a function of unusual brilliance. The Earl of Aberdeen, Governor General of Canada, presided, and delivered one of his characteristic speeches in welcoming the delegates. The Chamber, aside from the many Colonial delegates and visitors, was crowded with distinguished men from all parts of the Dominion, and with hundreds of ladies. It really presented a most splendid spectacle, in appearance as well as in the wide interests which such an assemblage embodied to the reflective on-looker. Lord Aberdeen's address was most effective, and patriotic in the broadest sense of the word. Sir John Thompson followed, and welcomed the delegates in a speech of exceptional eloquence. Stirred up by the occasion, he for once allowed his loyalty and Imperial aspirations to find full vent in a brief but really delightful effort. Friends and spectators say that the late Premier never looked so well, so dignified, so impressive, as he did on this historic day. In appearance and in speech, he appeared more than worthy to represent Canada before the delegates from so many parts of the British world.

After voicing the sentiments of welcome felt by all

Canadians, and speaking once more in their name, he said: "I can assure the delegates who are assembled, that our people, filled with zeal for the greatness and development of their own country, and for the strengthening of the Empire, are delighted to see the kindlings of the same ambition in the sister colonies throughout the world." He then expressed pleasure at the idea that the discussions of the Conference would be more immediately and chiefly connected with questions of prosperity, of commerce, and of communication, within the Empire, and not with disturbing problems of foreign relations, and of peace or war. But, and here his characteristic caution came in, "we realize that while there is ample field for the widest patriotism and the warmest loyalty, there are matters of pure business, needing the closest examination and scrutiny —matters connected with trade, with steamships, and with telegraphs." He went on to say that "the ocean which divides the Colonies should become the highway for the people, and for the products that the Colonies produce."

And then came an eloquent sentence which voiced his own views amid the enthusiastic applause of his audience, and will be remembered in all future records of the gathering: "On this happy occasion, these delegates assemble after long years of self-government in their countries, years of greater progress and development than the colonies of any Empire have ever seen in the past; not to consider the prospects of separation from the Mother Country, but to plight our faith anew to each other as brethren, and to plight anew with the Mother Land that faith which has never yet been broken or tarnished." He concluded by expressing the hope that this Conference would be but "the prelude of occasions on which we shall not only meet in Canada the statesmen of the other Colonies, but on which we shall be able to meet, with greater facilities than we now possess, the people whom they represent."

Lord Jersey spoke earnestly, and to the point, concerning the opportunities and possibilities of the Conference. In the course of his speech he turned to the Premier and said: "I should like also to express thanks to Sir John Thompson for having had the boldness and the foresight to call this Conference together in order to bring these subjects within the range of practical consideration.' He went on to say that the spirit which inspired him was one of "absolute sympathy with the far-seeing policy which has called us together"; and continued: "It is with wonder that I think of what Canada has done to bring the northern and southern parts of the Empire together. She has linked the two great oceans after an exhibition of courage and constancy and skill which has never been surpassed in the history of the world. She has made her country the half-way house of the Empire." Facing the Canadian Premier once more the speaker concluded: "Sir John Thompson, in the name of the country which I represent, the Mother Country, I take up the pledge of faith which you have so ably and eloquently tendered, in the full belief that the result of this Conference will be the strengthening of those bonds of affection and of interest which should always bind each part of the Empire together."

In the evening a great banquet was held. Sir John Thompson was unusually witty and graceful, and in the course of his speech made a reference which deserves to be recorded as being both effective and charming: "We have all been striving to express the heartiness of the welcome we desire to accord the delegates. For my part, I cannot do better than recall a greeting I observed was lately offered to the Countess of Aberdeen, during her tour of benevolence in Ireland: 'You are as welcome as sunshine.'"

After a loyal address to Her Majesty the Queen, the Conference settled down to business. Mr. Bowell delivered a lengthy and able review of the questions which might come up for consideration, and this address formed a useful basis for the ensuing discussions. Without going into the results in detail, the work of the gathering may be briefly summarised as follows :

I. A Resolution in favour of establishing a Customs Union between Great Britain and the other portions of the Empire.

II. An earnest expression of opinion in favour of preferential trade relations, between Canada, Australasia and South Africa.

III. A motion urging Imperial action in the removal of certain clauses contained in existing international treaties, which hampered reciprocal trade agreements between the Colonies.

IV. Approval of immediate steps for obtaining cable communication between Canada and Australasia free from foreign control.

V. A request to the Imperial Government to commence the survey of the cable route at once—the expense to be borne in equal proportions by the British and Colonial Governments concerned.

VI. A suggestion to the Imperial authorities that assistance be given to the proposed fast Atlantic line of steamships, by diversion of the subsidies hitherto granted to the American line from Liverpool to New York.

But the results which follow naturally from an increased acquaintance with each other's interests and industries, requirements and resources, were perhaps as important as the mere resolutions passed by the Conference. The Australians and South Africans came to Canada, saw the country, learned something of its vastness, its hidden and developed wealth, its institutions and productions. They told the Canadian Ministers in conference, and the Canadian people at the banquets tendered them in Ottawa and Toronto, Montreal and Quebec, something of the prosperity and possibilities, the loyalty and the aspirations after federal unity, which characterized the Australasian and other Colonies. The representatives of the countries concerned, found that the United States had gradually developed a trade with Australasia which was well worth being considered and diverted—a commerce which had increased from $4,200,000 in 1860, to nearly $20,000,000 in 1892.

And the great bulk of this trade was seen to be in products which Canada excels in manufacturing, or in articles of a kind which she now obtains largely from the United States instead of Australia. The Republic was found to export to those Colonies considerable quantities of agricultural implements, carriages, chemicals, fish, manufactures of iron, steel, leather and paper, petroleum, and manufactured tobacco and wood. Yet, although the Dominion can compete in nearly all of these products, it only sent them from $300,000 to $500,000 worth a year. Hence the very evident opening for a substantial interchange. During an informal discussion at the Conference, Mr. Suttor enumerated as the articles which Australia could sell to Canada: wool, which is produced in immense quantities, frozen beef and mutton, which can be got in Sydney for two cents a pound and costs twelve cents in British Columbia, canned meats, raw hides and skins, hard woods for railway ties and street paving, fruits such as lemons, oranges and mandarins, and sugar.

Amongst the things which could be taken from Canada would be paper, which is not made in Australia, cotton goods and frozen and canned salmon. Mr. Lee-Smith stated that the Massey-Harris Co., of Toronto, had already

Her Excellency The Countess of Aberdeen.

shipped 4,000 cultivators to New Zealand. That Colony could send woolen goods, superior gum and flax, and rabbit skins, and would purchase frozen salmon, hops and paper. Other articles mentioned by delegates were rough timber, matches, and petroleum, all of which could be obtained from the Dominion. Sir Henry de Villiers said that the Cape could offer wool, diamonds, wine and fruit, and would take lumber in large quantities, together with agricultural implements and paper.

The subsequent report of Lord Jersey to the Imperial Government was favourable to the proposals of the Conference, with the exception of the resolution which expressed a hope that England might be induced to herself enter some system of Imperial Customs Union. He referred to the greeting given by the Canadian Premier as having "struck the chord which vibrated throughout the proceedings," and went on to deal elaborately with all the questions discussed. He concluded with the statement that although commerce cannot be based upon sentiment, it is still possible for the latter to aid in clearing away obstacles and in diverting the stream of trade into new channels. The leading men of the Colonies "appreciate the value of the connection with Great Britain, and the bulk of their population is loyal. It is within the power of Great Britain to settle the direction of their trade and the current of their sentiments for, it may be, generations. Such an opportunity may not soon recur, as the sands of time run down quickly."

At a banquet given on July 8th by the Hon. Simon Fraser, M.L.C., of Victoria, but a native of Nova Scotia the Premier made a very pleasant after-dinner speech. The majority of those present were Nova-Scotians, and they could, therefore, appreciate the force of a portion of his remarks. He commenced by expressing great interest in the statement made by Mr. Fraser to the effect that in departing from Nova-Scotia, "the cradle of the earth." he had been moved to some extent by the predatory instincts of his race. "It was the Scotchman's characteristic to reach out to the ends of the earth in order to secure whatever he could lay hands on, and to lie down alongside of it, too." Then turning from the humourous to the serious, Sir John expressed great pleasure at the praise of Canadian development which their host and visitor had expressed. "That record of progress," he added, "will still continue, no matter what party guides the destiny of this country On this part of the continent the future belongs to Canadians, and the sentiment animating our people is that she shall be great in the Councils of the Empire."

With these and other similar words echoing in their minds, the representatives of many States of a vast Empire finally dispersed. Their mission had been a noble one; the occasion, a unique and historic event; the visit to the Dominion, a pleasant, and, it may truly be said, a profitable trip. The end is not yet; and as the Ottawa Conference recedes into the dim distance and is succeeded by other and seemingly greater gatherings, its importance may be somewhat overshadowed and its deliberations partly forgotten by the great mass of an Imperial people. But it is safe to say that history will do it justice: and that down through all "the ringing grooves of change" its resolutions and results will be carried as the first public political plank in the re-construction of the British Empire.

CHAPTER XXV.

Later Events in a Great Life.

In the middle of March, 1894, commenced Sir John Thompson's last Parliamentary Session. But neither he nor the public had any premonition of the fact, and the months, as they rapidly passed away, were as usual, crowded with work and busy achievement. Speaking in the House during the debate on the Address the Premier took occasion, with that courtesy which was so characteristic, to thank the Opposition and its leaders for having facilitated the despatch of public business at the previous meeting of Parliament, and thus enabled him to get away and perform the important duties to which he had been called at Paris: "I venture to say that they showed a high sense of patriotism and public duty in affording me that opportunity, and they have conferred an obligation upon me as a public man that I feel bound to recognize this evening."

A little later on Mr. Foster introduced his Budget, and explained the revision of the tariff which had been promised in the preceding Session, and pledged again by Sir John Thompson and other Ministers during the autumn tour of Western Ontario. He stated that his object in the changes made was the reasonable protection of Canadian industries, combined with due care for the rights of consumers. The speech was elaborate as well as eloquent, and it is not difficult to understand that its preparation and the tremendous work of revising a tariff composed of some 900 items had affected in some degree the health of the Finance Minister, and almost prevented him from taking part in the Inter-Colonial Conference. The whole tariff was changed; many of the specific duties were altered to *ad-valorem* ones; and a general lowering took place. Mr. Foster estimated the total loss of revenue at one and a half millions. The *Toronto Mail*, which would hardly be considered as too friendly at that time, thought four millions nearer the mark, and declared that the marked reductions in the new tariff "from the public and business point of view are to be commended."

While the Budget discussion was still going on, an interesting event took place on the 9th of April, when a committee from the Sir John Macdonald Club, of Montreal, presented to the Conservative members at Ottawa, a very handsome portrait of Sir John Thompson, to be hung in the party caucus room of the House of Commons. Sir John's speech in acknowledgment was most felicitous. He began by saying that "the genial and loyal spirit of the Club, in making the presentation is admirable beyond description, and the shortcomings of the picture are unhappily all my own." Then in a more serious vein and with a significance which could only be realized afterwards, he added: "That leads me to think that bye-and-bye my shortcomings may be forgotten, as more important questions arise on the political surface. Our hope for the future is not that I shall for all time, or for a very long time, continue in the leadership of the party, but that the party shall continue to be led by the lieutenants of Sir John Macdonald from time to time, the men who believe in his principles and are prepared to fight for them."

A few days later, on the 12th of the month, the Premier indicated his interest in all questions of moral reform, by attending a meeting of the National Council of Women, which was then being organized in Ottawa under the inspiring influence and Presidency of the Countess of Aberdeen. Representatives were present from Montreal, Toronto, Quebec, Hamilton, Winnipeg, London and other places, and an active part had been taken in the proceedings by Lady Thompson, Madame Laurier, Mrs. Drummond, of Montreal, Lady Ritchie, Mrs. Schultz, of Winnipeg, and Mrs. Grant Macdonald, of Toronto. Sir John Thompson left a crowded House and an important debate to be present, and seconded a resolution expressing the belief that the new organization would "conduce to the best welfare of the country, by promoting greater unity of thought, sympathy and purpose, amongst women workers of all classes and sections of the people."

He commenced a brief but pointed speech, by calling the assemblage a National Parliament of the women of Canada, and then referring, amid laughter, to "the brother Parliament on the Hill," which he had just left. "I hope," he continued, "that it will further be said of Canada, as the result of this movement, that we are not only the most law-abiding people—the most generous in our charities—but that we have the best organized system of charities in the world." After a reference to the appreciation which public men should feel in this matter, he expressed the belief that it would "bind together in sympathy and closer citizenship, all those who are interested in charitable work." He spoke of his pleasure in reading the resolutions regarding the consolidation of the Canadian people and the necessity of inculcating patriotism in the young, and concluded by declaring that "any movement which tends to bring together the people of the various Provinces, of different opinions, politics, and beliefs, will be patriotic in its aim and in its work, and Divinely blessed in its results."

During this Session the ever present Franchise question came up. It had already engaged the Premier's attention in the speeches made during the Fall, and he had everywhere denounced the Liberal proposal to apply the Provincial franchises in Dominion matters. At Arthur on October 2nd, he had pointed out that the Act was "founded on national principles and it is necessary for the national security that we should have a national franchise in this country, as every other self governed country has, with the single exception of the United States, whose example it is not always wise to follow."

It being necessary to have a revision of the lists, after an interval of three years, Sir John Thompson on June 14th, introduced an amendment to the existing Act, which, without in any way vitiating its general principles, improved it in detail and facilitated and cheapened it in operation. After dealing with the subject at some length; defending the position of the Government; and pointing out that the only way in which the Dominion franchise could be assimilated with the Provinces would be by the latter legislating themselves first into uniformity, he referred to the question of cost and observed that: "Hereafter, when the list is once framed we shall have the advantage of provincial lists to start from, that is to say, the very recent lists. We shall have the advantage of the more recent local revision, and to my mind these two circumstances together will make the construction of the lists from year to year very rapid and very simple, and if I am correct in this assumption we shall succeed in lessening the expense very much indeed."

The debate upon the French Treaty a month afterwards brought up incidentally the Prohibition issue and the temperance question, which for a year or two past had been creating wide discussion. Sir John Thompson's position upon this matter seems to have been one of evolution. As with every thing else, he believed in moderation.

WINDSCR CASTLE.

Speaking at Orangeville on November 29th, 1886, he declared it to be a moral and not a political question. But "the time is coming when it may be one of the great questions of the day." When the people had "understandingly pronounced upon it; it will be the duty of the Government —considering the interests of our country and fair-play to everybody whose interests may be affected—to obey the voice of the people." Later on, this hint at a plebiscite was taken up by Sir Oliver Mowat. In May 1888 he had strongly supported an amendment to the Railway Act making any person selling spirituous or intoxicating liquors to a railway employé subject to severe punishment. In reply to protests, the Minister of Justice declared it to be "just the same as selling to minors. Persons who are engaged in a business which we restrict must take the risk of violating the law."

Speaking at Owen Sound regarding the issue on October 4th, 1893, he was very explicit in reply to a query as to his views: "I am in sympathy with prohibition insofar as it is a move for the furthering of temperance in this country, and in remedying the evils which the temperance community are endeavouring to abate. If prohibition can be adopted and enforced in this country, I am in sympathy with that movement." In connection with subsequent questions concerning jurisdiction to deal with the subject, his opinion, as a constitutional lawyer of high rank, given in the same speech is most interesting: "My own mind has no doubt whatever. My own mind is that the power of prohibition rests with the Dominion Parliament, and I would not have thought that that could be contradicted if it were not that so great an authority as the Premier of Ontario has challenged that position and asked me to get the opinions of the courts of the country as to whether his Government or ours has power of prohibition." There is certainly no shirking of the issue here.

As to the Prohibition Commission which the Government had appointed in 1891, he stated at Durham on September 29th that "the object was to get information for the people as to what was going on in Canada with regard to the liquor traffic and the results of experience in other countries in the way of suppressing it." On March 29th following these speeches he received an important deputation of temperance people at Ottawa, but positively refused to give them any official promise or pledge. He pointed out that the Royal Commission had not yet reported, and that the matter involved a displacement of revenue to the extent of nine millions of dollars. Business considerations for the moment were more important than sentiment, and this he practically told the deputation; refusing to play in any way to the gallery of prohibition votes to which one delegate called his attention.

The discussion of the French treaty in the House during the early part of July was interesting apart from the allegations regarding differences in the Cabinet over its ratification. The temperance people did not at all like it, and the vine-growers were afraid of it. Sir John Thompson handled this part of the subject in his speech on July 10th: "I appreciate and endorse what has been said by several members of this House, with regard to the advantages which would accrue to this country from the increased consumption of the lighter wines instead of the whiskey and other spirits which are in general consumption to-day. . . . The wines of this country, I am informed, are sold more cheaply than the French wines of the same class, and the duty which will still remain, one would think would be a very considerable protection indeed to the wine growing interest of this country."

He appealed strongly to the House to sanction the Treaty, because it had been negotiated with and through

Imperial aid, invoked at the request of Canada. In any event it could be abrogated at twelve months' notice, should the arrangement not be finally satisfactory. Needless to say the Government was fully supported in its policy.

A debate dealing with the character and conduct of certain judges in the Province of Quebec took place in the House about this time. Charges of a more or less vague and inconsequential, but none the less unpleasant, nature had been flung at the French-Canadian judiciary by Mr. J. Israel Tarte. Sir John Thompson wrote a letter asking for proofs which would warrant him in submitting the allegations to a Committee, but these were refused. Meantime he obtained evidence that many, if not most, of the statements were baseless, or subject to explanation, and these particulars the Premier submitted to the House on July 17th, in a logical speech delivered in his usual judicial style.

But upon the whole he did not speak very frequently during the Session. A strong utterance upon the Manitoba schools, and his settlement of the long wrangle in the Public Accounts Committee as to the power of taking evidence under oath, were about the only matters he took part in, besides those already mentioned. He was in his place, however, every day, working hard, chiefly in the writing of letters. Always watchful of the proceedings, he was as quick as ever in detecting anything which called for a reply, and in directing attention to it through some one else, if he did not care to speak himself. His last act and practically his last words in the House of Commons, where for eight years his influence had been so strongly felt, and been so useful to his country and empire, was in moving on July 21st, seconded by Mr. Laurier, that "the House do concur in the address from the Senate to

Her Most Gracious Majesty the Queen, tendering cordial congratulations upon the birth of a son to Their Royal Highnesses the Duke and Duchess of York." His first speech in the House had been in defence of the execution of a rebel against Her Majesty's authority; his last words in the House consisted in an offering of its congratulations to the Queen; his last act in life was the receiving of a high honour from Her Majesty's hands.

On the 20th of August Sir John paid one of his somewhat rare visits to Toronto, in order to inspect the Island construction works at the request of the City Council. He came down from Muskoka, where he had been having an all too brief holiday, and was, of course, presented with a long address. Later in the day he was given a banquet at the Pavilion on the Island, amongst the guests being Sir John Gorst, Q.C., M.P., the distinguished English Conservative statesman, who happened to be in the city; Sir Frank Smith and Mr. Clarke Wallace. The Premier's speech was full of patriotic aspiration. He expressed the belief that sectionalism was disappearing; that the time had come for the young men—born in the days of Confederation—to take their place in the field of Canadian public life, and to realize that "the first principle of national life, national obligation and national hope, is that they are Canadians above and before everything else." He continued with a reference to Sir John Gorst's presence; to the statesmen of England, who are "the statesmen of the Colonies as well"; and to the recent Inter-Colonial Conference. He concluded with an utterance of unusual warmth:

"We are not ashamed or afraid to speak of our loyalty. It is not at all a mere boast. It is not a mere sentiment—great a sentiment as it is—but it is the sense that under the rule of our present Sovereign, this vast Empire is the empire of the colonies as well as of Great Britain herself."

The Toronto Industrial Exhibition was opened by Sir John on the 4th of September following, amid the usual ceremonies. Accompanied by the Hon. Mr. Bowell, he received an Address on behalf of the management from the President, Mr. J. J. Withrow, and delivered a speech in reply which indicated his steadily growing power of making a popular, as well as a judicial or Parliamentary, oration. His strong point was an appeal to the national British sentiment of the people:

"As one of the public men of this country, I assert that it is our duty to remove all possible causes of friction between the Mother Land and Canada, in order that we may, in these seven Provinces and in the fertile prairies of this Dominion, truly establish British polity and British institutions upon this continent. It is the interest of every true Canadian, if the time shall come, that we shall make all the sacrifices we can make to see that the flag which floats over us shall float over our children as well as ourselves. And it is the first duty, I say, of a public man to help to sustain the greatness of the Empire as well as of the Dominion, knowing that the greatest achievements which the people of this Dominion can accomplish are to be gained under British rule and in connection with the Empire of which we are proud to-day to form a part."

The loud and frequent applause which greeted these sentiments showed that he had touched the popular chord, and was at last learning to let the people into the secret of that strong inner loyalty, which his characteristic aversion to buncombe or display had hitherto made him so largely conceal from the public.

Hardly a week later the Premier performed his last public function in his native Province. On the 11th of September, in the presence of 5,000 people, and assisted by Sir Charles Hibbert Tupper, the Hon. J. W. Longley, and others, he unveiled a monument at Springhill, N.S., erected to the memory of 125 men who had met death by an awful explosion on February 21st, 1891. His words were few, but he took occasion to point out that the Canadian people were as fully prepared to face difficulties undauntedly as were ever the brave miners of Springhill. In conclusion Sir John read a poem in commemoration of the event, composed by Mr. W. E. Hefferman, as voicing his own feelings and that of his audience.

Following this came the unveiling of the monument to Sir John A. Macdonald, in Queen's Park, Toronto. It is a notable fact, that within little more than a year of his own death, Sir John Thompson performed the chief ceremonies at three memorial functions. And the comparatively few statues which are raised in Canada to the memory of departed greatness or present worth, adds to the force of this coincidence. At Hamilton on the 1st of November, 1893, he had unveiled the local monument to Sir John Macdonald and delivered a speech worthy to rank with the best ever produced by such an occasion. With him at this event were a number of the other Dominion Ministers; Sir Oliver Mowat; the Lieutenant-Governor of Ontario, and Lieutenant-Governor Schultz, of Manitoba. Senator Sanford, who had done so much as chairman of the committee, in obtaining the necessary funds, presided at the ceremonies and addresses were delivered by Sir Adolphe Caron, Sir Oliver Mowat, Sir Charles Hibbert Tupper and Mr. N. Clarke Wallace. But the Premier's speech was, of course, the pivotal part of the programme. It had evidently been prepared with great care, and perhaps reads better than it sounded amid the disadvantages of moving throngs and pouring rain. It was however, a cultured, patriotic and really beautiful eulogy of the chief founder of Canadian Confederation, and of Canadian Conservatism as understood in later days.

He spoke of the Canada of years' long past; of the struggles and successes met with by Sir John Macdonald, in the early days of the Dominion, and before the Dominion was a fact; of his work for the Empire; of his labours for the party. Sir John Macdonald had been "the master builder among the many who did noble work in the structure of the nation." His patriotism was the mainspring of his every action; his true and deep Canadianism was "the pillar of cloud by day and the pillar of fire by night," to multitudes of his followers. "It used to be a popular delusion," said the speaker, in referring to the Chieftian's amiability, kindliness and forbearance, "that when he took a new colleague he required from him his resignation in advance. I soon found that when he took a new colleague the new comer's relations to his Chief were regulated by affection and not by command." He was a great parliamentarian. He was "guided by the inspiration of heaven which falls upon truly patriotic men." He was ambitious in the best sense of the word. "Ambitious to infuse into the minds of his countrymen sentiments and ideas, that were wider than the issues of party; ambitious to make Canada great; ambitious to silence the voice of faction and the noise of discord; ambitious to leave this country and empire better off for the toils and sacrifices of his life."

The ceremonies in Toronto took place on the 13th of October, 1894, and constituted the last public function which Sir John Thompson was destined to perform in Canada. Great preparations had been made for the occasion; the troops had turned out in force; the school children in thousands; and the people in crowds, estimated as high as thirty and forty thousand. Many Cabinet Ministers from Ottawa and Toronto were present, together with distinguished people from all parts of the Dominion.

Mr. E. F. Clarke presided; Mr. Mackenzie Bowell paid a fitting tribute to the leader he had served with for so many years; Mr. G. W. Ross, the Ontario Minister of Education, offered a most eloquent and generous tribute to the great opponent of his party; Sir Adolphe Caron delivered one of his characteristic orations; Sir Charles Hibbert Tupper was brief and forcible; Mr. Hamilton McCarthy, the sculptor, was deservedly called upon for a few words.

The Premier's speech was necessarily short in comparison with the one delivered at Hamilton. But it was none the less inspiring and interesting. He spoke of the day being the anniversary of that "field of glory," the battle of Queenston Heights. Sir John Macdonald's was "the kind of loyalty which believes that the true interests of Canada lie in British connection and British institutions." He referred to episodes in the Chieftian's career when he had stood up for the Dominion; when he had dared great things for his country; when "the flood of patriotism had streamed through his undaunted heart." And then, Sir John Thompson concluded, in words, which two short months afterwards might well have been applied to himself.

"May the statue speak of one who was great because he loved Canada much, and loved and served his Empire well, and of whom it was truly said, in recollection of what he had accomplished for his country, and the example he had set his countrymen:

'He nothing fears,
The long to-morrow of the coming years.'"

Gateway of Windsor Castle.

CHAPTER XXVI.

Last Days and Dramatic Death.

Late in October it was announced that the Prime Minister of Canada intended to take a trip to Europe, partly in order to be sworn in as a member of the Imperial Privy Council; partly, as his friends knew, in order to place one of his daughters in an educational institution at Paris; partly for a rest after the arduous labours of a somewhat prolonged Session. The brief visit to the lakes of Muskoka in the course of the summer had been pleasant and beneficial, but it was understood that a still more complete rest and change of air was desirable.

No one, however, supposed that Sir John was in the slightest danger, or that his ill-health was anything more than the natural and temporary result of too much work, and too little exercise and recreation. His most intimate friends did not have the faintest conception that the end of that active and distinguished career was at hand. While the broad Dominion was looking forward with pleasure to the honour about to be given by Her Majesty the Queen to its leading and most representative statesman; while his personal friends were awaiting his return, crowned with Royal approval and vigourous in the enjoyment of renewed health and strength; the angel of death was in reality hovering above his head, and the shadow of eternity was sweeping slowly athwart the dial of a life which could ill be spared.

That Sir John Thompson was to a limited extent aware of his own dangerous condition is now known, though in spite of premonitions, he could hardly have expected such a sudden and startling termination. Before going to Muskoka he had found himself suffering somewhat from ailments which seemed natural to his physical condition—the stoutness which had been growing upon him so steadily during recent years—but he supposed that rest and change of air and scene would modify, if they did not entirely remove, the trouble. And with the reticence which was such a marked feature in his character, he did not talk of the matter, even to his friends.

Finally, however, he accidently mentioned it, and was at once urged to consult a physician. Later on this was done, first in Toronto, then in Montreal, and ultimately by a consultation in Ottawa. As a result of this, he received the strong advice of three leading physicians—Dr. Roddick, Sir James Grant, and Dr. Wright—to the effect that work should be given up entirely, and the winter spent in some warm country. The symptoms of kidney and heart disease were declared to be marked, but serious danger might be averted by taking the course outlined. Otherwise his life was liable to be the forfeit.

But here was displayed the personal patriotism of the man, and the devotion to duty which had always been such a prominent trait in his character. He told the doctors plainly, and no doubt with accuracy, that the course they urged would cause him so much anxiety and distress on account of the political complications it would create, and the disturbance it might make in public affairs, that the effect would probably be worse than if he remained at his work. The medical men finally agreed with this view, and consented to a compromise by which he promised the cutting down of his daily work, and undertook the trip to Europe which was shortly afterwards announced.

It is clear that he did not realize any special risk, and

had every hope of recovery. Otherwise he would never have left home without Lady Thompson's company or that of the invalid child whom he had always regarded with such a wealth of affection. Still, it is evident that an occasional premonition of the end did come, as it has so often come to others. Writing to the Countess of Aberdeen* two or three days before he left Ottawa on that last eventful journey of his life—October 27th—he made a most pathetic reference, and one which even then could not have been understood in its immediate application, to say nothing of its full prophetic meaning. After thanking Her Excellency for some papers which had been sent to him, and speaking generally for a few sentences, he continued as follows:

"It is as I said a year ago, you have all the hearts in the country with you, but I cannot help reflecting when I recall what was done by Your Excellencies in Ireland, in the Maritime Provinces and in the West, that there is an end to the burdens which the greatest energy and the strongest constitution can bear. I did not think this a few months ago, but I found it out before last Session was over and I see it now. Sometimes the warning to stop and rest comes very suddenly and sternly."

On Nov. 7th, Sir John Thompson reached London, and was examined by Sir Russell Reynolds, who corroborated the views already expressed by the Canadian physicians, and pronounced a hopeful opinion as to recovery if the advice given was acted upon. He then left for the continent with a party composed of himself, his younger daughter, Senator Sanford and Miss Muriel Sanford. They went from London to Paris, and after spending a few days at Nice and Monte Carlo, proceeded to Genoa, and

*Published by the kind permission of Her Excellency to the author.

thence to Rome. From there they journeyed to Milan, and afterwards visited Florence and Venice. During this trip it is understood that Sir John did some not altogether beneficial sight-seeing, upon one occasion climbing up the steep stairs of the lofty tower of St. Peter's at Rome. After three weeks spent in this way, he returned to London, reaching the metropolis on Nov. 29th. Here, again, he had done a rather unwise thing in hurrying from the Continent to keep an appointment with Lord Ripon at the Colonial Office, travelling all night and in some discomfort, in order to reach his destination on time. Upon several occasions during this brief tour he had suffered from shortness of breath and shown symptoms which appear, however, to have been hardly noticed at the time.

From the day he reached London until the night he left for Windsor Castle, Sir John seems to have become hopelessly involved in work. The Copyright question was in itself a most complex and difficult matter, and frequent interviews with the Colonial Secretary and others seem to have brought it almost to the verge of settlement. A little longer, and his clear head and great knowledge of the subject would have achieved the result so long desired and aimed at by the Dominion Government. Perhaps the appreciation of this fact drew him on imperceptibly into labours which he would have otherwise avoided. Finally, it was announced that on the 11th of December he would be present at the meeting of the Royal Colonial Institute, and would leave for Windsor Castle in the morning of the next day, where he was to be sworn a Privy Councillor by Her Majesty, and remain for dinner and the night. It was understood also that he intended to sail for home on the 19th instant, so as to spend Christmas, or a part of the Christmas season, with his family.

On the eve of the fateful day, and despite the advice

of Sir Charles Tupper, who was to preside at the meeting, he went to the Royal Colonial Institute in order to hear an address, which was to be delivered upon the Inter-Colonial Conference by Sir Henry Wrixon, one of the recent delegates So interested was Sir John in the subject that he seems to have been unable to stay away, although he had during preceding weeks refused the many social engagements which were pressed upon him. Of course, the audience would not dispense with a speech from the Canadian Premier, even though, with characteristic modesty, he had at first taken a seat in the background. He made the effort, but it was plain to all that he was decidedly unwell.

That last speech has a pathetic, as well as a practical, value. It showed Sir John Thompson's great interest in the subject, and breathed his strong Imperial aspirations. At the same time it pointed out the steps which it was necessary to take before sentiment could be chrystalized into action, and it revealed the policy which he would himself have pursued had Providence permitted. He began with a general reference to his health and to the subject under discussion:

"I wish the strength at my disposal this evening would enable me to express all I feel in sympathy with the Colonial Institute, and my appreciation of the paper we have just heard. The Ottawa Conference had for its primary and significant feature the appreciation of the whole people of the Dominion. It was impossible to have exceeded the enthusiasm felt with the objects of that Conference even in the most remote parts of the country. A good deal had been said about meetings of that kind being characterized by a display of sentiment and sentimentality. For my part, I look upon it as one of the great achievements of the Conference, one of the great justifications for the Conference, that the sentiment of the people of Canada responded instinctively at the first mention of the preparations for the assembly."

He then mentioned the tenders which had been received for the Pacific cable, and which indicated a cost of one million pounds less than had been anticipated, and went on to speak of the fast Atlantic service—in which he took so great a personal interest, and to which the Canadian Government had offered $750,000—as having success practically ensured.

Sir John concluded an earnest and greatly cheered speech, which he had evidently made longer than he intended at first, with the statement that "the possibilities with regard to trade with all these colonies, at the Cape of Good Hope and in Australia and New Zealand are very great. I have not the opportunity or strength to deal fully with them this evening, but in common with Lord Brassey, I venture to hope that the influence of this meeting and the influence of all who sympathize with our projects, will be liberally extended to us, and that the feeling may be increased here as it exists in the most distant portions of the Empire, that the day may come not only when the colonies will be united more closely together, but when they will have a more practically useful connection with the heart of the Empire itself."

It was indeed sadly appropriate that the last public utterance of Sir John Thompson should have been words of loyalty and the voicing of aspirations for closer Imperial unity.

After the meeting he seems to have recovered himself somewhat, and Sir Charles Tupper states, appeared in good spirits when he left him at his hotel, about 11 o'clock. The next morning he started for Windsor Castle, where, at half-past one, he was sworn in by Her Majesty as a member of the Privy Council. It was a romantic and significant scene apart altogether from the tragic result. Here, in the ancient home of the Sovereigns of England, where for centuries loyalty and valour had been rewarded by the bestowal of similar honours; where the great men of the land had knelt in homage to a long line of other monarchs; where Privy Councillors had been made before America was discovered, or the British Empire dreamed of; the greatest ruler of them all was calling to her Imperial Council a leader from the distant Dominion which had developed since her own accession to the Throne.

But the act of homage was hardly over; the well-won honour had only just been received; the ink was scarcely dry in the new signature to that roll of illustrious names which makes the history of England so proud a record, when the hand of death intervened, and closed a career of loyal and devoted service. The Court Circular of that night states, with the usual formal brevity, that

"The Queen held a Council at half-past one o'clock to-day, at which were present the Marquess of Breadalbane, K G., Lord Steward; the Marquess of Ripon, K.G., Secretary of State for the Colonies; the Right Hon. Henry Fowler, M.P., Secretary of State for India; and the Right Hon. Arnold Morley, M.P., Postmaster-General. The Marquess of Ripon acted for the Earl of Rosebery as President of the Council. The Hon. Sir John Thompson, K.C M.G., Q.C., Premier and Minister of Justice in Canada, was introduced and sworn in a member of the Privy Council. Sir Charles Lennox Peel was in attendance as Clerk of the Council. Lord Hawkesbury and Sir Fleetwood Edwards were in attendance as Lord and Groom-in-Waiting."

Then followed the equally brief statement that to Her Majesty's great regret, Sir John Thompson had died suddenly of syncope a few minutes after leaving the Council room. It was added that Sir John had felt unwell on his arrival at the Castle, and had mentioned having been under medical treatment. Those who witnessed the sad event testify to its sudden and startling nature.

Lord Breadalbane at the time gave a full account of the memorable occurrence. "After Sir John had been sworn, we retired to the luncheon room. While we were sitting there he suddenly fainted. One of the servants and I each took his arm, got him into the next room, and placed him beside the window. I got some water and sent a servant for some brandy. In a short time he recovered somewhat, and seemed much distressed at having made what he regarded as a scene, remarking, "It seems so weak and foolish to faint like this." I replied, "One does not faint on purpose; pray do not distress yourself about the matter." He begged me to return to luncheon. Of course I would not hear of this. I remained with him till he seemed completely recovered. He rose to accompany me back to the luncheon room. I offered him my arm, but he walked unaided. He cheerfully remarked, "I am all right, thank you." Meantime Dr. Reid, the Queen's physician, whom I had sent for, arrived. Within two or three minutes after Sir John's return to the luncheon room, and I believe before he tasted the cutlet or whatever was placed before him, I saw him suddenly lurch over, and fall almost into Dr. Reid's arms." The room was partially cleared and everything possible was done, but without avail. The end had come.

At a moment when Canadians were reading with pleasure the strong utterance of their Premier the night before; when his family and friends were looking forward to his announced return; when Miss Helena Thompson had just arrived in Paris again after her visit to London; there came the tidings of that dramatic death almost at the feet of his Sovereign and within the historic walls of Windsor. To quote from the elegy written by Mr. Lewis Morris:

> "Dead at the crest, the crown
> And blossom of his fortunes this strong son
> Of our great realm sank down
> Beneath the load of honours scarcely won."

In what followed can be traced the sympathy which has made the Queen so great a woman, and the tact which has made her so able and remarkable a monarch. Windsor's Imperial towers never, indeed, witnessed an event which so typified the development of British power, and at the same time so evidenced the real union of hearts existing amongst a world-wide and scattered people. The body of the deceased statesman was, late in the evening, placed in a coffin and removed to a room in the Clarence Tower. Meantime Sir Charles Tupper reached the Castle by command of the Queen, and upon Her Majesty learning, in the course of an audience granted him, that Sir John Thompson had been a Roman Catholic, a requiem mass was ordered to be celebrated, and was attended by the members of the Royal household and by various Colonial officials who had come down from London. The body was then taken to the Marble Hall, where it lay in state.

Early next morning the Queen gave instructions that the removal of the remains to the station should be accompanied with every possible ceremony and respect. Her Majesty with her own hands placed a wreath of laurels and lilies upon the coffin, bearing the words: "A mark of sincere respect from Victoria R. I." As the coffin was borne out of the Castle, placed in the plumed hearse, and taken to the special train which waited at the station draped in memorial black, the Queen stood at the window above St. George's gateway and watched the sorrowful function. At the last moment Her Majesty had placed another large wreath of laurel upon the coffin—one which was to lie on it throughout the voyage to Canada. Meanwhile, Sir Charles Tupper had been instructed to send a message of sympathy to the Dominion, which he did in the following cable to the Governor General:

"The Queen has personally commanded me to express to Your Excellency her deep sympathy with the people of Canada in the sad blow which the country has sustained by the sudden and untimely death of the Premier."

As soon as Miss Thompson could be re-called from Paris, she reached Windsor by the Queen's request, together with Senator and Mrs. Sanford, in whose charge she now was. She was received in the Council Chamber, where her father had so recently been sworn into the Privy Council, and was treated by Her Majesty in a manner not only sympathetic but affectionate. Drawing the orphaned girl to her, the Queen kissed her on either cheek and proffered the most deep and sincere condolence. On December 14th, the body of the late Premier was placed in state in the Chapel of Our Lady, in Spanish Place. The coffin, of which the outer shell was mahogany, bore the Queen's wreath and a heavy shield with the inscription:

THE RIGHT HON. SIR JOHN S. D. THOMPSON,
P.C., K.C.M.G., M.P., Q.C.
Premier and Minister of Justice of Canada.
Died at Windsor Castle, December 12th, 1894.
Aged 50 years.
R. I. P.

It was placed on a catafalque, which stood upon a carpet of purple and gold velvet, and was draped with a pall of rich black velvet surmounted by a large golden cross. Many prominent people were present at the memorial service, including the Marquess of Ripon, the Earl of Jersey, Lord Tennyson, Lord Mount-Stephen, Sir Charles Tupper and Mr. Cecil Rhodes. Miss Thompson was also present. The mass was celebrated, at the command of the Queen, by the Rev. Father Longinoto of the Town of Windsor. Here the remains lay in state for some days. Meantime it was announced that the Imperial Government had offered the almost unprecedented honour of having the body conveyed

Hon. Sir Charles Tupper, Bart., G.C., M.G., C.B.,

High Commissioner for Canada in England.

to Halifax—back to the Dominion which Sir John had served and ruled—in a British man-of-war. Lady Thompson accepted the proposal as presented through the Governor General, and on December 22nd commenced the last of the tributes of respect which the Queen and the Mother Land had showered upon the remains of Canada's lamented Premier.

The journey from London to Portsmouth was made a State funeral by Her Majesty's command. Arrangements were made that there should be no stoppage of the special train, in the centre of which was a splendid funeral car built of mahogany and teak, and containing a large compartment which was in reality a mortuary chapel. The ceiling was draped with Canadian flags; the walls were hung with black cloth dotted with silver stars, and caught up by silver cords. In the centre stood a magnificent catafalque, draped in black with silver borders; a large silver cross at the head, and a gold crucifix three feet high in front. The engine attached to the train was also draped, while immediately behind it was a car, full of the wreaths sent by prominent persons. The railway station platform was in black, and the officials on duty were all dressed in mourning garments. In addition to this the guards and other railroad men detailed to accompany the body to Portsmouth, wore a special mourning uniform such as would have been the case had the remains been those of royalty.

All along the route taken by the train, crowds of people waited in respectful silence and watched it pass by. As soon as it was sighted outside of Portsmouth, the many ships in the harbour half-masted their ensigns, the first of the twenty minute-guns boomed a salute, and the flags ashore were dipped. It was received by long lines of naval and military officers representing all branches of the two services, and drawn up in front of large detachments of marines and blue-jackets detailed as guards of honour.

The coffin was at once removed from the train, and carried to the ship by blue-jackets. On either side were the pall-bearers; in front walked the Roman Catholic Bishop of Portsmouth in full purple robes; together with a number of clergymen and priests. Behind the coffin came Lord Pelham Clinton and Major-General Sir John McNeill representing the Queen; then followed the mourners; the naval and military officers in full uniform; the Mayor and Corporation of Portsmouth in their robes of office; and a mass of people. Senator Sanford had accompanied the remains from London by request of Sir Charles Tupper, who was prevented through illness from giving the personal attention which was necessary. He also crossed in the *Blenheim*. As the procession commenced to move, the general silence was broken by a crashing discharge of guns from the *Victory*, Nelson's famed war-ship. The massed bands played the dead march, and all the sailors and marines reversed their arms. When the coffin was carried upon the *Blenheim* there was another crash of artillery and more funeral music, while the officers on board saluted.

A most impressive appearance was presented by the great war-ship. Her sides were painted black; her wide gangway was draped with black cloth; as was also the way to the mortuary chamber. Everything, even to the minutest detail, had been arranged in the most perfect and mournful harmony. A short and solemn service was held in the captain's room, which had been fitted up for the reception of the coffin. Here upon a handsome catafalque, draped with crape-bound flags and black cloth; surrounded by sentries and covered with Her Majesty's wreath, the remains of the Canadian statesman lay during the voyage to Halifax.

In this remarkable manner did Sir John Thompson, or all that was left of the statesman, the jurist, and the true Canadian, return to the land he had loved so well. But it can be truly said that in dying he had yet lived into his country's life. No event in history has done so much to enhance the bond of sympathy between Canada and the Mother Land as did the death of the Canadian Premier, and the spontaneous, universal and remarkable sympathy which it evoked, on the other side of the ocean which he had tried to aid in making a great British lake. The sentiment shown by the Queen, and the honours showered upon the head of the Dominion through its representative, could indeed be appreciated by the loyal people of Canada. And so also with the influence for good which Her Majesty's treatment of the religious side of Sir John Thompson's life and career would naturally have upon those who had once been prejudiced against the statesman for something which his Queen—and theirs—now marked out for special compliment.

Thus the *Blenheim* started with its burden of sorrow for the shores of the country which had still to confer the last of national honours upon its departed statesman. In the eloquent words of Mr. Nicholas Flood Davin, Sir John Thompson, "after being rocked as a child in a fifty cent cradle in a Haligonian cottage, had died in Windsor Castle as the guest of the Queen. One of the mightiest ships in the British Navy had become his bier, and the cannon of the greatest Empire in the world boomed his requiem."

CHAPTER XXVII.

A SPLENDID AND HISTORIC BURIAL.

The great British war-ship steadily and surely ploughed her way across the stormy Atlantic—timed to arrive at Halifax on the morning of the first day of the New Year. The deceased statesman was being borne from the shores of England with honours greater than those which have been accorded to many of the monarchs of the past and the heroes of history. Few indeed of the sons of men are privileged to have a war-ship for a hearse; a great sovereign as a mourner; a mighty empire as the onlooker at his funeral procession; two great countries and a rolling ocean as the scene of his burial.

As the British iron-clad steamed into Halifax harbour at the hour and minute appointed, the cannon boomed out the solemn news to the dense crowds who filled the streets and lined the wharves of the Cronstadt of America; and the flags of the forts and public buildings dipped in sympathy with those which were half-masted upon the Blenheim. Amid the firing of minute-guns and the strains of the dead march played by the ship's band, the coffin, still covered by the flag of Canada, was borne upon the shoulders of stalwart blue-jackets, placed upon the transport Lily, and received on board by the two sons of the late Premier and a number of his former colleagues and friends. As the sad music floated in over the waves, like the sobbing of the sea, the transport steamed into shore, where upon the landing stood a guard of honour, and the Governor General and Lady Aberdeen. Here the coffin was transferred to a gun-carriage drawn by four powerful black horses, and conveyed to the Provincial Building—where the remains were to lie in state—followed by a long procession through streets lined with the men of the 63rd Halifax Rifles, and packed with people who seemed to care nothing for the pouring rain. The day added gloom to the feelings of the spectators, while the mournful music harmonized with the surroundings of sorrow.

When the destination had been reached, the casket was lifted by twelve stalwart soldiers of the Imperial army, carried through another guard of honour, and placed upon the catafalque in the centre of the Legislative Council room, where it lay in state during the succeeding day. Here, for a few brief minutes, Lord and Lady Aberdeen knelt in silent prayer beside the remains of their departed friend and His Excellency's loyal adviser. The lofty and beautiful chamber was almost entirely draped in black and purple silk and cashmere, with silver trimmings; upon the walls hung historic portraits of Britain's monarchs and of Nova Scotia's honoured sons, looking down upon the remains of the Canadian Premier, who in death had so linked his native Province with the memories of his Sovereign's sympathy. The walls were draped in black cashmere; the windows were surmounted with an over-drape of purple, trimmed with silver fringe; the pictures were framed in crape and silver fixings; the ceiling was covered so as to form a canopy of black cashmere, surmounted over the catafalque by the Royal coat of arms, fitted into a smaller canopy of purple and black silk.

Upon the coffin lay the handsome pall worked by Lady Aberdeen with her own hands. It was a beautiful piece of work, made of rich Irish white poplin, lined with satin, with a large gold-thread cross running its whole length. It was bordered by a plain gold fringe and cord. Behind the catafalque was a raised dais on which rested the almost innumerable wreaths from all parts of Britain and Canada. Just below the Queen's memorial were the maple leaves and shamrocks from Lord and Lady Aberdeen, while near by were flowers in every conceivable form of beauty and abundance from Sir John Thompson's late colleagues; from the Governors of the various Provinces; from Conservative organizations throughout Canada; from the Marquess of Ripon; from the Royal Military College at Kingston; from the British Colonial Office. During the 2nd of January, thousands and thousands of people passed through the Chamber where lay the remains of the honored Canadian statesman. Around the catafalque stood a guard of honour composed of members of Parliament, who replaced each other in turn during the day and the succeeding night. Inside, the throng passed slowly, steadily and respectfully through the Chamber. Outside of the heavily draped building, other thousands patiently and solemnly waited their turn

All the arrangements of this memorable state funeral were splendidly carried out. At six o'clock on the following morning the coffin was quietly removed to St. Mary's Cathedral where it was placed upon the lofty catafalque prepared for the purpose. At an early hour the noble cathedral was filled with such a gathering of representative men and women as had never been seen in Canada—not even at the famed burial of Sir John Macdonald. The interior of the sacred building was in itself unique. It was magnificently draped in all the possible emblems of a nation's mourning. The walls were hung in black to within four feet of the floor, where the base was of purple cashmere. Over the windows were silver crosses. Between them were handsome banners, while above and surrounding the altar was the simple text:

"I am the Resurrection and the Life."

The massive Corinthian pillars of the church were draped in black cashmere, trimmed in white and purple, gold and silver. The ceiling formed an immense and sombre canopy, while the Bishop's throne was in purple and gold; the altar cloths were of black with purple velvet trimmings; the floor and the aisles were covered with purple cashmere; and the pews were draped in purple and crape. Behind the Episcopal throne, screened from public view, sat Lady Thompson; inside the altar rail and in the front pews were the Governor-General and Lady Aberdeen, the Lieut.-Governors of Ontario, Quebec, New-Brunswick, Prince Edward Island and British Columbia; Lieut.-General Montgomery Moore; Sir John's late colleagues in the Government; and representatives from very many of the leading legislative, judicial, political, religious, legal, scientific, military and national bodies of the Dominion of Canada.

Bishop Cameron of Antigonish, the warm and faithful friend of the deceased Premier, celebrated the requiem mass. The impressive ceremony was performed amid surroundings of regal magnificence and solemnity. With His Lordship were Archbishop O'Brien of Halifax; Archbishop Bégin of Quebec; Archbishop Duhamel of Ottawa; Bishop Howley of St. John's, Newfoundland; the Bishops of St. John, N.B., Alexandria, Rimouski, and Charlottetown, together with a great number of minor ecclesiastical dignitaries. The "Dies Irae" was exquisitely rendered by the choir, and had been specially translated by the Archbishop of Halifax for the benefit of the mixed congregation. It is impossible to do justice to the sympathetic, graceful and effective funeral oration delivered by Archbishop O'Brien. The career of Sir John Thompson was presented and embodied by the earnest words of one who had known him well and appreciated him thoroughly. His Grace dealt with "the integrity of life and the conscientious fulfilment of onerous duties," which had made that career so important, and so fitted to "adorn the annals of a nation and be an example and instruction to future generations." The late Premier had not succeeded by external influences; by pandering to passion or prejudice; by cunning arts or corrupt devices. It was rather by "a faithful observance of the law of labour imposed by the Creator on the human race, together with intellectual gifts of a high order, strengthened and made perfect by a deep religious spirit."

The Archbishop referred at some length to the Christain life and character of Sir John. His religion had been of a kind to develop and expand his intellectual attainments; give consistency to his actions; strength and vigour to his reasoning; "The way he sought the Lord in goodness and simplicity of heart is known to his friends. He recognised it to be the first duty of a Christian to follow the dictates of conscience and to make his life an outward expression of his inward convictions." At the conclusion of the mass and His Grace's memorial address, there occurred a most significant incident. By suggestion of Lord and Lady Aberdeen, in the midst of the highest Roman Catholic ceremonial, and in honour of a most devout son of the Church, a great congregation of mixed creeds united within the walls of a Roman Catholic Cathedral in singing that exquisite Protestant hymn commencing:

"Now the labourer's task is o'er;
Now the battle day is past;
Now upon the farther shore
Lands the voyager at last.
Father, in Thy gracious keeping
Leave we now Thy servant sleeping."

Then, as the vast audience stood in reverential silence, the solemn music of the Dead March pealed from the organ and the coffin was carried to the funeral car. Troops lined

H.M.S. Blenheim.

the streets from the Cathedral to the cemetery as the immense procession slowly formed and marched behind to the strains of mournful music and amid buildings draped in sombre hue. Thousands of people wore mourning badges, and many in the procession were clothed in garments of black. Three hundred blue-jackets and mariners; two hundred of the late Premier's constituents from Antigonish; Lord Aberdeen and his staff; the Governors of Provinces; officiating clergymen in their robes of office; senators, members of Parliament, judges, ecclesiastics and ministers of every creed; marched in that great procession.

The occasion served to illustrate that religious moderation and toleration which the dead statesman had so often and earnestly urged. Their was no precedence in the procession save by length of service, and mingled together in one common tribute to departed merit were men of such diverse religious views as the Roman Catholic Archbishop of Quebec and the Rev. Dr. Carman, Superintendent of the Methodist Church in Canada; the Episcopal Bishop of Nova-Scotia and the Rev. Dr. Saunders, Moderator of the Presbyterian General Assembly. Men of all political shades were there. The Dominion Conservative leaders and the Provincial Liberal leaders; the officers of the Canadian Pacific Railway and those of the Grand Trunk, joined in honouring the late Premier.

It is utterly impossible to describe the procession. Halifax was so full of people that not a tithe of them could take part, and they had to remain packed along the sides of the streets in serried masses. Fortunately the day was fine and clear. The funeral car was a splendid structure of the kind, beautifully covered with black silk, and draped with black velvet, trimmed with silver fringe. The coffin was placed upon a catafalque, surmounted by a canopy which rested upon four Corinthian columns festooned with flowers. It was adorned with handsome plumes and a silver cross and crown. The car was drawn by six horses, with coverings of black and silver, each guided by a man in uniform. The pall-bearers, who walked upon either side of the car, were the Hon. George E. Foster, Sir Charles H. Tupper, Sir Frank Smith, Hon. John Costigan, Hon. John Haggart, Hon. J. A. Ouimet, Hon. J. C. Patterson, and Hon. W. B. Ives. The route to the Holy Cross Cemetery, which stood in the centre of the city, had been arranged, so as to pass certain points of historic interest, and after an hour's march through lines of soldiers and throngs of people, and accompanied by strains of music and funeral airs from all the great composers, the cemetery was finally reached.

At the draped entrance stood a guard of honour. Within was a quaint, old-fashioned church surrounded by a not very large burial ground, crowded with the graves of those who had found a last resting place in the plot given fifty years before by the Imperial authorities to the Roman Catholics of Halifax. Hawthornes, and maples, and elms had grown up thickly in this sequestered spot in the heart of an important city. Another site for a cemetery had been obtained and was now largely used, but here it had been decided to lay the remains of Sir John Thompson, and here, after a few final prayers by Archbishop O'Brien, all that remained of the distinguished Canadian was hidden from sight in the soil of his native province; in the heart of his native city.

Sir John Thompson was now at rest. The active brain, the patriotic mind, the sturdy character, which had carved out so high a career, had gone from the country he served so well. But his character and achievements remained, written on the scroll of Canadian history. As the Rev. Dr. Barclay, of St. Paul's Presbyterian Church, Montreal, so eloquently phrased it: "The tragic ending of his earthly career shed a mingled gloom and glory on his life, on his family, and on his nation." But if it deprived us of a great leader, it endowed us at the same time with a noble memory.

In Canada and Great Britian the Press had done full justice to the life and work of the late Premier. Partisanship in the one case had been forgotten, distance in the other had been over-looked. The *London Daily News* had rejoiced in his labours for Imperial Unity, as shown in the Ottawa Conference, and declared that "his death will still serve the great purpose to which he devoted his life." The *Standard* said that "partly on account of his ability and tact the recent history of Canada has been one of uneventful prosperity." The *Times* declared that under his guidance "the position of Canada had been confirmed and strengthened." The *Post* joined with Canada in mourning "the loss of so able a man." The *Telegraph* was uncertain whether the loss was greater to Canada or to England. The *Chronicle* thought him "a man of sterling qualities, of whom the whole English-speaking race had good reason to be proud." The *Pall Mall Gazette* believed him to have been "the best type of a lawyer-statesman, cool headed, profoundly informed, earnest and sincere, and with the courage of his convictions."

In Canada the newspapers teemed with sorrowful comments. Black borders, and every possible expression of sincere regret followed his sudden death, and filled their columns during that prolonged and Imperial funeral. The remarks of the Liberal press were especially kind and generous—such indeed as would have given unspeakable pleasure to the statesman, when alive. The *Toronto Globe* referred to him as having given up "his plans and his preferences, and laid his remarkable talents at the service of his country. For the dignity of the Bench and the quiet of his study he exchanged the turmoil, the cares, the misrepresentations and the ingratitude of public life, and finally he gave his life."

The *Toronto Mail*, which had in other days so strongly opposed him, declared that "He will pass into history as a great Premier," and added that "no suspicion ever attached to Sir John as a politician. Sir Richard Cartwright once said of him that his hands were clean, and clean they certainly were. . . . The conduct of the late Premier with reference to offenders was unquestionably unprecedented. No other leader, Liberal or Conservative, has, in this country at least, been ready to act as Sir John Thompson did." The Woodstock *Sentinel-Review*, whose record is one of virile Liberalism, said that "as a statesman Sir John Thompson's name is likely to hold a high place among the men of Canada."

The Hamilton *Herald* declared that his career was an object lesson for young Canadians: "His character all through was above reproach. He was a thinker and a student, and spared himself no trouble and no research to master every detail of facts that he was called upon to deal with, and to acquaint himself fully with every phase of questions requiring his consideration. These issues with him were never questions of politics but questions of right and wrong. Men may not always have agreed with him, but no one who knew the man and his absolute honesty of conviction and sincerity of purpose, could fail to yield him the unquestioning respect which was his due."

And so with a long list from the old world and the new; from the Imperial country in which he died; from the home country in which he lies buried.

JOHN S. THOMPSON,

Editor of the Nova-Scotian; Father of Sir John Thompson.

CHAPTER XXVIII.

Characteristics and Home Life.

Sir John Thompson had inherited much of his ability, much of his patriotism, and much of his retiring nature from his father. The latter was not only "a writer of taste and genius" to quote his celebrated friend and colleague in the management of "*The Nova-Scotian,*" but was a patriot of the good old Liberal type represented in Ontario by George Brown; in Quebec by Luther Hamilton Holton; in Nova-Scotia itself by Joseph Howe. When Howe left him in full control of what had been such a powerful Liberal organ, John S. Thompson addressed his readers in words which were embodied in the life and policy of his son during many subsequent years:

"From early years I have been, I may say, instinctively attached to those principles of civil and religious liberty by which the mass of my fellow subjects would be left untrammelled, except by wise laws, in the pursuit of worldly honour and power, and in the service of their Great Creator. These feelings have grown with time; what unsophisticated youth adopted, riper years approved; and I feel wedded for life, through evil report and through good report, to that dispensation of freedom which is consistent with the British constitution, and which may be in most beneficial harmony with proper subordination of rank and the supremacy of the laws."

But unlike his son, Mr. Thompson never entered the stormy arena of politics, never sacrificed his preference for retirement, and remained to the last cultivating and instilling literary tastes in the quiet of his own fireside. The same desire for home life and quiet pleasures permeated the character of Sir John. Without a knowledge of that fact it is impossible to appreciate fully the sacrifice he made for his country in entering public life. The Hon. David Mills, a strong political opponent, but a man possessed of qualities which naturally inspired respect and esteem, in a speech delivered some weeks after the Premier's death, quoted words which fully express this feeling, and which were spoken to him upon one occasion by Sir John Thompson :

"Do you like this life? I confess it has no charms for me; and I cannot help feeling that any man of ability is a fool to come here. In private life you can be pecuniarily better off; you have peace of mind, domestic enjoyment and reputation about such as you merit; but here, what have you got? A blackened reputation, which bad as it may be, some think is better than you deserve. My advice to every man of ability and sense would be to keep out of parliament."

If, however, love of retirement could be considered a leading characteristic of the late statesman, love of country was a still more marked one. For this he was willing to give up the ease and luxury, the dignity and emoluments, the comfort and domesticity, which came from a high position on the Bench. For this he toiled at Ottawa; for this he laboured at Washington; for this he devoted many a weary hour to the Criminal Code or the Copyright Law; for this he went through the prolonged sittings of the Commission at Paris, and listened to the monotonous arguments of opposing counsel; for this he made political speeches which he detested and endured partisan abuse and sectarian attacks; for this he declined to take the Chief

Justiceship of Canada; for this he ultimately sacrificed his life, through overwork. In the words of His Lordship the Bishop of Algoma, at San Remo, on Jannary 3rd: "The sense of responsibility for his gifts seems to have been a distinguishing characteristic of Sir John Thompson. The talents with which he had been so richly endowed, belonged to his country, not to himself. They were a sacred trust committed to him for the public weal." It may truly be said of him, in the words of the poet, that he

"With Canadian greatness linked his own,
And, steadfast in that part,
Held praise and blame but fitful sound,
And in the love of country found
Full solace for his heart."

Love of work and appreciation of its importance in the struggle of life was another very prominent characteristic in Sir John Thompson. He was a severe, conscientious and thorough worker. To quote the *Toronto Mail* shortly after his death: "It was hard study that made him a lawyer. It was application that gave him eminence in his profession, whether on the Bench or at the Bar. It was thought, deep and long, that produced the Parliamentary speeches which made him famous. It was unremitting labour that conferred upon him what we describe as talent, and won for him the confidence necessary to his position as leader."

In Parliament he was always at his post. If the House sat till daylight, Sir John would keep his seat. Upon one occasion a debate lasted through the night and until 11 o'clock the next morning. When the members who were lucky enough to be allowed to go away to sleep "on call" returned next day they found the Premier sitting there, half asleep, but still on duty. At another time he remained at his post, although the little daughter in whom he was so wrapped up was known to be lying in a serious condition at home.

A stern sense of justice was one of the deepest traits in his character. It was this known sentiment which gave the House such confidence in the Minister, such respect for the man. Justice must be done, whether it affected wealthy contractors and Conservatives, such as Connolly, Murphy, and McGreevy, or the humblest clerk in a minor department of the Government. Many stories are told in this connection. In Nova-Scotia he had the reputation of being a very severe Judge, and especially when questions of fraud were involved. In such cases it was a common saying—"God help him if he gets into Thompson's hands." Upon one occasion he was visiting the Penitentiary at Dorchester, N.B, in his official capacity as Minister of Justice, when a man was brought before him who complained that his period of sentence had been too long; that the punishment was far too great for the offence—which he described. Sir John is said to have been greatly impressed by the story and to have exclaimed, "That does seem a long sentence for such an offence; who tried the case?" "It was Judge Thompson, your Honour," came the reply. He was inexorable in cases where cruelty to children was concerned. At one time, a woman had been convicted for some cruelty to a little child, and a great deal of political influence was brought to bear on the Minister to advise her release. On visiting the Penitentiary where she was confined, she brought up a further petition. Sir John said: "So you expect to be let out?" "I hope so, Sir John," was the reply. "Well, if in a hundred years from now you were living and I was still Minister of Justice, I would not let you out."

Love of religion and appreciation of the ordinances of his Church was another deep-seated influence in his daily life and public career. Reference has been made elsewhere at some length to this subject, but a little more may be said. Whole volumes were written and uttered concerning it at the time of his death. A very striking remark in this connection was made by the distinguished Presbyterian divine, Rev. Dr. Barclay:

"Whatever differing views we may hold, it is surely gratifying to know, that, alike in his private life and in the discharge of his public duties, he was not ashamed to own his Lord, and that when he went to Windsor to have an audience with and receive a high honour from his earthly Sovereign, he carried with him the symbols which could not fail to remind him that there, as elsewhere, he was in the audience chamber of the King of Heaven."

The symbols of his creed were thus with him in his sudden death, and surrounded him in his Imperial funeral, as they had been with him during his life.

The correspondent of a daily paper writing a few months before his last journey to the old land,* describes a talk with him amid the quiet of the Muskoka lakes, upon religious matters. So rare was it for him to say anything upon such a subject, that this little paragraph is doubly interesting:

"Do you accept all of the Apostles' creed, sir?"

"Yes," he said, and the little word was full of affirmation.

"Even the resurrection of the body?"—was it some unconscious premonition that moved me, I wonder?

"Whom I shall see for myself, and mine eyes shall behold, and not another," he replied with gentle gravity; and then he spoke about the difficulties of faith, and how he had come to realize that all vital belief centres about the solemn story of the Incarnation.

---

*Faith Fenton in the *Toronto Empire*.

Understanding that aright, we shall know all else, he said: "Christ did not come into the world merely to teach morality, that can be taught in other ways."

The home life of a public man in British countries is sacred. But in the case of Sir John Thompson the personal interest of the people was so greatly aroused by his tragic death; the sympathy of the Queen was so kindly and graciously tendered to the orphaned daughter; the sentiment of the country was so sincerely stirred by the lack of provision left for his family; that it is permissible to say that no more affectionate husband and father ever lived than the late Premier showed himself to be. His family consisted of two grown up sons and three daughters. The youngest of these was a beautiful and merry child, who was crippled a few years since by some sadly painful accident. Her father poured out money like water in the effort to have the trouble cured, but in vain, and friends of the family describe his devotion to the child as something touching. Some faint idea of the nature of the late Premier's home life crept into the papers during his summer stay in the charming Muskoka cottage lent him by Senator Sanford. And a writer already referred to may be quoted once more in this connection:

"Few are aware of the almost idyllic relations that exist in the home life of Canada's Premier. It is rarely given to see affection so strong, tenderness so great, sincerity and reverence so evident as that which is woven into the close bond that girds the family life of Sir John Thompson Between parents and children exist the clcsest possible ties, and one feels instinctively that all that the world could give of honours would weigh as nothing against this strong family affection."

And in spite of the stern justice which he endeavoured to mete out to criminals, and the apparent coldness of his manner and disposition, the late Premier was essentially warm-hearted and sympathetic. He gave freely to the poor, but always quietly and without ostentation. He contributed largely to religious objects, but in both these respects his right hand knew not what his left was doing. Lady Aberdeen, in a striking article contributed to the *Outlook* of New York, tells a story which illustrates his character better than many pages of eulogy: "It is understood that upon one occasion a woman, whose savings he had invested for her many years before, came to tell him that she had lost her money, and he contrived, with great inconvenience to himself, to give her back the money, conceiving himself in a measure responsible for the loss."

Sir John Thompson was often urged to take more exercise, but alleged that he had not the time. Of late years, it is understood, he walked, as a rule, from his house to his office in the Parliament buildings and back again. The story is told in connection with a well-known Ottawa character, that upon one occasion the Premier was spoken to in this matter, and replied, "Exercise! why the days are not long enough for all the work I have to do. About all the exercise I can get is the walk from my house up to the Hill and back. I go up Elgin Street one morning," he continued, with a twinkle in his eye, "and the next morning, in order to circumvent Henry Wentworth Monk, I go up Metcalfe Street."

It is sad to note that one of the pleasures to which he looked forward in his last trip to England and the Continent was never realized. It is understood that Sir John entertained a sincere admiration for Mr. Gladstone. Hearing of this from Lord and Lady Aberdeen, the Grand Old Man, despite his known desire to see only intimate friends or relations, wrote Sir John Thompson inviting him to pay a visit to Hawarden Castle. This the Canadian Premier had heartily consented to do, and proposed to go there after his visit to Windsor.

Statesmen and leaders of the people seldom die rich. Their emoluments are comparatively small. They are excluded from many means of legitimate industry. They cannot indulge in speculation or honestly take advantage of many ways of making money which come to them. They have numerous and great expenses in the shape of public and private contributions, entertainments and surroundings. Strict economy would be impossible, even if their minds could be sufficiently detached from the responsibilities of power and administration to look closely after matters of personal expenditure. Hence it was not unnatural that Sir John Thompson should have died poor. A couple of thousand dollars was found to be left of the money he had saved when on the Bench of Nova-Scotia, but including life insurance—which it is probable he found difficult to get in later years—the estate only totalled up to $9,727.

The Government were, therefore, justified in asking the people, for whom he had sacrificed so much, to contribute to a national testimonial. To this Sir Donald Smith wired $5,000 from London, and Senator Ogilvie, of Montreal, added $2,500; the Ministers of the Crown each gave $500, and the popular subscriptions very soon rolled the total up to $25,000. It would have been much larger had the public not been aware of the intention of Parliament to make an additional grant. An interesting and somewhat unusual feature of this spontaneous offering was a kindly letter from the dead leader's old opponent, Sir Richard Cartwright, enclosing a hundred dollar cheque

It is impossible, in conclusion, to do justice in a few words to the life and work of Sir John Thompson. But the leading features of his character—love of country and love of home, regard for religion and love of justice, loyalty to the Empire and devotion to duty—may be considered as the basis of his success in life; the root from which sprang popular approval and regard: the means by which his reputation grew; the source of the honours conferred by his Queen and country; the reason for the example which his career affords to all young Canadians and to all loyal citizens of this great Dominion.

APPENDIX.

CANADA'S LATE PREMIER.

An Article contributed by Her Excellency the Countess of Aberdeen, to the "Outlook" of New York, and reprinted by permission.

What manner of man was this whose death has stirred the heart of an Empire, whose memory was crowned with laurels by his Sovereign's own hand, and whose remains were borne across the ocean by one of Britain's proudest war ships, and followed to the grave by the representatives of army and navy, church and state, and of every party, class and creed, amidst the mouring of a people?

Some will attribute the feeling which has been evoked to the dramatic character of his death—and truly all the circumstances surrounding it were such as to leave an indelible impression. Here was a man, still in the prime of life, who had risen by steady and successive steps, to the highest post of honour in his own country, at the head of a powerful party, and enjoying the respect of both friend and foe, called by his Queen to her palace to receive from herself a signal mark of recognition of services which he had rendered to the Empire. And scarcely had he left her presence when the startling news came that a higher summons had called him to the presence of the King of kings, and his sorrowing family and country were left to realize all the greatness of their loss.

All that queenly thoughtfulness and womanly sympathy could do to soothe the grief of those who loved him and the country which trusted him, was done by Queen Victoria, who, in her respect for the religious persuasion of the dead, in her motherly tenderness toward the young daughter left fatherless far from her own home, and in her beautiful act of royal recognition of faithful service, in herself laying the victor's wreath of laurels on the coffin of the departed statesman, showed once more the secret of the power by which she has strengthened her throne and the British Constitution for well nigh sixty years.

Her government and her people caught up the note and honour after honour was offered to the remains of the late premier, and not only his own country, but every British colony throbbed responsively to this demonstration of the oneness of the British Empire and of the reality of the ties which unite all its component parts.

But when all this is said, and more than fully granted, can it be asserted that it was merely the accident of Sir John Thompson's death at Windsor Castle, and the consequences resulting therefrom, which occasioned the deep feeling perceptible amongst the crowds who attended his funeral, and which has left such a keen sense of bereavement from East to West in the wide Dominion, even after the first outburst of sorrow has spent itself?

What is the secret which has made the clergy of all denominations not only voice the sorrow of their people but hold up Sir John's life as a message to those who are left; and this, although in early manhood he had left the church of his fathers to join the Roman Catholic Communion?

What is it that makes his political foes speak as if they too have sustained a personal loss?

What is it that makes all patriotic citizens feel that they have been suddenly deprived of a national bulwark on which they depended for many years to come?

Why do those who were privileged to call him friend feel that a bright light has gone out and that a great darkness has overspread their lives?

There is but one answer to these questionings. The heart of the people is true to higher instincts when it gets a chance, and never has a man's career more exemplified the *power of character*, strong, elevated, trained *character*, than Sir John Thompson's.

He began life as a boy at Halifax, with but few advantages, saving those which lie in a public school education and in the influences of a cultured home, where all the proud traditions of mingled Irish and Scottish descent were cherished and made a means of inducing love and loyalty to the new country as well as to the old. His father, a literary man of no mean capacity, and a co-editor with Joseph Howe, was the reverse of wealthy, and the youth had to work his way upwards by his own personal exertions. From the outset a distinguishing feature of his character was a marvellous power of concentration and habit of industry, and it was the cultivation of these qualities which enabled him by degrees to give proof of his more brilliant intellectual qualities and which insured his rise from the reporters' chair to the lawyer's office. and thence to be Alderman of his city, Member of the Provincial Legislature, Premier of his Province, Judge, Minister of Justice for the Dominion, Premier of Canada, representative of Great Britain during the International Arbitration Conferences, and at last, Privy Councillor of Great Britain.

In each and all of these capacities he has left a record which any man may well envy, and one founded not on mere brilliancy of eloquence, or ability to evoke popular sympathies, or cleverness in manipulating party politics.

Search through his life, ask those who knew him best, and there is but one testimony. Thoroughness of work, intensity of purpose, singleness of aim, unflinching conscientiousness and a prevailing sense of the presence of God marked all he did or said. The poorest clients might depend on their case being gone into with the same thoroughness as was given in after years to a great legislative measure, or to the adjustment of an international question. Whether the matter was great or small which he had in hand, he considered it worthy of his best and his whole attention. and thus it has come about that during his comparatively brief tenure of office as Minister of Justice, he left the stamp of enduring work on the laws of the country, as for example, in the splendid accomplishment of the codifying of the criminal law, which he carried through with infinite pains and which has placed Canada ahead, in this respect, of many older countries. When listening to the details of a case, he would often sit looking immovable and irresponsive, but when the moment came for summing up, or charging the jury, it was found that not a point had escaped him, and that the just proportion and weight of all the facts were given with extraordinary precision and lucidity, and his arguments were so forcible as to carry all before them. His public speaking was eloquent, because of the matter which it contained and the strength of his reasoning, mingled with a quiet by-play of humour and kindliness. There was never any of that straining after effect, or the saying of words for the sake of saying them, which mark the utterances of weaker men. And in this, his speaking was after all, only typical of the man, who showed his greatness in his simplicity, humility, and entire absence of egotism or self-consciousness.

The success which he won in all that he undertook never spoilt him—to the end he was as a child—willing to learn from all and never so full of his own opinions as not to be able to listen to what others had to say But when his turn came to speak, there was no hesitation, and he could hold his own with the best of them.

The leading men who were engaged with him in the Behring Sea arbitration. and on other public occasions, whether in Canada, London, Paris or Washington, such as Lord Ripon, Lord Hannen, Lord Russell, Sir Richard Webster, Baron de Courcel, and Mr. Bayard, have all given their witness concerning the great influence exercised by Sir John's ability and strength, and calm judicial powers, and it was impossible for anyone to come into close contact with him without being impressed with his exceptional qualities.

But not all knew that beneath the calm, almost impassive exterior there raged a volcano, and that it was only by stern self-government that he had obtained the mastery which stood him in such good stead.

Many who knew him only as the inflexible judge, whose severity in cases where there was the slightest deviation from honesty and uprightness was proverbial, could scarcely credit the tenderness of his heart when he had to deal with the erring, the poor and the afflicted, in a private capacity, or know what he was as a husband, father and friend in the midst of his own home circle.

Of his personal scrupulous honesty and incorruptibility many instances could be given, but it is enough to point to the fact that he died a very poor man, although he had been in a position where he could have grasped at wealth, and that not his bitterest enemy can whisper a word against his memory. But even to mention the fact seems to insult him. What else could be expected from one of whom it is told that, when a woman whose savings he had invested for her many years ago, in what was considered a good investment, came to tell him that she had lost her money, he actually contrived with great inconvenience to himself, to give her back the money, conceiving himself in a measure responsible for the loss.

And when his change of religion threatened to wreck his worldly prospects, he faced the worst and was willing to endure poverty and toil for himself and his family rather than not be true to his convictions. And once again, only a few weeks before his death, he was warned that continuance in the public service might—nay, *would* probably mean death to him, whereas rest and change of climate would probably restore him to health. But to his mind his duty was clear. "It would be cowardly to resign now" he said. And so he remained at his post, and at his post he died, and to few has it been given to work so much good for their country by their death.

Is it then matter for wonder that Canada and the British Empire mourn, and that his country and his friends can only yield him to the great beyond with resignation, when they meditate on the abiding influence of his life and character and believe that it will surely inspire many young lives in the future to devote themselves thus also gloriously to the service of their country and their God?

SOME LETTERS AND DESPATCHES OF IMPORTANCE.

HER MAJESTY THE QUEEN TO LADY THOMPSON.

Windsor Castle, London, England,
December 12th, 1894.

It is impossible for me to say how deeply grieved I am at the terrible occurrence which took place here to-day, and how very truly I sympathize with you in your deep affliction.

VICTORIA R.I.

THE EARL OF ROSEBERY TO LORD ABERDEEN.

Please express to your Government my deep regret at the grievous calamity which has deprived your Government of its eminent Premier.

(Signed), ROSEBERY.

THE MARQUESS OF RIPON TO LORD ABERDEEN.

Downing Street, 12th December, 1894.

My Lord,—It was with feelings of deep sorrow and regret that I telegraphed to you yesterday, announcing the death, in circumstances so tragic, of Sir John Thompson. The grief which you and his colleagues and the whole of the Dominion of Canada must feel at the premature close of Sir John Thompson's career, which has been not only active and brilliant but marked by solid and useful statesmanship, is shared by Her Majesty's Government and the people of this country, who feel that the loss is a national one. The deceased statesman, while a strenuous supporter of the rights, and a firm believer in the future of Canada, was at the same time a loyal and eloquent advocate of everything that tended to the unity of the Empire to which, in the recent arbitration at Paris and on other occasions, he had rendered valuable service. With his personal character your lordship is of course much more familiar than myself; but even the brief acquaintance which I enjoyed with him impressed me with his genial temper and kindness of heart, his unassuming modesty, his candour and uprightness, and unflinching courage in maintaining his convictions. With Lady Thompson and her family I feel the deepest sympathy in the irreparable loss which has befallen them.

I have, etc.,

(Signed), RIPON.

FROM THE EARL OF DERBY, G.C.B.

LATE GOVERNOR-GENERAL OF CANADA.

Prescot, Eng., Dec. 13th, 1894.

Lady Thompson, Ottawa:

Accept the deepest sympathy with your great sorrow from your sincere friends, Derby, Constance, and all the other members of the family.

DERBY.

FROM THE EARL OF JERSEY, G.C.M.G.

Blatchley, England, Dec. 13th, 1894.

Lady Thompson, Ottawa:

I beg to offer you my deepest sympathy. The sorrow is universal.

JERSEY.

FROM SIR OLIVER MOWAT, PREMIER OF ONTARIO.

Toronto, December 13th, 1894.

Lady Thompson, Ottawa:

I desire to express my deep sympathy with you and yours in your great affliction I have not belonged to the same political party as your lamented husband, but I saw and learned enough of him to create an honest liking on my part towards him, as well as great esteem and respect. Canada has in his death lost one of her truest sons and greatest public men.

O. MOWAT.

THE MARQUESS OF LANSDOWNE TO SIR C. TUPPER.

Bowood, Calne, Wilts, Dec. 14th, 1894.

Dear Sir Charles.—Allow me to express to you the deep concern with which I have heard of Sir John Thompson's death. He joined Sir John Macdonald's Government while I was Governor-General, and I was much thrown into contact with him during the latter years of my term of office. It was impossible to know him without being impressed by his immense ability and statesmanlike power. That he had other qualities which made him a most agreeable and interesting colleague, no one is better aware than yourself. His loss is a very deep one to the Dominion and to the Empire. I cannot end these lines without saying something of the deep sympathy which Lady Lansdowne and I feel with Lady Thompson in the calamity which has so suddenly befallen her.

Believe me, dear Sir Charles, yours sincerely,

(Signed), LANSDOWNE.

FROM THE LIEUTENANT-GOVERNOR OF QUEBEC.

I can find no words to describe the shock I felt when the sad news came. Poor Thompson ! the cup of his life was filled with a mighty work manfully done ; with universal admiration and respect from friend and foe, with well-deserved Royal recognition of his services, when cruel destiny dashed it broken into an untimely grave Canada mourns over the loss of one of her most illustrious sons.

J. A. CHAPLEAU.

THE AMERICAN AMBASSADOR IN LONDON TO SIR C. TUPPER.

My dear Sir Charles,—I was not in London when I received the most painful news of the death of Sir John Thompson. I well knew his worth, ability and patriotism, and mourn his loss, not alone for Canada, but for the community and good government everywhere. I am glad to see Her Majesty's Government is paying fitting honour to him by conveying his remains in a national ship to the country he loved so well and served so faithfully ; and had there been any way of testifying my personal respect to his memory, I would promptly have availed myself of it. Will you not do me the kindness, when it can be done without intrusion, to make expression of my sincere condolence and sympathy to the bereaved widow and family.

Believe me, sincerely yours,

THOMAS F. BAYARD.

FROM SIR CHARLES MILLS, AGENT-GENERAL FOR SOUTH AFRICA.

London, S.W., 13th December, 1894.

Sir,—On behalf of the Government and people of the colony of the Cape of Good Hope, I offer to you this expression of their sympathy in the loss which the Government and people of the Canadian Dominion are now called upon to suffer by the sudden and unlooked for death of the late Right Hon. Sir John Thompson, the distinguished statesman and legist, who was but yesterday Prime Minister of Canada.

I am, sir, your obedient servant,

(Signed), CHARLES MILLS.

SOME RESOLUTIONS OF REGRET.

It is impossible to bring together within reasonable compass, the sympathetic resolutions called forth in every part of Canada, by the sudden death of Sir John Thompson. But a few are here given which may be considered of special interest as coming from the more important non-political bodies. It would be out of the question to give even a list of those passed by Conservative Associations.

UNIVERSITY SENATE, TORONTO.

The Senate of the University of Toronto, on motion of Mr. Mulock, M.P., seconded by Rev. Principal Caven, D D., passed the following resolution:

That the Senate shares in the universal sorrow caused by the death of the Premier of Canada, the Right Honorable Sir John S. D. Thompson, K.C.M.G., etc.

The Senate is deeply conscious of the great loss which the Dominion has sustained in the removal of a statesman so eminent for his abilities and whose devotion to the interests of his country is recognized by all.

Sir John Thompson's intellectual endowments were of a very high order, and had been diligently cultivated in early life by assiduous study.

He seemed easily and naturally to reach the highest position, whether in the profession of law or in the province of statesmanship. No sooner had he entered the public service of the Dominion of Canada than his great force of intellect and character began to be felt. His clear and comprehensive understanding, his mastery of facts and skill in arranging them, together with his power of direct, simple, statement, made him most able in debate. His capacity for work was great, and it may be feared that his untiring application to onerous duty may have shortened his valuable life. In his high position he had little more than time to show that in ability and devotion to the service of the country, he was worthy to stand beside his most eminent predecessors, when, in the inscrutable providence of God, he was called away, just as his Sovereign had placed the laurel wreath upon his brow

The Senate thankfully directs the attention of the young men of Canada to his example of the consecration of rare gifts to the service of his country, and looks back with pride upon a career which accumulated no wealth but the affection of his countrymen. It unites with the whole people in thanking Her Gracious Majesty for so fully recognizing his eminent talents and services, which will not be forgotten by Canada nor the great empire to which our country is proud to belong.

The Senate prays that heavenly consolation may be imparted to Lady Thompson and the members of her family in this the day of great sorrow, first and deepest of all, theirs, but also that of the country and the empire.

THE ALBANY CLUB, TORONTO.

At a meeting of the directors of the Albany Club, a letter of condolence was drafted and forwarded to Lady Thompson. The following is the text of the letter:

To Lady Thompson, Ottawa, Ont.

We, the officers and members of the Albany Club, Toronto, of which your deceased husband was honorary president, venture to intrude upon your privacy, in this, the hour of your terrible bereavement, with heartfelt sympathy.

To the members of this club, allied with him socially and politically, the decease of Canada's Prime Minister, in the ripeness of his manhood and the plenitude of power, is a matter for the profoundest regret. Outside and beyond us, the Conservative party at large, and the entire people of the Dominion, from his ocean home in the east to the shores of the Pacific, are mourning the death of one, trusted alike by friends and opponents. But to you and his grief-stricken family, the loss comes closer home and is irreparable. Fresh from the throne of our gracious Sovereign, where his life endeavours had just received recognition in the bestowal of one of the highest honours in Her Majesty's gift, death came to him in the very moment of fruition. The life full of promise was cut short, but time had been given him to show those qualities of head and heart, that will ever keep his name alive in the page of Canadian history, and in the memory of those who knew him. He had accomplished much. An able counsel, an upright judge, a wise representative in Parliament and a powerful Minister, enjoying the full confidence of his country, he ever bore himself bravely in the eyes of the public as a man without reproach.

In private life, with wife and family, a devoted husband and affectionate father, he has left to them and you the glorious heritage of a great and untarnished name.

And to them and you we respectfully tender this all too inadequate expression of sincere condolence.

C. H. RITCHIE,
President.

STAIR DICK-LAUDER,
Secretary-Treasurer.

THE MONTREAL BAR.

The following resolutions were unanimously adopted :

That the members of the Montreal section of the Bar of the Province of Quebec desire to give expression to the great grief with which they have heard of the death of the late Sir John Thompson, K.C.M.G., Q.C., Premier and Minister of Justice of the Dominion of Canada, and to place on record their sincere appreciation of his eminent abilities as a statesman and a lawyer, and of his probity and honour as a man.

That in the death of the late Sir John Thompson the Dominion of Canada and our profession have sustained an irreparable loss.

That we desire to convey our respectful condolences to the family of the deceased, and that the secretary be requested to transmit to Lady Thompson a copy of the foregoing resolution.

TRURO, NOVA SCOTIA, BOARD OF TRADE.

The members of the Truro Board of Trade, as Nova Scotians, share in the grief felt by our fellow-countrymen in the other Provinces of the Dominion, at the sudden and tragic death of Sir John S. D. Thompson, Premier of Canada.

His brilliant career in his chosen profession, and afterwards in the wider field of National Politics commanded the admiration and respect of all classes. When to rare intellectual gifts was united an evident and conscientious devotion to the country's interests and service, we realize more profoundly the loss that has been sustained. With gifts and opportunities for acquiring wealth, his unselfish sacrifice to duty left him a poor man, and he died rich only in the possession of the regard and esteem of his fellow citizens. We join in extending to Lady Thompson and her family our sympathy for their irreparable loss, and one which is felt most keenly not only throughout Canada but the Empire as well.

A TRIBUTE FROM THE METHODIST CHURCH.

At a meeting of the official board of the Truro, N.S., Methodist church, held on the 18th of December, Rev. W. H. Heartz, D.D., in the chair, after fitting remarks, it was moved by the recording steward, seconded by the financial secretary, and unanimously

Resolved,—That this board cannot but deplore the inexpressibly sad and immeasurably great loss the Dominion has sustained in the removal of one who, at so early an age, was regarded as the foremost statesman and jurist in Britain's colonial empire.

That the board take the opportunity afforded on behalf of the church to extend heartfelt expressions of sympathy and condolence to the widow and family of Canada's deceased Premier, with fervent prayers to the Giver of all good that He will bless and support them under their heavy affliction.

The Author desires to express his gratitude to Their Excellencies the Earl and Countess of Aberdeen, for kind assistance given.

He also wishes to sincerely thank His Grace Archbishop O'Brien, of Halifax ; His Lordship Bishop Cameron, of Antigonish, N.S. ; Mr. Justice Sedgewick, of the Supreme Court, Ottawa ; the Hon. Senator Sanford ; Mr. Martin J. Griffin, Parliamentary Librarian at Ottawa ; Mr. W. T. R. Preston, Legislative Librarian at Toronto ; Mr. F. Blake Crofton, Legislative Librarian at Halifax ; Mr. James Bain, jr., City Librarian, Toronto ; Mr. W. R. Young, M.A., Librarian of Canadian Institute, Toronto ; Mr. Sandford Fleming, C.M.G., LL.D., Ottawa ; Mr. Douglas Stewart, Private Secretary to the late Sir John Thompson ; Mr. David Creighton, Mr. A. H. U. Colquhoun, Mr. Christoper Robinson, Q.C., Hon. T. W. Anglin, ex-M.P., John A. Ewan, of the *Globe*, Mr. D. E Thomson, Q. C., Rev. H. J. Cody, Wycliffe College, Mr. B. E. Walker, General Manager of the Canadian Bank of Comm rce, Mr. J. P. Murray, Mr. W. D. McPherson, Mr. J. M. Clark, M.A., and Mr. Arthur Wallis, of Toronto ; Mr. Fred. Cook, Mr. W. J. Healy, Mr. George Johnson, of Ottawa ; Mr. F. B. Bligh and Mr. Alderman Wallace, of Halifax ; Mr. Nicholas Flood Davin, M.P., of Regina, and many others in different parts of the country.

www.ingramcontent.com/pod-product-compliance
Lightning Source LLC
Chambersburg PA
CBHW052340110726
47901CB00005B/1295

9783337096830